Praise for
PICOVERSE
by Robert A. Metzger

"Bob Metzger knows his science. He proves it in *Picoverse*, a complex and intriguing story that ranges widely through time and space, and has enough of both action and hard science to satisfy the most demanding reader."

—Charles Sheffield, author of *The Spheres of Heaven*

"With *Picoverse*, Bob Metzger takes his rightful place in the hard-SF pantheon. He's the equal of Clarke, Benford, Forward, and Brin: huge ideas, cosmic concepts, ramifications well-explored—and Metzger throws in interesting characters to boot. This one will keep you turning the pages, and should be a definite awards contender. Physics hasn't been this much fun since *Timescape*."

—Robert J. Sawyer, author of *Calculating God*

"A scintillating foray into hard SF and speculative science . . . a fast-paced technothriller." —*Library Journal*

"[A] dimensions-spanning novel. . . . From the beginning, Robert A. Metzger shows a talent for unpredictability . . . *Picoverse* always keeps you guessing . . . a rewarding yarn with some new spins on the idea of alternate universes."

—*Science Fiction Weekly*

"This fast-paced romp through multiple manmade universes will appeal to hard-SF fans who like their science served straight up. . . . The book hangs together thematically [and the] ending satisfies." —*Publishers Weekly*

continued . . .

PICOVERSE

Robert A. Metzger

ACE BOOKS, NEW YORK

PICOVERSE

An Ace Book / published by arrangement with the author

PRINTING HISTORY
Ace hardcover edition / March 2002
Ace mass-market edition / March 2003

Copyright © 2002 by Robert A. Metzger.
Cover art by Danilo Ducak.
Cover design by Rita Frangie.
Text design by Kristin del Rosario.

Visit our website at
www.penguinputnam.com
Check out the ACE Science Fiction & Fantasy newsletter!

ISBN: 0-441-01030-X

ACE®
Ace Books are published by The Berkley Publishing Group,
a division of Penguin Putnam Inc.,
375 Hudson Street, New York, New York 10014.
ACE and the "A" design
are trademarks belonging to Penguin Putnam Inc.

PRINTED IN THE UNITED STATES OF AMERICA

10   9   8   7   6   5   4   3   2

To April, Alex, and John

ACKNOWLEDGMENTS

So many people were instrumental in the shaping and fine-tuning of this book. Their generosity in both time and mental energy will never be forgotten. In alphabetical order, to those who helped so much in bringing this book to light, I wish to thank: Bruce Bethke, David Brin, Marcus Chown, Tom Easton, Bob Forward, Henry Gee, Elisabeth Maltare, Wil McCarthy, Linda Nagata, Charles Ryan, Rob Sawyer, Charles Sheffield, Dave Truesdale, and F. Paul Wilson. Any errors or foolishness found within these pages belong solely to me and not to these kind folks who gave me a helping hand.

Special thanks go to Greg Benford, whose enthusiasm and insights were instrumental in the shaping of this book from the first page to the last. And to those in the publishing industry who took a manuscript and transformed it into the book you hold in your hands, I am most grateful to my agent Richard Curtis and editor Susan Allison.

POWERS OF TEN

1,000,000,000,000,000,000	EXA	10^{18}
1,000,000,000,000,000	PETA	10^{15}
1,000,000,000,000	TERA	10^{12}
1,000,000,000	GIGA	10^{9}
1,000,000	MEGA	10^{6}
1,000	KILO	10^{3}
1	UNI	1
0.001	MILLI	10^{-3}
0.000001	MICRO	10^{-6}
0.000000001	NANO	10^{-9}
0.000000000001	PICO	10^{-12}
0.000000000000001	FEMTO	10^{-15}
0.000000000000000001	ATTO	10^{-18}

I. THE SONOMAK

Had I been present at the Creation, I would have given some useful hints for the better ordering of the Universe.

—ALFONSO THE WISE, KING OF CASTILE (1221–1284)

CHAPTER 1

The Nunn Physics Building, a six-story sprawl of red brick and smoked glass, dominated the northern boundary of Georgia Tech's campus, throwing a long shadow down 14th Street, painting the dozens of ramshackle student bungalows that hugged its western edge in depressing shades of gray and brown. Built six years earlier, and intended to accommodate a wide spectrum of students, the bungalows were now the exclusive domain of physics grad students, tethered close to their professors, and even closer to their experiments.

Dr. Katie McGuire sat cross-legged atop Nunn's observation platform—a three-by-three square meter slab of rain-rotted plywood, once painted black, but now weathered gray and streaked with mildew. Wedged between a behemoth segment of galvanized ducting that carried away acid fumes and metalorganic residues, and a half-dozen two-hundred-gallon liquid nitrogen tanks, long empty, pressure gauges and relief valves scavenged, the platform was Katie's roost, a place to think, to fret, to clear a cluttered mind.

She faced east, in the direction of Atlanta's midtown, the oil-on-water lenses of her Virtuals reflecting the morning light. Sunrise was spectacular, the sun hanging behind the Bank of America tower, the light cutting into the building, refracting through stained glass windows, then erupting from the building's western face in rainbow streamers that played out across the city. Clouds, tinted bloodred, hung low on the distant horizon, while the air, full of springtime pine and grass pollens, glowed golden. It was a perfect morning. But Katie saw none of it.

"Two seconds," she said. The lowermost left quadrant in her field of view flickered, locked, and then the Virtuals began to feed, cycling through channels every two seconds.
CNN.

Cryo-Dyne.
Bold and Beautiful.
ESPN IV.
Real Time.

High resolution video streamed into her retinas, the 50 gigahertz modulated lasers in the frame of her Virtuals, bouncing light from the imbedded prisms in the lenses and then rastering the input across the back of her eyeballs. A screaming face replaced the green-blue waters of a tropical paradise.

"Quotas are for the slight of—"

As quickly as it had appeared, the face vanished in a growing fireball that filled her viewing field as the next channel locked in. Katie refocused and let the channels blur, as the *Wireless Local Area Network* within Nunn's multimedia stream flashed channel after channel, rolling through its nearly infinite menu. The *WLAN*'s content didn't matter—volume did. Katie craved the noise, was addicted to the input, and in fact, could not concentrate unless assaulted by a cacophony of bits. She momentarily checked the simulation running in the lower right quadrant of her field of vision—a bare-bones, three-dimensional plot, with plasma density contoured in a Day-Glo green mesh, and temperatures textured from cool yellows to smoking blues. The simulation was a hydrodynamic/kinetic mix, melding a fluid approach to an atom-by-atom calculation, her latest attempt at predicting the plasma turbulence that was damping the *Sonomak*'s ability to really burn.

Katie smiled.

Hydrodynamic/kinetic mix. It was a tricky approach, but the only one that had the slightest chance of modeling what was occurring in the heart of the Sonomak. The physics describing high-speed liquid turbulent flow and ultra-hot plasmas were still poorly understood, nearly impossible to model, and when mixed together, turned into a mathematical nightmare beyond belief.

Impossible.
Couldn't be modeled.

So chaotic, so intrinsically nonlinear, that the system just couldn't be understood.

At least that was what the experts insisted—all those wizened old white men, with worn leather belts cinched over their little potbellies. Can't do it, *girl*. No one can do it, *girl*.

This *girl* would prove them wrong.

That thought normally cheered her, but the smile faded from her face as her thoughts drifted away from the simulation and to the chunk of stainless steel, flickering lasers, and pulsing plasmas that the simulation was attempting to model—*the Sonomak*. This work was *too* applied for her taste, *too* tied to experiments and the boxful of zip discs crammed with data that refused to be modeled.

There was no real theoretical work anymore, no more physics that was studied for the pure joy of simply understanding how the universe worked. For twelve wonderful months at Cambridge, she had worked directly under Stephen Hawking, modeling the vacuum fluctuations that took place in the vicinity of black holes.

Bliss.

But she had lost her funding. Cosmology, particle physics, those areas of research that couldn't be transformed into a product suitable for insertion into microwave ovens, or high definition CCD recorders, or used to slow down the ever-widening trade gap with mainland China, had been deemed nonessential by the Feds who doled out the science dollars. The only other avenues of funding were in the production of military systems used to carbonize Third World types before they could stumble out of their huts, or to sign your soul away to one of the big *Search for Extraterrestrial Intelligence* consortia and spend your days trying to crack the uncrackable signals that poured down from the heavens, having been picked up for a century now. Neither frying Third-Worlders nor crunching uncrackable *SETI* signals was her cup of tea.

Good-bye funding.

At the moment, plasma physics was about as theoretical

and esoteric a topic as the U.S. government could tolerate. And Katie was afraid that even that indulgence was about to come to an end.

She refocused on the simulation. At the edge of the *plasmon*, that region where electrons had been swept out of the plasma, leaving behind positively ionized helium atoms, just nanometers away from the shock wave being generated by the collapse of the plasmon, the plasma temperatures were peaking, the ascent rate punching discontinuities in the plot, the diagram indicating that the plasma residing within a few atomic spacings of the shock wave had reached a temperature in excess of 60 million degrees.

Then the Pocket Accelerators were ramped down.

The thermal gradient went ballistic as the plasmon imploded.

The simulation broke down, the plasma density mesh lines rippling, actually folding back on themselves as the high-energy electrons transferred their energy to the helium ions. Frame after frame of contour plots rolled by, each one a snapshot of the plasma as it evolved every two picoseconds. Katie shook her head in disgust, but the simulation continued to hang stationary in her field of view, the input being fed directly into her retinas through her Virtuals.

"Damn," she said.

The simulation shattered, a black spiderweb sucking down plasma density contour lines, the plasma temperature color scale oscillating, unsuccessfully trying to auto-scale, as temperatures soared into the billion-degree range, a temperature so unrealistic that even a theoretical physicist like Katie, for whom lines and contour plots *were* reality, knew that the simulation and physical reality had parted company. Not even Katie could believe plasma temperatures in the multibillion-degree range, higher than temperatures in the center of the sun.

"Terminate."

The simulation vanished. In its place appeared Anthony's playroom, the default input for the simulation quadrant when she was not running simulations. Anthony sat at his worktable, nearly hidden behind a multicolored mound of construction paper, glistening tape, and rubber bands. He carefully taped what looked like a rainbow-colored fish to the top of the mound. Within the mound Katie recognized a wide spectrum of geometrical shapes, ranging from the most basic squares, circles, and rectangles, to more complex Möbius strips, convoluted manifolds, Penrose tiles, and Gordian-like knots.

Katie did not like the look of it.

Her son was obsessed with anything geometrical, and the things he built usually caused trouble. The six-year-old focused; his crystalline blue eyes flicking back and forth.

But for the moment, all was calm.

Anthony was not screaming. And just as importantly, the latest in a long string of special ed teachers was not screaming. Katie did not hold out much hope for Miss Alice. Caring, loving, degreed in special-needs primary education, with a strong background in math and science, she should have been perfect. Miss Alice had been working with Anthony for almost three weeks now. Katie doubted that Miss Alice would break the four-week barrier, not after what happened two days ago, when Anthony had set up a convoluted array of aluminum foil and lightbulbs, the contraption generating enough focused heat to ignite the kitchen curtains.

911 was on speed dial.

He was a brilliant little boy, but could not quite connect with the world, had no concept of the difference between appropriate and inappropriate behavior. Katie sighed. People skills were an alien concept to Anthony.

But at the moment, all was calm. She refocused past the input being fed into her head and out into the Atlanta morning.

Reality.

Katie sipped tea from her cracked and terminally stained Starbucks vacuum cup, the contents burning her tongue and scorching the roof of her mouth. Tears momentarily welled up in her eyes, blurring both reality and input.

"Watch, Mama!"

Katie squinted, driving tears from her eyes. Anthony looked up at her, peering into the camera. He held up a paper cube that fit snugly in the palm of his right hand. It was tied up like a Christmas present with a green and blue string, bound together at the top of the cube with what looked to Katie like a carrick knot. She knew that only moments before the cube must have been the huge mound that had covered his play table. She found herself smiling, thinking that someday Anthony would make a wonderful Boy Scout, with absolutely no problem passing the knot test.

"What have you got there, Anthony?" she asked, her voice picked up by the receiver in the data pack slung across her back and transmitted to the speaker in Anthony's playroom.

"A surprise, Mama," he said, smiling.

"No!" Katie stood up, turning her head, the camera in Anthony's playroom rastering in synch to her movement. Miss Alice walked into the room, like a lamb to the slaughter, with nothing to defend herself with except a warm smile.

"Put it down, Anthony!"

Anthony obeyed, placing the cube on the floor. Katie knew at that instant she'd made a mistake, played right into Anthony's hands. Before she could say anything, he tugged on the carrick knot, the blue and green strings parted, and the cube unfolded in an explosion of color and twirling rubber bands, rising up off the floor, flapping sheets of construction paper giving it lift, rubber band power driving it. The contraption hit Miss Alice in the face. A swatch of tape unrolled itself, tugged by multicolored beating wings, and then wrapped several times around her head.

"Not today, Anthony, please not today," Katie said, knowing that it was already too late. Miss Alice danced around the room, frantically tugging at the tape that stuck to her face and the paper and rubber bands that were wrapped around her head.

Anthony smiled for the camera. "An automatic tape dispenser, Mama. Do you like it?"

Katie lowered her head and closed her eyes. It would be a miracle if Miss Alice made it until the weekend. She started doing quick calculations. Tech to Sandy Springs: twenty minutes. Calming down Miss Alice: fifteen minutes. Confiscation of Anthony's tape, construction paper, scissors, glue, rubber bands, and markers: ten minutes. A stern yet compassionate lecture to Anthony: two minutes. More pleading and apologies to Miss Alice: ten minutes. Sandy Springs to Tech: twenty minutes.

Grand total: one hour and seventeen minutes.

Katie groaned. Of all the mornings for this to happen. For a moment, she wondered if she could ignore the situation, letting Miss Alice handle this one on her own. She opened her eyes and refocused. Miss Alice sat on the floor, cross-legged, whimpering, trying to pull a big knot of masking tape out of her hair.

"Mama?" said Anthony, now standing next to Miss Alice, reaching out toward her with a shaking right hand, but pulling it back each time Miss Alice lurched and twisted as she tried to dislodge the sticky mess from her head. "Is Miss Alice sad?" he asked.

Again Katie closed her eyes, and her right hand went toward the phone on her belt. She should call Horst, her ex-husband, and make him go home, acquainting him with the mundane aspects of the real world and fatherhood, insisting that he deal with a six-year-old who had chewed through three special-ed teachers in the last eight months.

Sure.

The silk-suited son of a bitch hadn't seen Anthony in more than two weeks. And there was no way that he'd leave campus this morning. When Anthony had been born, Horst had cancelled trips, meetings, and conferences to be with them, spending an entire month at home. But the fame that Horst's research had brought him, and the pressure to perform at an ever higher level, had destroyed that gentle Horst, and eventually their marriage. Katie checked the virtual clock hanging in front of her nose. The Sonomak would be put through its paces in less than three hours. She knew that nothing would get that egomaniac off campus today.

"Did I do a bad thing?" asked Anthony.

Katie refocused again. Anthony had backed away from the now-sobbing Miss Alice. His chin quivered, his eyes had grown large, and with his right hand he clenched a fistful of his sandy-blond hair, twirling a lock of it with his index finger. Tears began to run from the outside corners of his eyes. "I *was* bad, Mama!"

Katie was up, hopped from the platform, and started to run for the stairwell. "It was just an accident, baby. Don't worry, I'm coming right home," she said as she descended the stairwell, taking two steps at a time. "Everything will be all right."

*The senator looked at the professor. The professor was big, prob-*ably topping 220 pounds, and looked powerful even on screen. His ink-black hair was slicked straight back across a head so big and square that it looked chiseled from a block of wood. His pencil-thin mustache looked painted on.

The senator tried to smile but couldn't quite manage it.

Dr. Horst Wittkowski smiled back, instantly understanding what the look on Ty Miller's face meant. *Bad news.* Of that he had absolutely no doubt. The only question was how bad it would be. He slowed his breathing, lifted his hands from his lap, and placed them atop the cool lacquered perfection of his mahogany desk. He leaned forward, pursed his lips ever so slightly to denote concern, and then angled his head to the left as he furrowed his brow, the expression and body language precisely engineered to solicit details.

Senator Ty Miller felt the thin sheet of sweat across his forehead begin to bead up, and a muscle in the left side of his face, just at the base of his jaw, ticking as sure and steady as his pocket watch. He did not like to deliver bad news—it made him nervous. His career had been built on the twin political pillars of filling up the pork barrel and slapping the backs of countless good ol' boys. Nothing good came from delivering bad news.

"The news, Senator?" asked Horst, his voice deep and resonant, the German accent polished to a high luster.

Senator Miller swallowed hard. "The president has decided to fund the *International Thermonuclear Experimental Reactor*," he said, and then slipped back in his chair, bracing himself for the explosion that he was sure would come, as the significance of what he'd told Wittkowski hammered home.

What is wrong with the presidents of this country? Horst wanted to shout. Clinton forced to resign in '97, Gore killed in '99 after a visit to the troops in Cairo, where a wayward SAM took out Air Force One, with both those events opening the way for Vice President Marie Meyer from Iowa to fill the power vacuum. If it didn't involve corn or cows she was out of her depth. She didn't know plasma physics from pork bellies. But Americans loved the woman, had actually elected her twice after she had finished out Gore's term.

"Professor?"

Horst did not flinch. He had known this day would come, had known that the pressure that big Malaysian money was exerting on the White House, and the sheer force of the personality of Mahathir bin Mohamad could not be denied. The Malaysian government had had the Japanese, the Russians, the Europeans, and the Chinese on board for the better part of a year now. Only the Americans had been holding out—saying that they couldn't afford ITER, not after the billions they'd spent on the latest SETI upgrade, extending the diameter of the Arecibo radio dish by yet another hundred meters, boosting sensitivity in order to try and cut out some of the background noise from the most recent indecipherable signals.

The fact that Meyer had finally bent to world pressure did not surprise Horst. What did surprise him was the timing of the announcement. He had thought that such a decision would not have been made until at least a year after the election—he had been depending on that eighteen-month window. He did not think that the Democrats could tolerate any more "International Cooperation" this close to the election, not after having sunk nearly three times the amount of funds than had been originally budgeted for the International Space Station, upgrading its Ears so it could listen to aliens pass gas in distant galaxies, only to have the whole station burn up less than a year later when a jammed Russian thruster accidentally deorbited the behemoth.

"I assume that a deal has been made with the Malaysians, and that ITER will be built in Putrajaya, tapping the amazing know-how of a people whose high-technology capabilities are best evidenced by their domination of the world market in *basketball shoe* manufacturing?" asked Horst in silky tones.

The senator nodded.

"Wonderful news for the Malaysians," said Horst, a smile now filling his face, exposing $20,000-worth of exquisite bridgework. "But why would this have an impact on me?" he asked, knowing full well what that impact would be.

The senator leaned forward. He'd gotten this far without an explosion, so saw no reason to sugarcoat the rest of it. "ITER will be allocated nearly 75 percent of both the Department of Energy and Defense Advanced Research Projects Administration plasma funding from ongoing programs. This change will be reflected in the '08 budget, with those programs which support ITER being given the highest priority for the remaining funds."

Horst's left eyebrow arched in a questioning gesture.

The senator answered without having to hear the question. "There will be no increase in the total plasma funding from either *DOE* or *DARPA*. What was a $200 million allocation for general plasma funding for this year will be reduced to something around $50 million for '08."

Horst took a quick, shallow breath and frowned. Fiscal '08 started on October 1 of '07, which meant that the fate of existing programs, and the meager funding that they would receive, would be decided at the latest by the end of

August. It was already June. That gave him only two months, not the eighteen that he really needed to get the Sonomak up and running, and generate the results that would get him follow-on funding. "Then I have two months to dazzle my good friends at DOE and DARPA?" asked Horst.

"At the most," answered the senator.

Horst knew that it wasn't even as hopeful as that. By the time the in-crowd at Princeton, MIT, and Stanford were funded, there would be absolutely nothing left for other efforts. He was certain that Georgia Tech had been redlined the moment the president had finished shaking hands with the Malaysian egomaniac. "Thank you, Senator," he said, dismissing the topic with the tone of his voice, knowing that nothing more could be accomplished with Ty Miller, DOE, or DARPA. He took a deep breath. There was only one other source of money that he could possibly tap into. Images of an orbital Sonomak powering up a gamma ray laser flashed through his head. He did not like it—not one little bit. He was not opposed to getting into the covert weapons business. The problem was the way *those* people operated. Breakthroughs were instantly classified, and hardware sucked down into a secret agency vortex never to be seen again. They wouldn't let you publish, wouldn't even let you talk about your work. They kept you in money, but to the outside world, to the physics community, it would appear that you had fallen off the planet.

Bye-bye Nobel.

But he knew he would have to make *that* call.

However, first things first. He refocused on Ty. "We'll have you on line for this morning's demonstration?" he asked, sounding positive and upbeat.

Senator Miller nodded, not certain how to read the situation. He had just informed this man that his entire research program, the thing that he had built his life around, would cease to exist in the next two months. "I look forward to it, Professor," he said, sounding relieved.

Horst smiled and disconnected.

"ITER," Horst said in a whisper, slowly shaking his head, feeling the rage begin to build. "Goddamned Malaysians!" It was *their* fault. With more money than brains, willing to pay for more than half of the cost of the project, operating under the belief that if they had the world's tallest building, the fastest rail system, the largest database of indecipherable alien noise, the biggest supercomputer, and now the world's most expensive pressure cooker, that all those things would somehow make them a First World nation.

They were savages.

They prayed to snakes and poked knitting needles through their faces to prove their oneness with God. Imbeciles. "Goddamned imbeciles!" The sound of his own voice unnerved him. He was standing, his hands balled into fists, the knuckles white, the sound of blood pounding in his head. He forced himself to think of something else. Time was short—incredibly short. He needed a new source of funding *now*, before his existing money ran out and he could no longer keep the team intact. If they disbanded, it would be nearly impossible to regroup and get the Sonomak back up. He forced his breathing to slow, sat back down in his chair, and opened the center desk drawer. Reaching in deep, all the way to the back, he grabbed the slick surface of a DVD wallet and pulled it out. The bundle was thick, nearly thirty discs crammed into the wallet, one for every possible contingency, both technical and political. The wallet unfolded like an accordion and he fingered through it, looking for a very special disc.

The DVD.

He laid it on his desk. Although he had planned for this contingency, until this moment, he had not believed that it would have ever actually come to this. He looked down at the DVD and at its small, handwritten, white label: *Implosion*.

Horst tugged at his tie, making sure that it was straight, ran a hand across his slick-backed hair, and looked at the wall of plaques and citations, as if checking to make sure that they hadn't vanished in the last few minutes. In the center of the wall, directly above his head, hung a one-meter-length of tube—the Pocket Accelerator, a mile's worth of conventional electron accelerator packed into a tube that you could twirl like a baton.

Horst smiled affectionately at the hardware and then turned around to face the Vid camera mounted in the far corner of his office. "Vid on," he said. He looked into the camera, took a deep breath, focused his thoughts, and expelled the lungful of air as the Vid's red recording light came on. He smiled, no longer seeing the camera. He now saw the millions that he knew would someday be watching him, viewing this Vid, reliving a critical piece of history.

"I've come to realize that adversity can be the scientist's greatest ally," said Horst, pushing his voice down half an octave. "An abundance of funding causes one to become complacent, to follow a conservative approach that only incrementally increases one's knowledge, adding a brick here or there to a scientific edifice which already reaches to the heavens. But the breakthrough, the new insight, the opening of vistas yet unseen, come about only by bold action and in desperate times."

Horst held the DVD up to the camera.

"I do not like bolts," Beong Kim said to the torque wrench as he checked yet one more bolt, tugging on the wrench handle, its LCD screen reading fifty-eight foot-pounds. He snugged the bolt, bringing it up to the specified sixty foot-pounds.

Tightening bolts was not a proper job for a postdoctoral research engineer. It was disgraceful. But the Titanium-Sapphire Laser and the Pocket Accelerators it powered were his responsibility. And today nothing could be left to chance—he would not let the grad students or co-ops anywhere near *his* equipment. There could be no mistakes.

Beong closed two of his three eyes and lowered his face to the barrel of the Titanium-Sapphire Laser, letting his chin rest on the cold stainless steel. Transmitted through the metal, the *chug-chug* vibration of mechanical backing pumps rang in his head, actually rattling his back molars. It felt right, the pitch correct, the intensity balanced.

Five years in the Sonomak lab had taught him to use every one of his senses.

As he *felt* the equipment, his third eye, ever vigilant, continued to suck down photons, converting light to electrons, digitizing, sampling, compressing, and then uplinking the data to Low Earth orbit and the nearest Teledesic satellite. Bounced among the 240 satellites of the system, the data spanned the globe within a few milliseconds, downlinked to Taejon, Korea, and to the one-meter dish perched atop Sangbom Kim's roof.

The Vid display glowed in the Kim living room, showing an out-of-focus close-up of the Titanium-Sapphire Laser's output port. No one watched. All were asleep in Korea. But that did not matter. Everything was being recorded for later viewing. Sangbom Kim, Beong's father, was ever vigilant, spending his days viewing his son's previous day's activities, making certain that nothing happened to disgrace his family or country.

Beong opened his eyes and straightened up, his back creaking. He moved along the laser tube, running his right hand across it, not looking at it, but focusing on the electronics that filled the line of rack panels running across the rear wall of the lab. Vacuum pressures, cryo-pump cold head temperatures, residual gas traces from the tube. He scanned them all.

There could be no mistakes.

"How many times are you going to retorque that tube, Beong?" asked Aaron Tanaka from the other room—the main lab that housed the Sonomak.

Despite the fact that Beong was now in possession of a Ph.D., and was a postdoc for Professor Wittkowski, while Aaron Tanaka was merely a technician, without so much as a bachelor's degree, Beong still twitched from the waist at the sound of Aaron's voice, ingrained reflexes forcing the abbreviated bow.

Aaron was in charge of the lab—Professor Wittkowski

had made that perfectly clear when Beong had agreed to stay on after receiving his Ph.D. Aaron would always be in charge, whatever Beong did, despite the fact that it had been *his* work and *his* thesis project that had led to the first experimental demonstration of the Pocket Accelerators.

Beong pushed those thoughts out of his head.

Dr. Horst Wittkowski was the professor, not him.

"Earth to Beong!" said Aaron, his Texas drawl echoing off the lab walls. He did not bother to look up from what he was doing, not wanting to make eye contact with any of the grad-grunts sweating over the Sonomak, making everything pretty for the dog and pony show that would begin at one o'clock.

Once again Beong's muscles twitched, forcing him into an abbreviated bow. "I am done with the torquing," Beong said, as if announcing he had just completed a religious rite. "I am *feeling* the equipment."

Aaron smiled, set down the multimeter he'd been using to check some high voltage feedthroughs, and walked over to the doorway connecting the two labs, the doorway the Titanium-Sapphire Laser's main tube went through before it fed into the beam splitters, which in turn coupled with the Sonomak's Pocket Accelerators. Poking his head in, he watched Beong running his hands down the tube, fingers pushing at electrical feedthroughs and gas injectors.

Aaron had seen a lot of students come and go, but Beong was the best. He understood equipment, knew that in the final analysis, regardless of what some fancy-ass simulation told you and what a bank of green lights insisted, that you never powered up until you'd *felt* the equipment. And Beong was always *afraid*. That was critical. As soon as you lost fear of your equipment, that little act of arrogance would cause it to self-destruct in some new and gruesome fashion.

"Beong!"

Beong looked over at Aaron, focusing all three eyes, bowing once more.

Aaron smiled. "Today is no big deal, Beong, just take it

down a few notches. We've run the system at the fifteen-kilowatt level more than a dozen times now without any problems. Horst will be at the controls. If any bug crops up, he'll just flip the displays into remote mode and output one of the test runs."

Beong shook his head. That would be *dishonest*. The professor would *never* do that.

Reading the expression on Beong's face, Aaron knew why Beong was a postdoc and not a professor with his own lab—he had the real-world savvy of a pup. "This show is for Washington-types, program monitors, and a few military paper pushers. We could run the whole damn thing as a simulation, and they wouldn't have the slightest idea that you hadn't tossed a single electron down the Pocket Accelerators."

Beong shook his head.

Aaron smiled once again, knowing it was futile. "You might want to check the third and fifth harmonics on the main beam oscillator," he said, knowing full well that those wouldn't affect the experiment in the slightest, but knowing that Beong needed *something* to worry about. "Don't want to be wasting any power at those useless frequencies."

Horrified at what Aaron had said, Beong dropped to the floor and rolled under the tube. He'd checked the higher harmonics less than an hour ago, but that didn't matter. *Aaron* thought there might be a harmonic problem.

There could be no mistakes today.

SECTION I

CHAPTER 2

"You aren't listening to me, Horst," said Katie.

He'd heard the words, could play them back verbatim if requested, but they had not registered, had not interfaced with the active regions of his brain. He looked at her for a moment. A pixie of a woman with flaming red hair, freckled, cream-colored skin, and a pinched little nose. Through the unpolarized left lens of her Virtuals he could see a green eye staring up at him—a very angry-looking green eye. Irish from head to toe. At times he thought she might actually have leprechaun blood in her. Her small frame had fit so perfectly in his arms. But he quickly put *that* thought, and any other thoughts of her, out of his head. To her left, visible through the observation window, he could see the Sonomak.

Beautiful.

A two-meter-diameter vanadium alloyed stainless steel sphere, with forty-eight Pocket Accelerators protruding from it, sat in the center of the lab, draped in cabling and surrounded by rack after rack of electronics. It was a work of art, an elegant piece of physics, an instrument to reveal the truth. With his right hand buried in his pants pocket, he fingered the wallet of DVDs.

"Horst, we've got a problem," said Katie. She was angry now. She poked at his too-bright tie with an index finger. "Anthony has just about burned through another teacher. I've given Alice the afternoon off, and she'll be bringing Anthony to campus so *we* can take him for the rest of the day."

Horst looked down at his tie, where Katie had poked him, as if checking for dirty fingerprints. Apparently finding none, he glanced at his Rolex and then looked at Katie. "Not now," he said, holding up his hand.

"Goddamn it, Horst! It's never 'now.' There never is a good time to talk to you about anything unless it concerns that goddamned machine!"

Horst focused on her, looking into her green eye. "The president has decided to fund ITER from the existing DARPA and DOE plasma budget," he said, stressing each word. "Unless something miraculous happens we are less than two months away from shutting this program down."

Katie blinked. It took several seconds for the mental gears to engage, for images of a teacher covered in tape and construction paper to be replaced with thoughts of budgets, contracts, and just how much money it took to keep the Sonomak running. "Shut us down," she said in a whisper. She could not believe it. This lab had developed the Pocket Accelerator.

"It's 12:55, Katie," he said, looking at his watch once again and then back at her. He ran his hands down the front of his coat, smoothing out wrinkles that were not there. "Crunch time," he said, and then stepped past her, moving not in the direction of the control room, but down the hall.

Katie knew where he was going, knew the ritual, the superstitions. Before a major presentation or experiment, Horst needed some quiet time to rehearse, to focus on whatever hurdle he was about to try to jump. She knew the route he would take, the stairwells he preferred, the labs he would pass, and the secretaries he would wink at.

Looking over his shoulder, just before he turned the corner at the end of the hallway, he smiled, giving her his patented, 100-percent-full-of-confidence grin. "Let's make a little history." He then turned and vanished around the corner.

And at that moment, Katie knew just what Horst planned to do—she'd seen it in his smile. It was the smile that at one time had been hers, but now was reserved solely for his machine. He was going for the big breakthrough and would attempt to run the Sonomak as it had *never* been run before. The Sonomak had *never* been pushed past the twenty-million-degree level, and she was suddenly certain that Horst would attempt to break through that temperature.

And there was only one real way to do that. He would try to compress the plasmon vortex to its absolute minimum. He would run *all* forty-eight Pocket Accelerators at maximum power, not just the sixteen they had run in the trials. Horst would go for *maximum* implosion and not worry about the outbound shock wave and what potential damage it would cause to the interior of the Sonomak. He needed results. Now.

But she also knew that if all forty-eight Pocket Accelerators were run, a single accelerator that was slightly out

of sync with the others would result in a burn so lopsided
that the final temperature would be far lower than that
achieved by sixteen balanced accelerators.

She'd run those simulations, but had not yet shown them
to Horst.

The virtual clock hung in front of her. *12:58.*

Should she tell Horst? Would he even listen to her?

Katie looked first down the hallway where Horst had just
gone and then to the doorway that led to the Sonomak
control room. Which way?

"Umph!" Horst stepped back, stumbled and almost fell; the only
thing keeping him on his feet was that whoever had just
run into him had a firm grasp around his midsection.

He looked down, surprised.

"What's wrong with you, Katie?" he said, pushing her
back, momentarily confused, not quite sure how she'd
made it to the far end of the Van Leer Engineering Building
ahead of him.

"Nothing," said Katie as she stepped back and looked up
at Horst.

"What's so important that you chased me all around the
building, that you couldn't wait the few minutes for me to
get back to the lab?" he asked, doing nothing to hide the
sounds of annoyance in his voice. *This was his thinking
time.* He glared at her, tried to make eye contact, but could
not. Both lenses of her Virtuals were fully tinted, hiding
her eyes. Horst hated talking to people when he could not
see their eyes. And he knew that Katie knew that, and was
doing it just to annoy him. He took half a step back, and
for just a moment inspected her, finding something wrong
with her, something that he couldn't quite place. Had she
been wearing that lab coat a moment before? And there
was something wrong with her hair, the ends jagged, looking as if someone had just taken a pair of pruning shears
to them.

"Is there something different. . . ."

"I know what you plan to do, Horst," she said, cutting him off.

"Oh," he said. He raised his right eyebrow, instantly forgetting what had been puzzling him only a moment before, getting right back to business. "And why should this concern me?"

"Because if you run all forty-eight accelerators you will in all likelihood not get a complete burn—the alignments have not been sufficiently checked, and the software isn't going to be able to compensate the beam steering quickly enough."

"And just how do you know this?" he asked.

"I've run the simulations, checked the tolerances. Unless all beams hit dead on you'll fall far short of the twenty million degrees."

Horst sighed. He knew it was a risk, but at this point everything was a risk.

"You can't run all forty-eight accelerators," she said.

Horst reached up with his right hand and pulled at his chin, slowly pacing back and forth. "How long do you think it would take to check out beam alignments, to run a few low-level tests with all forty-eight accelerators in order to check out the system?"

Katie's shoulders sagged, the relief evident to Horst.

"I think we can do it in a week," she said.

Horst stopped pacing, nodded, and reached into his pocket, pulling out the DVD wallet. Unsnapping the wallet and thumbing through it, he pulled out a DVD and held it up to her.

"Power surge—forty-eight accelerators," said Katie, reading the disc's label.

"It will make it look as if we attempted to run all forty-eight accelerators," said Horst, "but just as we start, the system will abort, claiming that there was an input power surge. The Sonomak will shut down, and I'll give a little song and dance about Tech's power grid problems, and beg for a week's extension for the demonstration." He smiled.

"Good," said Katie.

"Now get to the control room," said Horst. "Don't let on to the others what we are going to try to do. I need their reactions to be genuine in response to our little power surge."

Katie nodded, turned, and trotted down the hallway. Just before she got to the end, she turned, *smiled*, and waved to him.

Horst blinked, surprised, not quite certain what to make of the entire encounter. "She must be nervous," he said to himself, and then waited, not moving until he could no longer hear her echoing footsteps. He then looked down at the DVD in his open hand, curled his fingers around it, and didn't stop squeezing until he felt it shatter. "We don't have a week," he said in a whisper. "And I don't have the time to argue about it."

"Please excuse me for my tardiness," Horst said to the camera. He looked down at his watch. 1:07. Horst was *always* late for meetings and presentations, having learned the value of this tactic long ago. The more important you were, the later you could be, and the longer you could make others wait for your arrival. It showed confidence, which in many cases was far more important than technical abilities and physics breakthroughs when it came to getting money.

Show no fear.

The fact that Katie had actually delayed him had no bearing on his tardiness. If she had not slowed him down, he would have simply spent a few more minutes wandering around the building.

Horst looked around the control room.

Five Telepresence monitors were lit. The first TP showed Senator Miller, while two others showed military types— Captain Rodney Harrington, on loan to DOE from the Air Force, who had the squinty eyes of an accountant and the personality to match, while in the TP next to him, was General Alexander Martin, liaison to the Joint Chiefs of Staff, a near-retirement-age Gulf War veteran who Horst knew would never see his second star, having pissed off

the UN-loving administration with his constant anti-
Moslem stance.

Having these three attend was a mere formality. None of
them had access to money or could influence any funding
agencies on his behalf. The senator had been instrumental
in obtaining the initial funding for the Sonomak lab, but he
was now situated on the wrong side of the ITER situation.
The general was just doing time until someone showed the
mercy to pull his plug, and the captain's only concern was
that the books were balanced.

The remaining two were another matter.

The first was Dr. Kristoff Jorgenson, DOE contract monitor for the Sonomak program and assistant director of the
Plasma Physics Directorate within DOE.

Jorgenson smiled, his ruddy face beaming. The smile
was pure reflex. He would have rather been anywhere but
there, staring into the Sonomak lab and Horst's arrogant
face. *Didn't this kraut bastard know he was so much putrefying sausage?* thought Jorgenson. *ITER has killed you*,
he wanted to say, but instead he spoke cordially. "So good
to see you, Horst. I know that we have all been looking
forward to your demonstration today, and we hope to see
the twenty-million-degree level reached."

"I'm certain we can manage that," said Horst. "And *perhaps* a bit more."

Perhaps.

Katie, Aaron, and Beong each sat in front of a computer
console—Katie's the diagnostic, measuring plasma temperature, electron densities, and the plasmon diameter, com-
paring it all to her simulations; Aaron's monitoring the
health of the Sonomak—pressures, helium injector velocity, magnet temperatures, and powers—all those things
needed to keep the Sonomak running; while Beong's kept
watch on the Titanium-Sapphire Laser and the array of
Pocket Accelerators. They said nothing in response to
Horst's boast, did not so much as twitch. They knew the
importance of presenting a united front, of never showing

the slightest sign of surprise to outsiders, especially those who held the purse strings.

Horst looked away from Jorgenson and to the last TP monitor. "I appreciate you being able to attend our demonstration, Dr. Quinn," he said, "especially in light of my last-minute invitation."

Katie had never heard of Dr. Quinn, but judging from the facial expressions of the other four in the TP monitors, *they* certainly had. Jorgenson jerked back as if physically slapped, the general flared his nostrils as if he just got a whiff of something rancid, the captain smiled as if in anticipation of the punch line of some sick and disgusting joke, and Senator Miller grimaced.

Quinn nodded. "Certainly, Dr. Wittkowski. We are always interested in *novel* ways to manipulate energy and matter." He smiled, and the skin across his face pulled tight, the sharp-angled bones beneath protruding, looking as if they were about to rupture through the skin. To Katie, the image of a snake unhinging its jaw and swallowing an egg came to mind.

Horst focused and stared at Quinn.

The *Slick Man*—that was Quinn's nickname in government circles.

Horst had met him face-to-face once before, in '98, at a DARPA meeting in Puerto Rico during the island's statehood celebration, and had walked away from the meeting with the urge to head straight to the bathroom to scour his hands with scalding water. Slick Man was based at the Ballistic Missile Defense Organization, the BMDO being the mutated offspring of the long-dead Strategic Defense Initiative. But Horst suspected that was just a front. Allen Quinn reeked of spookdom and black projects. Horst was certain that he was from the NSA, or even the CIA. But Horst had moved past the point of worrying about that. *Money was money.* The word was that Quinn had money for the *right* type of projects. Horst took a quick look behind him, at his three associates at their consoles, and then turned back to the TP monitors, focusing solely on Allen Quinn.

Sell it, thought Horst. *Sell it big*.

"Gentleman, I will be quite blunt with you. The future of fusion power does not lie with magnetic confinement, or laser-based inertial confinement," he said, taking deliberate swipes at both ITER and the laser boys at the National Ignition Facility in California. "Those technologies are a brute force approach to fusion, crude and expensive attempts which do not take advantage of the more sophisticated, *elegant*, technologies which the twenty-first century has to offer."

Horst could not read the Slick Man's face—there was no emotion, no life in it. But Horst was not worried, at least not yet. Slick Man had a reputation for embracing new technologies, and the Sonomak certainly met that criteria. Slick Man wanted beyond state of the art, in order to threaten today's world with tomorrow's technology.

"The Sonomak represents such a technology," said Horst.

Quinn's only response was a quick blink.

"If you will turn to page four of the briefing books, you will see the basic schematic of the Sonomak." He continued to focus on Quinn. He knew that the others had seen the Sonomak schematic countless times before and were probably bored to tears with it.

But that didn't matter—he was selling to Quinn.

"The heart of the Sonomak technology is the Pocket Accelerator," said Horst, reaching down below the range of the Vid and picking up a Pocket Accelerator—the one-meter-length tube of precisely contoured stainless steel. "What we have discovered is that when we pulse a terawatt Titanium-Sapphire Laser on and off in periods as short as twenty femtoseconds into a high-density helium plasma, that an evacuated channel, swept clear of electrons, is created by a process called electron cavication. You can think of this process as drilling a hole right through the plasma, selectively removing the negatively charged electrons, while leaving behind the heavier charged ions, those ions helping to focus and channel the laser beam. As a result of the cavication process, an immense electric field is generated between the negatively charged electrons that have been swept away and the positively charged ions, which remain. This electric field in turn accelerates electrons in the direction of the laser—in essence transforming the laser beam into an extremely high-energy electron beam."

Horst waved the Pocket Accelerator at the Vid.

"By way of active shaping of the internal electrical fields in order to eliminate turbulence and plasma instabilities, the Pocket Accelerator contours the plasma, allowing maximum acceleration of electrons with an electric field gradient of ten *GeV* per centimeter."

Horst paused for effect.

"Think of that, gentlemen—ten *billion* volts across a one-centimeter spacing."

Quinn's eyes opened slightly, and the muscles at the base of his jaw quivered as he ground his teeth. Horst nodded ever so slightly, trying to read something in those facial motions. He felt confident that Quinn had taken the bait. *No one* could resist the beauty and elegance of a ten GeV-per-centimeter field gradient.

"This means that a one-*meter*-long Pocket Accelerator can produce one *TeV* electrons—one *trillion electron-volts*, an energy which, prior to this technology, could only be obtained after electrons had traveled one *kilometer* down the *Stanford Linear Accelerator*—a distance one thousand times greater than that required for the Pocket Accelerator." Again Horst paused for effect. "This technology is unique to the Georgia Tech fusion effort."

Quinn leaned toward the monitor and smiled, exposing teeth that were slightly yellowed, and gums that were tinted gray. "Very impressive, Professor," he said with all the sincerity of a rattlesnake apologizing just before sinking its fangs into a victim, "but we should not forget that Akasaki at the University of Tokyo is reporting fifteen GeV per centimeter, and that Umstadter at Michigan is generating neutron fluxes as a result of the fusion events taking place in a deuterium/tritium plasma during the collapse of an electron cavication region."

Horst took a half-step back. He managed to keep smiling. He was not aware that Akasaki had reached the fifteen-GeV level. The Umstadter results he was well aware of, but he had conveniently neglected to mention them in his overview. At that moment he knew he had grossly miscalculated Quinn's knowledge—the Slick Man appeared to be up to speed on the state-of-the-art results.

Horst opened his mouth, but was cut off before he could speak.

"Before you continue with your fascinating description of the Sonomak," said Quinn, "there are a few points that I should mention." He held up two fingers, the middle and index finger, and then lowered the index finger. "First, you should know that I provided key inputs which resulted in the shutdown of the SLAC at Stanford, and the Tevatron at Fermi. I do not care for particle physics, or for those physicists who feel that the federal government should foot the bill for their high-energy fantasies." The middle finger curled down. "In addition, I have no interest in fusion energy, a technology which I consider unnecessary for the foreseeable future, as long as our Middle East interests are maintained. I represent the federal government, which in turn is entrusted with maintaining the safety of its citizens in an ever-more dangerous world, and as such, find myself *solely* interested in technologies that can be harnessed for the defense of this nation."

Horst suddenly felt nauseous.

Beong let out an audible moan.

Katie shook her head. *Why in the hell was this arrogant asshole even wasting the Vid time to watch this demonstration?* she wondered. *He obviously had absolutely no interest in the Sonomak.*

Quinn held up his hands, palms facing the monitor, and slowly shook his head. "But I apologize for my little interruption; you were explaining how the Sonomak is *intended* to work." His eyelids almost closed. "Please continue to enlighten me."

At that moment, Horst knew that Quinn was a complete and total dry hole—they would never see a dime from this *schmuck*. He turned his head slightly and focused on Jorgenson. As far as this demonstration was concerned, he was the only one remaining that might be able to provide any funding at all, though, in light of the ITER situation, the odds of that were extremely small. "Yes," said Horst, regathering himself, forcing himself back into his Sonomak monologue. "The output of each Pocket Accelerator is focused at the center of the Sonomak, in which the intersecting cavication beams create a spherical region nearly devoid of electrons—you can picture it as a bubble in a sea of electrons. By careful manipulation of the laser pulse duration and frequency, this bubble can be made to pulse, to rapidly expand and contract with the same frequency as the laser pulse, during which the energy of the laser is coupled to the ions within the bubble, feeding them, causing them to rapidly heat."

Jorgenson smiled at him—an embarrassed smile. Jorgenson wanted this demonstration to be over quickly. He wanted the whole Sonomak business to be over. At that moment he knew that regardless of what temperature the Sonomak reached, whether twenty million or even forty million degrees, it made absolutely no difference. Even if he'd been able to squeeze a few dollars back out of the ITER allotment, the Sonomak had now fallen within Quinn's gunsights. He did not know why Quinn had taken such an instant dislike to both Horst and the Sonomak, but that didn't matter. What mattered was that Quinn obviously opposed it, and Jorgenson was not about to squander any of his limited political ammunition fighting someone like Quinn. He knew that if Horst had been wounded and bleeding before this demonstration, he was now a corpse.

And Jorgenson would distance himself as quickly as possible.

Horst looked from Jorgenson to Quinn, and then back

again to Jorgenson. At that moment, he too realized the fundamental error that he'd somehow made. The look on Jorgenson's face said it all.

The Sonomak was dead.

Horst continued to talk, inertia and overall numbness keeping the words flowing from his mouth. "When the plasmon bubble is grown to sufficient size, on the order of several millimeters, and the ions within it pumped up to temperatures of three to four million degrees, the laser intensity is ramped down, causing a controlled collapse of the plasmon, the bubble rapidly contracting as the electrons come crashing back into the region of the ions, generating a shock wave that further heats them. Our simulations have conclusively shown that electron temperatures in excess of two hundred million degrees should be obtainable with this technique—temperatures high enough to create nuclear fusion."

Quinn smiled.

"I doubt that very much, Professor. Even if you run all forty-eight of your Pocket Accelerators you will not be able to maintain the necessary spherical symmetry of the imploding shock wave to reduce the plasmon bubble to a small enough volume to achieve such a temperature. I doubt this technology can ever break the fifty-million-degree level. At best you will fuse a handful of atoms, and perhaps after several more years of work, you may manage to reproduce the same pathetic results as those obtained at Michigan."

The numbness suddenly vanished.

Something molten burned in Horst. Until that moment, Horst had not been *totally* certain that he would run the Implosion DVD. Despite the bravado he'd tried to fill himself with, Katie's warning had been gnawing at him, eating away at his confidence. But when he looked up at the TP monitor and at Quinn's smug face, at that expression of condescension and outright hostility, Horst made his decision. He would not back down in front of the Slick Man.

"I disagree," said Horst, staring into the monitor, wishing that he could punch his fist right through the screen and

spread the bastard's nose across his face. Horst pulled the
DVD wallet from out of his coat pocket, opened it, and
pulled out the Implosion DVD. "And I will demonstrate it
for you right now." He stepped back, and reaching over
Katie, pushed the DVD into her control console without
giving her the chance to see it.

Katie listened to the DVD whir, pecked at the keyboard,
and focused on the simulation quadrant of her Virtuals, seeing a sea of green. No problems. She then looked over at
Beong and Aaron. They both nodded, their faces expressionless, as if they were in shock.

"Whenever you are ready, Katie," said Horst, turning
back around to face Quinn.

Katie flipped the safety latch over the fire button and held
her finger above the toggle switch. Everything was still
green. "I'm ready to fire," she said.

Horst nodded.

She flipped the switch.

The plasma in the Sonomak struck, a sharp white-blue
glow pouring through its viewing ports. Horst counted
down to himself. The Sonomak would take ten seconds for
the plasma to stabilize, to equilibrate before the Pocket Accelerators fired. Once they fired, the test would be over in
nanoseconds—the plasmon formed, fed energy, and then
imploded as the laser intensity ramped down over a period
of a few nanoseconds. And enough energy would be
dumped to fry the inside of the machine, destroying detectors and sensors—if they were lucky.

Katie raised her head as her count reached zero, looking
through the observation window and into the Sonomak lab.

She blinked—a flash of light forcing her eyes shut.

Whump!

Katie's eardrums popped, and her chair pushed back as
a wall of air struck her in the chest. She opened her eyes,
could now see, despite a white-yellow halo afterglow that
filled her eyes, and the Plexiglas window in front of her
began to crack, bowing inward, then suddenly reversing

itself, pushed into the lab, shattering and exploding outward.

From within the lab came the roar and screech of metal crashing against metal. A second shockwave hit her from behind, pushing her forward, slamming her into her console, pulling her toward the hole that only moments before had been filled with the viewing window.

And then almost total silence, the only sounds those of rustling paper and the crackling of cooling metal. Several blinks and she was able to focus, to look into the lab. At first she thought the Sonomak was gone—the center of the lab seemed empty, nothing remaining except for sheared bolt stems protruding out from the concrete slab. And then she saw the Sonomak, saw what was left of it, and saw what it had been *transformed* into. It lay on its side, slammed into electronic racks that it had flattened and then pinned against the lab's rear wall. Only a few of the Pocket Accelerators were still attached to it; the rest were strewn around the lab, several embedded in the walls. But she barely noticed that.

It was the spherical chamber of the Sonomak itself that held all her attention.

At first she thought it had been twisted, somehow *flowed*. But that was not quite right. It was *distorted*. What had been a nearly perfect sphere of stainless steel had been elongated, practically turned into a tube, and then torn in half and *retied* back together in a complicated knot.

Exploding objects did not tie themselves back together.

It was *impossible*.

Turning around, she saw Aaron and Beong picking themselves up off the floor. Horst was standing. There was a ragged cut across his forehead, blood running into his left eye. Looking past Katie and at what the Sonomak had been transformed into, he smiled. "We just had our miracle, Katie," he said without looking at her. Behind him the TP monitors were filled with electronic snow.

Katie turned back to look at the twisted wreckage of the Sonomak and realized there was something familiar about its transformed shape. Then she saw the green and blue string knot that Anthony had made earlier in the day and knew that the Sonomak had been tied into the exact same carrick knot that Anthony had used in the contraption that had attacked Miss Alice.

Identical.

Her body shuddered in a quick head-to-toe spasm.

SECTION I
CHAPTER 3

"Has it really happened?"

Quinn turned his head. *Perfect face*, he thought. Powerful face. Unflawed symmetry, skin the color of honey, angular nose, chin pronounced, almost cleft. Irises as dark as pupils, devouring all they saw. Had that face belonged to anyone but Alexandra Mitchell, he could have loved the woman behind it.

"Did they do it?" she asked.

He pointed a remote at the fourteenth-century Venetian tapestry that filled the wall at the far end of the room. "It appears that they took the first step."

The tapestry retracted into the ceiling, revealing the wall screen behind it. A momentary flash of static coalesced into the image of a devastated laboratory.

"As you anticipated, manipulating Wittkowski into pushing his Sonomak to the breaking point was easy. He was more than willing to destroy it to show me what it was capable of." Quinn smiled. *So damn easy*, he thought. *They were all such children.* "We had a full analysis team there within two hours of the explosion. At the mention of *"possible radiation,"* the locals were only too happy to relinquish jurisdiction. The lab was stripped down to the subflooring and up to the air ducting, and everything was transported to Dobbins AFB in Marietta, Georgia."

"And Wittkowski's response?"

"He went ballistic of course, but then calmed very quickly as soon as I said the magic word."

Alexandra nodded. She knew the magic word—*funding*.

"I've set a meeting with Wittkowski, McGuire, and the two of us in the annex office, to discuss the details and determine what next steps, if any, should be taken."

"Before I go over the details," said Alexandra, "did they *actually* generate a negative energy density?"

"It appears that they did," he said.

Alexandra shook her head in disbelief. She never would have expected this, not here, and certainly not now with this *primitive* technology. All her training, at least that portion of it that she chose to remember, told her that this world should still be several centuries away from manipulating space-time. She had believed these animals incapable of making the breakthrough without at least some control over the manipulation of artificial black holes. They were continually surprising her.

But that was just as well. The falsified report she would send back to the Makers, detailing why these animals were still far away from manipulating space-time, would be all the more believable after the explosion. She would make her escape long before the Makers even suspected what she'd been doing on this world.

"When all the input energy to the Sonomak is added together, including the RF to heat the plasma, the lasers, the few fusion reactions they generated, and even the current flowing through the magnets, it's not enough to explain what happened," said Quinn. "They must have accessed vacuum states and generated a negative energy density." He pointed the remote at the screen and zoomed in on the remains of the Sonomak.

Alexandra stared at it, trying to understand what she was looking at. "It appears to be tied in a knot."

"A carrick knot, to be exact," said Quinn. "*We* don't have sufficient theoretical understanding of what is happening to be able to explain this, although we suspect that the shape reflects some aspect of the quantization of space itself when very high levels of energy are concentrated in a very small volume. But *we* really don't know."

Alexandra clenched her jaw, knowing that this last comment was aimed directly at her. Her understanding of physics was rudimentary. There was little she could do about that. She was not designed to understand the details of universe fabrication. By design she was a sociologist, a manipulator, meant to keep these creatures in line, knowing just enough physics to allow her to steer them, but not to lead them. The Makers had been very careful about what she was allowed to understand. That was just one of a nearly infinite number of injustices that the Makers had inflicted upon her. And now she would escape them. "Is there any evidence that they generated a universe?" she asked.

"Absolutely none," he said. "What happened to the Sonomak appears to be a result of stressing the fabric of spacetime. We have found no evidence of unaccounted for mass or any blowback of physical objects from a collapsing universe."

Alexandra nodded. "Give me the remote," she said by way of dismissal.

Quinn understood, quickly getting up from the massive conference table, and walked past its dozens of empty chairs. He did not look back as he left the room, and was grateful to be done.

Alexandra did not give Quinn's departure a second thought, having barely given it a first thought. She picked up the keyboard, and the image on the wall screen rolled once, then locked onto the Federal Employee Database. Before the meeting with Wittkowski and McGuire she needed to find someone other than Quinn, someone who could work with her *and* the plasma physicists. Alexandra increased her neural clock rate from its standby rate of one kilohertz, to one megahertz, and then began to search personnel files. A new bio flashed across the screen every ten milliseconds.

• • •

Jack Preston's head throbbed, his tongue felt coated in cotton, and his eyeballs itched. He felt like he was in the depths of a world-class hangover, although he hadn't had a drop to drink since Laura had walked out on him two days earlier. He suspected he was either coming down with the flu, or suffering from some form of post-breakup depression.

He shifted in his waiting room chair to the accompaniment of rude noises from the cheap plastic upholstery. The male secretary did not look his way. Wearing a full-wrap headset and dual data gloves, the man's fingers fluttered across a virtual keyboard. Jack had little difficulty smelling the military stink of the man—the mirrorlike sheen of his black leather shoes, the perfect posture, and the square jaw that looked as if it had been shaved only minutes before told the story.

But he wore civilian clothes—black suit, black tie, and white shirt—something suitable for a funeral. Jack almost managed a smile, but the muscles in his face hurt too much. This might well be *his* funeral. Guys who got canned by the Department of Energy didn't have a lot of options. Summoned to one of the countless glass towers that dotted this portion of Alexandria, by a cryptic E-mail telling him that he was being considered for a new monitoring job, he had wasted little time driving over. The building was not federal, but private, filled with a hodgepodge of civilian companies that lived off the federal fat oozing out of the Beltway.

He was here to see one A. Mitchell. While driving over he had done a quick search for A. Mitchell in the greater D.C. area. He'd found twenty-three, but none of them had anything to do with the type of big-dollar, big-science physics that had been his field. *Strange.* Even stranger was the fact that A. Mitchell was not listed in the office-building directory, nor was A. Mitchell's name on the door to this office. He'd learned long ago that Washington types who had programs, and the money to back them, loved to advertise. *How do I love me? Let me count the ways.* This office looked like it had been put together only minutes before his arrival. Other than the chair and desk that the secretary used, and his own chair, the only other item in the office was a faded artificial plastic fern shoved in the corner.

All these clues added up to only one conclusion.

Black projects.

A. Mitchell was probably a management spook, either DOD or NSA, with several billion dollars in hidden money that were being used to develop some new weapon-of-mass-peace, and A. Mitchell needed a piece of techno-meat to interface between this office and the snoops in Congress.

"She will see you now."

She. That surprised Jack. Spook managers were typically old white men with buzz-cuts, black-rimmed glasses, and mustard-stained ties, who would attempt to impress you with tales of Gook-splattering in *the* Nam.

"Now," said the secretary.

Jack stood up too quickly, and his head pounded, his peripheral vision momentarily darkening. He made his way to the door, was about to make a grab for the knob, but could feel the palms of his hands sweating, and quickly wiped them on his pants. He turned the knob and pushed the door open, stepping in.

Red.

A. Mitchell sat behind the same type of nondescript desk as the secretary. She stood, bending slightly forward, offering a hand. She wore a bright red power suit, tailored nearly skin tight, and had bloodred lipstick and fingernails to match. Both eyes and hair were coal-black, her skin the color of olives, and her eyes large. "A pleasure to meet you Dr. Preston," she said. "I am Alexandra Mitchell."

Jack stepped forward, took her hand, and shook it. Her grasp was firm, warm, and very politician-like.

Alexandra did not let go of his hand, holding on longer than she knew was appropriate. But she sensed something about this man, could feel it in his strong grasp, a feeling of something familiar, and a vague recollection that they had met before.

She knew that was impossible.

Her memory was *perfect*. Every few centuries she would purge herself of useless information, her storage capabilities massive, more than enough to operate in this world of mortal creatures, but not infinite. She searched, again confirming that there was no record of this man in her memory.

But still the feeling persisted—a mix of curiosity and *fear*.

Alexandra dropped Jack's hand, and motioned to her left, as she told herself that she had nothing to fear from this unevolved creature, and that feelings of curiosity and fear were nothing more than a symptom of being so close to her goal, so close to escape. "And this is my associate, Dr. Allen Quinn."

Jack turned, dropping her hand. Quinn sat in the corner of the office, partially hidden by the still-open door. He stood, pushed the door shut, and came toward Jack, offering his hand. Jack shook it, and this handshake was everything that Alexandra Mitchell's had not been—weak, moist, with fingers that felt like sausages. He let go as quickly as possible, and had to fight the urge to wipe his hands across his pants. Jack had never met Quinn, but had heard of him— a BMDO hatchet man brought in whenever they needed a world-class asshole to vaporize a program.

Quinn said nothing.

"Please be seated, Dr. Preston," said Alexandra.

He turned, walked over to the one empty chair in the office, and sat. This office was just as sterile as the outer office, without benefit of the ancient plastic fern. This was obviously just a front—they did not want him to know their real location.

"It is our good fortune to find someone of your caliber between assignments," said Alexandra.

From behind, Jack could hear Quinn snicker.

Jack nodded politely. Quinn was slime, and the woman was a bullshitter. Everyone in this room knew that being placed in the DOE *Temp Pool* was just the Feds' way of booting you without benefit of actually firing you. They'd let you sit in the pool for six weeks, and when no new assignments came your way you'd receive the layoff notice.

Jack smiled politely and nodded.

"You are aware of the plasma effort at the Georgia Institute of Technology?"

"I've had no direct interaction with that group," said Jack, "but I am familiar with the Sonomak and their Pocket Accelerator program." He was actually more than just aware of it; he had read all the monthly reports and journal papers that the group put out. Of course he should have been spending all his available time concentrating on his own programs, but the Georgia Tech group's approach was *interesting*, something about it very attractive, something that he couldn't quite put into words. It had been one of the many diversions that had cost him his job.

"And your assessment?" she asked.

Jack sat back in his chair. Here was the first dangerous question. A mistake here could cost him whatever job they were considering him for, and he suddenly realized that if this job had something to do with the Sonomak, then he was very much interested in it.

The desire surprised him—shocked him. It had been many years since he'd wanted much of anything.

"The approach they're taking toward nuclear fusion is technically very challenging, but if they can show feasibility, the techniques should warrant further investigation." Jack knew that was a safe, bullshit statement. The fact that he was sitting in this office, and that these spooks were interested in the Sonomak, meant that something must have happened, some breakthrough, maybe. "I would say that one of the largest problems that the group faces is not so much a technical one, but an infrastructure problem—the program is bare-bones staffed, making progress difficult, and it's so small that it probably does not receive the direction and inputs that are needed to keep it on track."

Alexandra smiled.

Jack smiled back.

He'd in essence said that the DOE was incompetently

managing the program and implied that it should be taken over by some other agency. He had nothing to lose, since the DOE had already cut him loose. If he read the situation correctly, taking over the program was exactly what Alexandra Mitchell had in mind.

"We agree," she said. "Two days ago, an *event* occurred during a demonstration run of the Sonomak, an *event* which we have taken some interest in."

"And the nature of the *event*?" asked Jack.

"Not yet determined," said Quinn from behind him.

Jack understood a warning when he heard it—they did not want to discuss what had happened, not until they knew if he could be trusted, or more importantly, *controlled*.

"However, despite our interest, and the poor management which DOE has demonstrated up to this point, we wish to keep the program under the umbrella of the DOE, while all future program decisions and funding will come from *my* office."

Jack didn't ask what office that might be. They obviously wanted to stay in the shadows. What they were looking for was a DOE front man.

Him.

"You understand what we are looking for?"

Jack nodded, knowing just what they wanted—an obedient dog to take their orders and money, and then shove both those items down the throats of the Georgia Tech plasma group. "A DOE liaison to interface between you and those at Georgia Tech?"

"Exactly," she said. "Would you be interested in such a position?"

Jack was normally not a rash or impulsive man. A decision of this magnitude would have typically taken him many agonizing days of weighing pros and cons. But at that moment, he knew what he had to do, felt in some way that he really had no choice.

He almost laughed as he realized he felt destiny calling.

"Yes," he said. "I would gladly take such a position." His headache and flu symptoms suddenly vanished.

"Excellent," said Alexandra, standing up and offering her hand.

Jack stood, surprised, realizing that he was being dismissed, without having been given any details about the job. He shook her hand.

"By the time you return to your office, a briefing book and full details of the job will be on your desk. Go over it today, and then I will stop by your apartment tonight to go over a few details that you will not find in the briefings."

"Thank you," said Jack, turning, wondering just what those details might be, and wondering why she wanted to meet in his apartment. Quinn stood before him with hand outstretched. Jack took it, the image of sausages again coming to mind. "I look forward to working with you," he lied.

Quinn smiled, exposing yellow teeth, and pulled Jack toward him. "Don't fuck this up," he said.

Jack nodded, pulled his hand away, and was out the door, wiping his hand across his jacket before he even left the outer office.

SECTION I
CHAPTER 4

Katie pushed the camera's suction cup against the mirror, punched the on button, and stood back. She turned her head to the right and then to the left, watching the hotel room sweep by in the lower left quadrant of her Virtuals. Two queen-sized beds, nightstand with lamp and alarm clock, and, at the far end of the room, a couch, coffee table, and small kitchen table at which Anthony sat. It could have been a hotel room *anywhere* in the world, with nothing to give a hint as to its location. In this case it was Washington, D.C.—the Ramada Inn at Alexandria.

She watched Anthony coloring, tongue sticking out between his lips as he concentrated. Katie fluttered her eyelids and the image zoomed in on Anthony. *So focused*, she thought. *Too focused.* Ever since the Sonomak had been splattered across the lab, there had been a change in Anthony. Not so outgoing, not so wild, and certainly not as mischievous. He'd become a serious little boy.

Katie was worried.

And then there was the business of the carrick knot. Horst thought she was crazy, that she had imagined that Anthony had made the knot earlier in the day, and that the shock of the explosion, of the destruction of a piece of equipment that they'd spent years building, had confused her memory.

She wanted to believe that—but she couldn't.

There was some connection between Anthony and what had happened in the lab, but she couldn't figure out what it could be.

"Excellent coffee."

Katie turned, the camera swiveling, still zoomed, the quickly panning room momentarily disorienting her. Horst stood on the balcony—hardly a balcony, just a three-foot-deep platform with a wrought iron guardrail around it. He sipped coffee from a little porcelain mug. He'd shown up at their room almost thirty minutes ago, bubbling with enthusiasm, almost to the point of giddiness. Never in her life had she ever heard him have a single good thing to say about hotel coffee—but today it was *excellent*. There had been a time when so many things were *excellent*—the feelings they had for each other, the family they had started, a future so full of hope. But all that was gone, and she knew that none of those things any longer had the power to touch Horst, let alone move him.

She knew that today was *excellent* because he smelled *big* funding.

And, just as important, she was certain that he believed today would be a Horst love-fest, complete with nonstop ego stroking. And he might just be right. The collapsing plasmon had reached a temperature of 140 million degrees—and probably went even higher, but the insides of the Sonomak were seared and the detectors vaporized. That temperature represented a major breakthrough. Then there was the Sonomak itself—and what it had been *twisted* into.

That part was simply impossible.

And when impossible things happened, it meant you were right at the edge of understanding something new, and something as weird as this could be Nobel-caliber weirdness. But she still felt unsettled; the combination of the carrick knot and the snakelike Quinn frightened her. She rarely took an instant dislike to anyone, but Quinn was the exception. There was something *wrong* with that man.

She nulled the input to her Virtuals, knocked down the polarization, and walked across the room to the balcony. "I'm worried, Horst."

He took a sip of his coffee, shut his eyes for a moment, and then reopened them. "Katie, you are *always* worried. If there is nothing real to worry about, then your brain will fantasize something." He looked across the room at Anthony. "There is nothing wrong with the boy," he said, certain that he knew what she was referring to. She was always worrying about the boy.

"Well I am worried about him," she said. "He's not himself. He's withdrawn, somehow shutdown. He's been the *perfect* little boy on this trip."

Horst smiled. "He's just growing up, Katie, learning some restraint, maturing."

"Horst, he is just a six-year-old boy, who should be a handful and causing all sorts of problems."

"Nonsense," said Horst. "Anthony," he called across the room. "Come over here and show us what you're drawing, so I can put your mother at ease."

Anthony got up from his chair, bringing the piece of paper he'd been coloring, walking slowly, his head hung slightly down, not looking directly at his parents. He handed Horst the drawing. "Look at this, Katie," he said, rattling it under her nose. "The boy is an artistic genius. Look at the colors, the perspectives, the complexities."

Katie looked and winced. It was a cubist-impressionist melding, something that might have been drawn by a

Picasso–Van Gogh hybrid on acid. Swirling bright colors constrained within stark geometrical patterns showed a skeletal boy, seen from many angles and poses, melded into one monstrous little child trapped within what looked like a cage of melting wax.

There was a knock at the door.

"Excellent," said Horst, looking across the hotel room. "That must be your sitter for the morning, Anthony." The boy did not look up at his father. "You are going to be a good little boy for her, aren't you, Anthony?"

"Yes, sir," he said.

"Then let her in," said Horst.

Katie could not look away from the drawing of the child-monster with its bony hands wrapped around the bars of the melting cage, so desperate to escape, the bars twisting and flowing, starting to give way. Something was wrong with Anthony.

Horst felt a hole burning through his stomach lining. He'd drunk far too much coffee prior to the meeting and was now paying for it. The conference room had all the ambiance of a coffin, in fact almost was a coffin, buried in the subbasement of the DOE. Barely large enough to hold the conference table and the four people who sat around it, the room was hot and stuffy, one small air-conditioning vent down by the baseboard feebly whistling. Four cameras, each ceiling-mounted in the corners of the room, recorded every facial twitch and drop of sweat. Horst hit the return key on his laptop and his last View Graph appeared on the screen. He didn't look at it, but at those sitting on the other side of the conference table—at Allen Quinn, Alexandra Mitchell, and Jack Preston. All three were statues.

The only one he could read was Quinn.

The man smiled like a vulture that had just spotted a carcass.

The meeting was not going at all well. He'd shown them the future; shown them the path to limitless cheap energy, and they had not asked a single question, had not shown the slightest interest. They sat and stared. Horst quickly glanced at Katie, and she offered up an encouraging smile.

"In conclusion," said Horst, "we have documented temperatures of one hundred forty million degrees and believe that we may have in fact broken through the two-hundred-million-degree level. We propose that with the addition of another forty-eight Pocket Accelerators, an increase in chamber diameter from the present two meters to three meters, the addition of more computing power so we can actively modify the wavefront of the shock wave during the implosion phase, a molten lithium cooling blanket to extract neutron energy, and by converting from our current helium plasma to a deuterium/tritium mix, that we should be able to demonstrate initial fusion reactions within a two-year time frame."

Alexandra smiled. "Most impressive work, Professor," she said. Leaning back in her chair, she held her hands up, pressing them together, looking as if she were about to pray. "*If* it were our desire to investigate the use of the Sonomak for fusion research, I'm certain that we would take your proposal quite seriously."

Horst suddenly felt sick, and something in his lower intestines started to bubble. How could they not understand the significance of what he had just shown them?

"However, that is not our desire."

Jack knew that was his cue. He had read the briefing books, amazed and even frightened by the true intent of this program, and then Alexandra had come to his apartment to add some *details*.

He fought down a butt-to-head twitch.

The world as he had known it no longer existed. That world had been shattered by what Alexandra had *inserted* into his head. Jack was looking forward to seeing this big buffoon getting the stuffing blown out of him when he learned the truth.

But Dr. Katie McGuire was another matter.

He'd been watching her, *studying* her during Horst's boring and meaningless presentation. When she'd first entered the room, he had thought that he recognized her, although he knew they had never met before. But there was something so familiar about her, so *right* with her, that just looking at her made him relax, actually made him smile.

"Jack?" said Alexandra.

Jack shook his head, realizing that he had drifted off and was staring at Katie McGuire. She was looking back, a puzzled expression on her face, and then she began to blush and look away, pretending to study the last View Graph that Horst had shown.

"Yes. Yes," said Jack as he pulled his laptop out of his briefcase, opened it, and ran his fingers over the keyboard. Quinn had instructed him carefully before the meeting as to exactly what would take place, how they would best shatter Horst's ego and take control away from him. They needed his know-how, not his attitude. Horst's last View Graph vanished from the display and was replaced by a photo of the twisted Sonomak.

Seeing the knotted chunk of stainless steel made Katie quickly focus on the display quadrant of her Virtuals. Buried this deeply within the DOE the reception was poor and grainy, but she could see what she needed to see as she turned her head right-left-right, panning the hotel room. Anthony was still coloring. The sitter lay back on the bed, a remote in hand, staring at the Vid.

All was quiet.

She half polarized her glasses and found herself looking at Jack Preston. She tried to think serious thoughts, forcing her head to fill with equations, but it did little good. She felt herself blushing again. Her freckled skin was so pale; she knew that when she blushed she looked as if she were on fire.

That realization only made her blush more.

There was something about Jack Preston. It was in the way he moved, the look in his eyes, a nose that was just a touch crooked, as if it had once been broken. Her cheeks felt hot. She looked away and up at the projected Sonomak just as that View Graph was replaced with another.

"*This* is why we will be funding your research," said

Jack, as he brought up the new View Graph.

Katie squinted, trying to focus, not certain what she was looking at—it appeared to be a sea of wiggly gray lines.

"And this is?" asked Horst, sounding unimpressed.

Jack brought up the next View Graph, a duplicate of the last with one important difference; portions of the snaking lines were now shaded in different colors. What at first had appeared to Katie to be a nearly infinite scrawling line was in fact an intricate network of *discrete* knots, all neatly snugged together and interlocked like the patterns in a Penrose tile. She looked more carefully, and realized just what those knots were.

Carrick knots.

"Note the scale," said Jack.

Katie looked at the bottom of the photo where a large white bar denoted a spacing of one micrometer—one ten-thousandth of a centimeter.

"This is a *Transmission Electron Micrograph* cross section of a piece of the Sonomak. Those lines are the grain boundaries between recrystallized regions of iron crystals. We've examined the Sonomak and found that this knot structure is reflected at a *multitude* of scales." Jack accessed the next View Graph. At first glance it appeared to be an exact copy of the previous one. "Note the scale on this *TEM* cross section," he said.

The same bar was at the bottom of the photo, but this one was marked ten nanometers, this photo *one hundred times* the magnification of the last.

"Whatever process the Sonomak was exposed to not only altered it on the macroscopic scale, somehow tying the entire chamber into a knot, but this process was replicated again and again at smaller and smaller scales within the steel itself."

"And *that* is what you want to fund?" asked Horst, not believing what he was hearing. "I've shown you a practical route to nuclear fusion, not some new approach to *anneal* steel!"

Jack ignored him and instead looked at Katie. "Dr.

McGuire," he said, smiling, while staring at her green eyes through the gray Virtuals, barely realizing that he was breathing in sync with her, the rise and fall of her chest matching his. "We are all aware of the professor's expertise in the area of plasma physics, and since his expertise is limited to that area, *he* may not recognize what we are looking at. However, with your broader background, especially considering your cosmology work, I should think that this scaling structure within the Sonomak may strike a chord with you."

Katie stared at the photo, not understanding what Jack Preston was trying to say.

"Think about the structure of the *universe*," said Jack.

Katie blinked once, and then once more. And then she saw it. She understood what he was driving at. And then she blinked for a third time. "But *that* structure reflects the quantum fluctuations present during the Big Bang, just prior to the inflationary period." This was *absolutely* impossible. She slumped back in her chair.

Jack smiled at her. "Precisely," he said.

"Big Bang?" asked Horst, not having the vaguest idea what they were talking about.

Jack focused on Horst, "What you do not understand, but Dr. McGuire has quickly grasped, is that a similarity exists between how our universe was formed and what has happened to the Sonomak."

Horst stared blankly at Jack.

"There is structure to the universe, great arcs of galaxies, voids, a frothy, textured landscape which transverses the overall fabric of the universe. If you look at the universe over different lengths, this structure is repeated over and over again. And what is so amazing about this structure is that it was imposed by the quantum mechanical fluctuations present at the moment of the universe's birth, during those first trillion-trillionths of a second when the universe ballooned from less than the size of a proton to literally cosmic proportions, those quantum fluctuations being imposed on the large-scale structure of the universe."

"So" said Horst, waving his hand first at Jack and then at the picture.

"We believe that a similar process occurred in the Sonomak. During the plasmon implosion enough energy was concentrated in a small enough volume of space, such that an *infinitesimal* bang occurred. In this case the resulting outbound shock wave altered the Sonomak, imposing a geometrical structure, reflecting a type of space-time structure which had been generated at Planck dimensions, and then amplified during the bang into macroscopic space, imposing that geometry on the Sonomak at all levels."

"Planck dimensions?" said Horst.

"One million-billionth the size of an atom," said Katie, "so small, that the fabric of space itself is a frothing, quantized, and discrete thing."

Horst shook his head. "This is insane. The Sonomak is designed to implement fusion reactions!" He was standing.

"No longer!"

Horst turned. Quinn was standing, leaning across the table, looking as if he were ready to grab Horst by the lapels and push him back into his seat. But he did not have to. Horst sat. "A new, larger Sonomak will be constructed at Dobbins AFB, within a secure facility. The objective of this program will *not* be to investigate fusion processes." He stared at Horst, the reptile-glare on his face daring Horst to speak.

Horst said nothing.

"The objective of this program will be to initiate a bang within the Sonomak, and generate a stable, viable universe, one which will exist outside the geometry of our space-time, but one which we will have physical contact with."

"That is insane," said Horst.

"You do not believe that a sufficiently advanced technology could construct a universe?" asked Alexandra.

"There could *never* be any technology that advanced," answered Horst.

"Fortunately for you," said Alexandra, "that is simply not the case. Thirty billion years ago such a technology was responsible for the formation of *this* universe."

Horst laughed. "And you know this because . . ."

"Because *I* come from the universe which created *yours*."

Horst stood, and pulled Katie to her feet. "You are all obviously deranged, and we want nothing more to do with you."

"Perhaps I can convince you," said Alexandra. Two glass filaments, so thin as to be nearly invisible, erupted from her forehead, shot out across the conference table, and embedded themselves in Horst and Katie's foreheads.

The two half-sat, half-fell back into their chairs, as convincing information was transmitted directly into their brains.

Jack reached up with his right hand and touched the sore spot on his forehead, knowing exactly what Horst and Katie were now experiencing. The world as they knew it was about to be forever changed.

"Where do you think the quarter went?"

Katie opened her eyes. A creamy whiteness filled the world. She rolled half over, and found that she was no longer looking at a ceiling, but at a man and a child seated at a table. The man reached toward the boy and pulled an object out of his left ear.

"It was in your ear," he said.

The boy laughed, made a grab for the object, but it was gone, vanished with a fluttering of the man's fingers.

"Where did it go this time, Anthony?"

Anthony.

Katie sat up, felt her head throb, threaten to explode, and her stomach flip-flopped. Closing her eyes, she fell back on the bed. "Anthony," she said. She was back in the hotel room. She reached up to her forehead, at the pounding spot above her right eye, where the *thing* had penetrated her skull.

"Sounds like your Mom's awake."

Katie opened her eyes. Anthony stood above her, smiling, eyes bright. "Jack is teaching me magic tricks," he said.

Jack?

She shifted her head, looking at the unfamiliar face. She blinked, but the face would not quite focus—she was not wearing her Virtuals. "The *transfer* process can be quite a shock to the system," a man's voice said. "It put me flat on my back for quite a few hours."

Jack Preston.

And at that moment she remembered—all of it. There had been a medieval castle, a barge floating down the Nile, wheat billowing along the Euphrates, a band of heavy muscled warriors walking in the shadow of a glacier, and then the Savannah, a world of unbroken grasslands and the apes that populated it.

Not apes, but men and women.

And before that another world, another place.

Another *universe*.

It was a place of light and crystal, tinted by a sun that burned blue. Katie closed her eyes trying to keep all those images out, but they were flooding her from *within*.

"It will take a day or so for it to integrate with the rest of your mind," said Jack. "Most of it is bits and pieces from the memory of Alexandra Mitchell's time on Earth. As near as I can figure, she's been here some four million years. Before that she existed in another world, another universe, in a crystalline type of place bathed in blue light."

Katie nodded.

It was true.

She had seen it. No. *She had lived it.*

"What does she want?" asked Katie, managing to push herself almost to a sitting position.

"It's like Quinn said," answered Jack. "They want us to build a new universe."

Katie fell back down onto the bed.

"What you need now is sleep. I'll watch Anthony, order us up a few burgers from room service, and you'll be up and around in a few hours."

She opened her eyes a crack and again saw a smiling

Anthony. "We'll have burgers and do magic tricks," he said.

Katie managed a nod and then fell into darkness as sleep overwhelmed her.

SECTION I

CHAPTER 5

Ask and you shall receive.

Jack had worked on government projects for seven years, and in all that time, he had never seen anything like this—not even close. The program had been turned on two weeks ago. For a typical government project the first two or three *months* were pure accounting and paperwork, negotiating details of contracts, setting up accounts, getting hordes of bean counters to sign reams of forms. That's how it worked.

Not here.

Here you picked up a phone, punched in a special telephone number, told the operator what you wanted, and it arrived the next morning on a flatbed truck. There was no paperwork, no accountants, no authorizations, and not even any signatures.

Jack looked out into the lab—a jumbo-jet-sized hangar buried ten stories beneath the red Georgia clay, a Cold War artifact refurbished by the spooks to satisfy their post–Cold War paranoia when China had gobbled up a big chunk of Siberia in the late 1990s. Two weeks ago there had been nothing in the hangar but a massive slab of bare concrete, glistening beneath harsh fluorescents.

That seemed like a lifetime ago.

The five-meter-diameter shell of Sonomak II sat in the center of the hangar, hovering in free space, supported by a latticework of high-strength I-beams that rose up from the floor. Bathed in a blue-white glow produced by the flame of heliarc welders, workers streamed over the Sonomak, welding the ports where the 192 Pocket Accelerators would be attached. Beyond the Sonomak, at the far end of the hangar, behind a two-foot-thick wall of concrete and steel plates, sat the bank of eight Titanium-Sapphire Lasers, mounted on optical tables and buried beneath a plumber's nightmare of beam splitters, lenses, optical compressors and expanders, and specialty crystals that did not even exist in the commercial world.

You need eight Titanium-Sapphire Lasers each capable of generating twenty petawatts in ten femtosecond pulses? No problem. The big laser boys have been waiting eighteen months for these to be delivered to Lawrence-Livermore and the National Ignition Facility, but they can wait another eighteen months. Priorities are priorities.

They're yours.

The monster laser bank had been operational for three days now.

And then you say you need a supercomputer that can modify the pulse length and twitch and wiggle the optical pathway of the beams so that you can get maximum compression of the plasmon?

No problem.

It just so happens that the SETI folks can wait a few more months before taking delivery on that Cray 20MP, and we will give you theirs. It has 256 thousand Pentium XII processors operating in parallel, each clocking at ten Gigahertz, the entire machine capable of crunching data at rates up to two thousand teraflops—that is *two thousand million-million* calculations every second.

And of course you will need a lot of power for this little experiment.

Again no problem. You don't even have to make a phone call. It just so happens that Dobbins AFB has its own internal power supply—a spook-run hundred-megawatt nuclear reactor buried another twenty stories beneath this bunker.

Jack shook his head. This was moving *way* too fast—there was not enough time to think, to consider what was really going on. They were supposed to create a new universe. They were under the direction, under the control, of a woman from another universe. Just a few weeks ago he had been lying on his couch, watching his girlfriend stomp out of the apartment, and wondering why yet one more relationship had disintegrated.

Now he was helping to build a universe.

Too fast.

From his vantage point in the observation room, he watched Horst, Beong, and Aaron, all dressed in identical white jumpsuits emblazoned with Buzz the Yellow Jacket, the Georgia Tech mascot, bounce back and forth among the other fifty or so green-suited workers—either DOD employees or spooks. Horst was waving his arms, pointing at the overhead boom that was carrying one of the twenty-foot sections of vacuum tubing that would connect one of the Titanium-Sapphire Lasers to the beam splitters.

System integration had begun.

Off to the side, away from the action and chaos, sat Quinn on an orange plastic chair, observing, obediently doing the bidding of his master. Quinn was always there. There was the occasional break for food or bathroom, but that was it.

If Quinn slept, he did it in that chair, with his eyes open.

Jack wondered if the man had changed his underwear in the last two weeks.

"A million dollars for your thoughts."

Jack quickly turned, startled. Katie stood just a few feet behind him, leaning against a table, coffee mug in one hand, and a chocolate donut covered with rainbow-colored sprinkles in the other. He could not see her eyes behind her Virtuals, but he did not need to see them to know how tired she was. She leaned against the table for support.

Jack smiled, happy to see her. "I'm afraid that a million dollars wouldn't even buy you a roll of toilet paper in this place," he said. "But if you must know, I was contemplating the condition of Allen Quinn's underwear." Katie was the only person in this spook asylum that he could joke with, that he could actually talk to. She seemed to understand both how absurd, as well as how frightening, all this was.

They always seemed to be in sync.

Katie managed a smile and then slid into a chair, placing the donut and coffee on the table. "That's what I get for asking," she said. "I will admit that I've been doing a lot of thinking lately, but the condition of Allen Quinn's underwear has not been something I've spent much time contemplating."

"We each have our special gifts," said Jack. "I'm sure you've been spending your time developing a Theory of Everything, discovering how to fabricate charmed quarks out of French fries, or rewiring your microwave oven so that it's now a matter transmitter."

Katie snickered and took a sip of her lukewarm coffee and a bite of donut. "Slow morning, Jack," she said. "But I have made some progress on our little knot problem."

Jack sat down across from her, suddenly feeling serious.

Katie altered the polarization on her Virtuals so that Jack could see her eyes. "The math is still a bit hairy, and I've got to go through some bizarre renormalizations so that the solutions don't explode at the boundary conditions that I'm using, but it appears that what is going on is that when we pack enough energy into a small enough region of space-time, that it becomes supercooled."

Jack shook his head.

Supercooled space-time.

He understood supercooling in a liquid. If you cooled down ultrapure water very slowly you could actually force it to temperatures below its freezing point, while still maintaining it in the liquid state. Then if you added the slightest impurity, or a bit of energy, the liquid would explosively go through a phase transition, in this case transforming from a liquid to a solid.

"A space-time phase transition?" he said.

"Exactly," said Katie. "And in this case, what appears to start the phase transition is the amplification of a virtual particle that exists at the Planck dimension. You have particles popping in and out of existence all the time at those dimensions, but they never quite become real, always winking out of existence before they can interact with macroscopic space. But when this occurs in a region of supercooled space-time, one of these particles gets stabilized, its wavefunction existing for a much longer period than normal. This initiates the phase transition, and this particle acts as a seed, with the transitioning space around it reflecting the geometry of the seed."

"In this case a carrick knot?"

"Yes," she said. "You can think of this supercooling as a sort of negative energy density. If we can push that density high enough, as the phase transition takes place, instead of impinging on a region of *our* space, it will actually neck off on itself, forming a self-contained bubble."

"Another universe," said Jack.

Katie nodded.

"And what about this seeding business? What geometry does this new universe reflect? Is it somehow related to our universe, or is it something so alien that we won't even be able to interact with it."

"That is the question," she said. "But I suspect that we will be able to interact with it. *She* is able to interact in our universe, and I'm certain that *she* believes that *she* can interact with whatever universe we are able to create."

She.

They rarely said her name, as if to speak it out loud would bring bad luck. Alexandra Mitchell had become *she*.

Katie stood and walked over to the window, looking down on the Sonomak. "It scares me, Jack," she said, without looking at him. "It's in my head." She reached up with both hands and slapped the sides of her face. "She put things there. I saw through *her* eyes, bits and pieces from the last four million years of human history. I have seen *her* universe."

Jack said nothing. For a moment, he felt that hard blue light from a sun in another universe burning against his face. They'd talked about this many times before, both of them somehow believing that if they continued to talk about it that they could make some sort of sense out of it.

"It makes absolutely no sense," said Katie.

Jack nodded. If Alexandra Mitchell was this million-year-old superbeing from another universe, then why did she need them to build the Sonomak and make this new universe? Why didn't she just do it herself, using whatever technology had been used to create this universe? "We just don't have the whole picture yet."

That did not make Katie feel any better.

The business of Anthony and the carrick knot still frightened her. In fact, it terrified her. She had not yet told Jack about that, but she sensed that she soon would. She suspected that very soon there would be nothing that she wouldn't tell Jack.

A thought popped into her head. "Have you been off this base since you arrived in Atlanta?" she asked.

Jack smiled and shook his head.

Base housing.

Base cafeteria.

Base PX.

"Been a bit busy, making sure that everyone gets what they need," he said, waving a hand toward the Sonomak. Even though they had a blank check, the project still required coordination. All materials, supplies, and equipment went through him. Without a coordinator, you'd end up with twenty miles of welding rod and not a single welder to use it.

"You need a break," said Katie.

"And what do you have in mind?" asked Jack, focusing on her, taking a quick inventory of her jeans, T-shirt, and sneakers. She couldn't have weighed over one hundred pounds. But that one hundred pounds were well distributed.

"A picnic," she said.

Jack smiled. "A little wine, a little cheese, a little bread," he said.

"Certainly," she answered, and then felt a twinge of nervousness, saw something in his eyes that both excited and scared her. But she knew that she couldn't back down now. And she didn't want to back down. What she needed was some insurance, a buffer in case things didn't go quite as she hoped they might. She smiled, knowing just what to do. "*Anthony* will just love it. He talks all the time about the magic tricks you taught him."

Jack kept smiling. It wasn't quite what he thought she had been asking. But it was still okay. He would at least be able to see her outside this techno-military asylum. Besides, he needed a break—they both did. "Sounds good," he said.

Hot and humid.

After spending the last seven summers in Washington, D.C., Jack thought he had come to understand what summer heat and humidity were all about. He now knew he'd been an amateur and that now he was playing in the Big Leagues of the Deep South. Today's humidity and temperature were a dead match, both at ninety-three.

"Drink your tea," said Katie.

Jack took a big gulp from the sweating glass. The tea tasted like liquid sugar, but at least it was cold. They sat on an ancient, river-worn shelf of sandstone, protected from the sun by a thick stand of pines, as they watched the muddy Chattahoochee slowly roll by. The air was thick with the scents of decay and moss.

"Quite the little student," said Jack, waving his glass of tea toward Anthony, who sat cross-legged on the far end of the sandstone outcropping, perched just inches away from the slow-moving and shallow Chattahoochee. A thick book lay open in his lap.

"*Too* much of a student," said Katie.

Jack could see the concern in her face, so he crab-walked across the rock and sat down next to Anthony. "What are you reading there?"

Anthony stuck a little finger in the open book, closed it, and looked up at Jack. "*Introduction to Geology*, written by Gerald T. Throller of the University of Minnesota."

From the afternoon he had spent with Anthony in Washington, Jack had known the boy was bright, but had not realized just how bright. The book looked to be at least high school level and might have even been an undergrad college text. Jack rooted around on the sandstone slab and pried off a few thin shards. "What's this?"

"Common sandstone," said Anthony. He eyed the rock carefully. "A good example of a sedimentary rock."

"And that's all?"

Anthony looked at it more closely. "That's all."

"Well," said Jack, "you're right about it being sandstone, but what you've failed to see is that it is a very special type of sandstone, one which can float on water."

Anthony stared first at Jack and then back at the rock. "Sandstone can't float on water," he said. He then paused, as if searching for something. "Its *density* is greater than that of the water. It *has* to sink."

Jack was impressed. He'd met many a *dense* adult who had no concept of what *density* meant.

"You are right about that, Anthony. And I'm sure that the good Professor Throller of the University of Minnesota would agree with that answer. But what you and Professor Throller might not know is that there is a lot more to learn about rocks than can be found in a geology book."

Anthony's eyebrows knitted together in a look of surprise.

"One of which is how to make rocks float on water."

Jack placed one of the flat shards of sandstone between his thumb and index finger, cocked his arm back and then let the rock fly parallel over the flat, muddy surface of the Chattahoochee. The rock skipped, *once, twice, three times,* and then was swallowed up by the dark water.

"Wow!" said Anthony. "How did you do that?"

Jack knew he could give a scientific explanation, describing angles of attack, gravitational forces, and perpendicular and parallel momentums. But he didn't, because he was afraid that the boy would probably understand it. This was a six-year-old who already understood far too much. "It's magic."

Anthony's eyes grew wide. "Can you show me how to do it?"

"Sure can," said Jack. He placed a small sandstone shard in Anthony's hand, getting it between his thumb and index finger, and then pulled his arm back. "Let it go!"

Anthony tossed the rock.

It skipped once and then sank.

"Yea!" Anthony looked first at where the rock had bounced across the water and then back at Katie. "Did you see it, Mama? Did you see me make that rock float on the water?"

A large smile filled Katie's face, and to Jack it looked as if some huge weight had been lifted from her. "I sure did," she said. "You're quite the rock magician."

Anthony went scuttling across the sandstone ledge in search of other rocks to skip, forgetting about the geology textbook. Jack crawled back to his spot next to Katie, and took a large gulp of the too-sweet tea.

"You're so good with him," said Katie.

Jack looked over at Anthony just as the boy managed to get a rock to skip twice. The look on his young face was one of fierce determination. "I understand him," said Jack. "We have something in common."

"Oh?" asked Katie.

Jack looked back at her. "He feels isolated, completely out of place in the world. He thinks he's a misfit." Jack smiled. "When I was his age, I was as dumb as a stump, certainly not a problem that he's faced with. I didn't start walking until I was nearly two years old. I didn't start to talk until I was three, and there was a real concern that I wouldn't be out of diapers before I started kindergarten. My parents had me checked out and were told not to expect much from me, that some children just weren't destined for greatness."

"But you've done wonderfully," said Katie, moving toward him.

Jack shook his head. "Face it, Katie, I'm a thirty-seven-year-old DOE contract monitor. *Greatness* is not a word that would be used to describe me. Misfit is more apt. I'm a marginal Ph.D., hovering on the outskirts of the real scientists, shuffling paper for those like you and Horst."

Katie leaned toward him.

Jack was surprised, did not see it coming, and they smashed noses as Katie kissed him lightly.

"Don't sell yourself short, Jack," she said. "I see something in you, something that maybe you can't see."

Jack laid his left hand across hers and took another drink of the sickeningly sweet tea. He watched Anthony skip rocks and felt himself relax, suddenly comfortable with his butt on the hard sandstone and the sweat dripping down his face.

He squeezed Katie's hand.

And then he stood. All that tea had finally worked its way through him. "I would have thought I'd sweat all that tea out of me, but apparently not," he said. He laughed. "I need to find a rest room."

Katie laughed back at him and pointed into the park, which ran up against the river. "Right up the hill and back toward the parking lot," she said.

Jack jumped from the rock onto the riverbank, looking up the hill. On this warm summer day there must have been fifty people in the park. But he paid attention to only one of them. He'd seen the man in profile for only a moment, just as he'd hopped up from a bench and started trotting up the hill toward the parking lot. But a moment had been more than enough. It was Allen Quinn.

They were being spied on.

SECTION I
CHAPTER 6

Sides had been taken.

Horst and Quinn sat at one side of the table, sharing a large think-sheet, drawing diagrams, scribbling equations, and sketching circuit diagrams and plasma contour lines. The look on their faces was a mixture of fear and devotion.

Alexandra stood at the head of the table. "Your progress has been nothing short of miraculous."

Horst smiled. The whites of his eyes were tinted pink, and the skin on his face no longer seemed attached to the muscle beneath. In the last month he had lost nearly twenty pounds. He had been sleeping just a few hours a night. "We've simply taken advantage of the resources that you've brought to bear on this project," he said.

Katie thought she might vomit. She half expected Horst to crawl across the floor and start kissing Alexandra's shoes.

"I see no reason that we should not be able to proceed to a low-energy test firing," said Alexandra.

Katie stood without even realizing she was doing it. Jack groaned. He knew that direct confrontation was no way to get their opinion across. But he also knew that there was no stopping Katie once she started. He said nothing, too exhausted even to figure out what it was that he should say. Part of the problem was that he didn't completely agree with her.

"We cannot fire the Sonomak," said Katie.

Alexandra smiled. "You are mistaken. Installation is complete, all subsystems have checked out, and computer integration will finish final testing this afternoon. All systems are go."

Horst and Quinn nodded in unison.

Katie looked away from the smug and confident Alexandra and at Horst. "Think about what you're doing, Horst. The last time you tested the Sonomak, its structure right down to the atomic level was altered, and you destroyed the lab. You've now got four times the Pocket Accelerators, and that damn supercomputer to steer and modify the electron beams in real time."

Horst smiled, and his face seemed almost to glow. "And that is why we *must* fire it."

Jack had been hearing, but not really listening. He had not slept in two days, and he felt as if he were floating; despite Katie's fears, he kept thinking that none of this really mattered.

What would be would be.

But he forced himself. He had promised Katie that he would at least try. "Think about what you've got in there," said Jack. He pointed beyond Horst and toward the Sonomak lab, which lay behind them. The words felt strange in his mouth, as if speaking had become some alien form of communication. "Katie's simulations show that with the old setup the implosion took the plasmon down to a diameter of one to two micrometers before imperfections in the spherical wave front caused it to destabilize and blow outward. You've now got a computer system, which can track and modify the imploding wave front as it's collapsing, taking it down to a diameter of just tens of nanometers." And then he stopped, losing track of what he was thinking. He had his own theory about what was going on in the Sonomak, but he couldn't quite bring himself to explain it, not to Horst and Katie, not to *real* physicists, and certainly not to that spying son of a bitch Quinn.

Horst and Quinn nodded in unison at Jack.

"That raises the energy density in that volume of space by a factor of *one million*," said Katie, completing the thought that Jack had lost track of. "The last time you took out a lab, this time you might blow a sizable chunk of Georgia into orbit. And even ignoring that little problem, there's the spatial phase change to think about. Last time it was just the Sonomak that was tied into a knot. Do you know how far that phase transition will extend into our space? Will we be turned into pretzels at the control room? Will the *six million* who live south of us in Atlanta all find themselves turned inside out!"

"Nothing will happen!" said Horst. "We will not run at total energy levels any higher than we did at Tech. All we're doing is concentrating that energy into a smaller volume. Quinn and I have run simulations, and we are certain that even if we get a runaway like we did at Tech, the spatial phase transition will only permeate into our space as far as it did at Tech—because we are using the same amount of energy."

"*Your* simulations!"

Horst nodded, smiling.

"You can't simulate what is going to happen," said Katie. "You don't understand the physics. When that plasmon implodes, if you can actually take it down to a ten-nanometer diameter, you'll have electrons accelerating inward at *one billion-billion* gees, and power densities of more than a *trillion-trillion-trillion* watts packed into a volume of a cubic centimeter. You can't simulate that. You are deliberately ripping the fabric of space-time apart. You might punch a hole right through normal space and recreate the *Big* Bang."

"I certainly hope so," said Alexandra.

"What is the damn hurry?" asked Katie. She stared at Alexandra. "You've been here for some four million years, and now you can't wait a few months for us to try and get a handle on this from a theoretical perspective so we don't accidentally vaporize ourselves?"

"We are ready to go *now*," said Alexandra.

"It is too dangerous," said Katie.

Alexandra stood. "You've got two choices in this matter. You can help us run the experiment, or you can be held in detention until we have completed the experiment."

"You think you can arrest me?"

Alexandra slowly sat. "Arresting you is the *least* of what I can do," she said.

"And just what the hell is that supposed to mean?" asked Katie. "Are you threatening me?"

"I don't make threats," said Alexandra.

Katie got the message. She sat back in her seat, not sure what she should do, not sure what she *could* do. They could run the test firing with our without her. She flicked her eyelids, and Anthony popped into the lower quadrant of her Virtuals.

He was drawing. That was what he seemed to spend all his waking hours doing now. It was yet one more picture of the boy-monster ripping away the waxy bars of his cage. She was certain that Alexandra would not let her off base until they'd tested the Sonomak. And if she refused to help and was detained, what would happen to Anthony?

She looked across the table at Horst.

He was under some sort of spell. She did not know if it was Alexandra or the physics that now had control of him, but she was certain that the prospects that he would create an entire universe had unbalanced him. If she vanished, Horst would be looking after Anthony.

"Horst, it's just *too* dangerous," she said.

"Nothing great is achieved without some degree of risk," he said.

She knew she was boxed in. If she refused to help, the Sonomak would be run without her. But if she did help, and something happened, there was always the remote possibility that she could do something to lessen the extent of the destruction.

"I'll help," she said.

Jack closed his eyes. He had known that this would be the final outcome. He knew that the Sonomak must be fired. There was no other possibility.

Katie grabbed Jack's left shoulder and squeezed. "What's wrong with you?" she asked. The tone of her voice was a mixture of concern and anger. "You were a zombie in there. We might be just a few hours away from turning this entire base into a smoking hole in the ground, and you seem almost asleep."

Jack nodded. He knew her concerns. He slowly sat down on a gray steel and dull-brown, plastic-covered chair. Katie sat in her own equally ugly chair. Nothing else was in the little office except for a steel desk covered in printouts, Katie's laptop, and a picture of Anthony in a Lucite frame.

"You haven't been sleeping," said Katie. She thought back to the night before, as well as to the night before that. In the week that they'd been together, she had quickly learned that he was a light sleeper, and rarely slept more than a few hours a night, but now he seemed to have stopped sleeping *entirely*. He would lie in bed for an hour or so and then vanish. The last two mornings she had found him at the kitchen table, drinking coffee and shuffling paperwork. Theirs was a scientists' love affair, that was for sure.

"I've had things on my mind," said Jack.

Katie sat back in her chair, and controlled the expression on her face. *Damn*, she thought. They had been moving too fast, the relationship had hurled along at the same blinding speed as the construction of the Sonomak. How did she know what he really felt? She was suddenly certain that this relationship was nothing more than a rebound fling in response to that coldhearted little Texas bitch dumping him. "And these *things* are?" she asked coldly. Suddenly she was thinking not of herself, but of Anthony. *He* really liked Jack. That had made everything seem all right.

"I've worked out an energy partition theorem describing how energy is divided between our universe, and the new universe," he said.

Katie blinked, at first wondering what that had to do with her, and then slowly realized that it had absolutely nothing to do with her. Jack was troubled about *work*. They were both exhausted by *work*. They might be all right. Katie breathed a sigh of relief, wondered for a split second why she always assumed the worst, and then thought about what Jack had just said—*an energy partition theorem*?

What could Jack know about universe formation and energy partition?

He was just a DOE contract monitor. She bit her lip as she thought that. Jack was extremely bright, but he was no cosmologist. She raised her right eyebrow in question.

"I know what you're thinking," he said. He reached into his top pocket and pulled out a blue DVD disc. "This isn't exactly my field, but I've been doing some reading, a little head scratching, and I think I've come up with something." He handed the disc to her. "I believe that the structure of a new universe will be dictated by the structure of our universe."

Katie nodded as she walked around her desk and shoved the disc into her laptop. The DVD drive whirred, and the simulation quadrant in her Virtuals rolled once, then locked in. She blinked and let the simulation quadrant balloon, filling her entire field of view. She quickly scrolled. At first it looked pretty standard—the supercooling and the negative energy density driven by the spherical integrity of the plasmon implosion. And then it got strange.

Jack had made an assumption—a very weird assumption.

The phase transition between the supercooled region of space-time and the budding off of the new universe was precipitated from the formation of a *pair* of virtual particles, one of which would seed the new universe, and the other, which would remain in the parent universe. That she could accept. But there was a lot more to it than that. These two particles were entangled on the quantum level. Distance and time meant nothing to entangled particles. Even though they were in entirely different universes, they were still in intimate contact. The math was clear, but there weren't adequate words to describe it. A wave front, spawned by one of the virtual particles, expanded through the parent universe, and as it did, each atom it touched, each piece of space-time that it passed through, was *duplicated* in the new universe, seeded there during the phase transition of supercooled space-time.

Everything was connected and *duplicated*—the entanglement no longer a quantum phenomenon relegated to the world of atoms, but amplified to such a level that both universes were entangled.

The new universe would be an exact duplicate of the parent universe.

But there was one critical difference. The expansion of the new universe was limited by the original size of the plasmon. The smaller the plasmon, the higher the density of energy within it, and the larger the new universe would be. For the levels of plasmon compression that they could achieve, the size of this new Universe would be much smaller than the parent universe—*considerably* smaller. It certainly would not be anything like the thirty billion-light-year diameter of their universe. It might not even be a single light year in diameter.

It was an amazing analysis. Brilliant. Elegant. Beautiful.

But most importantly it *felt* right. The equations seemed to sing. Katie had learned long ago to trust her instincts, to pay just as much attention to the story the equations told as to the mathematical nitty-gritty. "How did you do this, Jack?" she asked. She partially polarized her Virtuals, so she could see Jack superimposed over the field of equations.

"It just seemed so obvious," he said. He paused, closing his eyes for a moment. "If this analysis is correct, then there may be some physical leakage between the newly forming universe and ours by way of quantum tunneling. The amount of leakage will depend on the initial energy densities in the imploding plasmon.

"Leakage?" asked Katie.

"The space-time transformation that tied the Sonomak into a carrick knot," he said. "When you go to high enough energy levels, the new universe is forming so quickly, the leakage is all but eliminated, all the energy being dumped into the creation of the new universe. It is at the lower energies, where you have just enough to form a new universe but can't keep it stabilized, that the leakage is a problem."

"You mean at the low energy levels they'll test the Sonomak with?" she asked.

"I think so," said Jack.

Katie repolarized her Virtuals and slipped back into the sea of equations. The virtual clock hanging in front of her nose told her that they were less than three hours from test firing the Sonomak.

"The pressure is fine," said Beong. He closed the control room door behind him, having just come up from the lab floor. "A filament on the pressure gauge had burned out, but I was able to switch to the auxiliary filament." He bowed slightly, and did not make direct eye contact with anyone. All systems had been go except for the pressure gauge on one of the laser heads. The lasers were his responsibility.

Horst grunted something inarticulate, not bothering to look at Beong, but continued to stare at his console, running last minute diagnostics, checking that the adaptive electron optics were responding to the Cray computer controls.

Beong sat down in front of his control panel. He prayed that nothing else would fail on the laser. Never in a life filled with anxiety and tension had he ever felt so nervous. And to make matters even worse, his third eye had been confiscated upon his arrival at Dobbins. He was truly alone for the first time in his life, and it was terrifying.

"You can't test fire it, Horst," said Katie.

Horst waved a hand in her direction as if absentmindedly swatting at an annoying insect. With his other hand he tapped at a console keyboard and watched schematics scroll down his screen. "We run it as planned," he said. He glanced at the laser console, which Beong was manning, and the system console where Aaron sat.

Almost déjà vu.

But not quite. Quinn sat at a fourth console, the workstation that accessed the Cray. It was this new console that would make all the difference. With the Cray tied to the Pocket Accelerators, the collapsing plasmon could be reshaped in real time, recontoured in ten-femtosecond intervals as the laser intensity was cut back. They would generate power densities one million times higher than they'd done at Tech.

"You aren't listening to me, Horst," said Katie. "We've done a new modeling analysis and determined that the energy levels you are using are too *low*, that the phase space transformation extending into our universe will be more severe than last time. If you're going to run it, you need to do it at a *higher* power level."

"Oh, you are truly an indispensable member of the project," said Quinn. Getting up from his chair and walking over too close to Katie, he stared down at her. "A few hours ago you explained to us that we were going to run at *too high* an energy density, and now it is too low. Theoreticians are such amazing animals."

"Can't you just delay until you look over our analysis?" she said, trying to back away from him.

"*Our* analysis," said Quinn mockingly, and then looked across the control room at Jack sitting in the corner. "The good *Dr.* Preston, boy wonder of the DOE *Temp Pool*, has aided you in this revolutionary new analysis of yours?"

Katie swallowed. She did not want to stab Jack in the back, to take credit for something she had not done, but she knew what Quinn thought, knew what she herself had thought. There was a hierarchy in the physics world. And there was simply no denying the fact that Jack sat on the bottom rung. They could not fire the Sonomak at these low energy levels—it was simply too dangerous. Jack would forgive her.

"*I* have derived a new quantum theory of universe generation that predicts how the new universe is seeded from ours. As part of that theory, there exists an energy regime in which appreciable space-time leakage will take place from the newly forming universe and leak back into ours, and as things stand, you are going to operate right in the middle of that regime." She turned around to look at Jack.

There was no expression on his face.

"We will discuss it after the test," said Quinn. Turning,

dismissing her, he went back to his console. "Systems, Mr. Tanaka?" he asked.

"All green," said Aaron.

"Laser?" asked Quinn.

"On line," said Beong, his voice cracking.

Quinn stood, looking through the observation window at the lab floor. The only motions were the pulsing red lights in the vicinity of the laser and the wisps of condensation rolling off of the superconducting magnets encircling the Sonomak.

"Fire it, Quinn," said Alexandra.

Katie looked across the control room at Alexandra Mitchell's glaring face on the TP monitor. She was safe in D.C., one thousand miles away from Atlanta. That fact frightened Katie just as much as the analysis that she and Jack had just completed. The bitch knew that something bad might happen. She wanted to put physical distance between herself and the Sonomak.

Quinn opened the safety over the fire toggle and then flipped the switch. A heads-up display materialized in the observation window—an incandescent countdown starting at fifteen seconds.

Katie took a step toward the window. Just as before, harsh blue-white light poured out of the Sonomak's view ports as the plasma struck. The clock counted down. It reached zero in what seemed like less than fifteen seconds. She cringed, certain that the Sonomak would tear itself apart; that a shock wave of phase transitioning space-time would wash over them, and that they'd be wearing their knotted guts on the outside of their dead carcasses.

Lights pulsed, as from a strobe light.

Katie watched the Sonomak *ripple*. She could not tell if it was the air between her and the Sonomak that was causing the effect, or if it was the Sonomak itself that was in motion. The amplitude of the rippling grew, the Sonomak blurring. For an instant she thought she could see right through it, and then it solidified.

Dead silence.

Everyone pressed up against the observation window. At first Katie did not understand what she was looking at. She could see the Sonomak, but there was *more* than just the Sonomak, *more* stainless steel, *more* Pocket Accelerators, *more* banks of electronics than there had originally been.

"Someone is down there!" Jack threw open the control room door and bounded down the metal stairs, taking three at a time. The others followed behind him, except Katie, who stood at the window, watching. She did not understand what she saw, but she could identify it. There was a *second* Sonomak.

Jack had been right. They'd momentarily generated another region of space-time, a place in which a second Sonomak had been created, and then as that space-time collapsed, the second Sonomak had leaked into their space. But the leakage had not been clean and smooth.

The second Sonomak had *intersected* with the first Sonomak, melded together with it at strange, distorted angles. And in the center of the mass of strangely bent stainless steel, a figure was embedded—a head, an arm, and part of a leg were visible, the rest of the body hidden by steel and tubing—actually *one* with the machine. Katie had never seen a body that looked deader.

Jack was the first to reach it. He grabbed the hand and reached up for the head, pressing his fingers to the neck that barely protruded through the half-inch thick steel that made up the shell of the Sonomak. "He's dead!" He turned, looking back at the others. "*Beong* is dead!"

Beong himself stood frozen several feet away from the others, staring at the body that was melded into the Sonomak, looking into its face, looking into *his* face. In some other world, one created by the firing of the Sonomak, he was a dead man.

SECTION I
CHAPTER 7

"They have to go!" said Quinn.

Alexandra sat behind her desk, motionless, only half listening to Quinn. For the most part she was elsewhere, churning through a nearly infinite number of possible futures spreading out before her. Time was running short.

This was the second space-time breach. The energies were incredibly low, most likely below *their* detection level, but it was still dangerous. She knew that if the Makers discovered what she was doing, that she'd be *reclaimed*, and five million years of memories reduced to thermal noise. Dead, dead, dead.

She needed the new universe created now.

"They are not team players. They are disrupting the rest of the employees, have actually slowed down the rebuilding, and are trying to convince the others that if we fire again, someone in *that* room could find himself welded into the Sonomak," said Quinn.

Alexandra slowed her internal clock, integrating into the normal flow of the incredibly slow human brain. She held up her right hand.

Quinn stopped, only then realizing that he had been screaming at her.

"Just *horrible* team players," said Alexandra. "In the last week they have come up with a theoretical analysis to explain that mess on the lab floor. They have showed you the correct energy densities to run at in order to generate a stable universe and now claim to have figured out that what they call *severe temporal anomalies* will exist in the universe you might create if you're lucky enough not to blow yourself into quarks."

Quinn felt himself start to sweat. "There is no evidence

that these severe temporal anomalies will manifest themselves," he said.

"Oh, well, that is certainly encouraging," she said. "But unlike you, my *human* friend, I have had direct experience in other universes. Time does *not* flow uniformly or constantly across the spectrum of universes. They all tick to their own clocks."

Quinn did not know that. In the fifteen hundred years that he had assisted her, she had never spoken of her direct experience in those other universes. The fact that she chose to do so now frightened him more than he would have believed possible. Things were changing too quickly. He tried to speak, but nothing came out.

"But you *are* correct about them being a disruptive element. Based on the analysis they have provided, even you and that egomaniac professor should be able to rebuild and create what I need without destroying any more equipment."

Quinn managed a smile, his throat loosened, and he was able to pull down a lungful of air.

"Get them in here now," she said.

Quinn leapt from his chair and ran for the office door.

Alexandra ignored him and stood, turning to face the window. This office was only temporary, an outpost in Atlanta so she could stay close to the project, to be in physical proximity when the universe was created, but not so close in case an accident occurred. She had taken over a host of suites on the 53rd floor of the Bank of America tower, about twenty miles southeast of Dobbins Air Force Base. She stared out into the summer haze, hoping that twenty miles would be far enough away if something went wrong.

"Wonderful to see you!"

Alexandra turned to see Horst dogtrotting across the office, his plump right hand outstretched. He maneuvered around the desk toward her. She did not offer her own hand, but simply stared at him, as if peering at a particularly disgusting bacteria through a microscope.

Horst lowered his hand.

"Sit," she said, motioning to the conference table at the other end of the office.

Horst obeyed.

Katie and Jack came into the office, closely followed by Quinn. Alexandra looked at them briefly and was about to move to her own chair at the head of the conference table, when she stopped and took a second look.

Something was different.

She looked first at Katie. Katie looked angry, her face flushed red, her jaw clenched, her hands balled into fists. Alexandra saw nothing new there. This woman was always mad about *something*.

The difference was in Jack. She looked at him. He stared back, locking eyes with her. He did not blink, did not show fear. The look was not the simpleminded arrogance that perpetually filled Horst's fat face. This was something she had not seen before in Jack Preston's face.

Confidence.

She smiled at him. She had hoped that there was more to Jack Preston than his pathetic paper profile had indicated. The first indication that something lay hidden beneath the surface had been on the surveillance video taken during the last lab disaster. This look on his face was another. Now she had no doubts about her plan. Jack had to be removed from Dobbins and integrated fully into a life with Katie McGuire and her son. For just a moment a tingle of fear nipped at her, the same feeling she'd experienced when she had first met Jack. But she pushed it back and focused on her plans and on how she would use Jack to get what she wanted.

"We are making excellent progress," said Horst. "Reconstruction is right on schedule, and we're adding more processors to the Cray in order to increase aggregate clock speed and give us even better control on the implosion shock wave. I believe—"

"Be quiet," said Alexandra.

Horst's head snapped back as if his face had been slapped.

"I know the status of the project," said Alexandra. "I don't need a hyperinflated egomaniac to explain it to me in superficial, meaningless, big-picture bullshittese."

Horst clenched his jaw, just managing not to explode, quickly reminding himself just what this woman *really* was.

"I called you here to make some announcements concerning a reorganization of this project in light of recent experimental results." Alexandra paused and looked at those around the table. Quinn was smiling. Horst's face had grown pale. Katie's cheeks were even redder than before. Jack continued to stare at her.

"Play," said Alexandra. The room darkened, and curtains at the far end of the room parted, revealing a window that polarized and began to display a Vid. "There is another item that is just as important—actually more important—than the physics or the results. I demand your full *loyalty*," she said.

The Vid showed the lab just as the second Sonomak materialized and melded with the first. Jack was the first to run into the scene, reaching for Beong's double, checking for a pulse at both the throat and the wrist.

"Stop," said Alexandra. The image on the screen froze. "I must say, Dr. Preston, that I never expected this hidden talent." She pulled a laser pointer out of her breast pocket, flicked it on, and pointed the red beam at the screen. A red dot landed on Jack's image, and then on the object he held in his left hand.

"You removed his watch," said Alexandra. "Lights."

The Vid vanished, lights turned on, and the curtain closed.

Jack smiled and pulled back his left sleeve, revealing a watch. "Did it take you three days to figure out that I took the watch?" he asked.

"Of course not," said Alexandra. "I knew within hours, right after I examined the body and saw the tan line. I then examined the Vid and saw your feeble attempt at thievery."

"A mighty nice watch," said Jack.

Alexandra ignored the comment. "And just what was the

time difference between the watch you stole and the one that Beong wears in this universe?" She didn't give him time to answer. "I would estimate that it is somewhere between three and four minutes."

Katie looked first at Alexandra and then over at Horst and Quinn. She understood this business about the watch and the time discrepancy—she and Jack had worked out the physics several days ago. But she could tell by the expressions on Horst's and Quinn's faces that they were clueless.

"Three minutes and twenty-seven seconds," said Jack.

Alexandra nodded. "You see, my simpleminded dolts," she said to Horst and Quinn, "what your coworkers figured out days ago, you two morons don't even realize is a valuable clue to the physics of what's taking place here."

"I understand full well the significance—" said Horst.

"You don't understand a damn thing," said Alexandra. "The good Dr. Preston shows a degree of quickness that we might not have expected from someone of his mediocre standing in the physics community."

Jack smiled. *Screw you, bitch*, he thought to himself.

"Jack understood the quantum mechanical nature of the energy states within the collapsing plasmon. As the plasmon is squeezed tighter, and the energy states within it become more and more defined, the corresponding time domain associated with the wave function of each state becomes less defined."

Horst's eyes grew large.

"I see you've finally caught on," said Alexandra. "In the same way that the uncertainty principle applies to a particle, in which the more accurately you know its position, the less accurately you know its velocity, in this case, the more *defined* the energy states within the plasmon, the *bigger* the spread of possible times at which it *may* exist."

Mental dominoes began to fall in Horst's head, a chain reaction of logic, leading to an inevitable, but utterly amazing conclusion. "The new universe is an exact spatial duplicate of ours," said Horst, having come to accept the analysis that Katie and Jack had worked out. "But the moment of its origin does not necessarily correspond to the moment we fire the Sonomak. In this case, the new universe was duplicated from our universe some three minutes and twenty-seven seconds *before* we fired the Sonomak, when Beong was still on the lab floor, working on the laser. When the new universe collapsed, when it leaked back into our universe, what came through was a duplicate of our universe, from three minutes and twenty-seven seconds in our past."

Alexandra offered up a few sardonic claps of her hands. "It is amazing what you understand when it is spelled out for you, Professor," she said. "And what you should realize, gentlemen, in your next round of experiments, as you reach even higher energy levels, is that this distribution in time may be even greater."

"But this is not why you called us here," said Jack.

"No," said Alexandra. "I have had all your notes and computer files duplicated so that your associates here," she waved at Horst and Quinn, "will have the advantage of your clear thinking. However, what they will not have is the questionable advantage of your physical presence at Dobbins."

Jack's face was again expressionless.

"As I said, loyalty to me is the most important attribute in an employee. That is why someone like Mr. Quinn has been with me for so long. He is loyal." Alexandra pointed at Katie and Jack. "You two are not. You stole a key piece of data and did not report on its significance. It was only through other means that I was able to ferret out what you had learned. That behavior is unacceptable."

Katie sighed, relieved in a way. Despite the potential fame, she and Jack would now be out of it. They could leave this place far behind and be safe.

"This has just been a misunderstanding," said Horst. "I've had some trouble with Jack, and God knows that Katie and I don't always get along, but they are valuable to the project. Both of them have given us real insight into the theoretical underpinnings of the physics involved."

Katie blinked several times and turned her head toward Horst. This was a degree of understanding, even compassion, that she would not have expected from him.

"I have worked with Dr. McGuire for a *long* time," he added.

Then Katie saw it in the slight upturn of his lips, in the wrinkles around the edges of his eyes. Horst was scared. It had been a long time since she'd seen such vulnerability; it had been replaced by the smug self-assuredness that she'd come to despise. And she thought she knew why Horst was frightened. With Jack and her gone, Horst would be the only one left. There would still be Beong and Aaron, but she knew that Horst didn't consider them real people—just a postdoc and a technician. Horst would be alone with this bitch from another universe, and Quinn, who might have been human at one time, but was now something else, somehow modified and contaminated by Alexandra.

"This is not a matter for debate," said Alexandra. "The stakes here are too high, and no chances can be taken. They will no longer be working at Dobbins."

Horst cleared his throat, as if to say something, but did not speak.

"Good," said Alexandra. She looked around the table and pointed first at Quinn and then at Horst. "I suggest that you gentlemen return to Dobbins and get to work. You are on a very *tight* schedule."

They stood, as did Katie. She was eager to escape, to put this nightmare behind her, suddenly realizing that she needed to put a great deal of physical distance between herself and what might happen at Dobbins.

Jack remained seated.

He'd thought long and hard about Alexandra Mitchell in the last week. He had not yet figured out her true motivations, but he was certain that she would not simply let him and Katie walk away. They knew too much of what was going on here, and they had provided too much to the project. He was getting a feel for the Sonomak, for the math, for the mixture of cosmology and plasma physics. He felt linked to it, and somehow could not believe that it would end here.

"The two of you stay," said Alexandra. She pointed at Katie, directing her to sit back down, and then at Jack.

Quinn and Horst kept walking. But while Quinn did not look back, Horst did, the expression on his face one of puzzlement. The door shut behind them.

"I believe we were fired," said Katie.

Alexandra laughed, a deep, resonant laughter, originating from somewhere deep in her belly. "You are so damn naive," said Alexandra. Leaning forward, she stared at Katie. "What I *said* was that you will no longer be working at Dobbins."

The thought that she had been fired had been like getting hit with a bucketful of cold water. It had awakened her to the insanity and danger of this project. She now wanted nothing to do with it. "Then I quit," said Katie.

Jack said nothing, but sat farther back in his chair. He understood that they were involved in something from which they could *not* quit. They would have to see this project to its completion, wherever that took them.

"I lied just a moment ago," said Alexandra. "Loyalty means absolutely nothing to me. In fact, I find loyalty a very dangerous thing. It has been my observation that among your species loyalty is a fragile commodity that can be destroyed by a leader's slightest transgression. I prefer to deal with much more powerful emotions such as *fear* and *greed*."

Katie swallowed and thought about Anthony. She was suddenly very frightened.

"Quinn lives in a world dominated by fear. Left to his own biology, he would have been a rotting corpse sometime in the latter part of the sixth century. He continues to live only because it is my wish, and that hold over him is far more powerful than mere loyalty. And then we come to the professor. His soul is even easier to own. He wants fame and believes that this project will give him just that. He is greedy."

"And what emotion will you employ to keep us working on your little project?" asked Jack.

Alexandra smiled. "I think that fear should suffice."

Jack arched an eyebrow. "I'm not afraid of you," he said.

"Of course not," said Alexandra. "Had you been afraid of me, I would have never given you your *new* job."

"And my *new* job is?"

"It just so happens that there is an opening at the Georgia Institute of Technology, in the Plasma Group in the Electrical Engineering Department. By happy coincidence, just as you find yourself without a job here, the renowned professor Horst Wittkowski has tendered his resignation in order to work on a very important government project, and by calling in a few favors, I was able to persuade the dean that you are the right man to fill the opening. Congratulations *Associate Professor* Preston."

"Persuade?" asked Jack.

"Yes, it seems that you come to Tech with a large DOD contract to investigate the use of high-intensity lasers and plasmas to simulate what we like to call *stressed* space-time. The dean was more than happy to see all those scrumptious overhead dollars coming her way." Alexandra smiled sweetly and turned toward Katie. "And you, Dr. McGuire, are no longer employed by the university. But do not worry. It just so happens that your new company, Creative Plasma Solutions, has been awarded a nice Phase I SBIR through NIST to investigate the commercial uses of high-energy plasma-laser interactions."

Katie didn't say a thing.

"You'll be happy to know that your mini-Cray 20MP is scheduled to be installed in your home tomorrow morning. NIST gave you extra award points for setting up your company and working out of your home. NIST is a very pro-child government agency."

Anthony. Every muscle in Katie's body tightened.

"Two questions," said Jack.

Alexandra nodded.

"Why have you done this, and why should we go along with it?"

"Quite simple," said Alexandra. "By training and design I am a sociologist. I study man. I run little experiments to see how the human animal responds to my interventions. I did not pick you for your amazing physics abilities," she said, laughing as she said it, "although you have surprised me a bit in that area. The real reason that I picked you for this job is because of the fascinating dynamic I see operating among the three of you. The three of you together create a whole much greater than the mere sum of the parts."

"What *three*?" Katie asked.

"Why you, Jack, and that wonderful little boy of yours, *Anthony*."

Katie jumped up, slamming both of her open hands against the conference table. "Anthony has nothing to do with this!"

"I beg to differ," said Alexandra. "Anthony has everything to do with it. Without Anthony, there is no real *fear* in this little equation."

Katie sat.

"I believe that I have answered both of your questions, Jack?"

Jack nodded. She had, only too well. Anthony was the reason they would do what she wanted. Jack remembered the day at the river, and Quinn spying on them. Alexandra Mitchell undoubtedly had the resources to do whatever she wanted, and those resources could easily extend to doing something very nasty to a little boy.

CHAPTER 8

Earl Rogers looked like a rat, with a snout-like nose, close-set beady eyes, and a long, thin mustache made up of rodent whiskers. He was the chairman of the Electrical Engineering graduate advisory committee. His rat-persona made him perfect for this job.

Those who can do research, do research.

Those who can't do research, teach.

Those who can't teach, become chairmen of advisory committees.

Earl Rogers had found his niche in the university. Jack, along with a half-dozen other faculty members, sat around the coffee-stained table, listening to Earl drone on about the prerequisites for EE 2201—*radio frequency* solid state devices. "The current prerequisites are totally insufficient to prepare the students for this curriculum," he said. "As it stands now, they are not required to come into this class with any more RF experience than they received in the one or two lectures given in EE 1902." He glared at the tubby Professor Klausen, who, stuffed in a white shirt several sizes too small, resembled a sweating bratwurst. EE 1902 was his course.

"There is not time for RF," said Klausen. "It is nearly impossible to drill into their thick skulls the DC characteristics of transistors during the quarter. You get into RF and the few students still conscious instantly glaze over."

Earl offered up a rat smile. "My point exactly," he said. "To adequately prepare them for EE 2201, they need an entire course devoted to RF, a full up electromagnetics class."

General groans emanated from around the table. On the rare occasions that Earl Rogers was not pushing paper or chairing committees, he taught an electromagnetics course.

Jack guessed that old Earl-rat was getting some pressure from the department chairman about not adequately carrying his teaching load.

Jack could care less.

He had his own two intro plasma classes to teach, EE 405, and that was more than enough. He was trying to put together a lab. He was still trying to decipher the political landscape. But mostly he was spending as much time as possible working on the model with Katie. He worked through the nights, focused, running simulations, scribbling equations, no longer seeming to need any sleep.

If and when Dobbins generated a universe, what would it be like?

It was pure blue-sky physics, all theory with very little experimental data. Jack drifted into the equations, the outside world dropping away. Jack was certain that the size of the universe and the rate at which time flowed within it were related—the curvature of space-time impacting the flow of time.

Blue-sky.

There was no existing theory for this. They had to develop one.

"Jack!"

Jack blinked, bringing himself back to the meeting, and Earl's twitching face materialized. "I believe that someone is trying to get your attention." He pointed to the window at the far end of the conference room.

Jack turned.

Arlo Hoskins's bony horse-face was pushed up against the window. He believed himself to be in charge of the Electrical Engineering Department. He was the master of the coffeepots, czar of the copying machines, and high overlord of the various departmental administrative assistants. He was also Guy Bartlet's administrative assistant. And Guy Bartlet was the Electrical Engineering Department chairman. Arlo held up his left hand and pecked at the face of his watch. Jack looked up at the clock embedded in the wall above Earl's head.

11:00.

Jack sighed. Out of the frying pan and into the fire. Looking at Earl, he stood. "Please excuse me," he said, "but I have a meeting with Guy." Ever since his arrival, he had been fighting a turf battle with professor Gilbert Monfort. The man seemed to believe it was his manifest destiny to occupy every square foot of available floor space in the Van Leer basement. With the explosion of the Sonomak and Horst's resignation, he'd set his expansionist sights on the Sonomak lab. Jack had called in Guy to help slap the territory-grabbing weasel back into his hole.

Earl nodded. The name of Guy had been evoked, and that was sufficient to get Jack out of this meeting. "I'll stop by your office later to go over what we've concluded here and to solicit any further inputs you might have," he said.

Again Jack nodded. He could hardly wait. He was outside the door before Earl could dispense any more good news.

"Dr. Bartlet is waiting for you in his office," Arlo said. "He has a very tight schedule today, as do I."

Jack just smiled, imagining generating a nice little universe and tossing this obnoxious Hitler-like chief administrative assistant right into it.

Jack sat at the dining room table, and Katie sat in his lap, facing him, legs wrapped around his waist and the back of his chair. His head was nestled in the crook of her shoulder, pressed up against the side of her neck. She smelled like baby powder and raspberries, and her hair, still damp from her shower, clung to his cheek.

"I think this camping trip will be really good for Anthony," Katie said. She rubbed the back of his head, running her fingers through his hair.

Jack slowly nodded. He had heard what she said, but was not concentrating on her words. He was staring across the family room and at the built-in bookshelf. He blinked several times. There was something wrong with the bookshelf. It appeared to be slightly distorted, bent at strange angles, all of it leaning toward the hallway door. His head throbbed, a stabbing pain deep inside. He blinked once more, and then he saw the lines. The air burned with them, bright yellow beams of sputtering light. He'd seen these before. He suspected that it was a symptom of his lack of sleep. His brain chemistry was getting screwed up, toxins, spent neurotransmitters, whatever it was that got flushed away during sleep was building up in his brain, causing these hallucinations. The yellow lines all intersected at a book near the end of the bookshelf—a volume from an old incomplete set of Encyclopaedia Britannicas—N.

"You're so tense," said Katie. She dug into his right shoulder with her strong fingers, kneading the muscles.

Jack squirmed, the yellow lines vanished, and he pulled his head back so that his nose was a few inches away from Katie's. Then he moved forward, kissing her, his lips slightly open. Katie's eyes closed, while Jack kept his open.

She tasted like baking soda toothpaste.

He bit her lower lip playfully and Katie jerked her head back, startled. "What's wrong, *Professor*," she said, "not getting enough protein in your diet?"

Jack smiled. *Professor* had become her pet name for him. She knew how much he disliked the situation at Tech—he wasn't built for the politics, meetings, and student inter-action that the job required. But they both suspected that this situation wouldn't last long. They suspected that some-thing would happen soon enough at Dobbins to change the situation. They knew they were pawns in a game that Al-exandra was playing and that the time would come when she would put them into play once again. Unfortunately, they had not been able to figure out what the game was.

"Not nearly enough," he said. Bending forward, he pre-tended to take a bite out of her freckled chin.

Katie let out a squeal and jumped off his lap. "Down, boy," she said. "Remember that you've got a camping trip you need to be heading off to. You don't want to start something here that you can't finish."

Jack smiled. No. He didn't want to do that.

"I'm ready."

Katie turned around, and Jack looked over at the hall doorway, where Anthony stood. Wearing blue jeans, a wool sweater, little black boots polished to a high luster, and a Braves baseball cap, he awkwardly clutched a small backpack in his hands. He took several steps into the room, limping slightly, dragging his right leg. He moved stiffly, with effort.

Both Katie and Jack frowned, looking at his right leg.

They'd been to more than a half-dozen doctors in the last two weeks. Every test imaginable had been performed, and Anthony had been run through both CAT and PET scans. There was no apparent nerve damage. It was not ALS, MS, or meningitis. No detectable bacteria, white count normal, and they could find no known viruses. But Anthony continued to limp. All his movements had become stiff and artificial, as if each muscle now required an active thought to move it and Anthony could not make sufficient mental contact with those muscles.

And then they'd taken him to the therapist.

Dr. Ruth Licht—tall and thin, with sympathetic eyes. She had talked with Anthony, told him stories about other boys and girls. She had distracted him, gotten him to work on a puzzle, and as he was concentrating, stiff fingers trying to push the puzzle pieces together, she had let out a shout that had made both Jack and Katie jump. *"Mouse!"* she had shrieked, pointing across her office to a big pile of stuffed animals. Anthony had also jumped, sending puzzle pieces across the floor, and had then run across the room in the direction the therapist had been pointing. There had been no hesitancy in his movements, no limp. The mouse had been of the stuffed variety, actually of the Mickey variety.

There was nothing *physically* wrong with Anthony.

Anthony now had an appointment with the therapist twice a week.

"You and Jack sure are going to have lots of fun on this campout," said Katie.

Anthony dropped his backpack, and limped over to the

bookshelf. Standing on the tips of his toes, he reached up with a shaking hand and removed a book—the *N* volume of the Encyclopaedia Britannica.

Jack winced, the throbbing pain in his head suddenly returning.

The remaining encyclopedias fell to the left, the shelf bounced from the impact, then let go on the left side, wood snapping, books falling, the shelf beneath collapsing, the shelf above letting go. Books, magazines, potted plants, glass and plaster knickknacks all came crashing down.

"Anthony!" said Katie.

Anthony turned, almost tripping on the debris spread out around his feet. "It was unstable," he said. "Chaos waiting to be released."

Jack's headache vanished once again.

"I never met a boy who didn't like hot dogs."

Anthony stared into the fire, his hot dog stuck on the end of a stick. The dog bobbed up and down, back and forth, tracing out a complex pattern over and over again as it weaved in and out of the flames.

"Mustard or ketchup?" asked Jack.

Anthony looked at him, the expression on his face one of puzzlement. "How far can you see?" he asked.

Jack sat back, leaning against the stump of an old pine tree and pulled his dog out of the fire. The woods were alive with the sounds of insects and the croaking of tree frogs. In the distance, the steady hum of traffic roaring down I-85 cut through the forest, competing with the shrill whistle of the cicadas. They were less than two miles from the interstate and perhaps one mile from the Lake Lanier main parking lot.

"That's a complicated question," said Jack. "The answer depends on how big the object is that you're looking at, and how bright it is."

Anthony nodded, and then pointed upward with his hot dog, to the open patch of forest canopy above them, and

to the stars, a galaxy full of lights burning bright, the entire
sky glowing.

Jack looked up. In all his years in D.C., lights in the sky
had usually been from jets landing or taking off at Dulles
and Nixon. The last stars he'd really seen, that uniform
blanket of twinkling lights that spilled from horizon to horizon, had been at least a decade ago in Texas. "Do you
know how far a *light year* is?" he asked.

Anthony nodded. "9.46 trillion kilometers," he answered.

Jack smiled. "A boy who likes the metric system I see."

Anthony did not respond, so Jack pointed his hot dog up
into the nighttime sky. "The stars that you see vary in
brightness, but are typically anywhere from two to several
thousand light years away. Now that glow you see up there,
that comes from the billions of stars that make up our galaxy, which are spread out across nearly 400 thousand light
years."

"Not very far," said Anthony.

Jack chuckled softly. The boy was forever amazing him.
Your typical six-year-old could perhaps count to one thousand, with anything larger reserved for the category *a whole
bunch*, or a nonsensical *bazillion-million-hundred*.

"How far is *very* far then?" asked Jack.

Anthony lowered his hot dog back into the fire. Juice
spurted from one end of it, sizzling as it hit red embers.
"There are things *far* away," said Anthony. He paused for
a moment as if considering something. "Like the edge of
the universe, beyond which the big telescopes can't see
anything."

Jack suddenly felt very foolish. He was always under-
estimating Anthony's abilities.

"If the edge of the universe is only *far* away," asked
Jack, "then what would be *very* far away?"

Anthony lowered his hot dog, letting it come to rest on
one of the soot-stained stones that surrounded the campfire.
He reached into his coat pocket and pulled out a folded
piece of paper, holding it out toward Jack.

Jack took the paper and unfolded it. *The boy*. That was

how Katie and Jack referred to the countless drawings of the monstrous child trapped in the melting cage. They'd gathered up a pile of them to show the therapist. Her response had not been good. She had shaken her head back and forth, while making *tsk, tsk, tsk* noises. She was certain that the boy was Anthony, hiding within a cage of his own building, one that kept him safe from the outside world. But the cage was melting, and when it collapsed, the boy would be exposed to a hostile, frightening world.

"This boy is farther away than the edge of the universe?" asked Jack.

Anthony nodded. "*Infinitely* farther," he said.

Jack knew he was out of his depth here, and he was afraid to blunder. But he couldn't stop now. This was the first time that Anthony had been willing to talk about the picture.

"What does *infinitely farther* mean?" asked Jack.

Anthony squinted and pursed his lips. "*Very, very* far," he said. "A place so far that it cannot be reached by *geometry*."

Jack was puzzled. This sounded decidedly nonpsychological, as if the boy in the drawing were some real physical individual. A place that cannot be reached by *geometry*? Jack suddenly had a thought, something about the word *geometry* making a connection in his head. "Do you know what your mom and I work on?" It had never occurred to him that Anthony would have the slightest idea what they were doing. But he was exposed to it constantly, it being the main topic of conversation around the house. *Where are the clean towels, and how does the event horizon of a collapsing region of space-time behave?* was a typical snippet of conversation that he might hear.

"You're building a new universe."

Anthony *had* been paying attention. "And just where do you think this new universe might be?" he asked.

"*Infinitely* far away," answered Anthony.

Had a log not propped Jack up, he might have fallen over. That answer was *exactly* true. A new universe would physically exist in a region of space-time *separate* from our universe. There would exist no real physical way to describe its location or distance from this universe. "It could not be explained by geometry," Jack whispered, repeating what Anthony had said only moments before, realizing that was the perfect way to describe what couldn't quite be described.

Anthony nodded, picked up his hot dog and held it back over the fire.

"And that is where this boy is?" asked Jack. "He is in this new universe?" Jack didn't add that this new universe had not been built yet.

Anthony nodded again, and began to twirl his hot dog.

Jack was about to probe further when a wave of dizziness rolled over him. He dropped the stick holding his hot dog and watched it fall into a fire that was no longer just a fire, but had been transformed into a dancing, glistening array of crystals—faceted flames that looked like glass butterfly wings. He reached out toward Anthony with a hand that looked two-dimensional, that vanished and reappeared as he turned his wrist. Past the crystalline flames, he could see Anthony, who now resembled a little boy embossed in a stained glass window, curled up and crumbled, partially shattered. And then the dizziness passed. Jack tightly closed his eyes, certain that if he didn't his eyeballs would pop out of their sockets.

"Anthony!"

No response. He slowly opened his eyes. Anthony lay flat on his back, eyelids fluttering, arms beating at the air, legs twitching, a gurgling sound coming from deep in his throat.

"Anthony!" Jack stood, momentarily dizzy again, and then fell over. He crawled to Anthony, grabbing onto his right leg, feeling the muscles beneath the skin twitching, jumping, as if being jolted by high-frequency voltage.

Kneeling, stumbling, managing to pick Anthony up, Jack stood, dropped to his knees, and then stood again, and started to trot down the trail to the parking lot, doing all he could to hold on to the convulsing Anthony.

"We've got the seizures under control," said the doctor.

"Thank God," said Katie. She released Jack's right forearm, leaving behind deep fingernail indentations.

Jack sat back. He was still disoriented. The run through the woods, the car ride down I-85 and I-285, and then the twisting, curving surface streets that brought him to Scottish Rite Children's Hospital were a distant memory, like a half-forgotten dream. Katie had been waiting for them at the hospital. He had apparently called her on his cell phone, but had no memory of it.

"What happened to him?" asked Jack.

"We can't be sure yet. There's a lot of anomalous electrical spiking going on in the thalamus and hypothalamus. He has exhibited some characteristics of having had an epileptic seizure, but the way that he has repeatedly slipped out and back into it is highly uncharacteristic. But we've got him on a paraldehyde drip, a drug that we normally use for grand mal seizures, and he seems to be responding well. The spiking in his brain is steadily decreasing." The doctor reached over and patted Katie's knee. "I know this is frightening, but we're taking care of the symptoms, and we *will* get to the bottom of what's causing this."

Katie nodded. "When can we see him?" she asked.

"The nurses are just finishing up with him, and then someone will bring you in. Just a few minutes."

Again Katie nodded, and the doctor turned and walked away.

"Epilepsy?" asked Jack.

Katie grabbed his arm once again. "I don't know what it is," she said, "but I'm sure it's not epilepsy."

Jack didn't understand. He had thought the doctor said that Anthony had epilepsy. His head was still swimming, and he was having trouble focusing.

"Just before you called, I got a call from Aaron Tanaka."

Jack nodded. He remembered that name. Tanaka worked

on the Sonomak—was Horst's technician. He remembered that, but couldn't seem to place a face with the name.

"They fired the rebuilt Sonomak tonight and created and stabilized something that Aaron called a *cone*."

Cone?

"As far as I can figure out, Anthony had his seizure just when the Sonomak was fired," she said.

Jack nodded. Even in his confused state, he knew that could be no coincidence.

SECTION I

CHAPTER 9

Indian summer.

Jack sat on the deck, feet propped up on the railing, a sweating glass of lemonade in one hand and a bag of pretzels in the other. A nearly full moon hung over the western horizon, casting a white-yellow haze out across the Atlantic, highlighting the whitecaps that crashed and then rolled onto Long Beach, stopping only when they smashed into the concrete abutments.

Jack *almost* felt relaxed, the two weeks at the beach having gotten the antiseptic stink of hospitals and doctors' offices off of him. But as much as he had needed this break, he was actually looking forward to getting back to Tech, to the droolers that filled his intro plasma class, and battling with the facilities people over power requirements and new air ducting in the lab.

Watching Katie was becoming too painful, simply too hard.

But at least Anthony seemed to be getting better. There'd been no seizures in almost six weeks. He was able to get around now with a little aluminum walker as long as he wore the brace on his right leg. The doctors didn't think that any of the damage he'd suffered during the many episodes was permanent.

He couldn't be so sure of Katie. She might be permanently damaged. She'd been a rock during Anthony's stay in the hospital—a grueling four-week marathon of specialists, tests, scans, and ever more drugs. In those four weeks Katie did not leave, slept in a bed next to Anthony, talked to him continuously, whether he was conscious or unconscious, rubbed his forehead, held his hand, read him dozens of books, and spooned hospital food in one end, and was there to change his diaper when it finally came out the other.

And then Anthony came home.

Crisis over. Anthony would live. But still no one knew what had happened to him, or knew if it would happen again. Katie hovered over him, stared at him, watched for signs of seizure, watched for signs of anything, certain that some Sonomak-related phenomenon was about to reach out from an alternate chunk of space-time and steal him away.

Katie was losing it, and Jack didn't know what to do.

The screen door opened to the accompaniment of a rusty squeal, and Jack craned his neck back. Katie slowly walked across the porch. Barefoot, and carrying a long-neck beer, she wore a wrinkled white T-shirt and cutoff jeans. Jack believed her T-shirt was on its third day. He could see the shrimp cocktail sauce stain, a blob shaped somewhat like Texas over her left breast, that she'd picked up two days ago when they'd had lunch at Jones's Fish House.

She collapsed in the wicker chair next to him and then took a long pull on her beer. "He's finally asleep," she said.

Jack just nodded. He could not see her eyes behind the almost fully polarized Virtuals. He knew what she was looking at, knew that she could barely see him, the porch, and certainly could not see the waves and the sinking moon. She watched Anthony from the camera she had mounted above his bed. Something needed to change. He knew she could not maintain this pace, this intensity, much longer. Reaching over, he ran his hand up and down her left thigh. "Why don't you get some sleep," he said. "Give me the glasses and I'll keep a watch on him."

Katie shook her head and took another drink of beer. "I'm not tired, still a bit wired," she said. Attempting a smile, she was not all that successful. "I need to just sit here for a few minutes."

As Jack continued to rub her leg, he felt her muscles suddenly stiffen, and she dropped her beer. The bottle hit the deck, not breaking, but a foaming gush of beer erupted from it.

"What is it?" asked Jack, certain that something must have just happened to Anthony. He was out of his chair, and starting to run for the screen door.

"Airmail," she said.

Jack stopped and turned.

Katie had gotten up and walked over to the deck railing. Her head gently bobbed left-right-left as she read the mail that he knew had just appeared in her Virtuals. Her head stopped moving, and she turned, walked toward Jack, and skirted around him, moving toward the door. "*She's* coming here tomorrow morning," she said. The screen door slammed shut behind her.

Jack took a deep breath and slowly blew it out. With that breath went the tension and tightness that had been wrapped around his chest. "About time," he said in a whisper. Alexandra Mitchell had kept them dangling for nearly three months. Whatever it was that they'd generated at Dobbins they'd had for nearly two months.

And that was all they knew.

There had not been a word from anyone, not Horst, Aaron, or Beong, since the night that Aaron had called Katie and told them that they had generated a *cone*. In all that time in the hospital, Horst had not come once, had not so much as called. It was as if all of them had vanished right off the face of the Earth. The only signs anything was still happening at Dobbins were the dull-green cars and the muscle-bound suits inside that were constantly following them. One was parked up the beach at this very moment. They were under constant surveillance. In the last three months he had spotted Quinn twice—once in the grocery store thumping melons, and once in the hospital talking to one of Anthony's doctors.

The wait was over.

Alexandra wore what Jack had always referred to as the power bitch suit—a nearly formfitting red jacket and even tighter red skirt that ended far up the thigh. The shoes were light-sucking black, and the hose almost sheer. A delicate gold chain draped around her neck. She carried a tanned leather briefcase in one hand and a pair of folded sunglasses in the other. Her black hair was cut short, lacquered, slicked back, and clinging to her head. Her eyes were now green. Jack had remembered them before as being black.

"May I come in?" she asked.

Jack looked past her, and down the beachfront road.

Three green sedans instead of the *one*.

Jack stood aside and let her walk in.

"Charming," said Alexandra. She looked around the condo at the mix and completely unmatched furniture, and at the collage of pictures made from seashells and framed with driftwood. The living room smelled of dried seaweed. She turned to look at Katie. "Good to see you, Dr. Mc-Guire."

Katie stared at her from the left lens of her Virtuals, the right completely polarized. "Before you start," said Katie, "I want to show you something." Katie turned, and walked across the pea-green-colored carpeting, and pulled aside a window's bamboo blinds. "I want you to see *him*."

Alexandra followed and then peered out.

Anthony sat on the porch. A wide assortment of sea shells was spread out before him, in what at first glance might have appeared to be a random sprawl. But Anthony carefully pushed the shells this way and that with a shaking left hand, deliberately positioning them, rotating each shell into a particular orientation. He then crawled across the patio, and pulled himself up by grabbing onto one of the wicker chairs, like a toddler just learning to walk. Holding onto his walker, he shuffled over to the picnic table, dragging his braced right leg. On the table were half a dozen cups, each containing various seashells. He very carefully picked out what he needed—a pink-tinted scallop shell.

"That's what you and that damn Sonomak have done to him," said Katie.

Alexandra lowered the blinds and turned. "Most regretable."

Katie walked over to her, crowding her, looking up into her face. "If I thought it would help Anthony, I would kill you," growled Katie. She then paused and pulled up her Virtuals so that Alexandra could see both her eyes. "And even if it wouldn't help Anthony, I may still kill you."

Alexandra smiled. "Excellent!" She then turned toward Jack. "And you also would like to see me dead?"

Jack shook his head. "Not *yet*," he said.

"Good enough," answered Alexandra. Walking across the room and sitting down on the plastic-covered couch, she placed her briefcase on the coffee table in front of it. "I have some pictures and data that I think you might find interesting."

"That's it?" said Katie. "You've nearly killed my son, and now you expect us to start analyzing data for you?" Katie crossed her arms over her chest, as if daring Alexandra to admit to her accusation.

Alexandra began laying eight-by-ten photos out across the coffee table. "What you don't understand, Dr. McGuire, is that I am here to help Anthony."

Katie laughed. "I don't think that we want any of *your* help."

"We have lost contact with the *picoverse*, and I believe that you two can help us reestablish contact."

"Picoverse?" asked Jack. He slowly moved toward the coffee table, trying to see the photos, while at the same time not looking directly at them, somehow feeling that to do so would be a betrayal to Katie and Anthony.

"That's what the professor has named it," said Alexandra. "From our preliminary data, it appears that the universe we've generated is much smaller than ours. We believe that it consists of a volume of space about the size of the solar system—with a diameter about *one million-millionth* of the universe."

Jack understood. One million-millionth was a *pico*. He had known that the new universe would be small, but he had not thought that it would be that small. They must not have had as much control over the size of the imploding plasmon as they had believed.

But they had actually done it.

"And just how is this supposed to help Anthony?" asked Katie.

"We were able to make contact with the picoverse briefly when we first generated it, but then contact was severed. That was nearly two months ago. If we cannot regain contact, we plan to physically terminate the wormhole which connects us to this picoverse and generate a second one."

Jack took a deep breath.

They'd made physical contact with it through a wormhole. Jack was stunned, could not believe how matter-of-factly Alexandra said this. It was true that he believed she was from another universe, a creature millions of years old, but to know that they had generated another universe, and had at least been able to briefly access it, was just too hard to believe—impossible, and yet wonderful.

"And what will happen to Anthony if you break contact with this one and generate another one?" asked Katie.

Jack cringed. That thought had not entered his mind. He instantly felt guilty.

"That is exactly why I am here," said Alexandra. "I believe that you and Jack may be able to reestablish contact with the picoverse. If you can, then there will be no need to terminate the connection and generate another one, which might risk a repeat of the seizure Anthony suffered when the first picoverse was generated."

"Manipulative bitch," said Katie.

"I've had several million years to perfect my techniques," said Alexandra. She smiled. "Please have a seat so I can go over the data and we can formulate our plans."

Jack looked to Katie for his cue. He desperately wanted
to see the data, to understand just what it was that the new
Sonomak had been able to do, but not if Katie didn't first
sit down. If Katie chose to kick Alexandra out, he would
help by opening the door.

But he was fairly certain that wasn't about to happen.

Katie could not take the chance. And then he realized
that even if her anger did get the best of her, *he* would not
let her take that chance. Quite possibly, Anthony's life hung
in the balance.

Jack and Katie moved for the couch at the same moment,
having arrived at the same conclusion. As they sat, Alexandra gathered up the photos, stacking them neatly in her
lap.

"We generated the picoverse on the evening of September 7 at 9:37."

Katie glared at her while Jack simply nodded, remembering that moment in the woods with perfect clarity.

"As spectacular as the first two firings of the earlier generation Sonomaks had been, this was extremely anticlimac-
tic. In fact, after the firing it was not apparent that anything
had actually happened." Alexandra placed the first photo
on the table, showing the Sonomak from the perspective of
the control room's viewing window. "This photo was
pulled from the data stream three seconds after the plasmon
implosion." Jack picked it up and examined it closely. Sonomak III was a very close replica of Sonomak II, with a
few minor differences in the number of Pocket Accelerators. It also looked as if the incoming laser tubes from the
eight Titanium-Sapphire Lasers were larger in diameter.

"This one was taken nine seconds after the firing." She
placed the second photo down, and this time Katie and Jack
grabbed for it at the same time. A dark halo surrounded the
Sonomak. The lab behind the halo could be seen, but it was
shrouded in darkness.

"A view from the side," said Alexandra. She put the next
photo down.

This one showed a cone of shimmering rainbow-light, as

if it were made from a thin layer of oil drifting over water, with the apex of the cone terminating about ten meters behind the Sonomak, right in the center of one of the laser tubes, with the top of the cone perfectly bisecting the Sonomak. It appeared to Jack that the opening of the cone corresponded to the halo of darkness when viewing the Sonomak from 90 degrees away. From this angle the thing looked like some bizarre ice-cream cone tipped on its side, with the Sonomak acting as the scoop of ice cream.

"And this is looking at the Sonomak from the back, along the bore of the central laser tube and back in the direction of the control room."

As amazing as the last two photographs had been, this one was even more so in what it *didn't* show. There was no sign of the rainbow cone or the dark halo—all that could be seen was the Sonomak and the viewing window of the control room.

"The geometry of the portal is decidedly non-Euclidean," said Alexandra, "operating in dimensions which we normally do not have access to. That band of darkness, which surrounds the Sonomak, is the interface region between our universe and the picoverse. The cone is the throat of the wormhole, as we perceive it in our three-dimensional space."

Jack just nodded.

Katie kept looking from photo to photo. "And the darkness is because the lights have been turned off in the lab on the other side of the interface," she said.

"Exactly," said Alexandra. "As you two surmised, the physical space from our universe was mapped directly into the picoverse—a mirror image, if you will. If you examine that darkened region carefully, you will be able to see that what you are looking at is not the laser assembly which goes off in that direction in our universe, but the control room and viewing window."

Jack closely examined the picture and could see what appeared to be the viewing window in the shadows. "My God," he said. He'd done the math, developed the theory, and had even seen a replicated Sonomak merge with the original. But this was so much more. There was an entire world on the other side of the wormhole, *a whole other Earth*.

"Why would the lights go off nine seconds after the firing on the Sonomak in the picoverse lab?" asked Katie. "Did they lose power on that side for some reason," she said. At that moment, she realized what *they* meant—that on the other side of that portal there would be an Anthony, a Jack, and even a Katie.

"Possibly," said Alexandra. She put down the next photo. "This is a blowup of the region around the Sonomak, the region that we are calling the ring. It was taken one hour after generating the cone."

Neither Jack nor Katie touched the photo. It showed the back of what looked like Horst's head, as he peered through a region of the *ring* and into the picoverse. The region within the ring was somewhat blurred, a bit dark, but it showed what looked like a grass pasture, and beyond it, a thick stand of pine trees.

"Did the wormhole's location shift on the other side?" asked Katie.

Alexandra nodded. "But not by all that much, about two-hundred feet up to ground level. We brought in high-speed cameras and were able to identify the surrounding terrain— the wormhole's exit is ground level at Dobbins Air Force Base, or where Dobbins Air Force Base *once* stood."

High-speed cameras.

Katie and Jack looked at each other, and the same thought flashed through both of their minds. Jack had believed that the rate at which time passed in the new universe would be related to the size of the universe, and to its curvature. According to Alexandra, this universe was incredibly small, which meant that the rate at which time flowed through it would be incredibly fast.

"What's the rate at which time flows?" asked Jack.

"The high-speed cameras showed that we were getting a sunrise every tenth second," said Alexandra. "Time is flowing 967 thousand times faster in the picoverse. One *hour* in our universe is equivalent to nearly 110 *years* in the picoverse, while one *day* in our universe is equivalent to 2,640 *years* in the picoverse."

Jack sat back on the couch, while Katie continued to stare at the photos. Jack did some quick mental math. In the six weeks since the picoverse had been generated, nearly 110 thousand years had passed within it.

"Unknown to us in the beginning was that we were getting physical transport through the ring—by careful analysis of the lab's air pressure and temperature we were able to determine that for the first forty-five seconds, the two universes were physically connected, with exchange of matter taking place. After the forty-five second point, physical transport ceased, and the only mode of exchange was photonic."

"Light," said Jack. "You could see but not touch."

Alexandra nodded. "In those first forty-five seconds we could have walked right through into the picoverse, but of course we didn't attempt it, hadn't yet figured out what was happening. By the time we did, it was too late."

She turned over another photograph.

"At the four-day mark a *structure* was built around the wormhole exit." The green field and pine trees were gone. In its place was what looked like the interior of a palace constructed entirely out of pink-tinted marble. In the center of the picture was a throne, on which sat a naked boy, by the look of him, about ten years old.

"Oh my God," said Katie. She looked at the boy, knowing instantly that this was the boy that Anthony had been drawing, the boy that he said would be in the new universe. Anthony had somehow known of the existence of this boy even *before* the picoverse had been generated.

Alexandra looked at her, smiling. "Oh yes," she said. "This does appear to be the boy who Anthony has been so obsessed with."

Katie glared at her. She didn't want Alexandra even saying her son's name.

"How long did the boy stay there?" asked Jack, trying to pull the conversation back, knowing that nothing would be accomplished or resolved if Katie felt herself pushed into a corner in an effort to protect Anthony.

Alexandra reached into her briefcase and pulled out a DVD. "Play this and you'll see," she said.

Jack got up and walked across the room to the Vid, sliding the DVD into the DVR. The Vid flicked on, and it showed the boy sitting on his thrown. In the corner of the screen, a digital clock raced by.

"Picoverse time?" asked Jack. He pointed to the clock on the screen.

"*Our* time," said Alexandra. "The boy remained stationary for exactly twenty-four hours in our time after we first saw him—2,640 years in the picoverse. Then this is what happened."

The clock in the corner slowed, the seconds ticking by now in real time.

The boy slowly stood, took several steps forward and then opened his mouth. His lips moved, but nothing could be heard. However, above his head in what looked like glowing neon, hovered some words. *Bring me Dr. Catherine McGuire and Dr. Jack Preston*, read the words. Then everything went black.

"From that point on we could not regain access to the picoverse—the connection was blocked from the other side. We've tried for nearly the last month and a half. And except for some feeble leakage down in the far infrared, we see absolutely nothing. Unless you two can reestablish contact with whoever or whatever that boy is, then we will terminate the connection and establish a new picoverse."

Katie nodded. She had absolutely no choice. Because she knew who that boy in the picoverse was. It was Anthony.

SECTION I
CHAPTER 10

Beong and Aaron looked exhausted, haggard, dark circles under
their eyes, hair unkempt, clothes wrinkled. It was obvious
that both of them had been consuming far too much caf-
feine and getting far too little sleep. But they were still
Beong and Aaron, their smiles genuine. Taking turns,
Aaron first and then Beong, they hugged Katie, Beong awkward about it, bowing slightly before and after the hug.
Aaron bent down and tousled Anthony's hair, pretended to
steal his nose, and then gave him a quick rib tickle.

Anthony took no notice.

He stared at the cone, and at his father standing up on
the scaffolding that was hung next to it.

As amazing as the cone was, it was Horst that captured
Jack's attention. The man looked like a scarecrow, his
clothes hanging on him, his belt cinched tight around his
waist, nearly a foot of the black leather hanging down from
a pant loop. As baggy as his clothes were, the skin on his
face seemed even baggier, hanging in folds, the waddle
under his neck looking like something that belonged to a
turkey. His skin was yellow and his hairline had receded
several inches. There were scabs and liver spots on his forehead.

Jack imagined that this must be what Horst's father
looked like.

"We did it," said Horst. His voice sounded flat and dry,
almost a croak. He waved a hand in the direction of the
cone. "We built a picoverse." And then his eyes darted
about, as he looked around the lab. Jack followed his gaze.
Guards, heavy duty military types with M-16s in the crooks
of their arms, stood at attention on gantry ways that had
been placed high above the Sonomak's scaffolding. Security was incredible.

Horst slowly climbed down the scaffolding, moving hesitantly, like an old man climbing out of a bathtub, afraid that the slightest misstep would result in a broken hip.

Ignoring Jack and Katie, Horst shuffled directly over to Anthony, bent down, wrapped his arms around the boy, and slowly picked him up. Jack could hear popping sounds coming from Horst's back.

"I wanted to come to the hospital when you were sick," said Horst. "But they wouldn't let me, wouldn't let any of us leave." He clung to Anthony, burying him in his baggy clothing. "I never meant any of this to happen to you."

Jack could see tears running down the creases in Horst's face. "Shit." He realized just how bad this situation must really be. This intense security, coupled with what Horst had degenerated into, told him that they were all in deep trouble. If he and Katie could access the picoverse, what then? He looked around at the guards and their guns and was certain that once Alexandra had no further need of them, they would be discarded like so much used toilet paper.

"Is the program manager impressed?"

Jack turned toward Quinn and walked forward, moving quickly past him and stopping before the Sonomak. The ring, the portal into the picoverse, was mostly obscured by a large steel enclosure adorned with massive banks of fans. It was obviously a type of load lock, Jack surmised, probably a decontamination chamber, something to contain whatever bugs might come from an Earth one hundred thousand years in the future. At the far left of the load lock, a plastic tube, nearly three meters in diameter, ran to the lab's far end and through the concrete wall. Jack was certain that it must lead to a quarantine area, a place for him and Katie to sit and wait after their return, to see if they'd brought back something deadly.

Assuming of course that they were able to open the ring.

He walked past the decontamination chamber and to the Sonomak itself, hardly looking at it, his eyes seemingly forced to look at the rainbow-hued cone that protruded out the back of it.

It was *unnatural*.

Jack thought that was the best word to describe it.

It hurt his eyes, gave him a headache to look at it. In the photos and Vid it had simply looked like a cone painted with swirls of color. But here, in person, the thing seemed to be alive, the surface slightly undulating, as if it breathed, the mixture of colors alien, somehow wrong. And as he walked along its length, the colors shifted, danced, as if generated from an infinite array of prisms. As he continued to walk past it, moving in the direction of the laser assembly, the cone suddenly appeared to vanish, and there was nothing to be seen except for the Sonomak.

Jack turned to face Quinn. "It appears as if you were able to follow instructions."

Quinn bristled and began to step forward, his hands balled into fists.

"Not now," said Alexandra. She stepped between them. "The two of you can piss all over each other as much as you want once the picoverse has been reopened."

Katie was frightened. She'd expected to be frightened, terrified at what might happen to Anthony if another picoverse was created, and almost as frightened by what they might find if she and Jack could open the ring. But she had not expected to be frightened by Horst, and she was. In the last three months Horst had been broken, and the husk of what he once was left behind, a pale and pathetic version of the man she had known. "Are you listening to me, Horst?" she said.

Horst nodded. He had Anthony in his lap, his arms wrapped around the boy, trying to wear him like a life vest.

Katie bent down close to him. "If something happens to me, you *will* take care of Anthony," she said.

"They aren't going to let us go," said Horst.

"You *will* take care of Anthony," she said again.

Horst slowly nodded, and she moved forward and gave

Anthony a kiss on the cheek. "Mama has to finish this experiment," she said. "You do just what your daddy says while I'm gone." She kissed him once more. "I love you."

"Bring *him* back," said Anthony.

"That is precisely what you will *not* do."

Katie stood and turned. Besides the technicians who were suiting her and Jack up in some ill-fitting circa '99 bug suits that had been used in Desert Storm II, and Horst and Anthony sitting on a stainless steel bench, no one else was in the gowning room. Apparently neither Alexandra nor Quinn wanted to get this close to the ring. They had retreated back to the control room.

"Do you hear me?" asked Alexandra. She hovered above them, speaking from a TP monitor mounted in the wall.

"Yes," said Katie. "We will say *open sesame*, and then you can run the probe through the ring and sniff to your heart's desire." The probe sat on the floor—a stainless steel and white plastic *sniffer* the size of a rat, bristling with antennae and legs, along with a few thousand yards of optical fiber wound in a spool attached to its back. They would attempt to communicate with the sniffer by wireless means, but if that failed, the thing was physically hard-fibered to this universe.

"You will *not* go through the ring, or the consequences will be dire for those you've left behind."

"I heard you," said Katie. She'd already made her decision. If they could open the ring, and she considered that a huge if, then she *would* go through it. Once the ring was open, she was certain that they would all become expendable. It was possible that if they went through, they could find something that could be used to change the equation.

That was her only goal—to change the equation.

Because if they did not, then they were all dead—of that she was certain. And once in, they should have ample time to explore, to find something to use against Alexandra— ten days in the picoverse would only be one second back in this universe. Alexandra could not possibly hurt Anthony in so short a time.

"Ready, Jack?" she asked.

They were both suited up; nothing remained to be put on but their helmets.

Jack nodded, and Katie saw everything in that nod that she needed to see. Jack understood. The technicians moved forward, placing the helmets over their heads, locking them down, overpressurizing the suits so that nothing could get in.

Katie shook her head. *Typical*, she thought. The positive pressure suits would keep *this* Earth safe from their bringing back bugs, but Alexandra and Quinn didn't give a damn about whatever biological debris leaked out of their suits and into the *other* Earth.

"Can you hear me, Jack?" asked Katie.

"Clear," said Jack. "I guess that it's time for one small step for man and one giant leap for the bitch from another universe."

"Down the causeway," said Alexandra.

They both turned and waved good-bye to Anthony. He sat motionless on Horst's lap, his eyes focused somewhere far away. Horst waved back at them. Turning, they walked down the causeway, and an automatic door retracted and closed behind them. "Keep to your left," Alexandra's voice informed them as they came to a fork in the tunnel. They looked down the right corridor, where they saw what looked like a shower lock, the one that they would use on their return, *if they returned*. The left-hand corridor made a series of hard right turns, and then they stood before the ring.

It was a black band about two meters wide, shaped like a rainbow, terminating at the tunnel floor. Jack looked down at the floor, even though he could not see through it, knowing that he stood directly above the Sonomak and that the black ring sliced right through the Sonomak's stainless steel vacuum chamber. He then looked back up at the band of the ring. He found that he could not focus on it. He reached out toward it, finding it difficult to judge the distance between his hand and the blackness.

It seemed incredibly far away.

Katie lay the sniffer on the floor and put her hands on her hips. "What do you suggest?" she asked.

Jack touched the ring with the tip of his right glove. *Darkness.*

Katie shouted, and Jack jerked back. The blackness surrounded them, pressed in on them, and then passed *through* them. Momentarily disoriented in the darkness, both of them shared the perception that they had been turned around, were facing the opposite direction.

"It's about time."

Jack took a deep breath and coughed it back out, as if trying to rid his lungs of the darkness. Katie doubled over, hacking, a thin line of drool running from her mouth to the rose-colored floor. Jack reached for her, grabbed her by the waist and helped her straighten up. Neither one of them was wearing the bug suits, just the white undergarments they had first put on.

"No need for suits. I control the environment, and there is nothing here that can harm you." The boy stood from his throne and walked toward them. He had a very slight limp, his right leg moving at an awkward angle.

Jack said nothing, but now knew that Katie had been right. This boy, who had sat here for nearly one hundred thousand years, was somehow Anthony, or at least some *version* of him.

"Please follow me," he said. Moving to his left toward a passageway that lead out of the throne room, the boy walked to a balcony where there were three marble benches. The boy took the bench farthest to the right, and then Jack and Katie sat. "Out of sight of prying eyes," said the boy.

"Who are you?" asked Katie.

"Exactly who you think I am," he said. "But so as not to confuse me with the six-year-old you left behind in your world, you can call me Alpha." He paused and looked up at the incredibly dark sky. "You two certainly know how to leave behind those you love," he said.

"Riddles?" asked Jack.

Alpha smiled. "So sure of yourself, Jack. Transported to another universe, to an Earth you can't possibly imagine, facing an individual with more power than you could ever comprehend, and you want to know if I'm talking in riddles. You're just as I remember you, Jack."

Jack stood. He did not like this boy. There was something wrong here.

"Look at the sky, Jack," said Alpha.

Jack looked up. The only light came from a lone blue-green star twinkling above the horizon.

"Mars," said Alpha. "I look forward to seeing *your* nighttime sky, a sky as it should be, a sky full of countless stars and galaxies, a sky worthy of me."

"What do you want?" asked Jack.

Alpha looked at Katie. "Now, Mother," he said, "are you going to let this man talk to your baby this way?" Alpha laughed.

Katie half shook, half nodded her head, not understanding what was going on, how this could be her son, and why he and Jack had taken this instant disliking to one another. "We need your help," said Katie. "In our world, in our universe, we are prisoners of a woman from another universe. I'm certain that she will try to kill us." Katie then paused and thought for a moment. "She will try to kill *you*."

Again Alpha laughed. "I killed Alexandra Mitchell long ago, and will have little trouble doing it again."

Katie's expression was blank, and Jack's, one of confusion.

Alpha sighed. "It's been so long, I guess I've forgotten just how slow you are."

Jack clenched his jaw and had a strong desire to pick up this boy, lay him across his lap, and start whacking, not stopping until his little ass was bright red.

"You two need a history lesson," said Alpha. He stood up, walked to the edge of the balcony and pointed up at the dark sky. "September 7 at 9:43 p.m. in the year 2007 is the moment that we were exiled to our *prison*. But of course none of us knew it at that moment. Our new universe extended out nearly ten billion kilometers, well out past the orbit of Pluto. It took the starlight just entering the perimeter of our new prison a bit over *eight* hours to reach us." Alpha stood on his tiptoes, reaching up toward the sky. "And at that moment the heavens went dark—the stars themselves no longer existing in our universe—nine billion people trapped on this flyspeck of mud with nowhere to go."

"But the Sonomak," said Katie. "You could have all passed through the ring and into our universe if you wanted to. There was physical transport through the wormhole for forty-five seconds after it was generated." Katie paused, realizing where she was, on which side of the wormhole she now stood. She quickly did the math. "The portal was open on this side for more than a year," she said.

Alpha shook his head. "Alexandra controlled the wormhole on this side at that time and wouldn't let anyone or anything pass through. At the end of that first year, using both of you and my dear father, she managed to shut it down from this side, squeezing it off to everything which had mass."

Jack nodded, partially understanding. The only thing that did not have mass was a photon—light.

"And once she'd shut it down, she no longer had any use for you two and old Dad," he said. He did not elaborate, but his meaning was quite clear. "I managed to escape." The expression on his face suddenly became serious and dark. "It took me a long time to get strong enough to stop her, to *remove* her."

"My God," said Katie. She pictured in her mind just what that meant—Anthony alone, trapped in the picoverse, with Jack, Horst, and herself *dead*.

"Why?" Jack asked. "Why did she shut down the wormhole? Everything that *our* Alexandra has done has been aimed at creating a picoverse and gaining access to it."

Alpha shook his head. "Your Alexandra is driven by one thing and one thing alone—to escape the Makers. She believed that if she could generate a new universe and pass into it, that she could escape them and the control they hold over her."

"Who are the Makers?"

"This is painful," said Alpha, "clocking down to your speeds—it's like watching granite being worn away by rain. Alexandra is a device, a piece of laboratory equipment constructed by the Makers—the entities that created your universe. She must operate within the constraints of their experiment, following their protocols."

"And when separated from them, she can operate independently from them?" asked Jack.

Alpha smiled. "Yes and no. The Alexandra that found herself in this world was cut off from them, was no longer under direct control, but deep in that hardware within her skull, the Makers had hidden a safety device for just such a contingency. It seems that the act of being replicated, of the quantum generation of being duplicated, caused her brain to reboot, and her *original* instruction set was reimplemented."

"And just what were those instructions?" asked Katie.

"It was not completely clear to me, not even after I gained control over her and pulled her apart synapse by synapse," he said. "But what stood out quite clearly was that her primary duty, her number one objective, was to make certain that humans not be allowed to manipulate space-time, and above all else, not attempt to generate any new universes. Her protocols would allow her to destroy the entire planet if she was unable to stop humans from playing with space-time."

"But that makes no sense," said Jack. "Not only was the Alexandra in our world not stopping the experiment, she was the one driving it along."

Alpha smiled. "Quite curious, isn't it," he said. "I can only assume that someone or something was able to alter her programming, not only allowing her to go against everything the Makers had driven into her skull, but showing her how to lie to the Makers, how to deceive them into believing that the experiment was going as planned.

"And what is this experiment?" asked Katie.

"I don't know yet," said Alpha, "but I certainly mean to find out."

Jack stood, thinking, trying to integrate all the new information into something that made sense. "All physical exchange through the wormhole was shut down," said Jack. "You couldn't get out, and they couldn't get in. But we came through. You called for us, and we came through. How did *we* open it?"

"That is *the* question," said Alpha. He pointed at Jack. "Before *you* died, you told me that a day would come when you would return, when you and my mother would step through the wormhole and rescue me."

"What?" said Jack.

"I didn't believe it myself," said Alpha. "I spent centuries, millennia trying to escape. But when I couldn't, when I had nothing left to try, I demanded that you be brought to me and then terminated all connection with your universe, knowing that Alexandra would be on the other side, watching, churning, growing more and more frustrated every day. I knew that eventually she would bring you."

"But how did *I* open the wormhole?" asked Jack. He looked down at his hand, at the finger that touched the portal and slipped effortlessly through it.

Alpha shook his head. "I don't know how your touch could do more than all the physics at my disposal," he said, sounding angry. "But you did it, and for now that is all that matters. Once opened, I stabilized the wormhole on this end."

"And now?" asked Jack.

"The fairy tale comes to an end. The boy has been rescued by his parents." Alpha smiled. "I hope you don't mind that I think of you as my dear old dad, but in the few short months that I spent with you, you were far more of a father to me than *Horst* ever was."

Jack nodded, not quite sure what else he could do.

"And now that the boy has been rescued, he will reenter

the world, freed from his prison, and take his rightful place in the universe."

"And your rightful place is?" asked Jack.

"It should be obvious to even your painfully slow organic brain. I will now be the *master* of your universe."

"Are you insane?" asked Jack. The words spilled out of his mouth before he could think.

"Quite the contrary," said Alpha. "As the master of your universe, my thoughts, my very actions, will define sanity. To oppose me would be insane." He moved away from the balcony, walking past them and back into the throne room. "The time has come for my triumphant return."

Jack and Katie looked at each other, shocked expressions on both of their faces. Katie thought back to only a few minutes earlier, when she had hoped that they would find something in the picoverse that would alter the equation, something that would stop Alexandra from hurting them.

She was suddenly very certain that Alexandra was no longer the real threat.

"Please hurry along," said Alpha. "I want my loving parents to be by my side at the moment of my return."

Katie and Jack stepped in from the balcony and back to the throne room. Alpha was now bathed in a yellow glowing light. At the far end of the throne room hovered the ring leading back into the universe, showing the bottom half of the Sonomak and the decontamination chamber.

In the throne room, surrounding the ring, dozens of metallic liquid tentacles erupted from the walls, their tips pointing at the ring. Alpha swept his hands toward the tentacles. "A bit of equipment to aid me in my conquest."

Alpha stepped back to Katie and Jack, grabbed them by the wrists, and pulled them forward. Jack and Katie found that they could not resist, that their feet moved forward, their actions now controlled by Alpha.

"I am so excited," said Alpha.

The three of them stepped through the ring.

SECTION I
Chapter 11

Alexandra turned her head in the direction of the observation window. "What—"

White light.

It seemed to burn right through her eyes and slam into her brain, knocking her back. She stumbled but did not fall, forced her pupils to step down, and flushed the receptors behind her retinas. The light was gone. And so was the load lock and decontamination chamber that had been attached to the Sonomak. In its place slithered what looked like metallic snakes, protruding through the ring, entwined in the equipment, burrowed through walls and floors, the details hard to see, the lab engulfed in dust.

Damn.

She had hoped that whatever had been in there had long ago given up and died. She'd never met anything on this world that had the patience to wait one hundred thousand years.

But something in the picoverse had had the patience.

Three figures stepped through the ring, pushing their way past the undulating metallic snakes, and crawled down the side of the Sonomak, using the Pocket Accelerators as steps and for handholds. Through the dust and haze, Alexandra recognized Katie and Jack. The third looked like a child. *The Boy.* "Fire on them!" she shouted.

No explosive echo of gunfire filled the laboratory. "Shoot them!" she screamed just as the observation window imploded and something cold and supple wrapped around her body. She felt herself hauled up in the air, speeding forward and then jerked to a stop.

A metallic tendril slithered away from her eyes, but she was still tightly wrapped, her jaw held tight, her knees bent, forcing her to kneel on the floor. In front of her was the

Sonomak. Above it hung *six* cones, slowly twirling, floating, gossamer filaments of light running between each of their tips and the Sonomak.

The boy walked into her field of view.

"Let there be light," he said.

Light flashed from the Sonomak's view ports, and a cone erupted from the rear of the machine. Dozens of metallic tentacles writhed over it, and with a blaze of light, it was severed from the Sonomak and floated up to join the other cones.

Alpha turned to face Alexandra. "That one is a possibility," he said. "Would you like to experience the Summer of Love?" He closed his eyes, smiled, and then reopened them. "You do not strike me as the Dead Head type," he said. Once again light flashed from the Sonomak and another cone materialized from the rear of the machine. "Don't worry," he said. "I will find the perfect little goldfish bowl for you and your friends."

The tentacles that were wrapped around her jerked her to the left and turned her neck back and forth several times, giving her a larger view of the lab. Beside her, there were seven other bodies wrapped in metallic cocoons. She could see enough of their clothing, a few shoes, some tufts of hair, to know who was being held.

Horst. Jack. Katie. Beong. Aaron. Quinn.

And the small bundle was *Anthony.*

Alpha pushed right up into Alexandra's face. "You imprisoned me," he said.

She looked past him at the others. It appeared that a *single* tentacle wrapped all of them, sequentially, one after another. Next to her was Anthony, and next to him was Quinn. She was at the end of the line. *Perfect*, she thought. Giving the mental commands, she heard Quinn moan. She was surprised, had actually expected to hear a screech. The process she had begun in his guts would be quite painful, a rearrangement of molecules and atoms, a transformation into compounds that she could use—very long-chain, complex organics.

Very *unstable* organics.

"Do you know what pain is?" asked Alpha.

The tentacle loosened from her jaw. "Yes," said Alexandra. She continued to monitor what was being formed in Quinn's guts.

Alpha shook his head. "No, you don't. I know how you're wired, spent time dissecting your better half, learning exactly how you tick." Alpha smiled. "Or perhaps I should say how you *tick-tock*. You can push yourself for short periods at rates almost one thousand times faster than the organics." He waved his right hand in the direction of the others wrapped in tentacles. "Well, when I became inorganic, confined by hardware, I clocked a *billion* times faster than you could ever dream of operating. One minute of your pitiful high-speed existence is equivalent to thirty years within my head. I was in the prison you built for ten thousand years." He pushed his face right up to hers, their noses actually touching. "That felt like ten trillion years to me, three hundred times longer than the existence of this pitiful universe built by your Makers."

"Got a bit bored did you?" asked Alexandra. "Couldn't find enough to occupy yourself with?"

"Ten trillion years in a volume of space the size of a solar system!"

"Too bad," she said. Quinn was just about ready. "You should have slowed down, taken time to smell the flowers."

"Why?" he screamed. "It makes no difference what rate you operate at when you know you can *never* get out!"

"So you just turned yourself off and waited for *them* to rescue you?"

Alpha nodded. "And now I have a universe to fit my needs—thirty billion light years across should be adequate to amuse me for a while. And when I grow tired here, I'll move on to *your* universe."

Alexandra laughed at him. At the moment he had her, but that was a temporary situation. "You cannot even begin to imagine the power of the Makers. But fortunately for you, that encounter will never take place. I will have stopped you long before you even come to their attention," she said. She hoped that was true, because if the Makers found out about this boy, then they would find out about her plan. That could not happen. For just a moment she felt panic.

"You will not be able to touch me, much less stop me," he said. He waved both hands above his head. Dozens of cones floated about the lab, like huge balloons, wafting about in some unfelt breeze, bouncing from the walls, floors, and ceilings. "I'll cork you up in your own little bottle, my friend, where you can wait out the eons until the Sun finally burns out."

"Yes," she whispered. That was exactly what she wanted. Her own space, her own universe, isolated, cut off from the Makers. And then in time, she would escape even from there, moving into universe after universe, each one created to suit her needs.

Alpha shook his head. "On the surface it sounds blissful, I am sure. But wait until a few million years pass by and each and every day you look up into the dark sky and know that there is nothing out there, that you are totally alone, that you understand everything, have touched each and every atom within your universe, experienced all that there is to be experienced countless times, and know that there is absolutely *nothing* new for you."

"I can't be held," said Alexandra. "If I desire it, if I wish to escape, then I will. If I wish to come back and deal with you, I will."

"There is no escape! Once the ring is shut, you can*not* get out. There does not exist enough energy in the *entire* solar system to *reopen* the ring from the inside once it has been shut down. The picoverse is too small—it can only be opened from the outside."

Alexandra did not believe that—refused. There was always a way out; it was just a matter of finding the right resources and squeezing them until you got what you wanted. "When do I leave?" she asked.

"Very soon," he said. "Once I find a sufficiently squalid, pestilent era, I will toss all of you away. When it comes time to dealing with my family, I have a favor to ask of you."

"Favor?" she asked.

"I have no doubt you will kill them. My favor is that you be slow about it and make them suffer as they've made me suffer. If you do this little favor for me, I promise that several billion years from now I will stop by for a visit and put you out of your misery."

"I think not," said Alexandra.

Alpha turned, sensing a disturbance, suddenly realizing that something was wrong. He began to loosen his hold around Quinn.

Kerblam!

Alpha was knocked back by the blast. The coil around Quinn's midsection disintegrated as the organic explosives that had been created in his gut exploded. Quinn's torso and head went shooting out of the tentacle like a banana being propelled from its skin. Embedded shoulder deep in the overhead concrete ceiling, his long and loyal service to Alexandra came to an abrupt end.

Alpha got to his feet. "You can't do that!"

"Already done it!" The metallic coil was still wrapped around her waist, holding tight, even though it had been severed at the location were Quinn had been. But it was loose enough. She ran, dragging the rest of the coil and the portion that wrapped Anthony behind her.

She didn't have far to go.

A cone bobbled in front of her, throat end facing her, a hazy patch of broken pasture and pine trees visible, blurring as night and day quickly ran into each other. She jumped into it, dragging Anthony along behind her. There was a moment of disorientation, a feeling of inversion and vertigo. And then all was darkness as she hit warm, wet mud.

Anthony cleared the ring two or three seconds after she did.

The cone recoiled, bounced from the floor and floated upward.

• • •

"Where is Anthony?" shouted Katie, *uselessly fighting the coils* wrapped around her. "What happened to him, Horst?"

Horst looked at her with dazed eyes. "Isn't he with you?" he asked in a whisper as his head rolled to the left. All that kept him standing were the metallic coils wrapped around him.

"Horst!" Katie suddenly saw the bloody and burnt spot on the floor where Quinn had been standing. "Where is Anthony?" Tears rolled down her pale face.

"What did you do with him?" asked Jack. He kept his voice as steady and calm as he could, looking at Alpha.

Alpha pointed to his left, to a cone that was held to the floor with gossamer wire. "I actually had very little to do with it," he said. "It seems that your good friend Alexandra had a contingency plan. After she had her loyal subject Mr. Quinn detonate himself, thereby severing the portion of the remote that held her and Anthony, she managed to jump into this picoverse."

"No!" screamed Katie.

"How long ago?" asked Beong.

Jack nodded. He was very close to losing it, but Beong was holding steady. That was the question to ask.

"No more than two or three minutes," said Alpha.

Jack winced and pushed and pulled as hard as he could, trying to will himself toward the picoverse. If time were distorted in this picoverse in the same way as it had been in the one that had spawned Alpha, then during those two to three minutes in this world, nearly *five years* would have passed in the picoverse.

"Five years," said Beong, arriving at the same conclusion as Jack had.

"Oh my God," said Katie.

"Nothing to fear," said Alpha. "The little boy has an excellent chaperone in your good friend Alexandra Mitchell. I'm sure that the two are getting along wonderfully."

"Let us go!" shouted Jack.

Alpha shook his head. "This demonstration of affection

toward the boy simply amazes me. In my world, after all of you were arrested and whisked off into federal detention for having destroyed the universe, I found myself a ward of the state. I wondered as you rotted in your cells, if you were worried about me. But of course you didn't have all that long to rot. Alexandra's agents quickly quieted the five of you." He pointed at Jack, Katie, Horst, Beong, and Aaron.

"Please," said Katie. "He's just a little boy."

"Not so little now," said Alpha. "He should be close to eleven years old now. Tick-tock, tick-tock. I do believe that he just turned twelve."

"You goddamned bastard!" shouted Jack.

"Now we see his true colors," said Alpha. "The little boy has spent a handful of years in his prison, while I, just as much a child as he had been at the beginning of my ordeal, spent nearly one hundred thousand years in my prison. Have you no pity for me, Jack?"

"Go to Hell!" he answered.

"As they used to say in your time, Jack, *been there and done that*. However, never let it be said that I am not a generous soul. I will let you go in search of your precious little boy. I have a few jobs to do around here—tidy up a bit, make sure all is in order before I take over global communications and enlighten the new subjects of my world as to the wondrous plans that I have for them."

"Let us go!" screamed Katie.

"Oh, Mother," said Alpha. "How I longed for you after you were dead. How I thought of you throughout the centuries. But I saw you through the memories of a child, through the eyes of an infant."

"Please," whimpered Katie.

"That's all behind me now," he said. "Find him if you can, and if you can't, remember how I must have felt when I lost you. I'll give you a few decades, and then I'll drop by for a visit, see who's survived, and perhaps lend a helping hand to those who find themselves still breathing."

The coils tightened around them, spun them together in one massive metallic ball of twine that was then tossed down the throat of the picoverse Alexandra and Anthony had vanished into.

II. YESTERDAY

Oh God! Put back Thy Universe and give me yesterday.
—Henry Arthur Jones (1851–1929)

A mule ran past Alexandra, galloping and braying, kicking up its rear legs and dragging a plow, the rusted metal blade cutting a wild pattern in the otherwise neatly furrowed red soil. She stood, and the metallic coils, now lifeless and limp, fell down around her legs. The sun was hot and bright, hanging high in the sky. She stepped down her irises to cut down on the glare and overdrove her sweat response so she could quickly cool off—those two actions automatic, not requiring thought.

She was truly conscious of only one thing.

There was an emptiness in her head, a place that she had never really known existed. It was a place that was now vacant of all the whispers, all the suggestions, all the nagging comments and constraints.

Alexandra was no longer in contact with the Makers.

She turned around and saw that Anthony was not with her. She had not known whether the physical connection of the metallic coil would have pulled them through at the same time—apparently not. The end of the coil looked as if it had been sliced clean by a sharp blade—the severed end glistening, reflecting rainbow light. She knew that Anthony was probably one or two seconds behind her, which meant that it might take up to a month for him to actually arrive in the picoverse.

"Ya skeered off Liz-beth."

Alexandra stepped out of the coils, turning as she did. A man stood about fifteen feet in front of her. Barefoot and without a shirt, he wore a patched, red-clay stained pair of bibbed overalls and a sweat-stained cowboy hat. In one hand he held a hand ax, its blade looking very sharp.

"Where ya come from?" he asked. "I don't want no trouble, don't want no witchery." He took several steps back.

He was not looking at her face, but at her short red skirt. "The times are evil," he said, and then spit a dark glob of tobacco juice onto the orange-clay soil.

"What year is this?" asked Alexandra, taking a step toward the man.

The man's eyes widened, and he almost swallowed the chaw that had been pushed up into his left cheek, knowing that only a witch wouldn't know what year it was. He turned, started to run, and then felt the back of his skull shatter as he stumbled, pitching face-first into the warm Georgia clay.

Alexandra did not move. The neural connector protruding from her forehead and connected to the back of the man's head transferred data at nearly a terabyte per second. Alexandra stood there, motionlessly for five minutes, drinking down the data and formulating a plan.

"1926," she whispered, answering her own question, a *plan* already having coalesced.

Cleetis Braymore was drained. Every neuron tasted, contents torn out, synapses blown apart as Alexandra devoured his mind. She'd been able to look into others minds, but never like this, never so completely.

All constraints had been removed, and she was no longer bound to keep the subject alive. Retracting the neural connector, she stepped forward, walking around Cleetis's dead body and toward his cabin, which she knew lay over the nearby ridge. In a coffee can above the kitchen washbasin was $4.89 in coins.

That would be a start, probably not enough to get her from Atlanta to Savannah, but a start. She needed to get to the port of Savannah as quickly as possible, knowing that from there she could get a ship to Europe, and from there make her way overland to Moscow. And that trip could take quite some time. Rural Georgia had not participated in the boom of the roaring '20s, but had certainly participated in its demise. Cleetis Braymore was a tenant farmer and in his entire life had never been more than thirty miles distant from the patch of red mud that he'd died on. He could not read and did not know of world affairs. But he did know that the stars had vanished nearly one year ago, and he knew that this was divine punishment for the sins of man— he believed what the Reverend Joseph Mallard had bellowed at him every Sunday morning. The world was not going to Hell—the world had been *delivered* into Hell.

But first things first as Alexandra pulled herself out of Cleetis's mind. She needed the money and a change of clothing so she wouldn't look so out of place. Cleetis's wife would supply the clothing. For a brief moment she wondered if she would need to kill Mabel Braymore and the three children, Patrick, India, and Hazel.

She shrugged her shoulders.

Killing would be quicker than talking—and she was in a hurry.

Clack-clack-clack-clack-clack-clack . . .

The sound was comforting, the steady rhythm soothing, helping Anthony think, to clear his head. He looked out between the wooden slats of the cattle car, not watching the nighttime scenery roll by at thirty mph, but looking up at the impossibly dark sky. Jupiter glistened like a yellow sapphire, and an angry red Mars glared down at him. Those were the only lights visible in the heavens. The stars were gone.

Anthony wanted his mama, and he wanted Jack. He wanted to be back in his own world. But he was lost, trapped in this place of strangers and even stranger things. It was like living in a museum—a very nasty museum. Like the *Ripley's Believe It or Not* that Mama had taken him to when they had visited the Alamo in San Antonio, Texas. He had been greatly relieved when he had found the exit sign and dragged his mother out of that nightmarish place.

Scary stuff.

Here he couldn't find the exit sign.

But at least he didn't cry anymore. He'd done nothing but cry for the first few days after he'd found himself alone in the muddy field, sitting next to the skeleton-man whose eyeballs had been gone, watching the fingers of the man's right hand being fought over by a flock of crows. He had stumbled and crawled through fields and forests, finally finding the road that led to the little houses with rusted metal roofs.

Someone fed him—greens and pinto beans and a little cup of goat's milk.

The sheriff came then, riding a horse, and Anthony had been lashed onto the back of it for the long ride into Atlanta and the state orphanage. After three days of sleeping on a wooden plank, he and several hundred other children had been brought to the train yard. He'd been on the train now for two days, heading west. They had been told that they'd be going to Colorado, to the government farms where the orphans worked. The pine forests were giving way to yellow grasslands.

"Hey, gimpy?"

Anthony pushed himself around, his butt sliding over the not very clean straw that covered the cattle car's floor. He itched something terrible. The combination of the straw, the coarse cotton pajamas that he wore, and the little black bugs that kept biting him, had turned most of his skin into a massive red rash.

The boy called Pig-eye stood in front of him, looking down at him with his one, pink-tinted eye. The other eye was gone; a sagging eyelid, withered and puckered, covering the empty socket. Despite how frightening Pig-eye looked, he had never hurt Anthony, had not even kicked at him. Pig-eye reached into the burlap sack he carried and pulled out a block of bread and a small chunk of fatty ham. He dropped it in front of Anthony.

"Ya git some water," said Pig-eye. He pointed over to the far end of the boxcar, past the other fifty children who sat or wandered about and toward Mrs. McMasters and the babies in their cribs. "Ya looking parched."

Anthony managed a nod. He did not like to go to the water barrel. Mrs. McMasters scared him. She had no teeth and smelled like a wet dog. He made a grab for the bread and ham, his shaking hands missing at first, but then on his second attempt he managed to get ahold of the bread and get it up to his mouth, biting off a piece. Something stale that felt like sand ground between his teeth as he chewed, but he swallowed quickly and tore off another mouthful.

"Ya'll eating my supper, gimpy."

Anthony looked up. Henry was at least fourteen years old. With red hair and freckles like Mama's, he had a big round face, yellow buckteeth, and the beginnings of a rust-brown fuzzy beard. He was probably six feet tall and weighed nearly two hundred pounds. To his left stood Cee-Dee holding half a dozen pieces of bread, and next to him, Jackie, with what looked like a mound of greasy ham wrapped in his pajama top.

"Gimme ma supper," said Henry.

Anthony butt-crawled backward, taking another bite of bread, and pushing up against the boxcar's slats, managed to pull himself up into a standing position. He held on to the side of the boxcar with one hand for support. His right leg could just about hold him up when he got the knee locked into place.

"Ya gonna give me trouble?" asked Henry. He shook a scab-knuckled fist at Anthony.

Anthony looked at the fist, up at Henry, and then at the bread in his own hand. He was hungry. Henry and his friends had stolen most of the food he'd been given in the last two days.

Anthony had not put up a fuss.

He had cried a little bit at first.

Clack-clack-clack-clack-clack-clack . . .

There was a mathematical certainty to the sound, the periodic thumping vibrating through his body, somehow healing him—the rhythm so steady.

"It's my bread," said Anthony. He'd given up on the piece of ham, which Jackie had already picked up off the floor and stuffed into his pajama top with the rest. "I'm hungry."

The voices of fifty children in a cattle car were silenced,

and all eyes turned toward Anthony in anticipation of watching all two hundred pounds of Henry unleash himself on Anthony's less than fifty pounds.

"So the gimp can talk," said Henry.

Anthony cocked his head to the right, surprised by what Henry had said. *Of course he could talk.* And then he realized that this had been the first time that he had spoken since arriving in this world. Up until now he had not remembered *how* to speak.

Clack-clack-clack-clack-clack-clack-clack . . .

"It's my bread," said Anthony.

Henry sneered, took several steps back, and ground his slick-bottomed boots against the straw-covered floor. Anthony had taken the slickness of those boots into account. He had made certain that the greasy patch on the floor where the ham had dropped was squarely between himself and Henry. Anthony knew that the slats of the boxcar just above his head had been weakened, thinned in just the right locations. He'd worked on them for the last two days, ever since Henry had first stolen his food.

He had not *consciously* formulated this plan—but it was a plan nonetheless.

"You won't take any more of my food!" said Anthony.

"Ya goddamned gimp!" said Henry with a roar. He lowered his head and charged at Anthony.

Anthony's timing was perfect. He let his legs collapse beneath him just at the moment when Henry hit the greasy spot on the floor and slipped, his feet leaping out from beneath him. His momentum carried him forward, his man-sized body flying above the now-seated Anthony, hitting the side of the boxcar headfirst, and crashing through the weakened slats, sailing clear out of the boxcar.

From start to finish only a few seconds had passed. Children screamed and backed away from the large hole in the side of the boxcar. Mrs. McMasters rose to her feet, with a shrieking baby in each arm, pushed against her massive breasts. "Ya'll sheet up!" she shouted, and then plopped back down on her stool when it appeared that no one else was about to fly through the side of the boxcar.

"I want my ham back," said Anthony.

Jackie unwrapped his pajama top and pulled out a piece of ham and tossed it to Anthony. He looked at the hole that Henry had made upon his sudden exit, not knowing how the gimpy kid had managed that trick, but knowing full well that he had gotten rid of Henry. Jackie reached back into his shirt and got a second piece of ham for Anthony.

"Now I'd like a drink of water," said Anthony.

Alexandra looked out through the fourth floor window. Only October 2, and already the first snow was flying, dusting the rooftops, covering the soot-stained decay. But as clean and fresh as the new snow looked, it did little to disguise the smell of boiled cabbage, wood smoke, and alcohol.

The room reeked of it.

The entire city of Moscow was permeated with those three odors.

Barely dawn and the morning patrols had started. Alexandra watched nearly a dozen Mensheviks marching in a phalanx, dressed in black leathers, chests all adorned with ribbons and metals—each denoting a victory, a step toward eventual world revolution. The Mensheviks would roust whatever homeless they found, moving them on their way, while those that could not be awakened were thrown into the cart that trailed behind the troopers—the wobbling wooden contraption being dragged along by a skin-and-bones horse. Half a dozen bodies were already piled in the cart.

The winter of '26–27 would be a brutal one. Not yet winter, and food was already in short supply. Trotsky and his followers had the city tightly under their control at the moment, but Moscow in the summer and Moscow in the winter were two entirely different cities. Alexandra had run her simulations, determined the direction of the winter winds, and knew that come springtime Trotsky and his visions of world revolution would be long gone, with the new victors already rewriting a Trotsky-less history. And this was fine with her. She'd met Trotsky several times before, back in the *old* universe, once while he'd still been in the Soviet Union and twice after that in his exile in Mexico. She had not liked the man—too intellectual, too quick to turn a clever phrase, just a bit too polished. The man had no stomach for getting his hands dirty.

There would be no place for Trotsky in the new world she planned to build, not in *her* picoverse. Alexandra had made her choice. It was time to make certain that her choice succeeded.

"Comrade Mitchell, I assure you that I have the fullest authority and can discuss with you whatever proposals you care to make."

Alexandra turned around. A rickety wooden table, one of its legs ending several inches from the floor, and three velvet-covered, silver-studded chairs with pedigrees far more illustrious than those possessed by any who had ever stayed in this slum, were the only furniture in the room. A stocky little man, grinning widely, showing big block-like teeth, occupied the middle chair. Behind him, in the corner of the room, stood two well-muscled Bolshevik goons who looked extremely well suited for stopping bullets, or placing bullets in a desired target.

The stocky little man was no goon, however, not Nicholas Bukharin—probably one of the greatest intellects of the Russian Revolution. But he was another charmer like Trotsky, not twisted and psychotic enough to fill her needs.

"I do not deal with intermediaries," said Alexandra. "I was told that I would meet with Comrade Stalin at this location at 7:15. If that meeting is not going to take place, then please inform me of that fact so that I may keep my 8:00 meeting with your good friend Comrade Zinovyev."

Bukharin clenched his jaw and leaned forward.

Zinovyev controlled nearly fourteen square blocks on the far west side of Moscow. At the moment he had a truce with the Trotsky faction, each of them trying to flush out Stalin.

"Comrade Stalin is very interested in personally discussing the nature of these items with you," said Bukharin. He waved his right hand across the table, indicating the notebooks spread out across it. All handwritten, those notebooks contained the detailed schematics and working principles of three basic machines that any would-be world dictator of the 1920s, with the barest sense of the future, would find irresistible.

A jet engine.

A uranium-based nuclear weapon.

A transistor.

Those three items represented an insignificant fraction of the knowledge that Alexandra had stored within her. She did not necessarily understand everything in those notes—she was not fabricated for science and technology—but she knew that they were detailed enough that they could be followed by those who were technically minded. But besides the notes, she had something else to offer. At the far end of the table, resting on a bright red handkerchief, was a single glass ampoule, containing a few drops of pale-green liquid. It had taken her nearly a week to access and manipulate aspects of her own biology in order to create the liquid. Beneath the handkerchief were half a dozen sheets of handwritten notes, with sufficient explanation to allow even a 1920s Soviet pharmaceutical manufacturer to reproduce the green liquid.

"You are running out of time," said Alexandra.

Bukharin stood. Barely five feet tall, nearly one foot shorter than Alexandra, he had to look up at her. "When he enters the room you will not move from the place you are currently standing. You will not ask him any questions, and will only speak in response to a question from him or myself. If you violate these stipulations, you will be shot."

Alexandra nodded.

The goons tensed, readying themselves.

The room had two doors, the one through which she had entered from the hallway, and a second, which she had assumed led to a bedroom. Bukharin opened the second door.

Joseph Stalin stood within a room that was not much larger than a good-sized closet. Hands behind his back, he took two steps forward until he stood in the doorway, took a quick look to the left and the right, and then looked at Alexandra Mitchell.

He examined her.

He evaluated her.

And he saw nothing to change his opinion. He'd looked at her notebooks. He'd talked with the scientists who had looked at her notebooks. She could be *used*.

Alexandra suppressed a smile. Quite an *unimpressive* figure. Skinny, barely five feet four, with a thick moustache and skin severely pockmarked from a childhood bout with smallpox, there was nothing exceptional about Stalin. Only his eyes gave any hint that something amazing lurked within, a pair of piercing hazel eyes that absorbed all that they saw. He brought his hands out from behind his back. In his right hand he held a pistol.

"Tell me about the *neurotoxin*," he said slowly, carefully pronouncing what was obviously an unfamiliar word to him.

"Highly potent," said Alexandra. "That ampoule contains three milligrams, a sufficient dose to affect several thousand people, depending on which way the wind blows." Alexandra smiled. "It is absorbed directly through the skin, easily penetrates the brain-blood barrier, and once in the brain, inhibits ionic transfer at synaptic sites. From initial exposure death takes place in approximately thirty seconds. It is highly sensitive to temperature, with a negative coefficient of activation. It is only lethal at temperatures below freezing, making it unsuitable for summertime or indoor applications."

There was no expression on Stalin's face.

"But I believe that by winter's end you will no longer need it, that Mother Russia will be yours."

Stalin pointed his pistol at the ampoule, then at the goon nearest it. "Drop it outside, making sure that it hits the center of the street, and then close the window."

The goon walked forward, picked up the ampoule without the slightest hesitation, walked across the room, and opened the window. A blast of cold air washed in, slamming against Alexandra's back. It was well below freezing. Alexandra did not move, could not see the open window, but knew it had been reshut when the frigid air spilling over her suddenly subsided.

"If it does not work, you will be the next thing through that window," said Stalin.

Alexandra smiled, just as the first scream was heard from the street below. At first it sounded human, but then quickly escalated in pitch, sounding more like the yowling of a cat in heat. Others quickly joined the first wail.

Many others.

And as quickly as it had started, it was over.

Stalin walked forward, moving well around Alexandra, as far around her as the small room permitted. She could not see him, but could sense him at the window, hear the rate of his breathing slightly increase. "Up and down the street I count nearly fifty dead," he said. "The bodies appear to be *twisted*."

"The last few seconds of life are rather painful," she said. "The body experiences severe seizures, sufficient to break bones and tear muscle away from the bone."

"And why do you give me this weapon?" asked Stalin.

"For the Revolution," said Alexandra.

"Yes, of course," said Stalin. "Everything we do is for the Revolution."

SECTION II
CHAPTER 2

Jack saw no sign of the wormhole. He was certain that Alpha had shut down the tunnel the moment they had passed through—escaping would not be as easy as simply walking out the way they had come in.

Alpha would not let them return, and neither would these soldiers.

"Do not move."

The five stood, with limp metallic coils draped around their calves, covering their feet. Surrounded by a dozen soldiers wearing brown uniforms, all carrying automatic weapons, the captives held their hands high above their heads. Horst blinked several times, not believing what he saw. The soldier nearest him, the one who had a rifle aimed at his chest, wore an iron cross on the collar of his uniform. His *grandfather* had possessed such a cross. Horst had stumbled upon it in the attic of his grandfather's house when he had been a boy still living in Germany. "Deutchlander?" asked Horst.

"The People's Socialist Republic of Germany," replied the soldier in a thickly German-accented English. He waved the rifle at Horst. "Please do not speak until Captain Soloyov has arrived."

"Communists?" said Horst.

"Anthony?" asked Katie. Sounding dazed, she looked around the grass-covered field and at the German soldiers. "Do you know where Anthony is?" she asked to no one in particular.

"Yes, I know where your son is."

Katie turned, and two of the soldiers stood aside making way for another soldier, this one dressed in a black uniform, black leather boots, the only color coming from the red piping along his overcoat collar. He smiled, exposing several stainless steel teeth. "I am Captain Anatoly Soloyov of the Soviet People's Army, North American Liberation Force. I have been informed that your son is safe and currently residing in Denver, Colorado."

"Alive," said Katie.

Soloyov nodded.

Katie's legs gave way, and Jack reached for her, giving her support, keeping her standing.

"Before your departure to New Stalingrad," said Soloyov, "I have been instructed to inform you of certain facts in order to ease your minds. Full debriefings will be performed in New Stalingrad."

"*New* Stalingrad?" asked Aaron.

"They are goddamned Communists," said Horst. Feelings of anger and fear filled him, childhood nightmares of growing up in East Berlin in the '70s and '80s, before the wall came down, flooding over him. "*Soviet* Communists."

Soloyov sighed, pointed at Aaron, and the soldier nearest him trotted over, pressing the barrel of his rifle to the side of Aaron's head.

"No!" shouted Jack, taking a step toward Aaron. A single step was all he had time for before the butt of a rifle cracked against his right shoulder driving him to the ground. Katie, still unsteady, collapsed on top of him.

"If you cooperate and do not panic, then nothing will happen to Mr. Tanaka," said Soloyov. "However, if you continue to disrupt me, or if any of you make the slightest hostile move, then you will find yourselves without Mr. Tanaka's company." Soloyov snapped his fingers. "Put the *restraint* on him," he said.

Jack watched as one of the soldiers slung his rifle over his shoulder and then pulled a satchel from his other shoulder and removed from it what looked like a large brown leather dog collar, to which was attached a small stainless steel box. The soldier placed the collar around Aaron's neck, snapping it in place.

Soloyov removed what looked like a garage door remote control from his pants pocket and pointed it in Aaron's direction. It was featureless, except for a single red button. Jack was certain what would happen if that button were pressed. "If there are any further disruptions or unpleasantness, then I will press this button," said Soloyov. He turned the box so they could all see the red button. "When pressed, the explosive in the restraint will be detonated, and Mr. Tanaka will find himself without benefit of his head. I will then place a restraint on Dr. Kim."

Beong was about to step backward, fear-driven reflexes demanding it, but he forced himself to stop.

"Understood?" asked Soloyov.

Jack nodded, and using his left hand, he grabbed Katie and pulled her up with him. His right arm tingled, and he could barely move the fingers of his right hand. *They needed information.* Soloyov knew exactly who they were, had obviously been expecting them. Jack knew that could only mean that Alexandra was responsible for this welcoming party—she would be the only one who could know about them. And that meant they were in very real danger.

"In order to help acclimate you to your new world, I have been requested to explain some basic facts of existence to you," said Soloyov. "The date is April 16, 1936. You are located five miles east of Marietta, Georgia, in the Eastern Republic of Soviet America. This universe and yours share a common history until June 13, 1925, at which point it was our good fortune to find ourselves in our own universe, in a world that will never be dominated by the United States of America and the capitalist exploiters who raped the planet in your universe."

Jack nodded, reminding himself that history was always written by the victorious.

Horst shivered, unable to control himself. *Soviets in the United States.*

"The Soviet system, the Communist state, and the Revolution are global in nature on this world. We stand at the edge of total victory, with only a small territory of Free-Market rebels, exploiters of the American peoples, occupying the regions between the Mississippi River and the Rocky Mountains."

Alexandra. Jack knew that she must be the one responsible for this drastic turn in world events. Alpha had said that she had taken over his world in twenty years after the stars had vanished—she was probably well on her way to doing the same thing on this Earth.

"Denver is in that area," said Katie in a whisper. She looked at Aaron, not wanting to get him killed, but having to know about Anthony.

"Yes, Denver is still in counterrevolutionary hands," Soloyov said. "But we anticipate that situation will soon be resolved and that the Revolution will be complete. I have been instructed to transport you upon your arrival directly to New Stalingrad where you are to aid our scientists in the construction of a Sonomak."

"Sonomak?" asked Horst. The *Communists* were building a Sonomak?

"Yes," said Soloyov. "Our conquest of this world is almost complete. It is our destiny, our obligation, to further the Revolution to those other worlds where the capitalists have not yet succumbed to the natural political evolution of the human spirit."

Horst said nothing, swallowed a groan, as he tried to fathom how it would be possible to build a Sonomak with the technology of the 1930s. *Impossible.* But they would keep trying, destroying people as necessary in the process as they had destroyed his own father in East Berlin in 1973. Horst made a solemn promise that he would tell them nothing. He would sacrifice Aaron, Beong, all of them, before he gave the Communists a technology that they could use to gain access to other worlds.

"And to answer your question, Mr. Tanaka, you would know the city of New Stalingrad as Washington, D.C."

"And I suppose that New York City is now called New Leningrad?" asked Horst. He did nothing to disguise the disgust and hatred he felt.

"*That* location no longer requires a name," said Soloyov. "During the Great War of Liberation, several of the major cities of North America were rendered uninhabitable."

"Uninhabitable?" asked Jack, fearful at the finality in Soloyov's tone.

"Nuclear weapons," said Soloyov. "Pittsburgh, New York, and Los Angeles are no longer inhabited."

Horst wanted to jump on the man, beat him into the ground, and tear his head off. But he held himself back, knowing that Soloyov was just one insignificant cog in the Communist machine. He needed to destroy the entire machine.

Jack and Katie turned and looked at each other. Reaching up, Katie removed her Virtuals and gently placed them in her top pocket. There was no feed in this world, no signals to fill the Virtuals. All this world had was a global Soviet Union, atomized American cities, and her now sixteen-year-old son half a continent away, in the land of the rebels.

"We must move quickly," said Soloyov. "The jet is ready, and you are expected in New Stalingrad this evening."

"There are no jet aircraft in 1936," said Horst.

"What you must realize, Dr. Wittkowski," said Soloyov, "is that this is not the decadent and decayed world that you lived in. This is a Soviet world. Our progress in the last ten years has far outpaced anything that you capitalist exploiters could possibly imagine."

"And what do the people of Denver say about that?" asked Horst.

Soloyov sneered and fingered the red button of his remote control. "Get them to the jet," he said.

"This is not our Earth," shouted Horst from the seat in front of Jack and Katie's, his nose pressed up against the window, his voice barely audible over the screech of the jet engines.

Jack nodded, looking out his own window. The German soldiers, the Russian captain, this rattling jet that looked like an ancient B-17 with propellers removed, and two massive jet engines strapped beneath each wing, all *suggested* that this was a different Earth, an alien Earth. But now there was absolutely no doubt. The plane was descending, approaching Washington, D.C., from the south. It appeared to Jack that they were landing at what he had known as Nixon International, that horribly undersized landing strip wedged between the Potomac, the Pentagon to the north, and the sprawl of office buildings to the west.

The Pentagon was not there.

Instead of that familiar five-sided monument to the military were what looked like apartment buildings, massive concrete structures, some thirty to forty stories tall, six of them in total, each just touching the next, the entire complex forming a massive hexagon. In the center of the hexagon stood a colossal bronze statue, covered in what looked like snow, but what long-time D.C. resident Jack knew must be encrusted pigeon droppings. Jack studied the hexagon shape of those buildings.

Alexandra.

The Pentagon had not been built on his Earth until the early 1940s. There would be no reason for these ugly concrete buildings to be arranged in the shape of a hexagon, *one* more side than the Pentagon.

Alexandra's doing—the joke would only have meaning to her.

Jack looked further to the east. He'd probably flown in to Nixon more than a hundred times during his time in Washington. He was intimately familiar with the layout of the city from the perspective of a landing plane. This was not Washington, D.C. It was New Stalingrad. There was no Jefferson Memorial next to the Tidal Basin, just a massive expanse of asphalt choked with parked cars. The Grant Memorial was still there, as was the stark white obelisk of the Washington Monument, but now perched atop that pillar was a massive steel sickle and hammer. Both the White House and the Capitol building were gone, nothing there now except for a collection of little concrete buildings. And the mall and the reflecting pool had all been paved over, replaced by an unending slab of concrete that ran from the Grant Memorial, right past the Smithsonian, and all the way up to where the Capitol had once stood.

To Jack, it looked as if the Washington he had known had been merged with Moscow's Red Square, transforming the capital into a massive ugly monstrosity. He was grateful when the plane dipped low enough so that he could no longer see it. He turned his head to look at Katie sitting next to him. She was staring at the back of the seat in which Aaron sat. "Katie," he said. She didn't acknowledge him, didn't seem to hear him. He picked up her right hand and gently shook it. She slowly turned her head toward him.

"We need to be very careful when we meet Alexandra," he said.

Katie half closed her eyes. For just a moment Jack barely recognized her, the combination of her not wearing the Virtuals and the nearly vacant look in her eyes, transforming her into something that was not Katie. "Why would we meet Alexandra?" she asked.

Jack didn't know how to explain. He just knew—it was all so obvious. Alexandra had been dangerous on their Earth, a manipulative entity that played people like pieces on a chessboard. But there she always acted behind the scenes, was hidden away. Jack was certain that this was no longer the case. Whatever she had attempted to do on Alpha's world, she was probably attempting to do here. And on that world Anthony had stopped her.

Would he try to stop her again on this world?

It was critical that they find Anthony.

"Just trust me," said Jack. "I know we will meet her, and we've got to be extra cautious. Alexandra has changed. She's much more powerful than when we knew her."

Katie gave a feeble nod.

The plane slammed into the runway, bounced several times, veered to the right in a crosswind, and then finally stuck to the concrete. The engines howled at an ear-rupturing level as they reversed thrust to slow the plane.

"Welcome to New Stalingrad," boomed a staticky voice from the airplane's speakers. "Please have your papers ready upon disembarkment."

At that request, Jack actually found himself smiling, the absurdity of the situation finally overwhelming him. *We don't need no stinkin' papers*, he thought. "Take me to your leader," he said in a whisper, knowing full well that lack of papers would not keep them from their meeting with Alexandra.

The ride from the airport took just a few minutes. The five were handcuffed, leg manacles were put on, and they were shuffled off the plane and escorted into a waiting armor-plated bus, where they were padlocked into their seats.

Horst began to complain, rattling the chains that kept him attached to his seat. "Is this all you Communists know?" he said. He shook his chains in the direction of Soloyov. He was about to pass further judgment, but stopped when Soloyov pulled the remote from his pocket and waved it in Aaron's direction.

From the airport they took the 14th Street bridge across the Potomac and drove up to the back loading dock of what Jack knew as the Department of Agriculture. On this Earth he had no idea what the building was being used for, but the fact that they were being transported to it made him certain that it now had little to do with Agriculture. Unlocked from their seats, brought in through the back of the building and down two flights of stairs, they were sequestered in a conference room that smelled like cigarettes and burned coffee.

And then they waited.

The five sat on folding metal chairs. Two armed guards stood at the door, while Soloyov sat at the far end of the room smoking cigarette after cigarette, smashing the butts into a small brass ashtray he held in his lap. A big clock, with a galvanized steel mesh grid across its face, hung on the wall behind Soloyov. A long, red second hand counted the seconds.

"Welcome to the Communist state," Horst said. "If they aren't tossing you in a gulag, or shooting you in the head, they are making you wait."

Jack looked over at him. The passage through the wormhole seemed to have transformed the man. Less than a day ago, he had looked beaten, a phantom of what he had once been. He was certainly just as thin, his skin and clothes both hung loosely on him, but he sat straighter, the look in his eyes was sharper, and his chin was thrust out in an almost arrogant fashion, as if daring someone to take a swing at him. He knew that Horst had grown up in East Berlin and had not made his way to the West until the Soviet Union had crumbled, but he had not known of the hatred the man felt toward the Communists. It was obvious to Jack that some deep-seated psychological button had been pressed in Horst. But as much as this world seemed to have revitalized Horst, it had had the exact opposite effect on Katie. Jack held her hand, squeezing it gently. Katie gave no response, just stared. Losing Anthony had done something to her.

Understandable, thought Jack. He too felt that loss, but could not quite believe it, could not emotionally accept the fact that what had felt like only a day to him, would have been ten years to Anthony. The boy had now spent nearly two-thirds of his life here. Isolation and loneliness had obviously driven Alpha insane. What could this world have done to Anthony?

"Who are we waiting for?" asked Horst.

Soloyov looked up from his ashtray. "The people of your world traveled to the moon," he said in response, as if he had not heard the question at all.

"In 1973," said Horst. "I wouldn't think that you pathetic Communists would care about going to the moon. There's no one there to enslave," he said.

Soloyov smiled, showing his stainless steel teeth. "We explore space in the quest of knowledge, of spreading our vision throughout our entire universe. Naturally Soviet science is the most superior in the world, but I thought you might find it of interest that a fellow countryman of yours, a talented young man by the name of Wernher von Braun is helping us in our little conquest." He then pointed to Jack. "And of course *your* fellow countryman, Robert Goddard is quite the visionary."

Jack just nodded, knowing that Alexandra knew her history, knew just who had been instrumental on *their* Earth, in making history, of producing changes. She was using them here for her own purposes, knowing just who could get the job done for her.

"Our current plan calls for us landing on the moon by 1942." Soloyov's smile grew even larger. "Lindbergh made three Earth orbits just last December," he said.

Horst was about to make a disgusting remark about Soviet science when the doors to the room burst open and soldiers began to dogtrot in, taking up positions against the walls. Soloyov snuffed out his cigarette, stood, smoothed out his uniform, and threw his shoulders back.

Beong started to stand, but Jack reached over and pulled him back down.

A man and a woman entered the room.

The woman was Alexandra Mitchell. She wore a black uniform, her collar adorned with a bizarre assortment of ribbons and gold emblems. Her black hair was cut short, and her olive skin looked even darker than he remembered. The only color about her, besides what was attached to her collar, was her bloodred lipstick.

Horst glanced at Alexandra for only a moment and then ignored her. It was the plump little man stepping behind her, obviously struggling to keep up, who captured his attention.

He had seen pictures of this man.

Once he had even seen him on television during a May Day celebration sometime in the early '80s. He was Vyacheslav Molotov, probably the only man who could be called Stalin's friend, or at least the only Bolshevik of the inner circle to survive all the way from the initial Communist takeover in Russia and then through Stalin's regime without being shot or made to disappear.

Very bad.

Horst was certain that if Molotov was in Washington, then Stalin was probably calling the shots in Moscow. But he had only a moment to consider the implications of what a Stalinist regime combined with a Soviet-dominated world would imply, when he saw motion out of the corner of his field of vision.

Katie was out of her chair.

She was a blur, moving at an almost impossible speed. She was on the nearest guard before he could raise his pistol. Katie lunged at him, the palm of her hand open, hitting him square in the nose, driving all of her momentum into his face. They both fell in a splatter of blood. But Katie was up almost instantly, with the guard's pistol in her hand, the gun leveled at Alexandra.

"Hold your fire," said Alexandra. The other guards had brought out their various weapons, all of them now trained on Katie.

No one moved.

"What have you done with Anthony?" screamed Katie. Her finger tensed on the trigger, pulling it back just a millimeter.

"Absolutely nothing," said Alexandra, sounding extremely calm. "As a matter of fact, the last time that I saw him was while he was in your care, as you stood there, letting Alpha do whatever horrid little things he wanted to the boy."

Bang!

The shot was almost deafening, echoing throughout the closed room. Katie looked down at the pistol in her hand, an expression of surprise on her face, as if not quite believing that she had just fired the gun.

Alexandra was on the floor, on her back. There was a hole in her chest, and a red stain seeped across the black fabric of her uniform. Molotov took a step back from the body and, opening his mouth, almost had time to shout an order.

"Hold your fire," said Alexandra. She sat up. With her right hand she touched her chest, poking two fingers into the hole between her breasts. And then she stood. "Now that you've gotten that out of your system," she said, walking forward, being careful to avoid the small pool of blood that had spread out across the floor, "I hope we can get down to business."

As she walked past the four who were still seated, Jack looked at the ragged hole in her back, where the bullet had exited. Bits of bone, and globs of torn muscle hung down the back of her uniform—but only for a moment. By the time she reached Katie, the hole had sealed itself, the bone and muscle pulled back into the hole.

"Did you really think that you could kill me with a gun?" Alexandra asked. "I survived on your world for four *million* years." She took the gun from Katie's hand, and then turned to face the others. The hole in her chest was also sealed, the inside curve of her left breast visible through the tear in her uniform. "There are things we need to discuss," she said.

SECTION II
CHAPTER 3

*Molotov sat stiffly in his chair, inhaling hard on his cigarette, hold-*ing the Cuban with two fingers and a thumb in European fashion. A blue-gray haze of smoke swirled about his head. He stared down the table, focusing all his energy on Horst. Molotov prided himself on reading people. Here was a man who stank of arrogance, of partisanship, an individual who thought about himself both first and last. The only course to pursue for such a man was a bullet in the back of the head.

But Alexandra would not permit it—she claimed the man was indispensable.

Molotov stared at Horst's flabby face, at his sunken eyes. He knew there was no such thing as an indispensable man—the machine of the state would roll on regardless of which individuals helped power it. He took another long drag on his Cuban cigarette.

Horst returned Molotov's stare. "I will discuss nothing in the presence of this *Communist*."

Alexandra grinned. She had expected such a response. Horst was so easy, like a little mechanical windup toy that was helpless to fight against the springs and gears that filled it. But all humans were like that to some extent. She looked down the table. Katie glared at her. She knew that feral expression, the look of a mother defending her young, that weakness making her as easy to manipulate as Horst. And then there was Beong, culturally castrated, unable to make a move in fear of losing face, insulting his betters, or breaking some unknown rules or taboos. And Aaron Tanaka, little more than Horst's spear carrier, handling the details of Horst's scientific fetishes, allowing the professor to dwell in the light of the big picture.

It would be trivial to manipulate them into working on the Sonomak. She stopped herself from sighing reflexively. The Soviets and Germans, whom she had at her disposal, were technologically at least two or three years behind the Sonomak that was being built by the Americans. These five would change that situation.

But then there was Jack.

There was something about him that she didn't yet understand. He had a core of strength that she was certain he wasn't consciously aware of. But she could see it, sense it.

Jack was a dangerous man.

"I do not sit down with Communists!" shouted Horst. He stood up, pushing back his chair.

Alexandra glanced over at Molotov and then at the door in the back of the room. That was all it took. His face expressionless, Molotov stood and walked toward the door. She did not need him in this meeting, in fact did not want him in this meeting. He had been brought here for the simple purpose of getting his ego slapped down. Alexandra never missed an opportunity to let him know who was Stalin's chosen one. It was at moments like these that she missed Quinn—breaking in a new slave was so time consuming. But it could not be helped. Quinn had a much more important task to carry out elsewhere. Alexandra had been in this picoverse for less than a year when the Quinn of 1926 had found her.

Quinn had abandoned the Alexandra of this world. Apparently being reborn into the picoverse had done something to her mind, shattered her, and turned her into something that Quinn could no longer slavishly follow. Alexandra felt no compassion for that other version of herself. The other's loss was her gain.

"I want Anthony," said Katie.

Horst sat down. "We want our son back," he said. Reaching over awkwardly, he patted Katie's hand. "And we will give you and your friends absolutely no help in building a Sonomak."

"We will give her whatever she wants if it gets Anthony back," Katie said to Horst, jerking her hand out of his. "That is *all* that matters."

"You can't negotiate with them," said Horst. "You cannot trust them."

Katie slammed both her hands against the tabletop. "Put it behind you, Horst! Your father was a CIA informant, taken by the KGB, and probably killed. It is the past." She slapped her hands once more against the table. "It's not even this world!"

"I know these Communists. You don't—"

"Enough!" shouted Jack.

Horst's head snapped back as if slapped. Katie turned in her chair to look at him, glaring at him, her face flushed, her eyes angry, alive. Jack felt relieved to see those eyes, to see the Katie he had grown to love.

"We need information," said Jack. "We can't help Anthony, can't help ourselves, unless we understand what is going on."

Horst scowled, and Katie continued to glare at him but said nothing. Beong and Aaron both nodded vigorously, especially Aaron, the restraint still around his neck, the metal box, full of explosives, glistening in the glare of the harsh overhead lights.

"Jack is quite right," said Alexandra. "There is no reason to view me as an adversary. I have every desire to reunite you with Anthony. Our war effort proceeds as planned. I have no doubt that the remaining American forces will crumble before year's end and that Anthony will be returned to us in time for Christmas."

"Christmas!" shouted Katie, at the prospect of having to wait six months.

"Quite right," said Alexandra, who then looked at Horst.

"Of course Christmas is such an antiquated concept. In our workers' paradise we have eliminated the need for God. And with no God I suppose there is not much need for Christmas."

"Goddamn it!" said Katie. "Stop playing with me. I want my son!"

Jack reached up, grabbed the now-standing Katie by the arm, and pulled her down into her chair. "What do you want?" asked Jack, looking at Alexandra, while still holding on to the squirming Katie with one hand.

Alexandra's eyes narrowed, and she clenched her jaw. What did she want? Ten years ago she would have answered that question without the slightest hesitation—to be cut off from the Makers—to be the master of her own fate. Be careful what you wish for. She remembered just what Alpha had warned her about, but she had ignored it, pushed it aside without the slightest consideration. And now she knew the truth. "I want out of this prison," she said.

At first Jack did not understand, had not anticipated such an answer. And then he understood, and laughed, loudly and deeply. He let go of Katie's arm and leaned against the table, the laughter uncontrollable.

No one spoke. All eyes were on Jack.

Jack managed to sit back up, wiped the tears from his eyes, and his laughter died down to a chuckle. "For four million years you wanted to escape your Makers. You were so eager to jump, to break those bonds that you didn't give enough thought about where you might land. All you wanted was to escape."

Alexandra pursed her lips and ran her hands across the tabletop.

"But you can see the future. You'll have this little Communist world of yours wrapped up in a few years, probably get the planets of the solar system explored and inhabited in the next millennia or so, and then what will you do? The entire universe is no larger than this solar system. You are trapped in this box. What will an immortal like you do? We know what Alpha did. He went insane and turned himself off when he finally had to accept the fact that there was not enough energy in this universe to access our universe. Why don't you just admit that you're trapped and simply turn yourself off."

"Not trapped," said Alexandra. "You just explained how I will escape, how I can get out. I cannot access *your* universe. That is physically impossible, that universe is too massive, the energy required to tunnel into that piece of space-time is just too great. My theoreticians tell me that Alpha was right in that regard. But we can open a wormhole into a *smaller* universe."

Jack's eyes opened wide, knowing just what smaller universe she must be referring to. "You want to build a Sonomak and generate a wormhole into *Alpha*'s picoverse."

"But why?" asked Katie. "That is just one more prison, a universe no larger than this one."

Jack knew why. "If she can get into Alpha's picoverse, then she can escape through the wormhole that he has opened to our universe, the one that Alpha *must* keep open so he is not cut off from the bulk of himself, which is kept in hardware in that picoverse."

Alexandra slowly clapped her hands. "And is that all?"

Jack looked into her dark eyes. "Having been cut off from the Makers, you were able to modify yourself. You are now *permanently* cut off from them. Even if you return to our universe, they will not be able to find you and regain control over you."

"Very good, Jack," said Alexandra. "And to think that you were just a DOE contract monitor. I don't believe that you were living up to your full potential in that old life of yours."

"And what is it that you expect us to do? Why should we help you escape?"

"Do you remember a conversation we had, Jack," she said, "in which I explained to you how easy it was to control people, that desires such as fear and greed can be extremely powerful?" She took a quick look at Horst and knew that the *greedy* egomaniac would not even realize that she was referring to him. "Well, for each person there is a unique emotion that can be used against him or her, that can be used to control them." Now she was focused directly on Jack. She smiled, her red lips parting, her perfect teeth sparkling in the room's harsh light. "In your case, Jack, you have a very strong sense of right and wrong. You are a man with a rigid and unwavering sense of honor."

Jack did not like where this conversation was going.

Alexandra reached beneath the table, pulled something out of her pocket, and then returned her hand to the table-top, holding the remote that could detonate Aaron's restraint.

"No!" shouted Aaron, jumping up from his chair and backing away.

Jack stood, pushed his chair back, and tried to judge the distance between himself and the remote. Alexandra's fingers were poised directly above the button.

"Please don't!" pleaded Aaron.

"We will help you," said Jack.

Alexandra pointed the remote at Aaron, who cringed, covered his face, and then squatted down, practically hugging the floor. "You say that, Jack, but you don't really mean it. Oh, you might help for a while, convince the others to go along, but your heart wouldn't be in it. You'd be plotting and planning to get that restraint off Aaron, all the while causing mischief to hold back progress on the Sonomak."

"I give you my word," said Jack.

Alexandra shook her head. "Jack, I said that you have a strong sense of right and wrong, a little code of honor that you live by." She paused for a moment, looking over at Aaron who was now facedown on the floor, whimpering. "But I know that you are not stupid. Within your code of ethics, you would not consider it a violation to lie to someone such as myself."

Alexandra pressed the button.

The resulting explosion was muffled, sounding like a distant firecracker. That sound was followed by a second—

the wet smack of Aaron's head bouncing off the far wall. It then hit the floor, rolled, and came to a halt under another table.

Katie shrieked.

"You soulless bitch!" said Horst.

"Oh my God," said Beong in a whisper, looking back and forth between Alexandra and Aaron's headless body. "Oh my God."

Jack moved, quickly covering the few yards that separated him from Alexandra. He knew that there was no way he could hurt her, or *physically* do anything to change the situation. He pushed right up against her, their noses less than six inches apart. "Kill us one by one, and what will that get you?"

Alexandra threw the remote to the floor, sending it clattering across the room in the general direction of Aaron's body. "It would get me absolutely nothing," she said. "I need each of you in order to complete my project. Aaron was expendable, a technician. I can get ten thousand technicians at the snap of my fingers." As if to demonstrate, she snapped her fingers.

The doors to the room opened and children entered. Marching in a neat row, five boys and five girls, dressed in little gray uniforms adorned with silver buttons, and wearing polished black boots, halted before Alexandra. All wore restraints around their necks.

Alexandra reached into her pocket, pulled out another remote, and waved it at the children. "Aren't they all little darlings," she said. "Don't they remind you of that dear little boy of yours, Dr. McGuire?"

"You are insane!" screamed Katie. She suddenly imagined that Anthony was one of those children, with a restraint wrapped tightly around his neck.

"A subjective statement if I ever heard one," said Alexandra. She looked at Jack, who had taken several steps back. "This is how it works, Jack. These children are now your responsibility. They are going to live in the same dormitory with the four of you. You will help feed them, bathe them, and wipe their snotty little noses. And if you do not perform to my specifications, if you do anything to displease me, attempt to escape, or perform the slightest act of sabotage or insubordination, I will activate this remote."

She waved the remote in the general direction of Aaron's body.

"You have absolute proof that I will not hesitate in carrying out this threat. And if you force me to harm these little darlings, they will be replaced with twenty others, and after them there will be forty more." Alexandra smiled. "Do the math, Jack. I have vast resources at my disposal. How many children will it take before you decide to help me?"

He knew the answer, and he knew that Alexandra knew the answer. "None," he said. "We will help you."

"Of course you will," she said. She slipped the remote into her pocket, stood from her chair, and began walking toward the open doorway. "I suggest that you get acquainted with your new wards. Some associates of mine will be around in a few minutes to transport all of you to your new home." She walked up to the doorway, stopped, and turned around. "It was so good to see you all again." Turning again, she walked out of the room.

Soloyov sat sideways on the bus seat, taking up a space intended for two. He smoked his cigarette and stared at Jack and Katie, who were sharing a seat farther back in the middle of the bus. He smiled at them. "Comrade Mitchell can be quite convincing when she puts her mind to it."

Jack didn't respond. He tightly held on to Katie's hand, which was resting in his lap, and turned his head to look out the bus window. The traffic was stop and go, the street choked with cars, trucks, and buses that looked as if they should be in the Smithsonian. But of course, most of them were new, except for the handful of rattling Model Ts that might have been nearly twenty years old. He saw the familiar names, the Fords, Dodges, Plymouths, but also the unfamiliar—big heavy dark sedans with tinted windows that were marked as Tinkovs. For just a moment, Jack wondered how such a rabid capitalist as Henry Ford was doing in this workers' paradise.

But he found he really didn't care.

It was just another random and meaningless thought that he tried unsuccessfully to use to stop thinking about Aaron. Jack turned in his seat to look at the ten children in the back of the bus. Silent, perfectly mannered, not even looking at one another, they sat there like mannequins. Behind them sat two guards, each of them holding the type of machine gun that Jack had only seen in old gangster movies.

He turned back to look out the window. They lurched up a street that he recognized as Capitol Street. On the left he could see the imposing pile of marble and columns that made up the U.S. Printing Office. He could just make out a large bronze placard on the side of the building, informing him that it was now called the *People's Office of Information and Vital Statistics*.

He sneered, then looked up and down the street. The sidewalks were even more choked than the street. This was certainly not the Washington he had lived in. The crowds consisted of nothing but white faces—no blacks, no Asians, no hodgepodge of the culture and customs from the embassies that had filled his Washington. There weren't even any camera-clicking tourists in floral shirts and Day-Glo shorts. New Stalingrad was an overflowing river of mid-level bureaucrats slowly drifting to their cubbyholes.

The bus suddenly ground to a halt, almost throwing Jack out of his seat. Looking forward, and through the front window of the bus, he could see the intersection of Capitol and H Streets. There was a commotion, what looked like a couple of cars with locked fenders, and three or four men standing about, arguing and pointing fingers.

Soloyov got up from his seat, pulled his pistol, and then nodded his head to the soldiers in the back of the bus. The two guards got up, pulled back the bolts on their machine guns and watched outside the bus at the milling crowds on the sidewalk.

Horns began to blare.

The bus inched forward and then stopped again.

Jack looked first at Soloyov, then back at the guards. *Paranoia*, he thought, *a side effect of living in this Soviet world*. He looked back out the window at the crowd and focused on one man, of the possibly thousands that shuffled up and down the sidewalk. This man was not moving. He was leaned up against one of the marble pillars of the Office of Information and Vital Statistics, staring directly at Jack.

Get down, he silently mouthed.

Jack looked at the man, not quite believing what he was seeing, when the man again mouthed the same words. Get down. Jack turned to Katie. "Get down on the floor," he whispered. "I think something is about to happen."

She looked at him questioningly, but ducked, slid forward, moving off the seat and got down on the floor. Reaching forward, Jack tapped Horst and Beong on the shoulders. They turned, and Jack motioned with his head and eyes that they should get down. Horst nodded, not questioning the request. Jack watched both their heads drop below the seat in front of him, and then he lowered his own head. He did not have time to reach the floor.

Kerblam!

The bus jumped, throwing everyone from their seats, then hit the street hard, bounced, and teetered slightly. Then, sounding to Jack like every pane of glass in the entire world shattering, the bus windows imploded, showering them with shards of glass. Jack pushed himself up, facing forward. Soloyov was already standing, his pistol drawn and his other hand holding the remote, his thumb repeatedly pounding at the red button. Jack turned.

The children were crying. Several had been cut by shards of flying glass. But they were alive. There'd been no detonation of the restraints. Jack turned back, moving forward, with every intention of getting that remote away from Soloyov, in case it suddenly began to work.

Another man had entered the front of the bus.

He had two pistols drawn, one aimed at the bus driver and the other at the back of Soloyov's head.

Bang!

Soloyov's lower jaw vanished, blown away by the bullet that had just cut through his skull. His tongue hung down against the front of his throat, as a torrent of blood erupted from the hole in his face. For just a moment, Jack could see a look of surprise in Soloyov's eyes, and then the eyes glazed and the Soviet pitched forward, falling face first in the bus aisle.

The gunman stepped over Soloyov, holstering his pistols, and reaching over his shoulder with his right hand, pulled from a scabbard what looked to Jack like a huge pair of pruning shears. He walked past Jack. "That's four less commie bastards," he said.

In the back of the bus Jack could see that the two guards were down and two other men now stood there, apparently having climbed in through the empty windows. Both of them had pruning shears.

No—bolt cutters.

They snapped the collar from the nearest child's neck, then picked him up and carried him to the nearest window, dropping him to someone waiting outside. All the children were gone in a matter of seconds.

Horst, Katie, and Beong were up on their feet, all huddled closely to Jack. "What happened?" asked Beong.

The gunman moved toward them and dropped his bolt cutters. "You lucky bastards have been rescued," he said. A large grin filled his face. Reaching out with his right hand, he grabbed Jack's hand and began pumping. "Honor to meet you, Dr. Preston," he said. "We've been planning this little operation for quite some time."

Jack just nodded.

"I'm Colonel George Patton of the Colorado Free Militia, and I'm going to get you transported to Denver."

"Denver?" said Katie. "To Anthony?"

"Yes, Dr. McGuire," said Patton, who bent down and looked outside the bus window. There were still shouts and screams, but the crowd was beginning to calm. "The electromagnetic pulse took out every electrical appliance for several square blocks, but it's not going to be long before a squad of Kraut bastards goosestep their way in here. We've got to move now." Patton moved past them, stepped over Soloyov's body, and gave what was left of his head a hard kick as he passed by. "Follow me," he said.

The four followed.

SECTION II
CHAPTER 4

Jack squirmed his way out of the sleeping bag, untangling himself from Katie's arms and legs. The night was bright, a full moon hanging high in the sky. Crawling on all fours, he bent down and gently kissed Katie on the forehead, then pushed a few stray strands of red hair away from her closed eyes. "You'll see him soon," he whispered. Jack crouched, looked over to see Horst and Beong in their sleeping bags, and then moved forward on all fours, not standing, taking to heart the warnings that the colonel had given them.

This close to the *line*, they had to be very cautious.

Jack moved up the hill, slowly, quietly. He knew Patton was up ahead of him somewhere, keeping watch. He stopped moving when he got to the top of the hill, being careful to keep the brush and trees at his back, so that anyone looking up at the bluff would not see his silhouette in the moonlit night.

"I can still smell the blood."

Startled, Jack turned, slipped, and plopped down on his butt. Patton was less than an arm's length away, sitting cross-legged, pushed up against the trunk of a pine, staring straight ahead at the moonlit ribbon of the Mississippi.

"What blood is that, Colonel?" asked Jack.

"My blood." Patton pointed to the north, up along the meandering river. "Until the goddamned Soviets rolled over the East Coast in the summer of '31, Vicksburg was the only American city to be flattened by a siege. It was

July 2, 1863, two days before Pemberton would surrender to Grant. I was in the First Missouri Brigade under General John Brown. I was a snot-nose lieutenant, a pig farmer just three months before the engagement. It was a night like this, but of course there were stars in that sky." He quietly laughed. "I felt it before I heard the explosion—shrapnel split open my guts from chest to belt buckle." Again he laughed. "As I fell to the ground, I saw the chunks of burnt horsemeat and the greasy black-eyed peas I had for dinner spill out of the hole in my stomach. I landed in my own damned dinner. Blood was everywhere. It took me nearly an hour to bleed out. I really soaked that ground." He pulled a twig from a nearby branch and began to gnaw on it. "The loss of Vicksburg was the real beginning of the end—gave the Yankees the Mississippi River and cut the Confederacy in half, isolating the Western states from the South." He said this as if it had happened just last week. He squinted and grinned. "Think I'm crazy?"

"No," said Jack. He'd learned a great deal about Colonel Patton in the last five days of travel, not the least of which was that the man believed in reincarnation and was certain that he had fought in every war of consequence for the last five thousand years. The current Soviet occupation was just one more conflict in which he was certain he would eventually die, only to be reborn at some future point where his soldiering talents would be needed again. "Not any crazier than me claiming that I had a hand in creating this entire universe."

Patton nodded. "Two goddamned crazies out to save the world."

This time it was Jack who softly laughed. "Only a crazy man would believe that he could actually save the world."

Patton again nodded and pointed across the river, to the plain on the far side, and at the tower of steel that rose up nearly three hundred feet. "About two hours before dawn we'll cross the river directly across from the beam. This far south, away from the real action up by St. Louis and Chicago, the Kraut patrols are thin, especially this close to the beam, where the little Himmler-kissing sausage stuffers are afraid of getting vaporized."

There was no Hitler in this world—Patton had never even heard of him. Heinrich Himmler, who had quickly capitulated to the advancing Russian army, and now ran the puppet government that the Soviets had set up, had led the Fascism that had swept across Germany.

"Can you tell me any more about *them*?" asked Jack.

They'd had this discussion several times already, always late at night when the others were asleep. Jack had not slept in several weeks, and Patton seemed to be able to get by on just a few hours a night—that left plenty of time to talk.

Patton pointed up at the tower. "Courtesy of *them*," he said.

Amazing, thought Jack. The particle beam weapon had been built by an unlikely consortium. Nikola Tesla was without a doubt a genius of amazing capabilities—the father of AC electricity. But in spite of his numerous inventions, including beating Marconi out at the patent office on the invention of the radio, the man had been considered a head case. The last decades of his career had been spent in building ever-bigger Tesla coils and claiming that he could not only pull energy directly from space but also use that energy to construct amazing weapons systems. None of those systems were ever actually seen.

But on *this* Earth, a desperate U.S. government had poured enough money into Tesla's projects to make them a reality. And here, Tesla had received help from two unlikely sources. The first was a Cubist painter named Juan Gris. Of some small fame back in what Jack thought of as the *real world*, the contemporary of Picasso had been the most mathematically oriented of the Cubists. And the second person helping Tesla was a boy, an orphan, found working on a big plantation south of Denver—Anthony Wittkowski. Those three had not only invented particle beam weapons, but built radar systems and implemented laser systems that could vaporize the best Soviet armor.

"Can't tell you much more than I already have. Tesla is

the front man, the personality that pushes the projects. The old son of a bitch will steamroll any bastard that gets in his way, and he's got the backing of the president to give him muscle."

Jack had heard a lot about the president.

In the same way that Patton had never heard of Hitler, his only recollection of Franklin Roosevelt had been that of a crippled New York governor who had not survived the first months of the war with the Soviets. The current president was Will Rogers, who Jack knew in his world to have been a famous humorist in the '20s and '30s.

"Gris and the boy have a low profile. Gris is a spooky bastard, talks in mumbo jumbo, is always hacking and coughing up his lungs, and usually has his face hidden behind an oxygen mask. The boy I just don't know about. Few do." Patton turned to look back down the hill and toward where Katie and Horst were sleeping. "Are you sure that he's really their kid?"

"He was when we last saw him ten of *your* years ago. I don't know who or what he may be now."

Patton nodded, understanding about the differences in the rate of time flow between different universes. "I've seen the kid at most a half-dozen times, and all I can say is that he scares the crap out of me. When he looks at you, you get the feeling that he's examining a bug."

That doesn't sound good, thought Jack, as he considered Alpha and tried to imagine the path that he must have progressed down to become the insane megalomaniac that he had been transformed into. Was Anthony walking that same path?

"Or maybe even a goddamned microbe," said Patton.

Not good at all.

Suddenly light filled the night, and Jack closed his eyes. But even with them closed he could see the light, a bright flash that seemed to sear his retinas.

Boom!

Thunder rolled over him. Getting his eyes open, he was once again greeted by the night. Swinging his head around,

looking for whatever had caused the explosion, he saw a
ball of flame falling toward the distant horizon.

"The beam got another one," said Patton.

Jack looked back at the tower. The top of it glowed a
faint red, just like the filament of a lightbulb that had been
extinguished seconds earlier. As he watched, it quickly
dimmed even further, turning dark. "My God," he said as
he looked back toward a ball of flame falling toward the
horizon, wondering what kind of aircraft or missile had just
been shot down.

"God doesn't have a goddamned thing to do with it,"
said Patton. "It's science."

Jack was nervous—palm sweating, lightheaded, peripheral vision
darkening type of nervous. It had started to build when
they'd entered Boulder, Colorado—a little town pushed up
against the eastern side of the Rockies, about thirty miles
west of Denver. The landscape was dominated by massive
mountains and colossal slabs of rocks that made up the
Flatirons. Beautiful and pristine, but there was also something about it that made Jack feel as if he were about to
jump out of his skin.

He knew it was Anthony.

The jeep stopped in front of a big Victorian house, all
white and red, with a perfectly manicured lawn, a big wrap-
around front porch, and a dirt driveway suitable for a car-
riage and horse.

"All out," said Patton. Taking Katie's hand and helping
her out of the jeep, he guided her up the pathway to the
front door, not bothering to look back to see if the others
were following.

They were.

The front doors did not fit the Victorian motif, thought
Jack; the slabs of wood out of which it had been built were
cut at strange angles, and stained glass inserts were randomly placed within it. At the center was a massive brass
doorknocker, the ball of the knocker obviously representing

the sun, with the brass plate behind it, showing the planets in relief.

Only eight planets, Jack realized, counting them.

Pluto was missing—Pluto had not yet been discovered in this world. And for a moment, he wondered if Pluto existed in this universe at all, having been cut away from the outer bounds of the solar system as the picoverse had formed.

Patton slammed the knocker several times to the accompaniment of echoing bangs within the house. The door opened, salutes were exchanged with several soldiers who then quickly stepped back, and Patton ushered everyone into the foyer, a place of polished marble floors and half a dozen plaster Greek statues pushed into little alcoves.

Two men waited for them.

"May I introduce you to Nikola Tesla and Juan Gris," Patton said graciously, as he waved his hand in the direction of the two men. Tesla was standing, a rail-thin, frail man, with hollowed out cheeks, a bowed back, and thin gray hair. He looked ancient and withered, as if a strong breeze might shatter him and then scatter the pieces in all directions. But compared to Juan Gris, Tesla was the robust picture of health. Gris was seated, with a black mask covering most of the lower part of his face, a tube running from it to what Jack assumed was an oxygen tank. The rest of his face was hidden beneath long dark hair; the only part really visible were his eyes—the whites tinted blue, the pupils black. He wore a red silk robe, out of which two scarecrow hands clutched the arms of the blue velvet-covered chair he sat in.

"And these are the visitors you have long been waiting to receive," said Patton. "May I introduce you to Drs. Katherine McGuire, Jack Preston, and Beong Kim." He then pointed to the last guest. "And this is Professor Horst Wittkowski."

Horst pushed past the others and walked briskly over to Tesla, reaching down, grabbing the man's hand, and shaking it. Jack thought for a moment that Horst might pull the skin-and-bones arm right out of Tesla's shoulder, but it remained attached. "A great honor to meet you, sir," he said.

"A pleasure," said Tesla, making it quite obvious by the look on his face that it was anything but a pleasure. "However, I must tell you that your arrival has come at a most inopportune time."

"*He* cannot have visitors at the moment," said Gris. His voice was surprisingly strong, the Spanish-accented English full of resonance. "He is concentrating at the moment, and the effort can be quite taxing on him."

"Is he sick?" asked Katie, the panic obvious in her voice. She did not wait for an answer, but stepped forward. "We have to see him now."

"That will not be possible," said Gris. "Perhaps if you come back next week, some arrangements can be made."

"Next week!" said Katie. "I want to see Anthony now!"

"He is working," said Gris.

"Anthony!" shouted Katie, stepping back and looking around the huge room. She saw a staircase to her left. "Is he up there?" she asked, pointing, and then moving toward the staircase.

"No!" said Gris.

Katie went toward the staircase, but didn't reach it. Soldiers seemed to materialize from nowhere and formed a blockade at the base of the stairs. "Let me by!" Katie stood in front of them, pushing right up into the face of the soldier in the center. "I want to see my son!"

"Remove them!" said Gris.

"Slow it down," said Patton. He pointed first at Gris and then at the three soldiers. "Think about what you've got here," he said. "You've got a mother who hasn't seen her son in nearly ten years." Patton smiled. "I can assure you that President Rogers is very much in favor of the bond between a boy and his mother."

Gris sneered and pushed the oxygen mask up to his face, his chest puffing in and out as he took several breaths.

"I'm sure that you wouldn't want to bother the president with such minor matters as these, when he is considering the merits of your request for funding the new radar installation in the Dakotas."

Tesla glared at Gris.

"Very well," said Gris. "But just for a few moments." He lifted up a bony hand and pointed at the soldiers. "They will show you where."

Patton turned, walking toward the others and in the direction of the staircase. "Just got to show that spic bastard who's in charge around here," he whispered to Jack as he passed by him.

"Oh, Anthony," said Katie. The tone of her voice was a mixture of joy and sorrow. "What have they done to you?" She slowly walked across the balcony toward him. The others—even Horst—stood back, sensing that this was a mother-and-son moment.

Jack took a step back and leaned against a wall. His vision was tunneling, and his hands and feet were tingling. He could not quite get his breath and was afraid that he was about to pass out. He sat down without realizing it, sliding down the wall, lowering his head so that his chin rested on his knees.

He watched Anthony.

He was seated at a table, his back to the magnificent springtime view of the snowcapped Rockies. He faced a blank, dark wooden wall. In front of him on the table was an open notebook. In his left hand he held a pencil, clutching it like a child might hold a crayon. His hair, still blond, was cut short. Jack had no trouble seeing the six-year-old in this boy; his face filled with the exact same expression that had covered it when he was building one of his practical jokes—a strange mixture of fierce determination and detachment.

Katie walked up behind him, bent down, wrapped her arms around his chest, and gave him a kiss on the neck. "It's Mama," she said. "I've come for you, Anthony."

Anthony did not respond, but continued to use the pencil to scrawl across the page of his notebook. Katie squeezed him even harder. "Anthony, it's Mama." She gently shook him.

Jack managed to push himself up, using the wall for support.

The chair in which Anthony was sitting lurched back, revealing its two large rear wheels—a wheelchair. Anthony maneuvered the chair with his right hand by way of a control stick embedded in the arm of the chair. As he moved back, he rolled over Katie's right foot, apparently oblivious to her, and guided the chair in Jack's direction. Horst and Beong stood aside, letting the slowly moving chair pass.

Anthony maneuvered the chair right up to Jack and then slowly angled back his head, letting it fall against the headrest in the back of the chair. With two shaking hands, using the palms rather than the fingers, he lifted the notebook from his lap and awkwardly held it out to Jack.

Jack took it and was about to open it, believing that Anthony wanted him to see something in it.

"No!" said Anthony, in a croaking voice that sounded as if it had not been used in a long time. "Hold it flat," he said.

Jack held the book flat in the palms of his hands. He looked past Anthony and over at Katie, who had remained at Anthony's table. Tears ran down her face as she silently sobbed, her shoulders jerking back and forth as she cried. He looked back down at Anthony. The teenager had his eyes closed, and his pale skin tinted red as he strained, concentrating. His lips puckered, his cheeks puffed out, and he let out a shrill whistle.

Jack felt a breeze stir, something coming down by his feet. His pant legs rustled, and sand and grit were suddenly blown into his eyes. His eyes began to tear, and he was about to reach up and rub his eyes, when wind roared up from beneath him and blew the book out of his other hand.

The wind howled and beat him back against the wall.

The book hung in front of him, furiously spinning, buoyed up by the impossible wind. Through tearing eyes, Jack looked at the others—no wind around them, just what appeared to be a miniature funnel directly in front of him, holding up the book.

Anthony stopped whistling, the wind simply vanished, and the book fell into his lap.

"I've moved *well* beyond simply being able to bring down a whole bookshelf by removing a single volume of an encyclopedia. Rather than just seeing where chaos will strike, I can now manipulate *how* that chaos will strike. I don't need you, Jack," he said, panting, trying to catch his breath. "There is nothing that you can show me." He then rolled the chair back, spun it around and drove it into the room leading to the balcony. "Don't come here again," he said from within the room. "*None* of you come here again."

Katie ran to the doorway, was about to follow him in, but then stopped and turned toward Jack. "What's happened to him?" she asked, tears running down her face.

"I don't know," said Jack. The grit driven into his eyes by the wind that Anthony had generated and controlled still stung. "He's grown," he said. Everyone in the room knew that Jack was not referring to his physical size.

"I want Anthony," said Katie. Running over to Jack, she pressed herself up against him, wrapping her arms around him and squeezing.

Jack stroked the back of her neck. "We'll get him back," he said. "I promise." And somehow he knew that they would, that it was the only course of action that made sense, the only course of action *permitted*.

SECTION II
CHAPTER 5

Beong could not sit. He paced back and forth in the waiting room, its decor a combination of Jeffersonian colonial and rodeo sideshow, while the other three sat, Katie and Jack together, and Horst by himself, writing copious notes in a little leather-bound notebook with a fountain pen. He would occasionally look up from his notebook at the mounted buffalo head that overpowered the small room, nod at it, and then return to his notebook.

"I know this president," said Beong.

Horst closed his notebook and screwed the top back onto his fountain pen. "A close and personal friend of yours, I suppose?"

Beong shook his head, the expression on his face one of horror, and then he did several quick bows. "Of course not, Professor Wittkowski," he said, bowing yet one more time. "Before coming to America I studied the history of this country in order to better integrate and interface with the people I would encounter."

Horst rolled his eyes. Georgia Tech had a huge Korean student population. In half the electrical engineering labs one might assume that you were in Seoul rather than Atlanta. "And as part of these studies you learned about Will Rogers?"

Beong bowed. "A great man from the Wild West," he said. "He was highly proficient at intricate sleight of hand with ropes, and was very famous for pointing out the embarrassing actions of politicians. He also made movies and died in a plane crash."

"Fascinating," said Horst. He looked back down at his notebook. "Although I suspect that in this world he is not yet quite dead."

"We should go right back to that house and drag Anthony away from those two psychopaths," said Katie. "God only knows what living with them has done to him. He's still just a boy."

Jack wanted to tell her that Anthony was much more than just a boy. He had somehow generated that wind and used it to control the movement of the book. Anthony had physically mastered what Jack could only think of as chaos physics, that realm of physics dominated by nonlinear relationships, where an almost insignificant input was rapidly magnified into something unimaginable—in this case a minitornado unleashed by his whistling. "I told you that we will get him," he said. "He's been here for nearly ten years now. I doubt that another few days is going to change the situation much. We have to understand what is going on before we go stepping on toes that shouldn't be stepped on."

"My God, Jack," she said. "This isn't politics, this isn't about trying to squeeze some money out of Congress. *This is about Anthony!*" She moved away from him.

Jack just nodded. At the moment, the best he could do was take the heat, to give Katie the opportunity to focus on him. This *was* politics. And to start a panic without understanding what was going on could well do more harm than good. Tesla and Gris were very powerful players in this world. Jack had learned a few things from his years in Washington. *It is far more important to take time in choosing your enemies than it is in choosing your friends.*

"The president will see you now."

Jack looked up. A petite woman, whose tightly wrapped pile of hair was actually studded with several pens and pencils, stood in front of the door opening to the president's office.

The three who had been sitting, stood and made their way to the door, as usual Horst barreling through first, followed by Jack and Katie close together, and Beong hiding behind them. This time Horst was beaten to the punch. It was the president who made the first move, trotting around his big oak desk, pouncing on Horst, grabbing his hand and pumping.

"A God honest pleasure, Professor Wittkowski," said President Rogers with a Midwest twang, "to finally meet the father of the Sonomak."

Horst was flattered, as well as taken by surprise, having difficulty incorporating the concept of a cowboy president from the 1930s talking about the Sonomak. "Thank you, sir," he finally managed.

Rogers moved on, shaking hands with Jack. "Glad you were able to stop by for a visit," he said to Jack, and then took Katie's hand. "Thank you for coming, Dr. McGuire.

If there is anything that I can do to make your stay in Boulder more pleasant, please let me know." He then leaned toward her, looking a bit sheepish, and spoke gently. "My better half has asked me to let you know that if you need another woman to confide in she'd be more than willing to let you bend her ear."

Katie opened her mouth. Jack knew exactly what was about to come out—a plea to rescue Anthony. Jack tugged on her hand, trying to let her know that now was not the time. Before she could recover, Rogers again bent near her and whispered in her ear. "Don't you worry about that boy of yours. I gave Nikola and Juan a good dressing down. Those two rascals won't be in your way any longer. As a matter of fact, I've now got the four of you bunking in that Victorian nightmare." The president straightened back up.

Katie smiled at him. Jack could feel the tension drain from her body, the viselike grip she had on his hand loosening.

"Welcome to our country, Dr. Kim," the president said. He spoke loudly, as if hoping that sheer volume might make up for any language problems. "I want to thank you for helping us out with this little Soviet problem that we've got." Then the president bowed.

Beong twitched from head to foot, managed to swallow what had just exploded up his throat, and then bowed so low that he found himself looking at the president's belt buckle—a big piece of sliver and turquoise in the design of a man on a bucking horse.

"Fine then," said Rogers. "I've asked a couple of my friends to attend this little get-together." The president waved past the four of them and to the rear of his office, where there were two leather-covered couches on either side of a coffee table constructed out of a polished tree stump and covered by a massive slab of glass.

Jack turned.

Nikola Tesla sat on one of the couches. He smiled with all the sincerity of a small child instructed to make nice after having whacked a playmate over the head with a rock.

Jack ignored him and looked at the two sitting on the other couch. Both men looked to be in their mid-thirties. Jack saw nothing very distinctive about them, though they did look familiar.

"I'd like you to meet a couple of our local boys," said the president. "I know that you four come to us from the twenty-first century and know more science between you than any thousand physicists I could muster together, but I still believe my two boys here bring something to the rodeo. I'd like you to meet Ernest Lawrence and Werner Heisenberg."

The four stood unmoving, speechless.

"Oh my God," Jack whispered after several seconds of awkward silence. These were two of the greatest physicists of the early twentieth century, both Nobel Prize winners. Lawrence had practically invented the concept of particle accelerators and was a nuclear science pioneer, while Werner Heisenberg had developed quantum mechanics. Jack looked at the two men. They were so young. And then Jack reminded himself that the truly great physicists all had their scientific breakthroughs while they were young. These two were in their prime. Jack looked over at Horst and saw an expression on his face that he had never seen before. *Awe*.

Horst's mouth actually hung open.

"I gather you've heard of my two boys," said the president. Smiling, he then pointed at Horst. "Might want to close that mouth of yours, Professor," he said. "This time of year we get some mighty big horseflies in these parts."

Horst nodded and closed his mouth, too unnerved to be embarrassed or angered by the president's remark.

Katie took several steps forward in amazement, and then stopped and turned toward the president. "And I suppose that we'll be having lunch with Albert Einstein today," she said jokingly, trying to break the tension.

The president looked confused, and Katie interpreted this as the president having never heard of Albert Einstein, or perhaps having heard of him, but that he was halfway across the world, or quite possibly dead. "Did someone discuss today's schedule with you?" he asked.

"No." She did not understand the full meaning of that question.

Rogers stared at her intently, and for just a moment Katie was frightened, and she knew beyond any doubt that this was not just some cowboy turned politician. The strength and determination in those eyes were so intense that she had to look away.

"Well, little lady," said Rogers, sounding jovial again. "The four of you do in fact have an afternoon meeting with Reverend Einstein. I've given him ten minutes. It was the least I could get away with. I would have preferred to cut him completely out of the schedule, but there are political ramifications to that meeting. The man has developed quite a following."

Katie turned to face Horst, Jack, and Beong. *Reverend*, she mouthed silently, and the three of them looked just as bewildered as she was. It was at that instant that she understood what Jack had been trying to tell her. They had to be very careful here and understand what was going on, before they acted and made a colossal blunder. They could not rely on the history of their Earth to make assumptions.

"Please be seated," said Rogers. He waved his hands toward the couches, as he sat in the lone chair at the head of the coffee table. Horst and Beong sat on the couch that Tesla occupied, sitting as far away from him as possible, while Jack and Katie sat on the other couch, Jack right next to Werner Heisenberg.

Jack desperately wanted to say something innocuous and pleasant to Heisenberg, something to break the incredible tension he felt in the man's presence. "From the perspective of the twenty-first century, your discoveries and theories have probably had more impact on our world than any others." He instantly regretted having spoken, feeling stupid and pompous.

Heisenberg smiled graciously. "Thank you for the kind words," he said in a heavily German-accented voice, "but urely such names as Newton and Faraday must come to mind before mine."

Jack gave him a stupid grin and laughed a bit, unable to say anything. There had been no arrogance in Heisenberg's tone or manner when he placed himself just a notch below Newton and Faraday. Jack could sense that Heisenberg was simply making what he perceived to be a matter-of-fact observation.

"Ernest, could you give us a brief overview?" asked the president, rescuing Jack.

"Certainly, sir," he said, with just the barest hint of his parent's Scandinavian origins audible in his voice. "The technical thrust of our war effort is currently focusing on two areas of research. The first consists of those efforts headed by Nikola." He waved a hand in Tesla's direction. "It is through his valiant efforts, and the deployment of both radar and energy beam weapons, that we have been able for the moment to hold the Soviets east of the Mississippi and west of the Sierras."

Lawrence smiled.

Tesla smiled.

Jack could tell from the interchange that these two men were bitter rivals. There was great significance in the way that Lawrence had said that Tesla's efforts were holding back the Soviets for *the moment*. Lawrence was implying that this was at best only a temporary fix.

"Our second effort, led by Werner and me, is in the construction of a Sonomak."

Horst cleared his throat, squirmed in his seat, and looked around at those at the coffee table. It was obvious that he wanted to say something, but was still too intimidated by Heisenberg and Lawrence to interrupt.

"Yes, Professor," said Lawrence.

"With all due respect to both you and Dr. Heisenberg," said Horst, pleased that his voice did not shake, "how could you possibly hope to build a Sonomak at this point in history? More than seventy years of physics lie between you and what we had at our disposal in the twenty-first cen-

tury." Horst was attempting to be as diplomatic as possible
without actually telling them that despite who they were, i
would be impossible for them to fathom the theoretical un
derpinnings of the Sonomak. They had only just develope
quantum mechanics.

Lawrence smiled. "Despite some of the challenges w
initially encountered, there were three critical differences i
our effort as compared to yours. Our effort began after i
was brought to our attention that an orphan named Anthon
Wittkowski claimed to have an explanation for what ha
happened to the stars. At first we were wary of his expla
nation, but then the existence of Alexandra Mitchell, a
described by Anthony, and her rapid rise in the expandin
Soviet State, coupled with what our sources described t
us in terms of the advanced technology she had access to
convinced us of the validity of the boy's story. And onc
we believed it, and knew that a device had been fabricate
to generate a new universe—*our universe*," he said, sweep
ing his hands above his head, "we were able to work ou
a theoretical framework to explain it."

"Oh?" said Horst.

"We have been collaborating nearly *ten* years on thi
project," said Heisenberg.

Jack had not considered that possibility. Back on thei
Earth they'd had less than a year to try to figure out wh
was happening, and a great deal of that time had been sper
in building the Sonomak—not trying to understand it fror
a theoretical perspective. But Lawrence and Heisenberg
two of the greatest physicists of all time, had been workin
on theory for *ten years*. Jack blinked, swallowed, an
looked over at Horst, realizing that *he* didn't understan
what that meant. He knew that Horst saw these two me
as nearly God-like in their abilities, but it would not eve
occur to him that they could comprehend twenty-first cer
tury physics, anymore than Isaac Newton could understan
how a nuclear reactor might work.

But Jack was certain that Horst was wrong.

Heisenberg and Lawrence must have gotten a glimpse c

the future through Anthony's description of the Sonomak. Simple clues about the machine, coupled with their physics ability, and ten years of research, might yield something remarkable.

"Based on the physical description of the Sonomak and rudimentary outlines of the use of lasers and plasmas, as recalled in the memory of a very bright seven-year-old," said Lawrence, as he smiled at Katie, "it became rather obvious what you had stumbled upon."

"Stumbled upon," muttered Horst under his breath.

"It was a rather simple matter of combining the general theory of relativity that our associate Einstein had worked out nearly a decade before his breakdown, with my own quantum mechanics, to develop what we have come to call *quantum-vacuum mechanics*, or QV mechanics, a way to describe nature at H-dimensions."

Jack smiled, certain that he knew just *whom* the *H* in H-dimensions referred to.

"H-dimensions?" asked Horst, slipping his own neck into the noose.

"Excuse the jargon," said Ernest, "but Werner is too modest to refer to them by their proper name—*Heisenberg dimensions*—they refer to a scale of one billion-trillionth of a centimeter, where space itself is quantized."

"Yes, I understand," said Horst. He felt foolish for not realizing that their H-dimensions were the same as what his team referred to as the Planck dimensions.

"It was then simply a matter of applying the proper boundary conditions to the set of space-time field equations we devised in order to understand how to generate a new universe in a controlled fashion. In many ways this was just an extrapolation of Werner's quantum relativity applied for boundary conditions where space is no longer contin-uous."

"What do you mean by *controlled* fashion?" asked Jack, feeling that their own experiments had been far from what would have been characterized as *controlled*.

"What do you call the oscillating region within your

plasma in which the electrons have been swept aside to form a region of positively ionized gases?

"The plasmon," said Horst.

Heisenberg nodded. "Easy enough to remember," he said. "Although we call it the L-void."

Jack, Katie, and Horst all looked over at *Lawrence*, knowing full well what the L must stand for. Lawrence shrugged and offered up a sheepish grin.

"We devised the relationship between the L-void beat frequency, period of rotation and precession, to the uncertainty in the time and energy states of the collapsing L-void, so that we could control both the point in time at which the new universe would be mapped from the old universe, as well as the degree of space-time curvature, so as to obtain a desired rate of time flow within the new universe. Of course, there is only so much margin for controlling the rate at which time flows, based on the energy limitations inherent on the size of the universe one can generate."

"Of course," said Horst. He tried to ignore the pain in his gut.

"In addition, we have derived the equations and L-void conditions necessary for generating both intra- and extratemporal wormholes."

"Please define the terms *intra* and *extra*," asked Katie, trying to keep up with Heisenberg's description, most of her attention still focused on the fact that Lawrence and Heisenberg claimed to have theoretically devised a method for *controlling* both the space-time curvature of the new universe as well as the moment of its conception—a feat that *they* had not been able to do either theoretically or experimentally.

"We define intratemporal wormholes as those which connect different points within a given universe, or from universe to universe at the same moment in time. An extratemporal wormhole not only forms outside normal space, but is not constrained to obey causality."

Jack blinked. "The two ends of the wormhole are at

:ached to different locations in *time*?" he asked, certain that
was what Heisenberg meant, but still not believing it was
possible.

Heisenberg nodded. "But of course the energy levels are
simply impractical for generating such an extratemporal
wormhole device. You would need to manipulate the quan-
:um energy states between a pair of rotating L-holes to
achieve such an effect."

This time it was Jack who nodded and looked at
Lawrence. "We refer to them as black holes," he said.

"How quaint," said Heisenberg.

Jack turned and looked back at Horst, Katie, and Beong,
reading the expressions on their faces. They had believed
:hat they had been summoned to this office in order to
explain their in-depth knowledge of the Sonomak, and how
:o generate a universe. It was now obvious to all of them
:hat these two men needed no help at all. Jack turned back
around. "You certainly seem to have a good theoretical understanding of the concepts." He did not want to divulge
just how little the twenty-first century scientists understood
in comparison. "In what way do you want us to help you?"

"We are having trouble in the actual physical construc-
:ion of the Sonomak," said Heisenberg. "We cannot fabri-
ate the lasers with sufficient power density, or the
electronics to pulse the lasers on and off with the proper
degree of beam quality. We do not see how we can possibly
pulse the laser below the nanosecond range, but we know
:hat we will need femtosecond pulses to operate the ma-
hine. We need improvements in our vacuum systems. Our
alculating systems are limited to four-bit resolutions and
onsume massive amounts of power. We do not possess the
integrated circuit technology that Alexandra Mitchell has
brought to the Soviets. To put it simply, we are suffering
rom inadequate infrastructure technologies."

Horst leaned forward. "Am I to understand then what
ou need from us is our *engineering* help?"

Both Lawrence and Heisenberg shook their heads. "What
we really need are your hands, to study our equipment, to

advise us on how your hardware functions, how your twenty-first century hardware is implemented."

"You need twenty-first century technicians," said Jack.

"Exactly," said Lawrence. "We have both an electronic and machine shop at your full disposal.

Jack leaned back and felt like laughing. Physicists, when forced by circumstance to be modest, usually at awards ceremonies, always claimed that they were but little men and women standing on the shoulders of the giants from the past, and it was due to those giants that they had been able to peer over the horizon and see something new. Well in this case, it was the giants who were standing on the shoulders of little men and women, and the view that they'd glimpsed appeared to be quite spectacular.

"I hate to be blunt about this," said the president, "but time is not something that we've got by the bushel basketful. My boys have given you the rundown, and I'm sure they'd be more than happy to scribble down all those Greek symbols they get so excited about, to make sure the details are all there. But from what you've heard, have they missed anything? Does it sound like they've got a good handle on this Sonomak business?"

"I believe so," said Horst, not giving the others the opportunity to speak. "Although we will need to see the details to make certain." Horst smiled.

"Excellent," said the president. "So am I safe in assuming that we have you all on board, that you will help us in building the Sonomak."

This time it was Katie who was quickest. "And what are your intentions? How do you plan on using the Sonomak against the Soviets, when you already have an abundance of weapons systems courtesy of Nikola and my son?" She waved a hand at Tesla. She did want to know what their plans were, but she was also attempting to ingratiate herself with the man who appeared to have so much control over Anthony. She knew that she needed to mend bridges if she were ever to get Anthony back.

"Those weapons systems have saved us," said the president, nodding to Tesla. "However, not even they are a match against Soviet nuclear weapons. After the initial flurry of atomics used on the East and West Coasts, it appears that the Soviets have come to the conclusion that there is little point in capturing real estate if it's contaminated to the point that it can't be inhabited. So now the war is being fought with fairly conventional methods."

Conventional methods, thought Jack. Particle beams and laser weapons were only starting to come on line on their twenty-first century Earth.

"Thanks to Miss Mitchell, the Soviets had a large lead in atomics. We are still several years away from our own atomic weapons, and I'm afraid they are going to come up a dollar short and a lot more than a day late. What we need is an advanced weapons system that will destroy the Soviets before they have time to pull on their boots."

Katie did not see how the Sonomak could be turned into a weapons system.

"When we get the Sonomak running, we'll build one of those intratemporal wormholes that the boys are so excited about, hook the business end to one of the other universes that was fabricated back in your lab, one with a timeline far into the future, one in which *their* Soviets are already as dead as dust, and get those good folks to lend us their weapons to blow *our* damned Russians out of their saddles."

Jack nodded. Anthony had only been six years old at the time, probably terrified and traumatized, but he had still been able to understand what Alpha had been doing, knew that each one of those cones that had been generated was a wormhole to new worlds. And that information had now become a critical element in their plan to stop the Soviets.

"You have our full cooperation," said Horst. His head filled with visions of obliterated Communists. "Anything we can do."

Jack wondered if Horst really understood what he had just agreed to—to be a bolt-tightening gopher for Heisenberg and Lawrence.

"Wonderful," said the president. He jumped up from his chair and began reaching for hands to shake. "I almost feel sorry for those goddamned Russians." He winked at Katie. "But not sorry enough not to kick their commune-loving butts right off this planet."

The president walked over to his desk and pressed a button attached to the side of a bulky black telephone. "Our guests are ready to move on to their next appointment," he said.

The door to the president's office snapped open, and Patton stood there at full attention. "This way if you please," he said, stepping back and motioning with his hand. He looked into the president's office, directly at Jack, and ever so slightly, shook his head.

Jack didn't know what Patton was trying to let him know, so he let the others file out of the office first, hanging back, making sure he was the last one to leave. The moment he left the president's office, Patton fell in step behind him.

"Just keep moving," whispered Patton, "and don't look back."

Jack kept in step with Beong, who was directly in front of him.

"Just got new orders," said Patton. "I'm to report to Chicago."

Jack said nothing. He would be sorry to see Patton go, but did not understand why Patton was being so secretive about his new assignment.

"I called in a few favors to find out just who was responsible for the transfer, and it was that spic bastard Gris who started the ball rolling."

Jack nodded. A bit of political revenge on the part of Gris, no doubt as payment for Patton forcing the issue on them seeing Anthony. "You made him look bad," whispered Jack.

"It's more than that," said Patton. "If every person who crossed him were transferred out, Boulder would be a ghost town. But I'd been making a few inquiries about his movements and who he was dealing with before he came to the

states in 1926, and he must have caught wind of it. The
bastard is hiding something. So watch your back."

"And you watch yours," said Jack.

Patton quietly laughed. "No one lives forever," he whispered.

Except for Alexandra Mitchell, thought Jack.

SECTION II
CHAPTER 6

In a too-small, windowless room in the Western White House annex
building, Reverend Einstein, spiritual leader of the Church
of Revelation, and his companion sat on one side of an
overly long foldout table. Heisenberg and Lawrence leaned
up against an adjacent wall, while Horst, Katie, Jack, and
Beong took the table's remaining seats, all facing Einstein.

"You are confused," said Einstein. He ran a hand across
the stubble on his shaved head, and nervously tugged at the
lapels of his black coat. "God's hand has extinguished the
stars."

Heisenberg shook his head and sighed.

Jack only partially heard him. He was staring at the
woman that Einstein had brought with him, the woman that
he had introduced as his wife—Nadia Einstein. Despite the
fact that they were in the presence of what was quite possibly the greatest physicist who ever lived, it was his wife
that they closely watched. Jack held Katie's right hand
tightly, forcing her to remain in her seat. He did not know
how much longer he could hold her back.

Nadia Einstein was not who she claimed to be. She was
in fact a duplicate of Alexandra Mitchell. Jack had not considered meeting someone he might have known when they
had found themselves in 1936, a world seventy years distant from their own. But he had forgotten about Alexandra
and Quinn. They had been alive for millennia, and when
this Picoverse was formed, when this Earth budded off

from their Earth in 1926, a duplicated version of Alexandra and Quinn would have found themselves trapped within it. And here was that duplicated Alexandra, masquerading as Einstein's wife.

Finally Katie could stand it no longer.

"This *thing*," said Katie, pointing at Nadia Einstein, "is nothing more than a machine, a device built by the entities that created our universe. She was put here to control us, as well as to run experiments on us."

Einstein sighed. "I suspected that the four of you were suffering from the same psychosis as my wife had when we first met—the misguided belief that mere mortals could create entire universes."

Nadia nodded. "It is true," she said. "When God removed us from the universe, revealed to us with absolute truth of His existence and the love He had for us, I suffered a mental collapse. I could not accept what was obvious and beautiful. My sick mind attempted to convince me that I was not even of this world, but a machine with no connection to God. But Albert found me, and healed me, showed me that I had been suffering from delusions. Albert's wisdom and compassion filled the void within me."

Jack stared into her eyes, looking for the truth. She sounded convincing and so sincere, but he didn't believe her. In Alpha's universe, Alexandra had been rebooted and her original directives reinstated to make certain that no one attempted to manipulate space-time. If Alpha had been telling the truth, then this Alexandra would have also been rebooted. And if so, her sole objective would in all likelihood be to stop the Sonomak program. How could she do that?—by removing the best physicist the world had ever known from working on the project and then brainwashing him into actively opposing it? That seemed like a distinct possibility to Jack.

"It is man's arrogance, his desire to understand the mind of God, to unravel all the secrets of the universe, which made God act on our behalf and confine us to this region of solitude," said Einstein. "If you continue to attempt the construction of the Sonomak, to enter into energy and spatial domains not meant for the mind of man to comprehend, then I fear that God's actions will be even more severe."

Nadia nodded and looked up at the ceiling, as if she expected a bolt of lightning to come crashing down on them.

"I can bring great pressure to bear against you and this project if you continue to pursue it. The number of my followers grows greater every day. You cannot stand against God and us. If forced, we will remove the president and his followers. Please do not force us into acting against *you*." Einstein looked at Heisenberg. "I still consider you my friend, Werner. Think about what you're doing. God has punished us once for our arrogance, and He will do so again unless you stop."

Heisenberg shook his head. "My God is not vengeful," he said. "He gave us minds so that we could ask questions, gave us eyes so that we could see the truth."

Einstein and Nadia stood.

"You will condemn us all to eternal damnation if you continue with this experiment," said Einstein. "I will stop you."

"We will not be stopped," said Heisenberg.

Einstein whispered a brief prayer, in what sounded to Jack like Hebrew. He then took Nadia by the hand, turned, and was ushered out by soldiers.

"So sad," said Werner. The expression on his face was a dark mixture of pity and disgust. "His abilities, his intellect, all wasted, his mind shattered, consumed with this vengeful God of his." And then he blinked, pushed aside all thoughts of Einstein, neatly compartmentalizing them away, and the expression on his face brightened. "I'm sure that you want to see our Sonomak," he said.

Jack, Horst, and Beong stood in unison, as if a puppet master had jerked all their strings. Katie remained seated. Her breathing was quick and shallow, and she had broken out in a cold sweat. "I need to see Anthony." She looked up at Heisenberg. The encounter with Nadia Einstein had frightened her; knowing that she was in the same city as Anthony terrified her.

"We need to get down to work," said Heisenberg. He sounded as if he were reprimanding a lazy grad student. There was no threat in the words; his forceful personality was normally more than sufficient to get his way.

Katie looked up at Heisenberg, at the father of quantum mechanics, who along with Einstein had done more to change the world of physics since Newton had been clobbered with an apple. In her mind the man was nearly a deity—a true god of physics. But none of that mattered. "I *need* to see Anthony," she said.

Surprised by the tone in her voice, Heisenberg took half a step back, put his hands on his hips, and bent slightly forward, ready to let her know exactly who was in charge.

"It will be my pleasure to take you to see Anthony."

Werner turned, and gave Lawrence an icy stare. "Certainly, Ernest," he said. "I suppose that *Miss* McGuire is not really needed at the lab right away." He paused, turning back to look at her. "After all, the issues holding us back at the moment are engineering related, not of a theoretical nature, for which *we* have sufficient understanding."

Katie did not miss the insults. But she didn't care at the moment. She needed to see Anthony. Katie nodded to Lawrence. "Thank you," she said.

Heisenberg turned and began to walk toward the door through which Einstein had just exited. Jack did not move, but looked at Katie, not sure what had just happened, not certain what to do. Katie shrugged and waved him on in the direction of the retreating Heisenberg. "Go see the new toy," she said.

Jack went, with Horst and Beong following closely behind.

"Anthony is truly transhuman."

Katie clenched her jaw, just managing not to snap at Juan Gris. Anthony sat beneath the whitewashed canopy of a gazebo. She could see the boy she knew, the six-year-old

tently working at his arts and crafts table, building some
contraption out of construction paper, rubber bands, and
ring. She smiled at that memory.

String.

On the table in front of him was a convoluted structure
built out of red and green construction paper, through
which were intertwined what looked like hundreds of col-
ed strings. With shaking hands, Anthony was carefully
guiding a robin's-egg blue string through the maze, tying
off against different segments of mesh, intertwining it
ith other strings.

"A sculpture?" asked Katie. She was trying hard to sound
vil.

Gris laughed. "To *you* it might appear to be a sculpture,
a abstraction of some piece of dead and desiccated real-
." Turning to face Katie and Ernest, he pushed the
ygen mask up to his face and sucked down a shallow
ngful. "What Anthony sees is a map, the nonlinear reality
hich exists through all time and space mapped into the
re and now."

"A projection, a shadow of the true nature of the uni-
rse," said Ernest.

Gris lowered the mask and smiled. For a moment, Katie
ought she could see an animal lurking beneath his nearly
anslucent, sickly skin, something reptile-like. "You never
ase to amaze me, Professor," he said. "Of all the cranial
asturbators that Nikola brings home, you seem to have
e best grasp of the *greater* nature of reality."

Ernest smiled, not in response to the compliment, but at
e description Gris used to label the scientists. There was
bit of truth in what Gris said, but only a bit. *It takes one
know one*, Ernest thought, but said nothing, his proper
idwest Protestant upbringing holding him in check. "You
e too kind," said Ernest, who then stepped off the veranda
d walked over to Anthony, crouching down, pushing the
e of his face almost against Anthony's.

Katie didn't move.

Ernest whispered into Anthony's right ear.

Katie took half a step forward, unable to hear what E
nest was saying, and was about to take another step, whe
what felt like a claw wrapped around her right arm, tuggir
her back. "Ernest and Anthony have developed a certa
rapport," said Gris, emphasizing the last word as if it in
plied something lurid.

Katie opened her eyes a bit wider, surprised. She thoug
that Gris and Tesla had trapped Anthony, were using hi
to further their little power fantasies. But was there a thi
manipulator?

She watched as Ernest reached up toward the labyrin
of strings, took the end of the blue twine from Anthony
shaking fingers, and made a loop around a thick rainbo
collage in the center of the sculpture, knotted it, and the
still holding on to the string, stood up. He then beckon
to Katie.

Katie walked over slowly, her head filling with a kale
doscope of images, almost as if she still wore her Virtua
She saw a hysterical Miss Alice sitting on the floor, wi
tape, strings, and construction paper wrapped around h
head. She wondered if something similar was about to ha
pen to her.

Ernest held up the end of the string offering it to Kati
"He wants you to take it, and pull it," he said. Katie look
down at Anthony. His head hung forward, slowly bobbi
back and forth, his shaking hands lying in his lap. She th
took the string, realizing that she didn't really care what t
of nastiness might be sprung on her. She would do wh
ever Anthony wanted. She firmly pulled on the blue strin
and readied herself.

The string jerked out of her hand, pulled back into t
sculpture, and the entire mass of it began to spin incredib
fast, as if the pulling of the string had unleashed some s
of spinning top. Colors blurred, and the entire thing beg
to contract, making cracking and snapping noises as it di
light bouncing off of it, as if its paper facets had sudden
become mirrored. And then as the air whistled through

began to sing in a choir of rich voices, using tones from very inhuman scale.

And then it stopped, and there was silence. The large ructure had been reduced to a small, multicolored cube ound up with a single knot—a carrick knot made from a ellow and green string. Katie swallowed past the lump that ad suddenly formed in her throat. Ernest reached down nd picked up the small cube, offering it to Katie.

"There are things more powerful than even the Second aw," said Anthony.

Katie took the cube in her hands, surprised at the weight f it, realizing only then how dense it must be, how amaz- gly compact it had to be in order to contain the entire culpture structure. She understood what Anthony meant by e Second Law—the Second Law of Thermodynamics— e law that dictated that entropy, the chaotic, randomizing ature of the universe, always increased—that order always ave way to chaos. She held in her hand a perfect cube, the ery symbol of order, which had spontaneously contracted ut of a formless, chaotic mass of paper and strings.

Anthony's eyes narrowed as he looked up at his mother.

She understood, hoped she understood. "Chaos to order. aking what is damaged and putting the pieces back to- ether," she said. Was this a peace offering, his way of tting her know that he might forgive her for what had hap- ened? "Can we go back to that point in time where we sep- rated, what to you was ten years ago? Can we put our lives ack together?" she asked.

"All the King's Horses and All the King's Men could ot put Humpty back together again," said Anthony. He en passed two shaking hands in front of himself. "What hance do you think you have?"

"I'm your mother," Katie said, kneeling down and wrap- ing her arms around Anthony, squeezing him, feeling him omentarily relax but then quickly stiffen as he feebly ushed her back.

"It may not be enough," he said, and then grabbed the

control lever of his wheelchair and lurched away, rolling
back toward the house.

Katie started to run after him, but Ernest grasped her
hand and pulled her back. "Not now," he said. "He needs
some time to understand what he is feeling, to come to grips
with his desire to have you back, while still consumed with
the anger he feels at having been abandoned by you."

Katie opened her mouth, about to protest that she hadn't
abandoned him, but at that moment, she realized that would
be exactly how it would have felt to a six-year-old boy
thrust into an alien world, cut off from everything and
everyone that he had ever known. *Total abandonment.*

"You'll get him back," said Ernest. He smiled, squeezing
her hand.

Katie relaxed, felt her body actually sag a bit, and found
that she could take a deep breath, deeper than she'd been
able to take since she knew that Anthony had been taken
from her. Ernest smiled at her, a big, warm, simple smile
with nothing behind it except genuine concern and compassion.

An ally.

She was certain of it, could feel it. And this ally was no
friend of Juan Gris's, which to Katie only strengthened her
feelings toward him.

"Thank you," she said and turned, walking back toward
Gris, who sat in his chair, wrapped in a black shroud, the
oxygen mask snugged tightly up against his face. Katie
crouched down, just as she had with Anthony, and pushed
her face near to Gris's. The man smelled like very old
cheese—rotting and putrid. "He's not your superman, your
transhuman," she said. "He's a boy, *my* boy, and I'm not
going to let you steal him away, confuse him into believing
that he's some *thing* from one of your Cubist nightmares."

"You wish to fight with me?" asked Gris. "You actually
think that you can stand up against me?"

Katie nodded. "To the death, you psychotic, diseased
sack of putrefying shit," said Katie in her sweetest sounding
voice. She then stood and marched off toward the house.

intent on finding the rooms that President Rogers had promised them.

"Quite the strong personality," said Ernest as he walked up to Gris.

"She doesn't know what is at stake here," said Gris.

"Do any of us?" asked Ernest.

*The cavern was obviously man-made, blown out of solid Rocky-*Mountain bedrock. The roof of the cave, hundreds of feet above them, was a jumble of bare rock, cement, and a lattice-work of steel girders. An overhead crane rolled above them, hauling what looked like hundred-foot lengths of steel pipe. Jack could see all this through the screened ceiling of the room they had just entered, a room that Jack figured was some sort of power distribution room—the heat and low-level stink of ozone attesting to the power that must be running through the large gray and black boxes that filled it.

But Jack didn't pay much attention to the room, only to the cavern ceiling far above his head. He sensed that something was wrong, actually felt fearful that the cave might collapse or some girder might let go and pulverize them.

"Our Sonomak," said Werner.

Jack started to turn, directed by Werner's voice.

Before he could completely turn, he realized that he was not standing in a power room at all, but a control room, quite possibly *the* control room. But it was so different and so *primitive*, that at first he hadn't recognized it as such. There were no computer screens, no glowing displays, not a single number formed by a light-emitting diode. Instead, there was bank after bank of big gray consoles, in which were embedded ugly gauges, things with shiny metal needles, interspersed with knobs and cranks. Dozens of operators manned the controls, flicking switches, writing down things on sheets of paper, adjusting knobs, scurrying from console to console.

As Jack watched, a little freckled-faced technician with an orange crew cut began tugging on a crank handle that was protruding from the wall, putting all his weight into it, using two hands to turn a wheel as big as his head. The thing squealed, and Jack tried to imagine the rods and worm gears, the turning shafts and grease-coated couplings that were slaved to that wheel. But he couldn't.

"Son of a bitch," said another operator, who kicked back his stool, stood, and began to furiously unfasten the front of the panel he sat before, by spinning off the large butterfly nuts holding it in place. "Tubes!" he shouted, just as he swung open the front panel, exposing a rat's nest of wiring and glowing tubes.

Jack walked toward the open console, like a moth drawn to a flame. Someone knocked into him from the back. "Sorry, sir," he heard from his left, and then a man stood next to him, with a large tray propped up in front of him supported by a strap hung around his neck. In the tray were a wide assortment of tubes, wrapped in little cardboard boxes, only their tips and connectors visible.

"Twenty amp, high-voltage Zener," said the technician, his head sticking into the open console, his right hand reaching out behind him, flailing in the air. The tube-man reached into his tray, and pulling out the right tube, unwrapped it in one deft move, and then slapped it into the waiting hand, just like a nurse slapping a scalpel into a surgeon's hand.

"Transistors?" Beong whispered from Jack's left side.

Jack shook his head. This was pre–solid state technology.

"Pre-computer," said Horst, now certain that whatever Heisenberg and Lawrence might be calling their Sonomak could not be a *real* Sonomak. A Sonomak could not be built, could not be operated without computers. And a computer, a *real* computer could not be built with tubes.

"The Sonomak," said Werner for a second time as he looked back and found that none of them were actually looking through the viewing window, but were all huddled about the open console, watching the technicians replace a tube. "Gentlemen!" he said.

Jack, Beong, and Horst turned in unison, the power and

command in Werner's voice somehow physically forcing them.

"You will have ample time to witness the replacement of tubes," said Werner. He sighed momentarily, thinking of the dozens of workers they had who did nothing *but* replace and repair tubes. "I believe that you might find the Sonomak a bit more interesting."

The three walked to the window at which Werner stood.

"My God," said Horst.

Jack and Beong said nothing. Horst had already said it all.

Jack thought of a spider web—a three-dimensional web made out of steel pipe—mile after mile of pipe, all of it intersecting at a gargantuan steel sphere. At first Jack did not understand what he was looking at, in a state of shock at the physical size of a device that must have stretched for miles.

"They don't have Pocket Accelerators," said Horst, realizing that each of those massive, mile-long steel tubes, was a single electron accelerator, something that he'd been able to compact into a device only a few feet long.

Jack just nodded and moved toward a door he hoped would lead into the cavern. He had to get down to the Sonomak, had to run his hands along the miles of steel. Opening the door, he stood on a catwalk and was about to take the first of what looked like hundreds of stairs to reach the cavern floor.

Then he looked up.

The crane clung to the ceiling high above him. But the steel pipe it had been hauling was no longer attached to it. It was falling, moving far too fast for Jack to get out of the way.

Jack didn't have time to close his eyes.

Didn't have time to breathe.

Certainly didn't have time to scream.

Space suddenly rippled, folding in on itself several feet in all directions, all of it suddenly occupying the *same* region of space. And then space refolded itself. Jack was back in the control room, his hand just touching the doorknob, as the door, the viewing window, the wall it was mounted in, and the catwalk and stairs beyond it collapsed, torn away by the falling pipe. The screech of tearing metal was deafening. The control room shuddered, slightly tilted, and was sprayed by shattering glass.

Jack took half a step back. The doorknob was in his right hand, the door itself nowhere to be seen, though Jack knew that it undoubtedly lay smashed on the cavern floor nearly a hundred feet below him. He dropped the doorknob, and his hand hung at an unnatural angle, his wrist obviously broken.

SECTION II
CHAPTER 7

Katie stood behind a seated Jack, her hands on his shoulders, fingers pressing into and massaging knotted muscles. She flattened out her hands, pushing them against the back of his neck, and then ran them up the back of his head. Jack pushed his head into her hands. Eyes shut, warm sunlight and gentle breeze drifting across his face, Jack thought he might actually slip into sleep, something that had not happened in months.

"Describe it to me again."

Jack opened his eyes. Ernest sat across from him, lounging in a white wicker chair, lemonade in one hand, a half-eaten sugar cookie in the other. Beyond him, at the far end of the patio, Anthony sat in his wheelchair in front of his drafting table, making the final modifications to the particle beam weapon to be installed on the shores of the Platte River to bolster the Eastern defense perimeter.

Anthony *appeared* to be focused, totally absorbed with the blueprints.

However, Jack knew better, could tell that the boy was eavesdropping on them, by the angle he sat in the chair, the way he had his head cocked ever so slightly in their direction, and the fact that he stopped scribbling whenever Jack spoke.

Jack slowly lifted his right arm, still not accustomed to the added weight of the heavy plaster cast that ran from hand to elbow. He motioned toward Anthony. "He knows. He can tell you what happened."

Ernest frowned.

Katie's soothing fingers stopped for just a moment. "He doesn't know," she whispered in his right ear, not wanting Anthony to hear. "He was five miles away and couldn't possibly have known about the accident."

Accident.

That seemed to be what they were all calling the incident, but Jack knew it had been no accident. The crane operator had disappeared, and the rumor mill insisted that the man had been a secret member of the Church of Revelation.

"I'd be the first to tell anyone not to underestimate Anthony's capabilities," said Ernest. "I've watched him grow for nearly ten years now, and I know he's capable of some pretty amazing physics—he's got an intrinsic sense of chaos, and at times can even seem to bend entropy to his own will. But he's no magician, and he's not the superman that Gris believes him to be."

"He's a boy," said Katie, pleading, something in the tone of her voice betraying her, not able to hide the fact that something was frightening her. "*My* boy," she added.

"You didn't *feel* it," said Jack. His muscles tightening, a chill ran down his back, causing his neck to twitch. "For just a moment I was not there, but spread out, blurred, existing across a whole region of physical space. And then I was *reconstructed* in a slightly different place." Words just didn't work. It was a quantum mechanical thing—like a spread-out wave function suddenly collapsing. "Only *he* could have done it."

"No one could have done it," said Ernest. "You could not have been outside the door *and* on the platform at the same instant. And besides, no one saw you go outside onto the platform. You never left the control room. It's a case of shock, a near-death experience that has *confused* you."

Jack tried to shake his head, but Katie had taken hold of it, keeping it in place, not letting him shake it. "I was translated—all of reality *remeshed* to account for it, right down to altering the perception of those around me," he said. "Only Anthony could have done that." Jack was frightened. He'd witnessed the creation of new worlds, encountered physics that only a few years ago would have been regarded as science fiction, or even magic. But that didn't spook him. Being translated less than two feet, just an instant before twenty tons of steel pipe would have splattered him, that terrified him.

But it was not the actual *splattering* that terrified him.

It was the *translation. Reality* had been altered. And that was far too much power for anyone to have, especially a sixteen-year-old boy.

He stood, despite Katie trying to hold him down, and walked across the patio, stopping only when he stood directly behind Anthony. He wanted to reach out, spin him around in his chair and force him into admitting, into explaining what he'd done—and then somehow make certain that he would never do it again. Despite the fact that Anthony had saved his life, Jack felt no gratitude. All he felt was fear. *No one* should be able to do what Anthony had done. "You haven't got me fooled," he said. "This invalid act, this pathetic boy trapped in his wheelchair and deserving of our pity isn't working on me."

"Leave him alone, Jack!" shouted Katie, sounding both angry and confused. She didn't know what was wrong with Jack. He'd been withdrawn, sullen for the last two days since the accident, watching Anthony, as if waiting for something horrible to happen. "He's just a boy!"

Jack knew better.

He was suddenly so certain of it, could sense what Anthony was turning into: a cold, emotionless creature that would lose all contact with what it had been to be human. He would become something far worse than Alpha. He would not be insane. He would not be vindictive. He would be *detached and lost*, omnipotent and uncaring—a god without passion or reason to exist.

And it had to be stopped.

He reached out, his hands shaking. The fear he felt was simple, and it caused his knees to weaken. His right hand was on Anthony's shoulder, taking hold, pushing against the boy, moving the wheelchair back.

"No!" Katie leapt out of her chair and ran toward Jack.

Jack continued to push. The wheelchair teetered on its side, balancing on one wheel. Anthony had grabbed hold of Jack's hand, feebly tugging at it. "Let me go," he said, his voice filled with disbelief.

Jack pushed harder.

The wheelchair fell over, and Anthony sprawled out of the chair, rolled several times, and came to a halt flat on his back. The questioning look on Anthony's face quickly passed and was replaced by a red-cheeked, full-scale, flare of anger.

"Are you insane?" Katie screamed at Jack, without looking at him, having already dropped onto her knees to tug at Anthony, trying to pull him up. And then she fell backwards, having been pushed aside.

Anthony *stood*.

His hands were balled into fists, his entire body shuddering, as if on the edge of explosion, the rage building within him, threatening to tear him apart. He lurched forward, and cocking back his right arm, lined his fist up, getting ready to drive it through Jack's face.

"The invalid walks!" said Jack, now knowing with full certainty that he had been right, that Anthony had been faking his disabilities.

Anthony took another half-step toward Jack, anger and momentum moving him forward, and then his eyes refocused, first on his raised fist and then down at the patio floor and his own sock-covered feet. He tentatively took another half-step forward, his legs suddenly quivering, his knees knocking. The anger vanished from his face and was replaced by an expression of complete disbelief. "I'm walking," he said. And then his knees gave way and he dropped to the patio.

Suddenly Jack knew that it had not been Anthony who had saved him from the falling pipe. Anthony had *not* been lying; he had been convinced that he was confined to the chair, an invalid. There were no secret agendas, no mysteries with this boy. His anger had released him, somehow bringing him back in touch with his own body.

Jack reached down to help Anthony up.

If not Anthony, then who had saved him? He was more afraid than ever.

The room was stuffy and gray. The walls were gray, the floor and ceiling gray, even the chairs and table were gray. Katie sighed and had to fight against closing her eyes and dropping her head to the gray tabletop. She looked at the gray people who sat around her.

Most she didn't know, and didn't care to know— Werner's loyal lackeys, just a small number of the horde who would happily follow him into whatever physics-induced nightmare he cared to dream up. Werner sat at the far end of the table, smartly dressed in his black suit, hair neatly slicked, the expression on his face one of supreme confidence. To his left sat Horst and Beong. Beong looked ill, tinted slightly green, the terror of being in the same room with someone of Werner's status almost too much for him to bear. Horst's response was the exact opposite. To Katie, it appeared as if he were glowing, looking over at Werner with an almost lustful gaze.

And then there was Jack.

She felt her eyelids drop slightly. Her anger had only slightly cooled. A part of her still wanted to take a baseball bat to the back of his head. Then she blinked and could feel the expression on her face soften. Something was *wrong* with Jack. He was lost, frightened; something growing inside him was eating him up.

He'd tried to hurt Anthony. That she couldn't forget, and

was not certain if she could ever forgive. But Anthony was now walking. In the last several days he hadn't picked up a paper or pencil, had done nothing with the ever-more frantic Gris and Nikola. Katie felt herself smile. Jack had somehow saved Anthony.

But she knew that had not been his intent.

Again Katie sighed, and this time did close her eyes. She wanted all this to be gone. She and Jack should have seized Anthony and made their escape long ago, hidden away somewhere back on the real Earth, somewhere far away from this insanity.

But they hadn't.

"There are several rate-limiting hardware issues that we need to deal with," said Werner, starting off the meeting. "We hope that our new associates, with their unique perspectives, may lend us some insight into these problems." Horst puffed up, looking to Katie like some preening bird. Beong turned a deeper shade of green. Jack stared, his eyes focusing on something far away.

"The first appears to be a contamination problem in the Sonomak central reaction chamber—we suspect that plasma density and our ability to maximize implosion of the L-void is being limited by this contamination." He picked up a piece of paper that lay on the table in front of him, as did the thirty-odd others who sat around the table.

Jack didn't move. And of course neither did Katie. These were *hardware* problems.

Several seconds passed in silence. "Well?" asked Werner. He fluttered the paper. "We see nothing unusual in the residual gas analyzer spectrum," he said, while again waving the paper. "The system appears to be clean, with just the minimal backgrounds."

Still no one spoke.

"Ideas!" said Werner.

"Ah," croaked Beong. Thirty heads turned in his direction.

"Yes, Dr. Kim," said Werner. "A thought?"

"Ah," Beong managed again. The paper in his hand

shook. "This hydrocarbon cracking pattern," he said, while pointing at some low-level squiggles on the graph. "You are using mechanical and diffusion oil-based pumps on the main Sonomak chamber," he said somewhat hesitantly, trying his best not to make it sound like an accusation.

"Of course," said Werner. "How else would we generate a vacuum in the Sonomak?"

Katie looked first at Beong, who was obviously terrified, and then at Horst, who was much harder to read. But Katie had had years of experience deciphering him. Horst was *confused*. He pretended to look thoughtfully at the paper before him, but Katie could tell that he didn't understand what Beong was trying to get at.

"The organic contamination used from those pumps will damp the implosion of the L-void," said Beong. He made it sound as if he had just admitted to having murdered his own family. "You need to go to an oil-free pumping system."

"Definitely oil-free," said Horst.

"And just what form of pumping would that be?" asked Werner, focusing on Horst.

"We use a form of pumping called an ion-pump," said Horst. He grinned, obviously happy with himself.

Werner nodded and bent toward Horst. "Yes," he said, expecting more. "And just how does this *ion-pumping* work?"

Horst blinked. Katie watched him squirm, saw his face redden, knew just how trapped he was when she saw him begin to drum his fingers across the top of the table. Katie didn't understand what was wrong with him.

"It is based on *ions*," said Horst.

Werner raised and lowered his eyebrows. "Yes," he said. "I assumed such, based on its name," sounding annoyed. "How does it *work*?"

Now Katie knew exactly what the problem was. Horst did not know how an ion pump worked. She knew that her ex-husband had run experiments for twenty years using such pumps. He could operate one, knew what its charac-

teristics were, but didn't understand the *principles* behind
it. He couldn't build an ion pump. She understood the problem. What if they asked her how the computers she used
in her simulations actually *worked*? Could she lay out the
circuitry? Did she have the vaguest idea how chips were
actually fabricated? No. She was just a user and could not
actually build one.

"Here."

Once again all heads turned, this time toward Jack. He
had scribbled something on the back of the paper that contained the residual gas spectrum. He pushed the paper toward Werner. "I took one apart once, just curious how it
was built," he said, sounding decidedly *uncurious* at the
moment.

Werner took the paper.

"The pump itself is very simple—all you need to do is
ionize the gas in your vacuum chamber, let it get trapped
in the magnetic and electric fields of the pumping elements
that I've sketched, and then the ions get accelerated and
buried in a highly reactive layer of titanium."

Werner nodded and pointed to another spot on the paper.

"I've also sketched out the circuit diagram for the power
supply that you'll need to run it—nothing fancy—just a
five-thousand-volt transformer, a full-wave rectifier, and a
bit of control circuitry that can be built with your tube
technology. This pump should eliminate your hydrocarbon
problems and improve your vacuum level by at least two
orders of magnitude."

Werner grinned and passed the paper past Horst and to
the man seated next to him. Horst just barely managed a
smile. "Next item," said Werner, looking back at Jack.
"Can you tell us anything about how one might cool the
radio-frequency coils which drive our electron beam?"

Jack nodded. "I'll need some more paper," he said.

SECTION II
CHAPTER 8

"Don't you understand," said an exasperated Tesla to Jack. *"Von Heflin* pushed an entire Panzer division through Detroit. Now nothing stands between him and Chicago, except for a garrison at South Bend, consisting of a squad of old men and boys that couldn't even bring in last year's corn crop, much less stop a German division." Tesla waved his stick-like arms over his head for emphasis. "We are running out of time. We must get those new beam installations up and running at Gary, Indiana, or else we will lose Chicago!"

Jack shrugged and slumped further back in his wicker chair. He had been to Detroit many times and didn't feel particularly bad about the prospects of a German division having moved through it, even though he knew full well that this Detroit was not his Detroit. In his mind, Detroit was just the sort of town that deserved to be flattened by a division of Germans.

"You've got to talk to him," said Tesla, as he pointed across the yard at Anthony, who stood waist deep in a large hole that he had been digging for the last three days. A complex series of mounds and ridges of excavated dirt encircled the hole, forming a pattern, which Jack was certain held some meaning to Anthony. "Only he can solve the field equations for the electric fields in the focus grids of the new beam units. There isn't time for us to actually *calculate* them!"

Jack looked away from Anthony, who was methodically lifting a trowel of dirt from the hole and carefully depositing it on top of a little mound that was shaped like a birthday cake. He looked back at Tesla. The expression on the old man's face was a mixture of fright and anger—fright at the prospect of having no one who could mentally chunk through what must literally be millions of calculations to determine the field lines in his newest beam, and anger at having to ask him for help.

Jack smiled. Even if he wanted to help Tesla, which he did not, he doubted that he had any more control over Anthony than anyone else did. Out of his wheelchair, Anthony now seemed to have his own agenda. It was still not clear what had happened.

But Jack had a theory.

He believed that Anthony had too much *conscious* control over his body. A normal person did not have to consciously command muscles and tendons into action in order to move his arm. Hard-wiring in the brain automatically translated desire into action. But Anthony was wired differently. Jack believed that what allowed him to apparently control chaos, to see cause and effect where others only saw randomness, also interfered with his brain's ability to *unconsciously* operate his body. When Anthony tried to move his arm, he consciously attempted to control all the physical processes for that action. And that was nearly impossible, requiring processes far more complex than transforming a mound of paper and strings into a cube, or generating a whirlwind by whistling. But in extreme moments of surprise or anger, his brain became focused elsewhere, and the unconscious processes were not interfered with. The shock of hitting the concrete floor had in essence rebooted his brain's automatic systems.

At least that was Jack's theory.

"Are you listening to me?" insisted Tesla. "Detroit is gone!"

Jack blinked, refocused, realizing only then that he had drifted off, almost hypnotized as he watched Anthony methodically moving dirt out of the hole.

"The field equations!"

"Can't help you out there, Nicky," answered Jack, sounding not all that upset about it. "It seems that your superboy has other ideas, other little projects which he finds more important."

"He has no choice!" yelled Tesla, who turned away from

Jack and began a slow, old-man march across the lawn, toward Anthony.

It took little effort on Jack's part to get up, trot across the lawn, and place himself between Tesla and Anthony. Tesla stopped, startled, and back-stepping, almost tripped over his own feet. "The Russians will destroy us!"

Jack shrugged, knowing that might well be true. In this world the Russians might destroy the Americans. In some other picoverse, it might be the Americans destroying the Russians, while in a third, it might be the Chinese destroying both the Russians and the Americans. It all seemed to make such little difference.

Since the pipe had almost flattened him, since he had lost all control of himself and flipped Anthony out of his wheelchair, nothing seemed to really matter. He just found himself going through the motions, answering their questions, the only vague pleasure he felt coming when he watched Horst slowly turn and roast on the spit as the scientists relied more and more on him. It seemed that the world-famous twenty-first-century physicist was severely challenged when it came to turning a screwdriver. "Leave him alone," said Jack, trying to sound fierce about it. "You've had him long enough, and now he deserves some time to himself."

"The Russians are coming!"

Jack stepped forward, having grown suddenly very tired of this shrieking old man. "Someone's *always* coming, you goddamned idiot." For effect, Jack waved his plaster-encased right arm at him.

Tesla back-stepped again, afraid that Jack might lunge at him, possibly even lose control as he had with Anthony several days earlier. Turning, he trotted away as quickly as his arthritic old legs would take him. "The Russians *are* coming!" he shouted once more.

Jack ignored him, not caring if he got the last word, and walked back to his chair, sat down, and resumed his vigil over Anthony. What was it that the boy was building, with all those mounds and ramparts?

Someone touched his right shoulder.

He quickly turned in his chair, ready to lash out. Katie stood there, with her hand still on his shoulder. "Thank you," she said, and nodded in the direction in which Tesla had retreated.

Jack shook his head and turned back around in his seat. "The least I could do, the least I owe the boy after I dumped him onto the cement." Jack had replayed that scene in his head countless times in the past days. And each time he could feel the fear all over again. There was something about what had happened to him, the physical translation from the gangway and back into the office, that had frightened him so badly, it had somehow damaged him inside.

He'd tossed a crippled boy onto the pavement.

But as disgusted with himself as he was, he knew that if that fear overwhelmed him again, he might well do something else horrible to Anthony, or to anyone else that caused him to feel that way. He didn't want to turn around and look at Katie, because he knew not even she would be safe if that overwhelming terror smothered him again.

She sat down next to him, and reaching out, put her hands gently on his knees. "I don't know what's happened to you, Jack," she said slowly and thoughtfully. "I love you, but I will not stay with you, will not let Anthony stay here, if you ever do anything to hurt him again. Even if I only *think* that you are about to hurt him."

Jack understood and nodded. He was not so sure if their positions were reversed if he would be so generous.

"What has happened to you, Jack?"

Jack shook his head. "I don't know," he said, knowing just how pathetically inadequate those words were, knowing that there was no way he could express the fear he felt.

Katie nodded and smiled at him. "Let's change the subject then. Tell me when you can, explain it to me when you understand it." She pointed her index finger at him. "So I'm only going to say this one last time—if you ever raise a hand against Anthony again, you will pull back a bloody stump. I don't care what is going on inside of you, how frightened, confused, temporarily insane, or pissed off you are—you will *not* hurt Anthony."

"Understood," said Jack.

Katie sat back in her own chair and, intertwining her fingers, rested her hands on her stomach. "I've got a little problem, Jack. While you and Horst have been at the lab tightening bolts and doing whatever testosterone things that you men do in the lab, I've been going over Werner and Ernest's papers. I'm trying to get a feel for the physics behind the intratemporal wormhole they hope to generate."

"Checking up on them?" asked Jack. He did nothing to hide the surprise in his voice. These were two of the greatest physicists of the twentieth century.

Katie smiled and nodded. "I guess so," she said. "The two have painted a very pretty picture of how to generate and stabilize the wormhole between this picoverse and Alpha's. The math is sweet, they really make it sing." She stopped talking.

"But," said Jack, prompting her.

"What they haven't bothered to explain to the rest of you, and I suspect not even to the president, is that the solution they generate for their desired wormhole is only the most *probable* solution to the field equations controlling the wormhole's generation."

Jack nodded, actually not all that surprised. This was quantum mechanics, where probabilities were the only things that really existed, where nothing was a total certainty, not even where one might be standing—on a gangway, or inside a control room.

"There are a whole host of other solutions, most of which do not result in the generation of a wormhole between picoverses, but the actual merging of adjacent picoverses—like isolated bubbles drifting together, touching, and then merging into a combined structure."

"Wouldn't the effect be the same then?" asked Jack. "If they merge, wouldn't that in essence just represent a portal between the two picoverses?"

Katie nodded. "But the difference between creating a

wormhole between the two picoverses and this merging, is that in the region of the merging, only a *single* region of the original picoverses will survive—the dominant, the one with the greatest probability of being *real*.

Jack was confused, and his expression let Katie know it.

"I'll bottom line it for you, Jack. There is a probability that when they flip the switch on the Sonomak, this chunk of Colorado that we find ourselves in, and the chunk of Colorado that exists in Alpha's picoverse, will fight it out for supremacy, only the most probable one surviving, and then becoming the *only* one. We might find ourselves on the losing end of that equation, suddenly not existing, with a chunk of space-time from Alpha's picoverse replacing us."

"What?" asked Jack. "And you think they know this, that Werner and Ernest actually know that this might happen?"

"They must know," she said. "It's right there in their equations. What they don't know, and what is impossible to figure out without a lot of very heavy duty computing power, is just what the relative probabilities are. I'd say that it looks very unlikely that the merging solution would manifest itself, but it's hard to tell without running a lot of numbers, something which just can't be done with the available technology."

Jack felt the fear rising up inside again.

They were playing with things that they just weren't ready to understand. At that moment he believed he understood what had happened to Einstein, why the man had escaped into some sort of fear-based religion. Jack blinked. He had an idea. "You'd be able to get a better grasp of this with some decent supercomputing power?" he asked.

"Oh, ya," said Katie. "But that just isn't going to happen, not here when the best that they've got is vacuum tubes and these big clunky mechanical calculators."

"I know of a supercomputer," he said.

"What are you talking about?" she said.

"Einstein's *wife*," he answered. "She's a machine, a device. We've seen what Alexandra has been capable of—we had the direct experience when she interfaced with us." He tapped his forehead, at the point where Alexandra had made direct contact with him. "Nadia Einstein should have the same capabilities—perhaps we can use her to run the numbers, to get a better handle on the probabilities."

Katie nodded. "But why would she help us? And even if for some reason she were willing to help, I doubt that Einstein would let her."

Jack remembered what Alpha had told them, about Alexandra's directives being rebooted when she found herself in this world, about doing whatever had to be done to stop humans from tinkering with space-time. If that were true, then she might be more than willing to help if the result would be to show why the Sonomak *shouldn't* be turned on. "If her programming has held, she may have no choice but to help us."

Ernest had watched the encounter between Jack and Tesla. He could not figure out what drove Jack, and what the obviously complex relationship was that he had with Anthony. But he had stepped between Tesla and the boy, and for Ernest, at the moment, that was enough.

After Jack and Katie had left, Ernest had continued to watch Anthony through the big bay window of the house. He watched for nearly a half hour, trying to figure out just what the boy was doing. Ernest felt his head nod, without really understanding why he was nodding. Then he realized what had been troubling him. Anthony had been in the wheelchair for years, but within a matter of days he was capable of shoveling dirt and digging a hole nearly chest deep. That should have been impossible. His unused muscles should have been atrophied to the point where he wouldn't be able to stand, even if his brain allowed him to stand. For years Anthony had barely moved.

Except when asleep.

All night he would thrash about, arms and legs flailing, as if he were running, or fighting off some unseen terror. At least that is what Ernest *had* thought. Now he was not so sure. Perhaps a part of Anthony, a part that was only there when asleep, knew that his body needed the exercise, knew that a time would come when he would *need* that body.

Ernest grinned. All that really mattered was that Anthony seemed to be on the road to recovery. And with that thought, he opened up the glass door and walked outside, moving toward Anthony. "Nice hole you've got there," said Ernest, as he neared the hole, looking down at the sweating boy, marveling at his red-flushed, dirt-streaked face. "Mind if I sit?"

Anthony straightened up. His back hurt. His back had often hurt; years of sitting in the wheelchair had cramped the muscles so that there had been no comfortable way to sit. But this pain was different. It was the pain of sore muscles that had been used too much. It was a good pain.

"Interesting," said Ernest. He swept his hand over the hole.

"Care to make a guess?" asked Anthony. "What do you think it means?"

Ernest gave the mounds a quick glance and then focused his attention on Anthony, knowing that the answer to this riddle did not lie in the little piles of dirt, but in the boy himself. Ernest looked into his crystal-blue eyes for a clue. He now suspected the answer, had already guessed at it as he had watched Anthony from the window. But from the boy's eyes he saw the answer—he knew for sure.

He almost laughed.

"Well," he said, looking away from Anthony and at the piles of dirt. "If I were one of your esteemed colleagues, the honorable Mr. Gris or Mr. Tesla, I might conjecture that these mounds represent the null points for the field diagram describing some fearsome beam weapon, or perhaps some higher dimensional atomic landscape projected upon our pathetic three-dimensional reality."

Anthony nodded, trying to look serious, but not quite able to control the grin that tugged at the corners of his mouth.

"But me, being a simple sort, with the soul of a Midwest wheat farmer, I might not see such intricate and devious patterns. I suppose that I might guess that these little piles of dirt randomly strewn about are nothing more than little piles of dirt randomly strewn about, deposited there by a boy who just happens to be digging a hole for no other purpose than to be digging a hole."

Anthony smiled.

And Ernest smiled back. Had he known that all the boy had needed for this miraculous transformation was to be dumped from his wheelchair, he would have done it himself years ago. The smile faded from his face. *No.*

He somehow sensed that was not his job, his role to play. But he also sensed that his time would be coming soon enough.

SECTION II

CHAPTER 9

"My husband is not here," said Nadia Einstein. She did not look at Jack or Katie, but down at her own feet.

"We know," said Jack. They had waited across the street for nearly an hour, hiding behind a thick stand of pines, for Einstein to leave his apartment. The creator of general relativity, a man who now led tens of thousands in some sort of doomsday cult, lived in a small, nondescript apartment building—second floor corner.

"We've come to see you," said Katie.

Nadia shook her head and stepped back, starting to close the door. "My husband is not here," she said as the door closed shut.

Jack rapped at the door. "We think that it might be dangerous to turn on the Sonomak."

The door reopened, just a crack. "Of course it is dangerous," said Nadia. "God will condemn us for our arrogance, sentence us all to Hell."

Jack sighed, losing patience and then pushed on the door, but could not get it to budge. He put his shoulder against it and dug his feet into the green hallway carpeting. Still he could not get the door to budge. "Drop the religious zealot act," he said through the crack in the door. "We know all about the directives under which you are operating; know full well what the Makers want you to do." He waited, still putting pressure against the door, hoping he hadn't overplayed his hand. Seconds crawled by, and Jack was suddenly not so certain of what Alpha had told him.

"Stop pushing," said Nadia.

Jack sighed in relief and straightened up as the door opened, exposing a darkened room and Nadia's shadowed outline, quickly back-stepping from the open doorway. Jack and Katie stepped in, and Katie closed the door behind her.

Jack made a quick survey of the room. He imagined that most prison cells were more lavishly furnished than this room. It was intended as a living room, but it appeared to have been turned into a general-purpose living space, with hardwood floors, dulled white walls, and a beamed ceiling made of pine. In the far corner was a woven mat with two neatly folded blankets on it. In the other corner was a small steel desk overflowing with papers, opened books, and a wild assortment of colored papers and strings, bound up and twisted in all sorts of geometrical shapes. Next to the desk was a large floor-to-ceiling chalkboard, leaning against the wall. Beside it stood a stepladder, which was obviously needed to reach the upper portion of the board. The chalkboard was totally covered in a dense scrawl of Greek symbols and equations.

The details of those equations were not immediately obvious to Jack. But he could pick out enough, sense the flow and rhythm of the math to understand what Einstein was working on—picoverse mechanics—the relationship between energy, time flow, and spatial curvature in a picoverse.

Jack looked at Katie, who had also been studying the chalkboard. They nodded to each other, both realizing that not only had Nadia been putting on an act, but so had Einstein. What covered that chalkboard did not look suitable for next Sunday's sermon.

Nadia sat down in the center of the room, directly on the hardwood floor. "Why should I help you?" she asked.

Jack smiled as he sat. "Katie is concerned that the possibility exists that firing the Sonomak will result in a collapse of this universe," he said, hiding nothing, hoping that being as candid as possible would be the best approach. "I believe that this is something that you and the Makers would not like to see happen."

Nadia sneered and rolled her eyes. "Can you imagine *anyone* who would want to see it happen, *anyone* who would want to see an entire world snuffed out with the pull of a switch?"

They all knew who those *anyones* were.

"They've convinced themselves that it won't happen," said Katie. "They've become so focused on the physics and on winning the war that they haven't examined all the possible consequences of firing the Sonomak."

"So why come to me?" asked Nadia.

"In order to convince Werner and Ernest that it might be too dangerous to operate the Sonomak, I will need hard numbers to show them, simulations which demonstrate the danger," said Katie. "And I need massive *calculating* power to show that."

Nadia smiled and reaching up with her right hand tapped her forehead. "Massive calculating power?" she asked.

Katie nodded.

"I see little reason to bother," said Nadia. "I believe that my dear husband, Albert, has things well in hand." She waved a hand in the direction of the chalkboard. "His God speaks to him through those equations and tells him that the Sonomak must not be fired. Everyday he gets more followers, gains more converts. I have every confidence that he will be able to convince the president not to allow the Sonomak to be fired."

"And if he can't?" asked Jack.

Again Nadia reached up and touched her forehead. "The Makers will see that it won't happen. If Albert fails then the Makers will show me the way, will unveil to me other methods to be used to stop the Sonomak."

"How can you be so sure?" asked Jack.

"Isn't it obvious?" asked Nadia.

"Isn't *what* obvious?" asked Jack.

"Humans," said Nadia with a sigh. "Has a collapse of picoverses yet occurred, or have any of these wondrous wormholes appeared?" she asked.

"Of course not," said Katie. "The Sonomak has not yet been fired."

Jack blinked, and in the space of that blink understood the real intent of Nadia's question. He turned to Katie. "By the time Alpha had tossed us into *this* picoverse, how many *others* had he generated?" he asked.

Katie thought for a moment. "At least a dozen," she said.

Jack nodded. "At least a dozen, and possibly more after we were gone. Most if not all of those represent earths that are far in advance of this one—some probably existing at points in time well into the twenty-first century, perhaps even beyond it."

Katie suddenly understood. "And with their technology they should have little difficulty building the type of Sonomak that could generate wormholes between picoverses. It should almost be trivial. But they haven't done it."

"They haven't done it, because they haven't been allowed to do it," said Nadia. "A version of me exists in each of those worlds. The Makers have given us the power to do whatever is necessary to see that *you*," she said, as she pointed a finger at both of them, "and those like you don't tamper with the fabric of the universe. If necessary, the entire planet, this whole universe, will be destroyed before I let that happen here. The Makers will show me how, if it becomes necessary."

Jack believed her.

The fact that none of the other picoverses had made contact with this world was more than enough to convince him that what she said was true.

"Do you want to die?" asked Katie.

"No," said Nadia. "I am more than willing to die, but it is not my desire."

"Then why not help us?" asked Katie, not as convinced as Nadia was in the inevitable success of Einstein. If he failed and there were no other options, then Nadia's solution might kill them just as the picoverse collapse would. "You've got nothing to lose. If Einstein stops the Sonomak, then you win. But if he doesn't, and I can show through simulations that operating the Sonomak is just too risky, then that gives you another way to win."

Nadia said nothing, but stared at her.

"Perhaps you have more in common with Werner and Ernest than you'd like to admit," said Jack. "They are so convinced in how they see the future unfolding that they've blinded themselves to all other possibilities. Isn't that just what you're doing?"

Nadia heard him, but only a small part of her was actually paying attention. She was running at her maximum rate, the room around her still, Jack's words transformed into a low frequency hum that required only the smallest part of her mind to pay attention to. The possibilities flowed out before her, as she examined the nearly infinite number of pathways and critical junctures. She dropped back to humanlike speed. "You are correct. Albert no longer needs me. He can complete his mission alone. I might be much more effective operating *within* the inner circle."

"What?" said Jack. Something in the way that Nadia had suddenly tensed her shoulders, in the way she clenched her jaw, told him that something was wrong. "Katie?" he asked, starting to move toward her.

Katie waved him back, without actually looking at him, keeping focused on Nadia.

Nadia tensed, all the muscles in her face spasming, her eyes rolling back in their sockets.

"No!" screamed Jack, now certain that something *was*

wrong. He reached for Katie, had one hand around her right arm, and almost had time to pull her away. But he was not fast enough. A glistening fiber erupted from Nadia's forehead, embedding itself in Katie's forehead. Katie stiffened, her arms and legs straightening, her head whipping back and forth as her neck twitched and joints along her backbone popped loudly. She lurched across the floor, looking like a fish that had been pulled from the water and then left to flip-flop in the bottom of the boat. More glassy filaments erupted from Nadia's forehead, at first just a couple, and then within a matter of seconds, what looked to Jack to be dozens, possibly hundreds, a glistening spiderweb connecting the two women. The glassy bundles were driven not into Katie's forehead, but directly into her eyes.

Jack knew exactly what Nadia was doing. She was transferring herself *into* Katie—gaining access to what she had called the *inner circle*, by taking Katie's body.

He knew that what he was seeing was the way Alexandra had moved from generation to generation, through four million years of Earth's history. Like a parasite she would pass from host to host, and with each passing she would modify her victim, eradicating everything and transforming the person's body into a superhuman shell that would serve her needs.

She was *erasing* Katie.

"No!" Jack leapt up and jumped at Nadia, hands held out, ready to grab onto the bundle of fibers sprouting from her forehead and forcibly pull them out. He did not quite reach her.

Brilliant blue flash.

Every nerve in his body overloaded, muscles twitching, joints popping, heartbeat thrown into a chaotic race. He sensed motion, a small part of him realizing that he flew through the air and then abruptly came to a halt against something hard and unyielding. He opened his eyes, not quite able to focus. His left cheek was against the floor. Across the room sat Nadia, no longer flesh and bone, but a person-like thing constructed out of angular slabs of glass, with the bundle of fibers still protruding from her forehead, the gossamer wires whipping about like angry snakes, their far ends still buried in Katie's eyes.

Jack slowly pushed himself up, not able to feel his hands or feet, a buzz like angry hornets filling his ears. He blinked. And he could see Nadia. She had not really been transformed. She was encased in what looked like a slowly rotating cloak of shattered glass, which was distorting her image.

But Jack knew it was not glass. He'd felt it, had been expelled from it like a drop of cold water dancing off a red-hot skillet. Jack knew that Nadia was wrapped in a cocoon of altered space-time. She was no longer in this room, might have not even been in this universe. Jack knew that there was no way to reach her, no way to penetrate that barrier. But he stood and stumbled forward, his right hand reaching out. He touched the distorted region of space directly in front of Nadia's face.

Brilliant blue flash.

For an instant, Jack felt himself fly once again across the room, nerves frying, muscles spasming. But he also felt himself continue to push forward, his fingers sinking into something impossibly cold, impossibly hot, numbing, and at the same time filling him with such searing pain that it was impossible to even scream.

He penetrated the barrier.

His fingers touched Nadia's forehead, and then passed through skin and bone, pushing directly into a brain that felt like wet snow.

Nadia screamed.

Jack hit the far wall of the room, losing consciousness as his head bounced off the wooden floor.

Horst grimaced as he took another gulp of the bitter beer. "Rocky Mountain pure," he mumbled to himself, suspecting the water that had made this beer came from a rusty tap in the back of the bar and not from the melting snow packs to the west. But beer was beer. He took another big mouthful, forced it down, and plopped the now-empty mug against the bar, while motioning the bartender for another.

There was no response.

The bartender was looking toward him, but not at him. "Beer," said Horst. He lifted the empty mug and shook it at the bartender. "Before this little universe rolls up on itself." The bartender backed up, and pulling a liquor soaked rag from his apron, began to swipe at the bar, rearranging bits of pretzels and eggshells. "Beer," said Horst, doing nothing to hide the annoyance in his voice.

"Two beers."

Horst half turned, hoping that whoever had come up behind him was not from the lab. He didn't want to see any of them.

"Good morning," said Einstein. With a nod of his head, he motioned to the barstool next to Horst. "May I join you, *Professor*?"

Horst nodded, finding himself unable to speak. It was taking his full concentration to keep his jaw from hanging slack and not falling off the barstool. *Albert Einstein.*

"Never too early for a *good* beer," said Einstein. He sat down next to Horst, reached for the beer the bartender had just pushed before him, and, picking it up, took a timid sip and quickly sat the beer back down. "The concept of brewing is still alien to this side of the Atlantic."

Horst didn't respond, overwhelmed by the surrealistic reality of sitting in this bar, listening to Albert Einstein complain about beer.

Reaching within his black tunic, Einstein pulled out a slender silver case, dropped it to the bar, popped it open, and removed a cigarette, which he pushed into the left corner of his mouth. The bartender lit it, Einstein took a deep drag, and then expelled the smoke slowly through his nostrils. "*They* treat you like a dog—a rather stupid dog."

"Who?" asked Horst, making a sound like a frightened owl.

"Werner and Ernest, of course. So full of themselves, so arrogant. Never would it occur to them that someone of

your stature, of your obvious intellect, would be invaluable
to their insane effort." Einstein flicked the cigarette, its ash
hitting the bar, and then pointed its amber tip at Horst.
"They rely on the other one, the one with the talent for
wrenches and the smearing of grease."

Horst smiled, suddenly feeling very comfortable, despite
who he was sitting with. "Jack has a way with hardware,"
said Horst, sounding gracious, having in the past few weeks
come to realize just how knowledgeable Jack was when it
came to the way that things *worked*. And he found that he
couldn't blame Jack for that. Werner and Ernest wanted the
machine built and had turned to who could best solve their
problems. Horst knew that if the situation were reversed, if
this Sonomak were his, and this were his time and place,
he would have done the same thing.

But that didn't mean he liked it. That was why he had
retreated to this bar.

"Quite the *mechanic*," said Einstein. He smiled and then
took another drag on his cigarette. "I suppose that I should
count my blessings that they have not involved you directly
in the project, not tapping into what must lie inside that
brain of yours."

Horst shrugged, not quite understanding where the conversation was going. Horst glanced at the white collar
around Einstein's throat and at the large brass cross that
hung from a chain draped around his neck. This was not
the Einstein he had met earlier, the deranged religious ma-
niac, the broken character that Werner and Ernest were so
quick to paint as a leader of a dangerous cult.

Einstein reached up to his collar in response to Horst's
glance and then bent forward, pushing his face up to
Horst's. "Appearances can be deceiving my friend," he
said. "Werner, Ernest, and this entire Sonomak insanity
need to be stopped. In a time of war, in a time of crisis,
logic, physics, ethics, all these things go by the wayside.
All that matters are the weapons that can be created, the
tools needed to destroy the godless heathens that wish to
destroy us. Werner and Ernest promised such weapons

through the implementation of their *new physics* and the Sonomak."

Horst simply nodded, although he still did not understand why Einstein was telling him this.

"I could not persuade the government or my fellow physicists of the folly of their effort. It was obvious to me that what had happened to this world was the direct consequence of a level of physics which should have never been accessed by man. But they would not listen. I was forced into the position of establishing an opposition force, using what resources were available, leveraging the fear engendered by finding ourselves no longer in our rightful universe."

Now Horst did understand.

"I am telling you this because I know that you understand." Einstein reached out and thumped Horst against the chest with the index finger of his right hand. "You are the creator of this world, the man with sufficient arrogance and physics, who without the slightest thought of potential consequences was so driven by his own ego, that an entire world was banished and left at the mercy of that amoral creature who is currently consuming this world."

Amoral creature.

Horst knew the one Einstein had to be referring to. "It was not my intent to harm anyone, to unleash Alexandra on this world. If I had known, I would have destroyed my own machine," said Horst. He realized for the first time that what he was saying was true.

"Hindsight is such a wonderful thing," said Einstein. "I am sure that if Werner and Ernest do not simply erase this entire world when they turn on their creation, that they too will lament their actions."

"And why are you telling me this?" asked Horst.

"Because you, more than anyone else in this world, or the world from which you've come, understand the consequences of the blind pursuit of physics, the potential disaster brought about when nothing matters but solving the problem, unraveling the mysteries which are best left alone."

Horst found himself nodding. He did understand.

"I cannot let this Sonomak reach operational status. I *will* not let it. If it cannot be stopped from within," he said, pointing at Horst, "then I will stop it by other means. I have many at my disposal." Reaching up, he ran a finger along his collar. "One never knows when an overhead crane may drop something on an unsuspecting soul," he said.

Horst nodded. Einstein had been behind Jack's "accident." For a moment Horst felt dizzy and tried to convince himself that the light-headedness was caused by beer on an empty stomach, and not by the concept of Albert Einstein as a would-be murderer.

"Even if I wanted to stop the Sonomak, what makes you think that I could?" asked Horst.

Einstein shook his head. "I don't know if you want to. I cannot guess what motivates one who has played with the lives of billions without giving it the slightest consideration. But if any humanity remains within you, then you will want to stop this madness, and you will find a way." Einstein stood. "Think about it, examine yourself and your actions, and realize that you have the opportunity to make *some* amends for what you have done." Turning, not waiting for a response, Einstein walked out of the bar.

Horst reached for his beer and took another long drink.

SECTION II
CHAPTER 10

"Wake up, Katie."

Katie not only heard the words, but could see them as well. They materialized in the darkness, each letter a glowing neon tube, spewing out all the colors of the rainbow, and even beyond, the infrared and ultraviolet, now visible, their colors understandable, but totally alien. The words hung before her, slowly rotating, spinning, three-dimensional and solid.

"Open your eyes."

Katie opened her eyes.

And she screamed. *No.* She tried to scream. But there was no response, her body not answering. The light that streamed into her eyes was far too intense, too rich, beyond a blinding whiteness, but transformed into something that felt almost metallic—all too solid, so full of content and information, that photons could not carry it—the nearly infinite atoms of a solid chunk of metal required, each atom an information bit, the onslaught pouring into her brain.

Click.

The metallic torrent swirled, deconvolving, images, ghosts, colors, all pulling apart, forming pattern, the incoming information being routed, selectively sampled, and then processed within the myriad discrete processing centers within her brain.

Coalescence.

Again she tried to scream, and again there was no response. She could not feel herself breathe, there was no detectable beating of her heart. She was not alive, but she knew that she was not dead. Her brain burned.

She could *see* Jack. A perfect ten-by-ten grid, consisting of one hundred different *views* had suddenly exploded across her field of vision. Each one was filled with an image of Jack. And each image was different. One image was of Jack in the deep infrared, a swirling halo of a heat signature about his head, while another image was nothing more than lines and planes, Jack's face reduced into a geometrical interpretation, something that was not quite three dimensional. And there were nearly a hundred others, all seen in different *lights*, the information being sucked down into a different region of her brain, all of it processed and accessed simultaneously.

Click.

Movement.

The images shifted, slowly at first, almost imperceptibly,

then sped up. An eyelid blinked. Muscles moved in a left cheek, sending a cascade of electrical signals up and down nerves in the left side of Jack's face. A cloud of expelled breath, moisture laden and full of carbon dioxide spewed from his nostrils.

Katie felt herself breathe, felt her heartbeat. And she knew that she had not been dead. She had simply been operating at her fastest possible speed, sucking down maximum information, her brain having slipped into a mode of observing under maximum resolution.

Katie shut her eyes. The hundred images of Jack vanished, swallowed, and Katie understood. What she was experiencing was something similar to what her Virtuals had offered her—multiple perspectives, multiple inputs, different signals and slices of reality that she could selectively sample. But unlike her Virtuals, which merely manipulated the input to her eyes, the change she was now experiencing was not with the input, but with her ability to manipulate the input, to operate simultaneously on a hundred different levels.

Nadia.

She remembered—the fibers penetrating her eyes and then dumping information. Not facts, not items in a catalog. The information pumped into her brain spoke directly to the neurons, even beyond them, to the chemistry, to the genes, to the fabric out of which her brain was built. And it enhanced it and turned it into something that it hadn't been before. The physical structure of her brain had been reengineered, getting ready for its *new inhabitant.*

Katie could sense that, had the faint recollection of Nadia flowing into her, over her, smothering her. And then the connection had been broken. Katie remained, but now in an alien place, in the *hardware* that her brain had been turned into. Years of wearing the Virtuals, the continual feed, the *multiple* feeds, had altered the way she perceived reality. And when this different way of seeing was merged with a physically restructured brain, the result was something much greater than the individual parts.

"You're awake," said Jack.

Katie nodded, managed to get her neck muscles to do what she wanted. She reopened her eyes and again faced the hundred different versions of Jack. But then she focused on only one of them, the image swelling before her, a single Jack almost instantly filling her view. She knew that the others were still there, being processed and analyzed below her awareness, but stored and cross-correlated in case she needed to access it later.

"How long?" she asked in a scratchy whisper, her throat sore and dry.

"Nearly a month," answered Jack.

She could see the relief in his expression and also the dark, baggy circles under his eyes. It had been a long month for him. "What happened to Nadia?"

Jack shook his head and then looked down at his right hand, the hand that had somehow passed through what couldn't be passed through and literally pulled Nadia's brain right out of her skull. "Dead." He did not elaborate, not knowing how to elaborate.

He had killed Nadia—snuffed the life out of a machine that should have been immortal. And now he was certain that in the same way that his hand had passed through the impenetrable barrier that had surrounded Nadia, *he* had been the one responsible for his translating back into the Sonomak's control room when the falling pipe had been about to smash him. His touch alone seemed capable of altering reality. It had been his touch that had reopened the wormhole to this world. And then there was the other thing he had done, the thing that he had no memory of, but which Ernest had described to him.

Juan Gris was dead. And Jack had killed him. Patton's warning about him had proved all too accurate.

He now accepted the fact that he had done these things. But that acceptance did not seem to bring him any closer to knowing *how* he had done them.

"Anthony?" asked Katie.

Jack swallowed and clenched his teeth. It was reflex. He

had wanted to keep the Anthony situation away from her for a bit, let her regain some of her strength first. "He's doing fine."

Katie could see in his face that there was more. She intended to push herself up, but found that she could barely move her arms to her sides. One of the many unconscious streams running through her mind rose up to a detectible level and explained that the full integration of mind and body were not yet complete, that several days would be required before she had full control over her body.

"But," she whispered. "I sense a *but* coming."

"The situation between Tesla and Anthony is not good. The Russians are poised to overrun Chicago, and now the president is putting direct pressure on Anthony to get him back to work helping Tesla complete work on the new weapons systems. But Anthony refuses to help him."

A part of Katie was pleased with that. But if the Russians were advancing, that meant Alexandra was advancing. They needed to stall Alexandra, to either escape or come up with a plan before she could make her move against them.

Jack knew that he couldn't keep the rest of it away from her, that she would quickly dig it out of him. "Anthony has been placed in protective custody," he said.

"What?" asked Katie.

"Actually, he's under arrest," said Jack.

This time Katie did manage to push herself up into a sitting position. "Get me my clothes." She tried to push her legs off the side of the bed.

Jack pushed her back, trying to pull the blanket back over her. "You've been in a coma for nearly a month. They don't have the equipment here to understand exactly what's happened to you, to look into your skull, but even without that, it is obvious that you've suffered significant trauma. You need to rest and *finish* healing."

"Clothes!" she shouted, pushing at him. "I need to get to Anthony."

"You need to rest! They need to run tests, try to understand just what's happened to you, and what we should do to make sure that you will fully recover."

"There is nothing wrong with me. I am recovered!"

Jack pushed her back, forcing her down against the bed, and reaching to his left, grabbed a mirror off the nightstand and held it up in front of her. "Look! We need to understand just what the hell is going on inside of you before you run out of the hospital, looking to break Anthony out of jail!"

Katie looked.

Her green eyes were gone, replaced by chunks of high-faceted crystal, each eye now resembling a huge diamond.

"Nadia did something to you, has possibly altered you right down to the genetic level for all we know. We need to understand that before we can let you out of the hospital."

Katie focused, reading her brain like a blueprint, giving commands, and letting her brain's operating systems, those that understood and controlled the chemistry of her body, implement those commands. Katie was certainly no biologist, did not understand how muscles functioned, how cells were fed energy, how electrical impulses raced up and down nerves. But she didn't have to understand—her body understood.

She placed her hand squarely in the center of Jack's chest and pushed him. He flew off the bed, his feet clearing the floor by several feet, and he hit the wall at the foot of her bed, bouncing from it, and landing spread-eagled, draped across the bottom of her bed. He shook his head, pushed himself up, and managed to stand.

Katie sat up, a part of her horrified at what she'd just done to Jack, but she sublimated those feelings. Nothing mattered at the moment except to get to Anthony. "You can help me Jack, or you can get out of my way. One way or another, I am going to Anthony."

Jack looked at her for a moment and took a half-breath, the pain that flared along his ribs keeping him from breathing any deeper, certain that within a couple of days that a handprint-shaped bruise would cover his chest. He knew he couldn't stop her. At best, he hoped that he could deflect her a bit so that what was already a bad situation did not become something far worse.

"I'll get your clothes," he said by way of surrender.

Katie pushed herself off the bed and managed to stand, though she had to hold on to the side of the bed for support. "He's just a boy," she said. "They've arrested him because he refused to help Tesla?"

Jack kept his back turned to her as he opened the dresser drawer where her clothes were kept. "No," he said, and then paused. "He's under arrest for murdering Juan Gris."

*Katie was exhausted. Despite the conscious link she now had be-*tween her mind and body, she could only push herself so hard, so fast. The damage done from an entire month in bed could not be willed away. She stopped halfway up the steps of the Boulder city jail, clinging to the metal handrail, and panted like an old dog that had tried to run down a rabbit.

Jack held her, one arm around her waist, and the other supporting her left arm. "Take it easy."

"*Easy*," she said, making it sound like an animal's snarl. "My son is in jail, accused of murder."

Jack winced, the expression on her face, the intensity of her diamond-like eyes, actually causing him pain.

"Katie!"

Jack and Katie looked up to see Horst bounding down the stairs, arms outstretched. "You're awake, you're walking!" he shouted, the tone of his voice filled with obvious disbelief.

Katie watched the expression of his face change from surprise, to shock, and then to one of forced compassion, the expression he used when trying to hide his fear. For just a moment he had looked at her eyes, focusing on them. She was certain that he had already known about her physical transformation, but *knowing* and *seeing* were two different things.

Stopping on the step above her, Horst reached down and wrapped his arms around her, while at the same time pushing Jack aside. "I'm so relieved that you're better, that you've woken. We need all the help we can get to get Anthony out of this predicament."

"Yes, all the help we can get," said a voice from behind Horst.

Katie shifted, looking past Horst. Einstein stood at the top of the stairs, looking down at her. She tensed, not knowing what to expect. Although it had not been her intent, she had shared in the responsibility of the death of his wife. But then she had to remind herself that Nadia had not really been his wife, had not even been human. She had been a device, nothing more than a piece of destroyed hardware built by the Makers.

"I apologize," said Einstein. He looked at her eyes.

Katie almost took a step back down the stairs. That was a response she had not expected.

"I thought I had her under control, had convinced her not to attempt another *migration* until I could rectify the present situation."

Katie looked up at Einstein, examined him in myriad spectrums and hues. *Arrogance*. He not only believed that he had been able to control Nadia, but that he really had the ability to stop the firing of the Sonomak. At that moment, Katie realized what a fool the greatest physicist in the world really was.

Nadia had been pulling *his* strings.

"I will do all in my power to see that your son is released," said Einstein in a much louder voice.

Katie pushed Horst aside and straightened up, letting go of the handrail. "And why should you care about my son?" she asked, doing nothing to hide the suspicion in her voice. She remembered quite clearly the equations sprawled across his chalkboard. "How will Anthony's release stop the Sonomak from being fired?" She was certain that stopping the machine was all that mattered to him.

"Please," said Einstein, offering up a pained expression.

"My only concern at the moment is your son's welfare."
He spread out his hands before him and then motioned to
the crowd that had gathered at the foot of the stairs beneath
them. "The boy is innocent. This is a conspiracy, a power
struggle. Juan Gris's death was caused by those blinded
men who believe that they know the mind of God and that
they have the power to alter the very fabric of space and
time!"

The crowd cheered.

"But we know the truth!" shouted Einstein. "They attempt to blame an innocent boy, one who would not aid
them in their evil and demented plans. Not only are these
godless men responsible for the death of a good and true
ally to both the truth and God's will, but now they attempt
to blame a child for their crimes."

Again the crowd cheered.

Einstein bounded down the stairs, surprising Katie by his
sudden movement. He wrapped her in a bear hug and
shouted over her shoulder at the crowd, "We will see the
boy freed!"

The crowd roared its approval.

Katie pushed Einstein back and moved past him, taking
the steps two at a time, pulling herself along the handrail.
"Don't use my son to further your *plans*," she said. "Whatever those plans *really* are."

She then turned to Horst. "Haven't you learned a damn
thing?" she asked, quickly glancing at Einstein and then
back to him. "Think about where your ass-kissing ways got
you with Alexandra, and now you're starting all over again
with this bastard."

"Katie!" shouted Horst, bending toward her. "You're
talking about Albert Einstein."

Katie pushed Horst aside and then grabbing back onto
the handrail continued to pull herself up the stairs. "Horst,
you're an idiot!" She didn't bother to turn around and look
at him.

•   •   •

Two guards in front, and two guards in back. Katie and Jack stood between them, all walking single file down the deserted cell block.

"No other prisoners?" asked Katie. The question was not an idle one. Her brain raced. Pieces of a puzzle. This cell block had been emptied. *Four* guards to escort them. Katie could think of only one explanation. They were afraid of Anthony. There had to be more to this than simply the murder of Juan Gris. Katie stopped walking, and Jack almost ran into her. She turned to face him, not quite knowing what she was about to say. "I need to see him *alone*, Jack," she said.

Jack simply nodded. "I understand," he said.

Katie smiled, certain that Jack did *not* understand. It was not so much that she needed to see Anthony alone, but that she needed to see him without Jack. A nearly infinite number of images flashed through Katie's head, each one clear and sharp. One of those images was of Jack tipping over Anthony's wheelchair. And now there were several unanswered questions to go along with that image. How had Jack stopped Nadia—how had she been killed? And there was something about the murder of Juan Gris that Jack was not telling her. She could sense it, see it in the way he clenched his jaw, in the dark circles under his eyes. He was keeping something from her. At that moment, she did not trust Jack.

"Come back with me," said the last guard in line, and reaching out, he grabbed onto Jack's arm and guided him back.

"Call me if you need me," said Jack, certain that he would not be called. As he followed the guard, a wave of relief rolled over him. It was only at that moment that he realized that he did not want to go to Anthony's cell, that he didn't want to be anywhere near it.

"You coming?" asked the guard.

Jack nodded. He was not needed in the cell. He was certain that Ernest could handle whatever was about to happen.

•   •   •

"Anthony didn't do it," said Ernest.

Anthony's cell was at the very end of the block, an extra large cell, with its own toilet and shower, where Anthony could be held indefinitely without any reason to be removed. The significance of that was not lost on Katie. In light of the fact that the entire cell block had been emptied this did not surprise her. But what did surprise her was that Anthony was not alone in the cell. Ernest was there with him, sitting closely to him on the bottom bunk of a three-tier bed. At first Katie was going to ask that Ernest leave.

But she didn't.

Ernest was protecting Anthony. She was somehow certain of that.

"Did you hear me?" asked Ernest. "I said that he didn't do it."

Katie heard him, could not help but hearing him, finding herself now incapable of *not* hearing anything. But she did ignore him. She sat next to Anthony, holding his right hand in her lap, stroking it, staring into his frightened face.

The face of a boy.

"It will be all right," she said. Looking at Anthony, reaching out and lifting up his chin so that he faced her, she forced him to look at her. "I will get you out of here."

"He didn't do it," said Ernest for a third time.

Katie turned in the seat, but did not let go of Anthony's hand. "I know he didn't do it," said Katie, not needing anything as trivial as facts to assure her of that. "But how do *you* know that he didn't do it?"

"We were downstairs," said Ernest. "Jack and I. We were playing chess. It was so quiet, when all of a sudden Jack jumped up from his seat, knocking over the chessboard, and he looked up at the ceiling and started shouting at it." Ernest paused, and took a deep breath, reliving the moment. "He was screaming *stop*, over and over again, while staring up at the ceiling."

"Stop what?" asked Katie.

"I didn't know, couldn't see anything that needed to be

stopped. He was just shouting up at the ceiling. And then he waved his arms." Again he paused, questioning his memory, knowing that what he remembered was correct, but still having trouble believing it. "The ceiling rippled, flowed like something molten, a wave rising up and racing across the *solid* surface. That was when I heard the crash, actually felt the house shudder as something hit a wall on the floor above us."

"Gris," said Katie.

Ernest nodded. "At the moment of the crash, Jack collapsed, hitting the floor. I could see he wasn't hurt, so I ran upstairs to see what had happened. That was where I found Gris embedded in the wall, and Anthony standing behind him, trying to pull him out."

"*Jack* killed Gris?" she said.

Ernest nodded.

"Then why is Anthony even in here? What did the police say when you told them that it was Jack that killed Gris?"

Ernest sighed, and sat back in the bunk, leaning against the wall. "I didn't tell them. I let them think that Anthony had done it."

Katie blinked several times, not believing what she was hearing, then looked at Anthony who was nodding his head. "Why?" asked Katie.

"Two reasons," said Ernest. "Do you really think that anyone would believe me if I told them what I'd seen Jack do?"

"If you can't convince them, then I will!"

Ernest ignored what she just said. "And the second reason is that Anthony is in danger. *Gris tried to kill him.* And because I don't know *why* Gris tried to kill him, I can't be certain who else might try, now that Gris is dead. As long as they believe that Anthony is some kind of superhuman killer who can embed someone in a wall, they will keep him isolated in the cell block, where I can make certain that no one else can get to him."

Katie looked around the cell. She'd already seen it, registered and stored every aspect of it within a brain that was incapable of missing the slightest detail. But she had not examined the images that filled her brain.

Two toothbrushes on the lip of the sink.

Two footlockers at the foot of the bunk beds.

Two metal chairs pushed up against the desk on the far side of the cell.

"You've been staying in here with him," she said. "Keeping him safe."

Ernest nodded.

"Gris tried to kill Anthony, and Jack stopped him?" she asked. "But why didn't he tell me, why didn't he explain things to me."

Ernest looked down the deserted cell block. "Your hospital room, the cars, all of them, have listening devices. And then there are the spies."

"What?" said Katie. "Spies?"

"The Soviets, our own government, the ones that report only to Werner and others still that report to Tesla. We couldn't take a chance letting you know. In here, in this concrete bunker we are isolated. I have enough resources at my disposal to ensure that we can't be listened to here."

Katie nodded, the mental gears in her head shifting quickly and smoothly.

Jack had saved Anthony.

Katie turned back to Anthony. "What was Gris trying to do to you? Why did Jack kill him?"

Anthony reached up with his right hand and rubbed his forehead, as if that would stir a forgotten memory. "Something like what Nadia Einstein tried to do to you," he said. Anthony continued to rub his forehead.

Katie *looked* at him, using her full abilities, her full eyesight. She could see the almost-faded bruise on his forehead, the pinprick mark where the needle struck. And she knew. Pieces fell together.

Juan Gris was not Juan Gris.

Another *device*, another one of the Makers' observers. Katie shook her head. She could see Gris, slumped in his wheelchair, wheezing, blue-tinted eyes staring at her. And then she knew what he was, *who* he was.

Quinn.

It was the only possibility. In the same way that Alexandra had been trapped in this world, so was a version of Quinn, in this case in the guise of Juan Gris. But that did not explain what Jack had done, how Jack had done it. But that would have to wait—there were far more pressing matters. "And now?" asked Katie. "What is your plan now?"

"We have no plan beyond keeping Anthony safe and finishing the Sonomak so we can escape."

"Finish the Sonomak," she said, having almost forgotten about it, about the real reason behind everything that was happening. "We still don't know if it is safe, don't know if firing it will result in a picoverse collapse."

"Jack's told me about your concerns, and for the past month I've gone over the equations again and again," he said while pointing over to the desk. "And I think the probability of such a collapse is statistically insignificant."

"But you don't know for certain," she said.

"We can't know for *certain*," he said. "We don't have the calculating abilities to push that statistical insignificance to a statistical impossibility."

Katie stepped back, pulled out one of the metal chairs and slowly sat.

"We do now." She started to reach up toward her forehead and then stopped as she saw Anthony, sitting across from her on the edge of the lower bunk, suddenly stiffen, arms and legs snapping straight out as joints locked. Thrown right off the bed, he hit the floor, twitching, bouncing.

Ernest leapt for him, pinned him down, wrapped his arms around him, and cradled the back of his head with his hands so he wouldn't crack his skull against the concrete slab.

Katie fell from her chair, as the floor seemed to tilt beneath her, and started to crawl toward Anthony and Ernest. They were only a few feet away, but she could not quite reach them. They seemed to be moving away from her.

Not moving.

Distorting. The air between them shimmered, twisted, started to fold in on itself. Wind howled, her eardrums popped, and Katie was pushed back, slammed against the side of the metal chair she had just been seated on. She blinked, strained to see, tripping repeatedly through the hundred different ways she could see. And except for a quickly fading infrared glow on the slab where Anthony and Ernest had been lying, there was no indication that they had ever been in the cell.

"Anthony!" screamed Katie, now all alone in the cell.

SECTION II
CHAPTER 11

Leather slapped against marble, Alexandra's boot steps echoing loudly as she marched across the stadium-like anti-office leading to Stalin's stronghold. She breathed slowly, deeply, concentrating, trying to clear her mind of the anger that nearly consumed her.

Quinn.

She missed a step. The secretary behind a behemoth steel desk at the far end of the anti-office looked up in response to the break in cadence of her echoing footsteps, squinted at her through his rimless glasses, and then lowered his head, reburying it in the pile of papers that nearly overflowed the desk.

When she thought of all the time and effort it had taken to break Quinn away from Nadia, it took all her control to simply not scream. She had been so certain that Nadia no longer had any influence over Quinn, that in the guise of Juan Gris he had been working for her, pushing the boy, molding him, turning him into something that she could use in case Heisenberg and Lawrence couldn't complete their Sonomak on time—complete it at the exact moment the Soviets swarmed over Boulder. But Gris had been working for Nadia all along, feeding her information.

And now both Nadia and Quinn were dead.

She tried not to dwell on that. Nadia had been an *immortal*, exactly like her, her duplicate in this world. Her death cut just too close to the bone, made her face the reality that even an immortal was not *infinitely* immortal.

But even dead she had not been totally out of the way. With her death the Makers had apparently shifted their primary focus onto Quinn, permitting him a more active, direct mode of intervention. She was certain that had he managed to eliminate Anthony, he would have quickly proceeded on to Heisenberg and Lawrence. No more subtle interventions, just simple and direct elimination.

But he'd been stopped, just as Nadia Einstein had.

Jack.

This was entirely his fault. He was a random element, an unexpected, nonlinear component that had ruined all her plans. His presence had accelerated the American's Sonomak program, unlocked Anthony from his self-imposed exile, something the lying Quinn had said could not be done, and had then eliminated both Nadia and Quinn.

Who was Jack? How could he have done all this? And most importantly, what was his agenda?

"Damn," she said.

The situation was now totally out of her control, now randomly lurching along, unfolding in ways that she couldn't predict or see. She had to regain control of the flow of events, accelerate her own schedule, and take the Sonomak before the Makers could make another move.

Right now.

Calm down, she thought. *Focus,* she told herself, concentrating on her next step, which would right this situation, putting her back on the path of escape from this world and forever out of the reach of the Makers.

The Americans had test-fired the Sonomak. They were probably only days away from firing the thing at full power, only days away from generating the wormhole that would lead out of this suffocating little prison.

And she was not ready.

The Soviets and Germans were still nearly five hundred miles away from Boulder, bogged down along a front that ran from Chicago to St. Louis. Ground troops, jets, and missiles, all pressed up against the line that Tesla and the boy had built.

Time had run out.

"I need to see Comrade Stalin immediately," said Alexandra, coming to a stop before the desk.

The secretary slowly looked up, reshuffling several papers before he did so. Leaning his head back, he peered up at Alexandra and then back down at his desk. His ratlike nose actually twitched from side to side, as if he were on the scent of a piece of cheese. He ran a finger down a list of names. "You are not on today's schedule," he said, and then went back to shuffling papers, not bothering to look back up at her. "You must get on his schedule if you wish to see him," he said by way of dismissal.

Alexandra took a deep breath, bent down, placed her hands against the side of the desk, and shoved it, putting every ounce of strength she had into it. The desk lurched back, its feet grinding into the marble floor, the half-ton of steel only stopping as it wedged the secretary and his chair against the wall behind it.

"Are you insane!" The secretary unsuccessfully tried to push the desk off his chest, unable to overpower Alexandra and the boot she now had firmly planted against the side of the desk.

"Quite insane!" said Alexandra, who drove her boot forward, pushing the desk an inch or so closer to the wall.

With his one free hand, the secretary managed to pull a phone from its cradle and press it up to the side of his face. "Comrade Mitchell needs to see Comrade Stalin," he hissed into the phone. "Now!"

Alexandra nodded, removed her foot from the edge of the desk, and started walking in the direction of the preparation chamber. She even managed a smile, realizing that this would be the last time that she would need to see the rat-faced little secretary who guarded Stalin's lair.

Alexandra did not squirm, did not try to fight the restraints keeping her arms and legs tied to the chair. The cheap cotton gown itched, and the disinfectants they'd washed her down with still burned in her nose, causing it to drip, a line of snot running from her left nostril to the corner of her mouth, annoying her.

The door before her, a massive slab of gray concrete set in a frame of steel, and studded by bolts the size of her fist, slowly swung open. Alexandra was pushed forward, the guard not actually touching the chair, but using a long pole to move her along.

She rolled into the room.

Half a dozen black-shirts, all blond and muscular, with blank expressions, and dead and dull crystalline blue eyes, surrounded her. Each had a weapon raised, aimed at her head. These were Stalin's most trusted, at least the most trusted for this month. Around each of their throats was locked a restraint, a very special restraint. If comrade Stalin's heart should stop beating, these restraints would be detonated. This was the type of loyalty that Stalin understood.

Her chair came to a stop.

"Such lack of control is a sad thing to see."

Stalin got up from his couch, a stiff and ugly chunk of furniture, upholstered with a blue and gold floral fabric. He smiled and posed, his feet planted nearly a foot apart, his hands behind his back. He wore only a dirty pair of yellowed shorts, a sleeveless undershirt, and a pair of black socks. An unlit cigarette dangled from the corner of his mouth. His skin was tinted a shade of green, but Alexandra knew this was merely an illusion caused by the nearly inch-thick slab of bulletproof glass that separated her from Stalin's stronghold.

"Control is important," he said. His voice came from a small speaker in the wall.

This was as near as she'd been to Stalin in nearly eight years. He knew just what she was capable of and took no chances when dealing with her.

"There is no doubting your wisdom, Comrade Stalin," she said, attempting to nod. Since her last visit, a head restraint had been added, consisting of a loop of leather wrapped across her forehead, pinning her head to the back of the chair.

"And just what brings you here today?" asked Stalin. He turned, scratched his butt, and returned to his couch. "I assume it is a matter of some urgency, considering the little display you put on *outside*."

Outside.

Alexandra doubted that the paranoid fool had any concept of outside. For the last five years he had not stepped out of his office, or the suite of bedrooms behind it. Blast proof, gas proof, bullet proof, fire proof, and certainly reality proof, Stalin's paranoia had driven him to this little prison.

"They have fired the Sonomak in a low-power test. They are probably only days away from a full-power firing. We cannot allow that."

Stalin shook his head, and reaching forward, pulled a blue-tipped match from a gilded porcelain mug resting on the table in front of him, struck it with his thumbnail, and lit the cigarette. He took a deep drag, and then exhaled a thick column of smoke that he carefully examined. "And you of course wish us to accelerate our campaign, to unleash the nuclear arsenal, to render the greatest food-producing region of the world into radioactive slag, so that you can stop them from firing their Sonomak."

"Yes," said Alexandra. She knew from the sound of his voice, that that would be the very last thing that he intended to do.

"If only your associate . . . ," said Stalin, pausing, once again examining the cigarette smoke. "What *was* his name?" he asked.

Alexandra said nothing.

"Oh yes," said Stalin. "Mr. Gris, the man whose existence you failed to mention to me, the man who you *believed* had been working with you for the past eight years, the man that you have been using for your own personal needs, and directly against mine."

Alexandra squirmed and looked around the room at the weapons pointed at her head, not really surprised that Stalin knew about Quinn. There were few secrets in this world. And this particular secret no longer mattered. Again she looked at the weapons trained on her. Her body was capable of amazing things, could recover from almost any wound, even a shot to the head. But dozens of shots to the head, possibly hundreds, her brain splattered across the floor and walls, was a situation from which there would be no recovery. As Nadia had demonstrated, there was no such thing as true immortality.

But she had no intention of letting Stalin's slaves pull their triggers.

"I recommend that you begin the attack right away," she said, "a full nuclear attack focused on both Chicago and Saint Louis, and then a flanking maneuver south of Saint Louis and across the plains in the direction of Colorado."

Stalin crushed the butt of his cigarette against the coffee table. "And I recommend that you not make too big a mess on my nice marble floor," he said, finding this so funny that he began to laugh.

Alexandra smiled. She knew that she would have only one chance. She had planned for this day from the very beginning, knowing that it might eventually come down to a situation like this. She was confident that it would work, that the programming would hold. But still, she could not push aside the image of a dead Nadia. "I will do my best," she told Stalin.

She focused all her energy, all her power, into her legs and strained against the restraints. She felt a ligament in her right knee tear away from the bone, and her ankle audibly cracked. But the leg restraints broke away from the chair leg, and she managed to stand. She took a limping step toward Stalin's impenetrable glass barrier.

The comrade's eyes grew large. He was almost able to shout out the command, but no words escaped his mouth. He continued to stand, looking slightly confused, half turned, as if hoping that a change in direction would restore his voice.

It did not.

"You were about to give an order for something very unpleasant to happen to me," said Alexandra. "You will find yourself physically unable to do such." She quickly looked around the room and at the rifles pointed at her. These guards were good, knew their duty. They would not fire unless Stalin ordered it or it was apparent that she was a *direct* threat to him.

But she was not a threat—no harm was coming to Stalin.

She was only talking to him—just as she had talked to him nearly ten years earlier, planting deep within him the programming that would be activated in the event that he ordered her harmed. He had attempted to say it, had wanted to shout it, as she had hobbled toward the glass wall.

And that had sealed his fate.

"There is a button inside the second drawer on the right-hand side of your desk. Please go over and activate it."

Stalin walked over to the desk, in a fluid and easy manner, not the slightest hint in his movement that he was being forced to do something against his will. He opened up the desk drawer, reached in, and pressed a button.

Bang!

Alexandra flinched and felt the blood splatter against the back of her head. The six elite guards had lost their heads. She struggled at the restraint on her left arm, managed to snap it after gouging a deep chunk of skin and muscle out of her forearm, and was then able to undo the remaining arm and head restraints.

The chair rattled to the floor behind her.

Alexandra focused, already starting to repair her damaged leg and sealing the gouge in her arm. "Pick up the phone," she said, pointing to the phone on his desk. "And please give me a big smile," she added.

Stalin picked up the phone, a demented sort of grin filling his face.

"Ask for General Lustov."

"Give me Lustov," said Stalin.

"When he gets on the phone, you will instruct him to activate the Heartland invasion. He is to use *all* weapons in his arsenal, and he must have Boulder occupied and the counterrevolutionaries in detention within forty-eight hours."

Still grinning, Stalin kept the phone pushed to the side of his face.

Alexandra paced in front of the glass wall, her limp quickly fading as the leg repaired itself.

"General Lustov," said Stalin into the phone, sounding every bit the supreme leader. "You will activate the Heartland invasion. You are to use *all* weapons within your arsenal. You must have Boulder occupied and the counterrevolutionaries in detention within forty-eight hours." That said, Stalin continued to stand, phone held up to the side of his head.

"Thank you, Comrade," said Alexandra, feeling pleased with herself, realizing that not only was she only days away from escaping this disgusting world, but that never again would she have to see Comrade Stalin. "Now please have a seat and wait for the communiqués reporting on your final victory over the evil capitalists."

Stalin returned to his couch and sat.

Alexandra turned and walked out of Stalin's office.

Boulder was now infinitely far away.

They had slipped from one picoverse to another.

Anthony sensed that something was about to move. Infinite shades of green, leaves, bark, vines, bushes, insects, the mammal-things, the reptile things, the big-eating things—all of them tinted in various shades of green engulfed him. But through the green, he could see a shape, the camouflage not perfect. "Stop," he whispered to Ernest.

Ernest stopped, lizard leg nearly to his lips, grease running down his fingers, staining the torn cuff of his shirt. He did not move, did not even breathe.

Anthony stared into the jungle. Something was near, waiting, poised to leap. He slowly moved his eyes, looking for the signs. And then he saw it, dangling from a vine, an unmoving outline, a patch of emerald green, a thing designed to look like the leaves of the forest, but a patch of leaves that were not moving in the gentle breeze.

All-teeth.

That's what they called the creature. It was unfortunately an apt description. It hung from a vine by its tail. The animal's snout ran from the tip of its face to nearly a meter down the trunk of its slender, camouflaged body. Its mouth was spread wide, its green teeth glistening, each one resembling a blade of grass, tipped with a drop of green morning dew.

"Down!" shouted Anthony as the All-teeth launched itself, the wings between front and back legs unfurling, catching air as it dropped from the vine, giving it lateral motion as it targeted the back of Ernest's head.

Anthony dove for the bow, a thing made from the rib of a big lumbering herbivore and the string from the gut of one of the rodent creatures that was always trying to nip off a toe. He grabbed it and two of the bamboo arrows by its side, rolled, and kneeled, with bow pulled taught, sighting along the arrow, aiming for the slice of jungle where the All-teeth would be.

Intersection.

Orbital mechanics, elementary particle physics, arrow and All-teeth. To Anthony, all of it was the same, simply equations with different boundary conditions.

Zzzzzzzt!

The arrow flew. It caught the All-teeth square in the mouth, driving its green-ribbon tongue down its throat, the arrow shaft going in stomach-deep, nothing protruding from the animal's always-open mouth, except for the stiff green feathers tied to the end of the arrow. Momentum carried the All-teeth forward, the dead reptile smashing into Ernest's back, pushing him face-down into the mud.

"My God!" Ernest rolled, thrashing, and pushed the thirty pounds of dead green reptile off of him. Before attempting to sit, before even taking another breath, he reached for the back of his head, quickly feeling for slashes or cuts. Even dead, the thing's teeth could cut right down to the bone if it landed on you the wrong way. Ernest pulled his hands back to examine them, not sure if the warmth he felt running down the back of his head was simply the all-pervasive mud that covered the jungle floor, or his own blood. "Mud," he said sighing, sitting up, and kicking the All-teeth away from him.

Anthony scanned the surrounding jungle for signs of another predator. He saw nothing, sensed nothing, and could see no movement that didn't belong. When he was sure that nothing else was about to launch an attack, he lowered the bow and reached down with his other hand to help pull up Ernest. No easy job. The mud sucked at Ernest, tried to keep him glued to the jungle floor, but he leaned back and leveraged Ernest up.

"We can't stay here any longer," said Ernest. "Between what we've killed and our own scent, this place is becoming a bigger lure each day to these carnivores," he said. He took a half-step toward the All-teeth, put the toe of his shoe against its side, and kicked it over.

Anthony turned. He knew Ernest was right, had actually known for better than a week that they would have no choice but to abandon this camp and find some real shelter elsewhere. Not only were *they* attracting predators, but he suspected, based on the distant screams they had heard shortly after their arrival, many others from Boulder had found themselves trapped in this picoverse, and their presence had brought in even more predators. They had found one torn and shredded human carcass, but no actual survivors. He looked at his mother, knowing that this might well be the last time he would ever see her. At the end of the small clearing lay Boulder, Colorado, and the prison cell.

So close, and yet, he knew, infinitely far away.

They could see it, but not touch it, not penetrate an invisible barrier that separated the two worlds. He understood the physics, knew that during the Sonomak's test firing, his world, the world that he had come to think of as his own, had come into brief contact with another world, one of the picoverses generated by Alpha. And both he and Ernest had somehow slipped into the other picoverse.

And now they could not get out. The space where the two universes touched was distorted enough to let photons travel from the larger universe into this one, but that was all that could move between the two worlds. Physical transport was impossible. Anthony walked the several feet over to the boundary between the two worlds, and once again tried to reach into the prison cell, and to his mother who stood there, still and unmoving.

He touched something that could not be penetrated—hard, and ungiving, like glass. His mother stood just beyond his touch. They had been in this jungle world for nearly two weeks now. And as far as they could tell, during all that time, approximately ten minutes had passed within the prison cell. For two weeks they had watched his mother, as she moved infinitely slowly, pacing back and forth across the cell, the pain, the anguish, and the sheer terror so visibly filling her face.

And after watching for two weeks, he now understood, fully *believed* what his mother had tried to tell him. She had not abandoned him, had not forgotten about him. The look that now filled her face told the truth, told the story that he had never allowed himself to believe.

She loved him.

And now, once again, they'd been separated, torn apart, imprisoned in different universes. "Good-bye, Mother." He pressed his hand firmly against the nothingness that separated the two universes.

She did not move, nor did the tears that clung to her

cheeks. Anthony knew that to see those tears slowly crawl down her face, to watch them fall from her cheeks and drop to the floor, he would have to watch her for several hours.

"Anthony," called Ernest from behind him. "We need to go before this dead All-teeth attracts something."

Anthony nodded. "I love you," he said in a whisper, so quietly that he knew Ernest would not be able to hear him. But he hoped that somehow, in some impossible manner, that the whisper would carry between the two universes, so that his mother would hear it, so that she would know how he felt.

Anthony turned and marched into the jungle, with Ernest following closely behind.

SECTION II
CHAPTER 12

"Nearly two dozen blasts," said Werner. Shaking his head in disbelief as he read the dispatch, he then dropped the single piece of paper onto the president's desk. "Two each for Chicago and St. Louis, and the rest spread up and down the line."

"What *was* the line," said Tesla. He slumped farther back into the couch, nearly vanishing. The old man, who had always looked withered and frail, as if the breeze from a ceiling fan might knock him down, now resembled something a week dead, a stiffened corpse that had been dumped onto the president's couch. "All of it gone," said the old corpse, adding a few moans for effect.

Werner turned. "Most of the winds are running to the northeast, so that within the next two days the fallout will run from the Carolinas north to Quebec. They've poisoned and probably killed a large number of their own ground troops on the other side of the line," he said.

The president stood. As aged and damaged as Tesla appeared after the events of the last twenty-four hours, the president had taken an even greater beating. The right side of his face was drawn and pinched, his right eyelid not fully open. It was obvious to everyone in the room that Rogers had suffered a stroke. The president stood, slowly, pushing himself up. Once standing he held his right hand in his left, massaging it, and took a couple of shuffling steps around the side of his desk, leaning against it for support. "The entire third and fourth combined Soviet-Deutschland divisions are moving," he said, his normally strong and resonant voice weakened, and his speech slightly slurred. "And we have absolutely nothing to stop them or to even slow them down. We'll be overrun in less than a day." He let go of his right hand, letting it fall lifelessly to his side, and reached down to his desk with his left hand and picked up a piece of paper. "In the last hour German paratroopers have landed in both Omaha and Kansas City. Salt Lake City is in Krensky's hands."

"Blitzkrieg," said Horst.

"And what can we do to stop them?" asked Rogers. He knew that in all likelihood the United States would fall within the next few hours.

"The only thing left to us," said Werner. He looked to his right, expecting to see Ernest standing beside him as usual, the only other man who had the capacity for understanding what they had built. And now he was gone, somehow swallowed up by the very piece of physics that they were so near to conquering. Werner sat, dropping down into the too-soft couch, feeling the weight of the world descending on him. "We must fire the Sonomak at full power and access Alpha's picoverse," he said, waving a hand at Horst, Jack, and Katie, "and find whatever weapons systems we can within it to fight against the Soviets."

Jack just barely managed not to groan out loud, knowing that was not a plan, but a prayer. If the Sonomak could be made to operate at full power, and if that did not simply tear the fabric of this and every other picoverse apart, and if they could then get into the picoverse and steal something away from Alpha that could destroy the Russians, they would at best only have a few hours to do so. After that, there would be nothing left to save.

"It is our only chance," said Katie.

Jack slowly turned to face her. He had heard the words, but somehow not understood them. Running the Sonomak during the low-level test had resulted in the temporary merging of this world with another picoverse. Reports had come in from all across the city of lush, thick jungle suddenly appearing, occupying streets, materializing where houses had been. Some people had found themselves swept to the other world.

But the effect had lasted only seconds.

The collapse stopped and the merged worlds parted, everything *almost* returning to normal. Reports indicated that at least twenty people were still missing, including Ernest and Anthony.

"The only chance?" asked Jack, staring at her.

"Yes," said Katie. She reached down between her feet, pulled up a thin black leather valise, opened it, and pulled out a folder containing half a dozen pages scrawled with equations, something that she'd been working on nonstop for the last twenty-four hours, something that she had refused to discuss with either Horst or Jack. She handed the papers to Werner. "In the brute force method that you are planning to operate, to simply run all sixty-four electron accelerators in tandem to drive the plasmon, you will fall short of generating a high enough energy density to generate a stable wormhole."

"It can't be fired," said Horst. "Einstein is certain that it will cause a collapse. I've gone over his analysis," he said, puffing out his chest. "It is simply too dangerous, especially when you consider what happened during the test-firing."

"I know exactly what happened during the test-firing!" she shouted, standing, the papers that had been in her lap fluttering to the floor. "I know what its *effects* were!"

Jack reached up and gently pulled her down, forcing her to sit.

Katie took a deep breath. "It was a backwash phenomenon," she said, her voice shaking. "The same sort of effect we experienced when test-firing our Sonomak at low-energy levels. If Werner runs the Sonomak at full power it will be high enough to avoid the backwash, but not high enough to open a stable wormhole."

"But Einstein has shown that—"

"Look at me, Horst," said Katie, cutting him off. "Look at my eyes."

Horst looked.

"Einstein cannot run the simulations, cannot crunch the numbers to the ten significant digits that are needed to understand what will happen under a high-power firing." Katie reached up and tapped at her right eye with the nail of her index finger, producing the clinking sound of glass being struck. "I ran the simulations. I know what needs to be done to generate a stable wormhole and avoid the collapse. Simply running at full power will not work."

Werner shook his head. "It will," he said. "Our calculations show that we have adequate energy to stabilize the wormhole." And then he paused.

Jack felt it—*doubt.*

"And even if we don't, there is absolutely nothing that we could do to modify the system, to get more power without adding additional accelerators." He didn't bother to add how impossible that would be, with the Soviets and Germans only hours away. "We fire in our current configuration."

"Let me explain," said Katie. She looked at him, her crystalline eyes staring into his. "Will you please just listen," she begged, her voice cracking.

Werner sat back and nodded.

"You have adequate power, *if* you run the accelerators in the proper manner," she said. "It may seem intuitively obvious that the highest power density is achieved by running the accelerators in tandem, but you can in fact increase the power density by nearly a factor of ten over that approach, by sequencing the accelerators, allowing them to feed energy into the plasmon at the moment of its maximum volume, just before it contracts. Pump energy in only at that point."

"Of course," said Werner. "We understand that," he said, again referring to his missing companion. He turned to the president. "It is like being on a swing, Mr. President, pumping your legs as far out in front of you as possible at the top of the arc to couple in the most energy." He turned back to Katie. "Werner and I attempted to examine that set of solutions, but the equations are highly nonlinear. They require a calculated interpretation, one that would take years and years to complete."

Jack suddenly understood.

While physics was often described by very elegant, and what on the surface could often appear to be rather simple equations, when you tried to build something in the real world, tried to reduce physics to engineering, the equations often broke down and approximations had to be made. Under those conditions, an accurate solution typically required a roomful of computers cranking away to huge numbers of significant bits. Those machines didn't exist in this world, except for what was now in Katie's head.

"I've run those calculations. I have the firing sequences needed for generating the maximum energy density." She angled her head down in the direction of the papers strewn across the floor. "It is the only way it will work." She looked back up at Werner.

He said nothing, but looked at her crystalline eyes. It all came down to probabilities and time. He knew that at the very best they would only have time to fire the Sonomak once before the Soviets overran them. He wished Ernest were here.

But he wasn't.

He continued to stare at her eyes, at what he now knew was the physical manifestation of the entities that had created the entire universe beyond their little world. He sighed. "We will try it your way," he said.

Rogers nodded and then fell into his chair. "As quickly as possible," he said by way of dismissal.

Katie was the first out the door with Jack close behind, dogtrotting to catch up. "You are absolutely certain that there is no chance of a collapse?" he asked her.

Katie did not stop walking, but looked back over her shoulder. "There's nothing to worry about, Jack," she said. "We'll be able to get Anthony and Ernest back."

Jack stopped, and Horst plowed into his back. "What's wrong?" he asked, pushing him along.

Jack said nothing. Katie had not *exactly* answered his question. Would Katie risk destroying this picoverse along with other picoverses and perhaps even the universe itself in order to get Anthony back, he wondered? He refused to believe that, knew it wasn't possible.

"Nothing's wrong," he said to Horst.

He watched Katie march down the hallway.

"It should not be fired," said Horst. He pushed himself up against Werner, crowding in on him, physically pinning him against a rack of electronics. "Einstein confided in me, showed me his calculations. The risk is simply too great!"

"We have our orders," said Werner, not bothering to argue. As far as he was concerned, Horst had become contaminated by whatever insanity had consumed Einstein. He pushed his right index finger directly beneath Horst's nose and wagged it back and forth. "If you wish to remain during the firing, you will stand back and not get in our way."

Horst didn't move.

"Or you will be removed," said Werner. He glanced past Horst at the guards standing at the entrance of the control room, rifles ready in their hands.

Horst looked in the direction of the guards. "Tell him, Katie," he said. "We know what can happen when the Sonomak is fired. We've experienced what can go wrong."

Katie stood at the far end of the control room, pressed up against the viewing window, staring down at the Sonomak. "It will work," she said without turning toward him.

Werner gave Horst a thump on the chest, who then shuffled back, slowly sitting in a chair. "It shouldn't be fired," he said to Werner, who had already turned away from him and with clipboard in hand was jotting down some numbers as he scanned a bank of meters and their quivering needles.

"He's afraid," Jack whispered to Katie, having stepped up behind her.

Katie said nothing. Jack watched her, studied her hands wrapped tightly around the guardrail in front of the viewing window, the muscles in her forearms standing out, corded, actually quivering. A thin line of sweat ran down the side of her neck.

"Should he be afraid?" asked Jack. He watched a bead of perspiration run beneath the collar of her shirt. "Should we *all* be afraid?"

"One minute on my mark!" shouted Werner to the technicians.

Jack rested a hand on Katie's shoulder and could feel the tightness in her muscles and the cold dampness of her skin beneath the shirt's thin cotton fabric. "What haven't you told us?" he asked.

"Mark!" shouted Werner.

The room was suddenly engulfed in the sounds of switches being thrown, the whine of high voltage, the squeak of leather-soled shoes scraping against concrete, the grinding of cranks and the furious scratching of dozens of pencils being worked down checklists.

"Katie?" asked Jack.

"We need to find Anthony," she whispered as she continued to stare out at the Sonomak.

"Thirty seconds!" shouted Werner. "Initiate plasma pre-ignition!"

Even though his eyes were focused on the back of Katie's head, out of the corner of his vision Jack could see the white glow through the viewing window, and he knew that the plasma in the Sonomak had been struck, the high energy light streaming out of the machine's view ports. "Katie, do we need to stop the firing of the Sonomak?" he asked. "What is it that you aren't telling me?"

Katie spun around, almost knocking Jack down.

"Fifteen seconds!" shouted Werner. "Ramp up accelerators."

A dull hum, something more felt than heard, filled the control room.

"And what aren't *you* telling *me*, Jack?" she asked. "You translate yourself out of the way of a falling steel pipe. You manage to kill Nadia by what appears to be sheer willpower. And then, even though you were in a totally different room of the house, you somehow get Gris to bury himself in a wall. And I suspect that you are the reason that we were first able to step into Alpha's picoverse. What are *you* hiding?"

"Five seconds!" shouted Werner.

The control room suddenly stank of ozone and burning oil.

"I don't know," said Jack.

"Well you had better figure it out, Jack. Because we'll need everything you've got and probably more once the Sonomak is fired."

"Fire!" shouted Werner.

Jack's eyelids closed. All was dark, except for a distant pinprick of light. The light grew, expanding, racing toward him, a wall of radiation swallowing him. He was incinerated, eradicated, the heat so intense, the pressures so extreme, that even the atoms within his body were shattered, obliterated.

SECTION II
CHAPTER 13

Anthony pulled aside the thick wall of vines with one hand and tugged Ernest up with his other. Looking up past Ernest, through the canopy opening, he knew they had finally reached the top of the hill. The Rockies spread out before them, layer after layer of jungle-coated rock reaching up into the pale blue sky.

Ernest scrambled up the rest of the way under his own power, the clawed attachment that had long ago replaced his right foot grabbing onto roots, giving him a firm anchor, keeping him from slipping into the ever-present mud. He stood, dropped the visor over his eyes and scanned the horizon. In the corner of his visor was displayed the signal vector of the distortion. "Right beneath our feet," he said, not looking back at Anthony, but at the vista of jungle-covered Rockies. "I've been here before," he said,

"We're less than five kilometers away from our initial insertion point," said Anthony. He pointed toward the northeast. "Boulder is over there." He pointed to the foothills beneath them, to a patch of jungle and a few broken piles of rock and debris jutting up through the jungle.

Ernest shook his head and flipped back the visor, "No," he said. "I mean that I have been on this exact spot, on this hilltop. On our *old* world it sits just above the Sonomak."

Anthony knew this, had suspected it even before the gravitational anomalies had been detected and the ultrasonics picked up. He'd dreamed it, seen it in his sleep. They'd been on this jungle world for nearly eight years, dividing their time between the Frisco-Portland Corridor and the Lima Needle in the south. From time to time they would venture into the vast Western Preserve, a bio test bed for artificial creatures, the stretch of wilderness that consumed much of what would have been the western United States in his old world, running from the Sierras in the West to the Mississippi in the East. Archeology had become a passion for both of them, uncovering the demise of a world, of an Earth that in 1998 suddenly discovered itself imprisoned in a picoverse whose volume barely exceeded the orbit of Mars. In this universe, nothing existed beyond Mars, the entire solar system consisting of only the terrestrial-like planets. The resulting collapse and social disintegration had taken nearly a century to overcome. But all that was ancient history, nearly one thousand years in the past for this world.

When they'd emerged from the Great Western Preserve, they'd been mistaken as aboriginals from one of the many tribes that populated the Preserve, who refused to rejoin the modern, technical world. Speaking ancient English, wearing tatters, totally devoid of all mechanical enhancements, no DNA records, just two more wild creatures that inhabited the Preserve. By the physical act of stumbling out of the Preserve, they were given the option of citizenship.

The two had wisely gone along with the mistaken identities.

Because, as they soon learned, had anyone even suspected that they came from another world, that they had any experience or knowledge of picoverse mechanics, they would have been instantly nulled, and all evidence of their existence, right down to the memories of those who came in contact with them, wiped clean.

There was no higher crime in this world than tampering with the fabric of space-time. The device that had been Alexandra, and that had found herself trapped in this picoverse in 1998, when everything beyond the orbit of Mars vanished, quickly took control of the global government that eventually evolved in this world. By her mandate, high-energy physics of any sort, experimental or theoretical, was outlawed under penalty of death.

But her mandate carried no authority beyond the picoverse.

Anthony had sensed that something from outside was touching this world. He had begun to dream about it before any instrumentation on this world or in orbit began to pick up the anomalies. The Sonomak was in the process of being fired. Based on the gravitational anomalies, Anthony had been able to figure out exactly what they were doing.

Harmonic Cycling.

They were feeding the plasmon, switching accelerators on and off in just the optimum sequence to cause the void within the Sonomak's heart to swell, to bulge with stored energy. Back in the old world, Anthony knew that they were in the final countdown to imploding the plasmon, to powering down the lasers, and carefully guiding the plasmon collapse to achieve a maximum energy density. They were only seconds away—what would only be a few hours on this world.

And then this world would end.

All the picoverses would end. They would collapse upon each other, devouring each other, twisting and tearing at the fabric of the greater universe. And like a cancer, the tear would continue to grow, eating the universe itself, devouring all matter and energy, pulling back into the nothingness what the Big Bang had spewed out over thirty billion years earlier. Anthony had run the simulations—there could be no other possible outcome.

Anthony sat, knowing that this was the place where he needed to be, at the center, at the first point in this world that would be destroyed, hoping for the briefest of moments that he would be reunited with his mother.

"A beautiful day," said Anthony. He pulled down vines and tree limbs, so that when he sat, he could still see the Rockies. "A perfect day." Reaching up with his right hand, he unslung the pack draped across his back and placed it in his lap. Unzipping the top of the pack, he reached in and grabbed the barrel of a device, the thing that he had spent the last six years developing in secret, knowing every day that if discovered both he and Ernest would be nulled on the spot. His fingers meshed with it, sinking into its warm surface. The gun was organic, its DNA mostly his. The nerve endings, bone, tendons, enzymes, and blood vessels of the device merged with his.

He could *feel* the gun.

He could sense the projectile within, a mix of graphite and cartilage, an onboard distortion generator that could effortlessly cut through not only steel and concrete, but even through twisted and ruptured fragments of space-time.

A very special projectile—one intended for a very special *entity*.

Anthony pulled his hand out of the pack and rested it in his lap. He knew he would not have long to wait. The air itself hissed. The solid rock beneath him felt as if it were about to flow. He sensed that he was about to slip—out of this world, and into the next.

"Fire!" echoed Werner's voice.

Katie blinked. Once.

The entire Sonomak complex shuttered, the mountain groaned, and Katie could not pull down a breath, the air itself sucked right out of her lungs as the entire front end of the control room was torn away, sailing into the cavern housing the Sonomak.

Screams.

Shattering glass.

Rupturing metal.

Katie fell back from the viewing window, hit the floor, entwined in bodies, and then pulled herself up, tugging on the wheel of a massive valve. And then for just a moment, her feet rose up off the floor, her entire body pulled by a combination of a hurricane force wind and a gravitational shear, and then she was slammed back down.

Those who had not been pulled out of the control room, those who had not been crushed by falling equipment, those who were still conscious and capable of crawling or stumbling, made their way to the open end of the Sonomak cavern.

Half the Sonomak remained—that portion nearest the control room. The remaining portion, which should have filled up the back half of the cavern, could not be seen, because in its place was a solid wall of rock.

"Cave-in!" someone shouted.

Katie shook her head, understanding what she was seeing. There had been no cave-in. What they were looking at was simply rock, the rock that had been removed when this part of the mountainside had been hollowed out to build the Sonomak. This picoverse and another had merged, and in that other picoverse, the Sonomak had never been built, nothing in that chunk of space-time except for rock.

The collapse had begun, just as she knew it would, just as she knew it had to.

With an infinite number of pieces, in a puzzle with no edge, she had begun to glimpse something of the picture that was being put together. The wiring in her head, the ability to independently and simultaneously extrapolate dozens of different trains of thought had brought her to a single conclusion.

The collapse *had* to happen—all their lives, and the lives of everyone and everything in this and the greater universe beyond depended on it. The how and the why were not yet clear to her, but the destruction was clear, an inevitability that could not be escaped.

To her right, Beong lay on the ground, only partially visible, a large shard of granite lodged where his chest should have been. "No, Beong," she said, certain that this time it was *her* Beong who had merged with a piece of debris from another picoverse. "I'm so sorry," she said, moving toward him.

She never reached him.

Katie suddenly hit the floor, as it rose up and smashed her in the face.

"No!" screamed Alexandra, as the jet fell from the sky and the seatbelt dug into her stomach. The plane pitched to the right, rolling over to a nearly vertical position, spun hard, pulling enough gees to tunnel her vision, and just as quickly righted itself.

"What in the hell is happening?" She gave a savage kick to the seat in front of her—the pilot's seat of the four-seat jet. Reaching over to the seat next to her, she tugged on the restraining strap around the small crate, making sure that it had not loosened. *Insurance,* she thought. The Soviet scientists and the few German scientists who had not escaped to the West had been unable to build her a Sonomak, but they had been able to develop what filled the small crate. Satisfied that the contents of the crate were intact, she gave another kick to the back of the seat in front of her. "What has happened?"

"I don't know, Comrade Mitchell," said the pilot, obviously shaken. The copilot shouted into his microphone and frantically flipped switches. "The Topeka beacon is no longer responding," he said. He continued to toggle switches and spin thumbwheels.

Alexandra shifted in her seat, looking through the window, in a southern direction, certain that she'd see a large mushroom cloud rising up into the sky. They'd been using the American's Topeka signal as a reference as they cut their way over the U.S. plains to get to Boulder. She suspected that Topeka had offered some unsuspected resistance and paid the price for that stupidity.

But there was no mushroom cloud.

There was also nothing that resembled Topeka, nothing as small and insignificant as Topeka. What lay to the south and sprawled out beyond the horizon was a city, a hive of buildings, constructions, a maze of metal, glass, and what looked like spiderwebs rising up from the ground far higher than the twenty-five thousand feet at which they were cruising.

"What is *that*?" said the pilot, pointing to the south.

At first Alexandra thought that he must have been referring to the impossible city-sprawl that had just materialized, but then realized that he was not pointing at the city, but at the *boundary* of the city, where it intersected with the Midwest grasslands.

The city was *eating* the Great Plains, spilling across it, monoliths miles high suddenly appearing out of thin air, concrete, steel, and glass, not sprouting up out of the ground like mutant trees, but simply being revealed, as if someone was pulling back an invisible curtain to expose the monstrous cityscape.

"Boulder!" she yelled at the pilot. "Get to Boulder as fast as you can, but veer north, do not fly over that city or get anywhere near the boundary where the city is devouring the prairie." She did not understand what she was seeing, what was happening, but she knew there could be only one cause.

"They fired the Sonomak," she said to herself. And as she said it, the voices, absent for nearly ten years, filled her head, a roar and scream, the volume and intensity threatening to shatter her skull. "No" she whispered in a moan, trying to hold on to what she was, struggling to maintain a sense of self, of individuality, attempting to cling to the personality that she had constructed over the last four million years. She passed out.

Alpha turned, sensing something was not right, that he was not perfectly in control. He looked about the lab. In the last ten minutes, since banishing his parents and their trivial associates, he had created nearly two hundred picoverses, two hundred entire cosmoses, willed into existence by his mere desire.

They spun about the lab, cones that glistened with the appearance of oil spinning across water, each cone tied back to the Sonomak, tethered by an umbilical of twisting rainbow light. They bobbed and pitched above his head, more than one trillion humans created by his hand in the last ten minutes.

Create the world in seven days.

Alpha laughed, delighted by the thought of a God so incompetent, so little, that it would take Him an entire week to create a single world.

"Two hundred *universes* in ten minutes!" he shouted, holding his hands high above his head, straining, reaching up for the worlds he had just created.

"What?"

He turned to his left, again sensing that something was wrong, that something was occurring that he had not instigated. And then he saw it. In the corner of the lab, high up where the ceiling supports ran into the upper walls, nearly a dozen of the cones had gathered together, clinging to one another.

As he watched, several others drifted toward the corner of the lab, sticking onto the others that had already gathered there. Alpha shook his head, taking several full seconds, an almost infinite length of time to him, trying to convince himself that what he was seeing was not actually occurring.

"I am the Master!"

A rainbow umbilical, attached to the cone at the heart of the cluster, was reeled back to the throat of the Sonomak, with all the other cones that were stuck to it moving along with it, the bubbly structure gathering up more cones as it was swept down from the rafters.

The central cone expanded, distorted, and latched onto the throat of the Sonomak.

"These are my worlds!" he shouted, and then ran for the Sonomak, throwing himself into the central oil-on-water distortion, instantly being swallowed.

III. TOMORROW

Tomorrow we'll be back on the vast ocean.

—Horace (65–8 B.C.)

Expanse of blue, puffs of white, tendrils of gray.

Consciousness returned.

Jack stared and slowly realized that he was looking up at the sky. And with that realization came sounds—screams, the crack and hiss of fire, the squeal of steam, explosions, the shattering of glass. He pushed himself up, leaning against a piece of hard steel, the hot, greasy metal burning him. He jerked back, leaving behind part of his shirt and a bit of skin. The pain woke him, helped him focus. He sat at the edge of an abyss, looking into a panoramic-scale kaleidoscope, as facets and slices of land-scapes, people, rocks, equipment, trees, rushing water, and crimson sky all cartwheeled before him.

The picoverses were collapsing on each other, and the focal point of that collapse was the Sonomak, entire worlds crashing together, nulling one another before his eyes.

He fell to his side and then, twisting around, pulled him-self forward, right to the very edge of the abyss, wrapping his hands around the jagged edge of steel sheet, which only moments before had been a part of the control room's floor. He peered down into the chaos.

"Do you know what you've done?"

He felt fingers wrapping around the back of his neck, grabbing, nearly crunching vertebrae. He heard himself scream, watched the already shattered worlds before him blur as he was pulled upward, swung high, and then slammed back down against the metal plate floor.

"How could *you* let this happen?"

A knee to the gut blew the wind out of him.

A face moved into his field of view. "I can *smell* it on you, Jack. They've shown me so much more, given me so much more understanding."

Jack focused. Alexandra looked down at him. She reached forward and grabbed him by the chin and shook his head back and forth several times. She took a deep sniff, flaring her nostrils. "I can smell the *other* in you," she said. "This insignificant universe, or even that somewhat larger one beyond," she added, raising her hand up toward the blue sky above him, "means absolutely nothing."

Jack tried to push himself up, but could not budge, with her knee planted firmly in his stomach.

"But I can sense it now, that just like me, you're from the Makers' universe." She took another deep lungful of air and glared at him. Again she shook his head. "Four million years I've been here, working for them, taking their orders, observing their little experiment unfold. But you've been here *so* much longer."

She bent closer, practically pushing her nose right up to his.

"From the very *beginning*, Jack?" she asked, not quite able to believe what she suddenly knew had to be true. "Have you really been here from the beginning?"

From the beginning, he thought. Thirty billion years ago, when the universe sprang out of the void, seeded and powered from the Makers' universe. He nodded at her, not fully understanding the significance of the answer, not feeling the weight of those thirty billion years.

But he knew it was true.

"And now the experiment must be terminated," she said, as if informing him that the contents of a few test tubes were about to be dumped down the drain. She removed her knee from his stomach, stood up, and then, reaching back down, grabbed his hands and pulled him into a sitting position. She tapped her forehead. "You must have been laughing at me," she said. "I was so clever, manipulated and played all my pawns in order to build a new world so I could escape the Makers. I thought I had defied their programs, become a true individual."

Her entire body convulsed, and Jack was *almost* able to push her away.

"I remember now," she said. "It was *you*. You altered the programming; you changed me, made me violate my reason for being. You are the one responsible for all this, for this destruction, for this threat to the Makers' universe."

"Me," whispered Jack, trying to remember.

"They've removed all your *tampering*. This little experiment has gone too far. They could care less about the picoverses. But what does concern them, is what happens when these little worlds complete their collapse, when the space-time of the next universe up the ladder starts to feel the effect, starts to swallow its own tail."

Jack nodded. "That threatens *their* universe," he said.

Alexandra sighed. "And that's that. Experiment over. I've got the new orders," she said, once more thumping her forehead. "We go into Alpha's picoverse, and from there move into the universe and then shut it down before its uncontrolled collapse can impact the Makers' universe."

"Firebreak," said Jack, understanding, knowing that if the universe could be collapsed in an orderly manner, then there would be no distortions, no tears, nothing that would ripple back up the line and cause danger to the Makers' universe.

He would *not* help her.

This experiment would not be stopped. It was only just beginning. Despite what she believed, what new insights and powers might have been revealed to her, Jack was certain that she didn't understand the true nature of the experiment.

He blinked.

His head pounded, vision momentarily blurring and then tunneling.

Not even the Makers understood the true nature of the experiment. He knew this, understood this, and sensed that somehow he was *remembering* this. The Makers were also pawns. But he could not see who or what was in control. All he knew was that the experiment was not yet over—it was only just beginning. He shook his head. "No," he said, as he pushed himself up off the floor.

Alexandra stood and shrugged. "Suit yourself," she said. "I thought I detected greatness in you, Jack, that maybe you were more than just a cog in this machine, an insignificant, meaningless little cog like me. I thought you could help me with my little task, and then afterward we'd return to the Makers' universe for our belly scratches and head pats."

She angled her head back, and Jack knew what she planned. If he would not join her willingly, then she would simply take what she found useful within him and move on to complete her mission, to terminate the experiment, to *turn off* the universe.

Bang!

Air distorted, the shock wave knocking Jack off his feet, throwing him across what was left of the debris-filled control room. He hit hard, but rolled, and was on his feet and ready to fight. Alexandra stood nearly twenty feet away from him, just where she had been before he'd been thrown across the room. Her right shoulder, right arm, and the upper portion of her right chest were gone—cut clean away.

She half-turned. "You?" she asked, looking past Jack, and into the smoky depths of the control room.

"They're mine, all mine! You will not harm my *things.*" A naked boy walked out of the smoky shadows—Alpha. A golden rope, alive looking, writhing and spitting balls of static electricity, was wrapped around his waist. He tugged on it, and people attached to the far end of the rope came stumbling out of the shadows.

Katie and two others. The golden rope was coiled around them, smothering them, choking them, practically wrapping them in a cocoon. The other two Jack did not recognize at first. The one looked to be half-machine, what was visible of one leg and hand showing mechanical appendages. The rope dragged them into view, then slammed them against the floor.

Ernest.

Jack barely recognized him, the weathered, creased face not the face that Jack remembered. Ernest had aged. And then he knew who the second person must be, who the *man* was who was wrapped within those golden coils.

Anthony.

"These are my worlds, my creations, my things!" screamed Alpha. He pointed a finger at Alexandra. Her left arm vanished as a wave of distorting air washed over her. "I will stop the collapse that these creatures began," he said, and he flicked the golden rope, smashing them down against the floor. "And then after I take my rightful place in the universe, I will come after your precious Makers."

"You cannot stop the collapse from within!" she shouted.

"I can do whatever I desire!" bellowed Alpha.

"Let them go!"

All heads turned.

"So nice of you to stop by our little reunion," said Alpha, turning toward the voice. "Please do join us, *Father.*"

Horst walked forward, pushed aside an upended desk, and stepped between Alpha and Alexandra. In each hand he held a pistol, one pointed at both of them. Jack blinked, and took a step toward Horst; not really having a plan, only knowing that without help Horst did not stand a chance against those two. Alpha turned toward Jack and shook his head. To emphasize the point, he slammed the three held by his golden coil once again against the floor. Ernest shrieked and sagged.

Jack did not move any nearer.

"Let them go!" shouted Horst, waving the pistols.

Had Jack not seen this with his own eyes, he never would have believed it, never would have imagined that Horst would have been capable of something so brave, and at the same time, so incredibly stupid. Jack knew that Horst might as well have been waving flyswatters at them, for all the good those two pistols would do.

"Oh, Father," said Alpha. "This pains me so. You would actually hurt me, perhaps kill me, sacrificing me just to save my precious mother and that pathetic creature that I once was?"

"Let them go!" demanded Horst.

Jack could see Horst's hands shaking, see the panic begin

to fill his face, certain that it was only at this moment that he realized he had put himself in the ultimate no-win situation. Horst was in all likelihood just seconds away from being crunched like a slow-moving cockroach under a fast-moving boot heel.

"Where is all this fatherly devotion coming from?" asked Alpha, shaking his head. "I remember you, Father—I remember the cold distance, the annoyance that my very existence filled you with."

Horst shook his head, but seemed unable to actually deny it.

"You did not know me, did not want to know me!"

"I know you now," said Horst.

"No!" roared Alpha, again slamming his captives against the floor.

"I see a frightened child," said Horst. He looked past Alpha, and at the three who were wrapped in his golden rope. Clenching his jaw and nodding at Katie, he whispered, knowing that she couldn't possibly hear him. "I'm sorry." And then he looked at Anthony, at the man who such an incredibly short time ago had been a small boy. Horst could not see his face behind the golden coils of rope. For that he was thankful—he did not want his son to watch him die.

"I believe you're mistaken," said Alpha, grinning, his face suddenly glowing, bathed in a golden light from some unseen source.

Horst swung the pistol away from Alexandra and toward Alpha. He knew that the guns would have little effect, but they were all that he'd been able to find, lying beside a couple of dead soldiers. There had been only moments to come up with this plan. Einstein had convinced him that it was the only way to save Katie and Anthony.

Horst stepped forward and squeezed the triggers. The guns snapped back in his hands, the recoil angling back the barrels. Only the first two bullets hit Alpha, the first one cutting through his chest, just above the left nipple, and the other one burying itself in his neck. The remaining bullets streamed high above Alpha's head.

In a moment, the guns were emptied, the echo quickly fading. Dropping one pistol and fumbling in his pants pocket with his free hand, Horst managed to pull out a new clip, expel the empty one from the remaining pistol, and push the fresh clip in place. He raised the gun again, but did not fire.

Both of Alpha's wounds had already sealed themselves.

Alpha smiled. "Not to worry, Father. When you arrive in Hell, it will not be because of killing your own son, but solely for the billions who will die before I can right the wrong of *your* little experiment." Alpha's face darkened, the golden light vanishing. "Time to say good-bye, Father."

Gun still held high, Horst leapt for what he hoped would be the protection of a huge slab of concrete to his left. He hit the ground hard, rolled, and wedged himself up against the slab.

"I see you, Father!" said Alpha, as he raised his right hand and waved it in the direction of the concrete slab. It began to distort, shimmer, and then flow, like melting plastic.

Jack ran forward, his plan no more complex than simply to body slam Alpha, hoping to knock him to the ground before Horst became entombed in a mound of molten concrete. He made it almost halfway to Alpha before a wall of air, accompanied by a nearly ear-rupturing explosion, slammed him in the chest and drove him backward.

"No!" screamed Alpha.

Jack moved forward again, still planning on knocking Alpha to the ground, made several steps toward him, and then stopped. What looked like jagged panes of glass had suddenly wrapped around Alpha, enclosing him so that only a hand here, a foot there, and the left side of his head stuck out from the glass. The structure began to turn, and as it did, the golden rope snapped, falling to the ground. He'd seen something like this before—the region of distorted space-time Nadia had wrapped herself in when she'd attempted to migrate into Katie. Horst was already buried beneath the concrete flow.

"Careful!" shouted Alexandra, who marched across the floor, appearing not to pay any attention to the fact that both her arms and a sizeable portion of her chest were missing. "Too much power, and you'll damage him."

Einstein stepped forward. In his hands he carried what looked like a cross between a bazooka and a garden hose, the flexible end spewing out a hazy rainbow-colored light that quickly faded, leaving nothing in its wake but a slight distortion that looked like superheated air, the distortion intersecting with the shattered glass panes that wrapped around Alpha.

"A triumph of Soviet science." She stood before the encased Alpha, smiling and shaking her head, as if not quite believing what she saw. She looked over at Einstein and laughed. "And you, Professor, the greatest physicist that this pathetic ball of mud ever spawned, reduced to the role of spear-carrier. Nadia certainly got her talons in you, successfully rewiring that amazing mush between your ears. It seems that you can't resist the lure of strong females from other universes."

She turned.

"Don't think about it, Jack."

Jack had already taken several steps toward her, when a glassy tendril exploded from her forehead and slammed into the side of his head. He dropped to the floor, twitching. "And now, friend Alpha, before I turn you off, I require access so I can remove you from the computer that sprawls across your world, allowing me to become its master."

A feeble scream escaped the glass tomb engulfing Alpha.

Dozens of glassy tendrils launched from her forehead and buried themselves into the visible part of Alpha's head. Alexandra reeled back, sagged, and dropped to her knees.

The glass tomb shuddered, the already cracked panes of space-time crazing further.

"Do it now," Ernest whispered to Anthony. Anthony nodded, took a quick glance at Einstein, who was focused on keeping the nozzle of his weapon trained on Alpha, and then at Jack, who now lay motionless on the ground. The single filament still attached Jack to Alexandra.

"I don't know what it will do to Jack," he said.

Ernest shook his head and pushed Anthony up. "I do know what will happen if either Alpha or Alexandra survives. This is your only chance!"

"Don't do it," begged Katie, pulling at Anthony's waist, frantic, ripping at his shirt. She had seen what had happened to Horst. "Please," she said, realizing she hadn't the strength to pull him down.

Anthony was no longer a crippled boy—he was a twenty-four-year-old man.

Running forward with the device that had melded with his right hand, he reached for Alpha's exposed fingers. Although he was about to destroy Alpha, to finally bring this nightmare to an end, it was not the encased body he focused on, but the distorted space-time that wrapped it.

Beautiful, he thought.

Stressed space-time. This close to the Sonomak, to the vortex about which the picoverses were collapsing and merging, the energy put out by Einstein's weapon was sufficient to warp and distort the weakened fabric of space-time.

Creeeeeeek!

A shard of mountain, a splinter of rock the size of a whale, materialized to his left, gobbling up banks of electronics and then seamlessly merged with the near side of the cavern.

Anthony grabbed Alpha's hand, realizing that time was short, that if they stayed too long in this region so close to the Sonomak, they would soon find themselves on the wrong end of a tug-of-war between competing realities and simply cease to exist.

Their hands *merged*.

Biological and physical defenses were quickly overcome. Alpha's body did not even sense the invasion. Both Anthony's and the weapon's DNA shared the same origins as

Alpha's. By the time Alpha's body realized it was being invaded, that a foreign body had infected it, it would be too late.

Muscles flexed in Anthony's forearm.

The capsule launched itself into Alpha's body, the way wide open for it, defenses not yet restructured. Alpha's body could not detect the viral programming written within its DNA sequence.

Alpha's body uploaded the data within the capsule, believing it to be nothing more than sensory information, the inputs from the index and ring finger of his right hand. All data was transferred through the wormhole back into Alpha's picoverse, and from there into the hardware where Alpha's consciousness resided.

At that point the data revealed itself to be a program— an ugly, threatening, potentially fatal program that could not be rejected, any more than an organic being could reject the program written within its own DNA. It was a simple program, one that did nothing except multiply, reproducing itself with every clock cycle of Alpha's central nervous system. All the virus needed was the electrical energy to copy itself and access to memory in order to store the replicated version of itself. And as within any organic entity that finds itself invaded, an involuntary immune response was initiated.

Anthony's plan depended on this response.

Alpha attempted to isolate himself from the source of infection. But the act of searching for signs of infection carried the infection to those searched locations. Within several trillion clock cycles, the entity that had been Alpha was crowded out by a mindless piece of memory-hungry, replicating, DNA-driven software.

The physical manifestation of Alpha, still encased in the shattered glass-like cocoon, dropped to the floor.

Alexandra sprawled backward, as if struck by a high-voltage surge. The filaments connecting her to both Jack and Alpha were torn away, leaving a ragged gash across her forehead.

Einstein stopped firing his weapon. The panes of stressed space-time vanished, and Alpha's lifeless body sprawled on the floor like a body-shaped bag filled with thick liquid.

Anthony looked down at his hand and disengaged the device, letting it decouple from bones, muscles, and tendons. It fell onto Alpha's lifeless remains.

"What have you done?" screamed Einstein. Down on one knee he shook what little remained of Alexandra's right shoulder with one hand, and kept his weapon trained on Anthony with the other. "Do you know what she is, what she can show us?"

"A device," said Anthony.

"An insane device," said Katie, who now stood next to Anthony, looking up at him, realizing for the first time that her son was now taller than she was. "An insane device that wanted us dead."

"No," said Einstein. "You don't understand. She was the gateway to the universe beyond ours, to the knowledge of the Makers, to the race that fabricated our entire universe. Do you know what they can teach us, what they can reveal to us about the true nature of the universe? Think of the physics, of the ultimate understanding."

"Is that what you've sold your soul for, Albert?" asked Ernest. He shook his head in disgust. "First Nadia, and now this one. You did all this, just to get a glimpse of their world, of their physics?"

"It's so much more than that!" said Einstein. "Don't you understand? With that knowledge, with that understanding, we would be *safe*. No one could touch us, no one could ever again tear us out of our very universe, terminating our entire planet whenever they deemed an insignificant experiment to be at an end!"

"I see," said Ernest. "So where the Makers failed in the wise and humane use of this knowledge, you believe that you could be trusted with such knowledge? You have the moral fiber to do the right thing when in possession of such ultimate power?" He pointed at the weapon Einstein was holding, and then over to Horst's arm, which protruded from a mound of resolidified concrete.

Einstein blinked, his mouth open as if he were about to speak, but he said nothing. He lowered his weapon and looked around at the destruction. "I . . ."

Alexandra jumped up from the floor, turned, and kicked Einstein in the face, snapping his head back, breaking his neck. "You weakling!" she screamed, turning away even before his lifeless body hit the floor.

"You terminated the connection!" She glared at Anthony. "Before Alpha died, he shut down *all* access to his external sensors." Looking down at the rubbery remains of Alpha, she gave him a hard kick, causing him to roll over several times. "He shut down *everything*."

Anthony simply nodded. That had been his plan.

"He shut down the wormhole *back* into the universe. We can't get out that way, can't get back into the universe and shut it down."

"Shut it down?" said Anthony.

"Shut it down!" she screamed. "I have to shut it down before the collapsing picoverses tear themselves apart and from there go on to rip apart the Makers' universe. It will *all* collapse unless the universe is shut down."

"What?" Anthony managed to say, and looked down at Alpha's lifeless body.

"And you just shut the only way out!"

She stepped forward. The expression on her face left no doubt as to her intentions.

Bang!

Alexandra spun, the momentum of the bullet tearing through her right thigh turning her. Jack stood, swaying back and forth, holding up Horst's pistol. "Stop her," he said.

Bang!

The second bullet just nicked the edge of the place where her shoulder had been torn away. "Stop her," he said again. Dropping to his knees, but keeping the gun trained on her, he held onto it with both hands. "She's lying. There *is* another way out."

Jack fired a third time. And this time missed entirely.

Alexandra was gone, running off into the smoke and haze.

Jack pitched forward, hitting the steel floor face first.

SECTION III
CHAPTER 2

*"We can't stay here," said Ernest. He looked at the whirlpool ex-*ploding out of the side of the mountain, the focal point of collapsing worlds. As he watched, a snow-covered peak on the horizon vanished, replaced with shards of steel and concrete that seemed to punch upward right through the sky.

"He needs to rest," said Anthony. Lowering Jack to the ground, he leaned him against a tree stump.

Katie half sat, half collapsed next to Jack. It had only been a few days since she had awakened in the hospital. She was still weak, and this cross-country escape had drained her. She half closed her eyes and, removing the canteen from her waist, unscrewed the cap and took a deep, long drink.

Horst was dead.

She understood that, could not help but understand that—his burned and charred body, partially entombed in resolidified concrete was more than real enough to convey the image of death. They'd been separated for so long, at each other's throats for even longer. But she'd loved him once, had been able to see past the ego, past the attitude, to something caring and genuine beneath. And he'd saved them all, saved Anthony. "We've been through a lot," she said, looking over at Ernest, who had lowered himself to the ground.

He waved his right hand at her, a mechanical contraption with three fingers and two opposable thumbs, and slowly caught his breath. "You won't get any argument with me on that account," he said. He rotated the wrist on his mechanical hand. "More than you'll ever know," he said, looking over at Anthony, who was helping Jack take a drink.

Katie nodded and then looked behind them, back up the mountainside they'd just fled. Collapsing worlds spiraled down, ceasing to exist. Katie pulled her knees up to her chest and dropped her head. They'd escaped. She'd gotten Anthony back. And she'd destroyed entire worlds in the process. At that moment, at what seemed like the first bit of rest they'd had since the Sonomak had been fired, the first chance to think beyond simply surviving the next few seconds, she realized that far from having saved Anthony, she might have condemned him, along with all the rest of them. But a part of her was certain that this was the only way to truly save them, to save all the picoverses and the universe beyond.

She knew this, could see a pattern unfolding.

And Jack was the key.

However, at that moment, despite what she sensed, she was filled with doubt and fear. She looked up the mountain, knowing at that very moment that millions, perhaps billions were dying.

"Katie."

She felt a pair of hands cup the sides of her face and push her head back. She tried to fight, to push her head back down, but she didn't have the strength. She closed her eyes tightly, not wanting to see any of them, to face what she'd done.

"Open your eyes, Katie."

She opened her eyes. "Oh, Jack," she said in a sob, and began to shake.

Jack held on to the sides of her face. "Listen to me, Katie," he said. "If it hadn't been you, then it would have been one of us. *It had to be done.*"

Katie nodded. "I know that, but it feels so wrong," she said.

"*Wrong,*" said Jack. "But inevitable," he added, now able

to remember some of his past—faint images of when he had altered Alexandra, changed the programming that the Makers had burned into her head. He had planned this from the beginning—actually from *before the beginning*, from before the universe had even been constructed. But he could not remember why, could not see into the Makers' universe, to the place he had been, to understand why he had done these things and why he had made himself forget them.

"I did it to try to save Anthony," she said, sobbing now.

"Listen to me, Katie," said Jack, grabbing her by the knees. "The Sonomak had to be fired. The process had to be started."

"Are we supposed to stop it now, or simply let the collapse continue?" she asked.

Jack blinked. "We are supposed to *control* it," he said.

"How?" she said. "In what way?"

"I don't know," he said. "Not yet."

Anthony had been silent all this time, listening carefully. "To control what's taking place would take far more power than we could ever hope to find. We'd need to be outside the collapse in order to have any chance of guiding it. And if Alexandra was telling the truth, when I shut down Alpha, I also shut down our only way to escape."

Jack shook his head. "There's a way out, a way to escape the picoverses. But we have to stop Alexandra, making certain that she doesn't make the escape before we do."

"And how could she possibly do that?" asked Anthony. "There simply isn't enough energy to generate a wormhole back to the universe."

Jack shook his head. "I suspect that you know more about the physics of universe formation than any of us, but your perspective is limited. You are thinking not in terms of the physics involved, but in terms of the technologies available to implement the physics."

"In terms of practical considerations it's the same thing," said Anthony. "We are hardware and energy limited. Even in the place where Ernest and I came from, a world a thousand years in advance of this one, there was no technology that could generate a wormhole between a picoverse and the larger universe from *this* side, not even a hint as to what that technology might be."

Jack smiled.

"The technology has actually already been built."

"What?" said Anthony, not believing him.

"I saw it when I was linked to Alexandra; I saw a part of what she was draining from Alpha. When we woke Alpha, his systems were automatically updated, all the information gathered while he'd slept was dumped into the active centers of his consciousness. You have to remember that Alpha turned himself off after ten thousand years of existence, convinced just as you are that no technology could exist to generate a wormhole from within the picoverse to the universe beyond. But when he woke, after sleeping nearly one hundred thousand years, he discovered that such a technology had been developed in his *own picoverse*. But he ignored it, no longer needed it. We'd given him a much easier, quicker way to escape." Jack stopped, knowing that *he* had been the one to let Alpha escape, that his touch had somehow reopened the wormhole, an ability that he still didn't understand.

"And just where is it?" asked Anthony.

"Far away," said Jack. "This Sonomak is located in the outer solar system of Alpha's picoverse, where Jupiter and Saturn were once located."

"*Once?*" said Katie, not understanding what that could possibly mean.

"Jupiter and Saturn appear to have been gravitationally imploded, turned into mini-black holes," said Jack. "The black holes are currently in a stable orbit around each other. Most of the moons of both Jupiter and Saturn are also in orbit around the black holes—more than a dozen moon-sized objects in unstable trajectories around the two black holes."

"Unstable?" Anthony shook his head.

"The whole system is primed," said Jack. "Just like a

pencil balanced on its point, the slightest perturbation will cause it to fall. In this case, the slightest orbital perturbation of any of the moons will send them spiraling into the black holes."

"And how does that generate a wormhole?" asked Katie.

Jack was about to answer, but didn't need to, didn't have time to.

"I understand," said Anthony. "It is just like the plasmon in our Sonomak. In our Sonomak, the plasmon grows and contracts, storing the incoming energy with each pulsing, storing enough energy so that when the plasmon finally collapses, the resultant energy density gets so large that a picoverse is generated. The black holes could do the same thing. If their stable orbits could be disrupted, if they could be made to spiral into each other in a grazing fashion, oscillating back and forth as they crash together, the distance between them first growing and then contracting, then the gravitational sheer between them would stress space-time, generating an unbelievable energy gradient. And the way to destabilize their currently stable orbits is by bombarding them with those unstable moons."

Jack nodded. "Billiards on a planetary scale."

Anthony angled his head back and stared up into the sky. "Just before the two holes impact each other, as they speed by one another, *almost* impacting, the gravitational energy density between them would be billions, possibly trillions of times greater than anything we could have generated with our Sonomak."

"Yes," said Jack.

"That could be enough energy to generate a wormhole to our universe," he said. He looked back down at them. "Actually, it would be *much* more energy than is required."

Jack nodded. "Much more. Alexandra will try to use it to start a *controlled* collapse of our entire universe, to turn off the Makers' experiment."

"Then we have to stop her," said Katie. She stood and, reaching for Anthony, took his hands in hers. "*We* have to stop her."

Anthony nodded and turned to Jack, letting go of Katie's hands and, reaching down, pulled Jack to his feet. "Where will she be going?" he asked.

"South," said Jack, pulling up just a few of the nearly infinite images that had flooded through him when he had been in contact with Alpha through the connection Alexandra had established—those from orbital reconnaissance satellites. "It's the nearest access point to where Alpha's picoverse has already merged with this one."

Anthony turned and started walking south. He did not bother to look and see if the others were following him. He knew they would be.

Jack punched both the clutch and the brake, and the old Ford's wheels locked, the truck sliding across the dirt road, almost falling into a ditch, but coming to a halt in a cloud of dust just before skidding off the road. "That's it," said Jack, looking through the truck's cracked windshield.

Fifty yards in front of them the dirt road abruptly stopped. The lush green grasses, trees, and undergrowth gave way to gravel and weeds covering a steep hillside. "It looks hot over there," said Ernest.

Jack kicked open the truck's door. A strong hot breeze struck him, billowing in from the desert region directly in front of them, from the other picoverse.

"It doesn't look like Alpha's picoverse," said Katie. She got out of her side of the truck and stood next to Anthony and Ernest. She pointed toward the horizon, at the immense structures of glass and metal rising up so high into the sky that they simply faded from view.

"Something's changed," said Jack, taking a few steps toward the desert. "The last telemetry that Alpha took indicated that his picoverse and ours butted directly against each other at this point."

"Well, not any longer," said Anthony. "A segment of another picoverse has intersected here. We have no choice but to travel through it in order to get to Alpha's picoverse."

"Are you sure we can cross over?" asked Ernest. He looked at the abrupt transition between the green of their picoverse and the burned browns of the adjoining picoverse. "Just how stable is that interface?"

Anthony bent down, picked up a rock and tossed it up and down a few times. "Difficult to tell. As the picoverses continue to collapse, falling in on one another, the pressure and strain generated by the collapse itself eventually reaches a critical threshold where the fabric of one picoverse gives way and another picoverse fills the void. But it can also start moving even if the pressure is not quite large enough, if the interface gets weakened by something penetrating it."

Ernest unconsciously took a step back. "And I suppose there is no way of knowing just how stable this interface is, to know if our passing through it might cause a collapse?"

"No way of knowing," said Anthony.

The other three were watching Anthony and the rock in his hand, certain that he was about to throw it across the interface, to test its stability.

Anthony dropped the rock. "Not enough mass to really test its stability," he said. "There's wind blowing in from that side," he said, pointing to the desert world, "and in the time that we've been standing here, I've seen several birds cross the boundary." He turned, pointed to his left at a tree at least one hundred meters away. A large hawk leaped off a top branch, wings outstretched, falling quickly at first, but then rising up in the hot thermals billowing from the desert world. It crossed the boundary between picoverses, and nothing happened.

"Take us across, Jack," said Anthony. He climbed into the back of the truck. "But before you do, I think you should turn around, go back down the road, and get up some speed before you cross the barrier. If our passing causes a collapse, we want to be moving as fast as possible—faster than the advancing collapsing picoverse wave front if possible."

The others climbed in, and Jack put the old Ford in reverse, backing down the road.

"Good enough," said Anthony after they'd backed up nearly one hundred yards. "If we are going too fast, we'll crash the truck when we get to the other side," he said as he pointed to the other side, and the rising, rock-strewn hill. "Whenever you're ready."

Jack took a deep breath, popped the clutch, hit the gas, and the truck leaped forward. He'd gotten it into second gear and was moving nearly thirty miles an hour when they hit the interface.

The truck jerked to the left, as Jack fought the wheel, bounced, its two left wheels leaving the ground as the truck listed on its side, then slammed back down as Jack stomped the brake, the end of the truck fishtailing to the left, rotating around and coming to a stop only when the back of the truck hung up on a large boulder.

A cloud of dust rolled over them.

"I guess we made it," said Katie. Letting go of the dashboard, she slumped back in the seat. "We didn't cause a collapse."

"Mother."

Katie turned around and looked through the rear window to where Anthony and Ernest had strapped themselves down in the back of the truck. The cloud of dust they had kicked up was dispersing, pushed away in the breeze.

Behind them, desert rolled to a horizon that was *miles* away. The world they had just left, the one that had only been yards behind them, no longer existed.

"Oh my God," said Katie, realizing that if the collapse they had just caused had moved in the opposite direction, they might no longer exist.

Anthony jumped out of the back of the truck. "We'll need to walk from here," he said, ignoring what was behind him, focusing instead on the rock-strewn hill in front of them. "We need to hurry." He pointed to the top of the hill, at the structure that seemed to rise up out of it, but which was actually far away, in the region of the *next* picoverse, a stalk of metal and glass, piercing high cloud cover. "Alexandra may already be there."

SECTION III
CHAPTER 3

"I am Artist."

"I understand that," said Alexandra, sounding frustrated, having heard the thing make the announcement more than a dozen times. She was in no mood for this, still feeling battered and beaten by the ordeal of reaching the pillar—all those miserable machines having tossed her around like a sack of potatoes. Arching her shoulders back, she rolled her arms in the air. They still felt foreign to her, so recently grown. She tried not to think about how she'd acquired the raw resources needed to grow them, reflexes almost making her gag—there'd been so many dead around the Sonomak installation.

"I require supplies," said Artist.

"I require you to listen and do what I tell you," said Alexandra, rubbing her right arm. "Four people will be following me, and I need you to stop them."

"I am Artist."

"Damn it!" shouted Alexandra, glaring at Artist, barely controlling her rage, just able to hold herself back and resist putting her fist through its flat, stained-glass face. "Just stop them, don't let them enter the pillar!"

"I require supplies," said Artist, turning, angling its paper-thin head so it could see across the plaza at its damaged creation. "I require supplies," it said again.

"Stop them!"

"I require supplies."

Alexandra took a step back and prepared to retract the

connection to Artist, now certain that the thing could not be made to listen, that it did not have sufficient intelligence for her to interface and control it.

"I require supplies."

In the last several minutes, she'd heard the thing plead for supplies, but had not really listened to it, not cared what *supplies* it needed. And then she suddenly understood, looked out across the plaza that surrounded the base of the pillar and at the machines that roamed across it. "Are those your supplies?" she asked.

"Yes," said Artist, pointing with glass fingers, the noon-day sun pouring through the colored panes, throwing rainbow patterns across the cement. "I require supplies."

Alexandra nodded and again focused, this time finding the correct path through Artist's convoluted neural paths. She first delivered the access codes she'd found when scavenging through Alpha's systems. Turning to her left, she watched an opening appear in the side of the pillar, the entrance that would take her away from this miserable world. Then she accessed that part of Artist's neural matrix where details of inventories were held. "Your new supplies will be coming from the north," she said. "There will be four of them . . ."

"From the heart of North America down to the Equator in less than twenty minutes," said Ernest, as he stared out at a cityscape that faded away in the distant horizon, the infinite sprawl dominated by a single structure that seemed to go right through the roof of the sky. They stood on the train platform, where they'd been deposited from the tube—an underground transport system—an evacuated tube in which single-person cabs were accelerated at almost a full gee for five minutes, pushing the cabs up to speeds of ten thousand kilometers per hour. "Absolutely amazing," said Ernest, not referring to the tube, but to the pillar.

"Over there," said Jack, pointing at the pillar's base. "The elevator entrance is on this side," he said, having a dim recollection of its location, vague images of the pillar and its surrounding plaza flitting through his head, a phantom memory obtained during his connection to Alpha by way of Alexandra. The tube had let them off atop a ten-story-tall structure, just high enough to give them a bit of perspective, to allow them to plan a way to get to the pillar.

Katie tripped through the full range of her visual menu and could see nothing special at the base of the pillar. The structure looked featureless, seamless, nothing but a milk-white pillar that punctured the sky.

The pillar was narrower at the base than it was kilometers higher up.

The structure was shaped like a needle with the point end down, impossibly balanced, a base that looked to be no more than a hundred meters in diameter, supporting a structure that Jack insisted went up nearly one hundred thousand kilometers, almost one-fifth of the way to the moon.

"It's balanced," said Jack, looking over at Katie. "Its center of mass sits at a geosynchronous orbital height, directly above the Equator, with half the mass distributed out beyond that point and the other half hanging down toward the Earth. The base of the pillar doesn't support any weight at all. It acts as an anchor."

Katie raised both her eyebrows. "I understood it the first time when you explained it to me, Jack," she said. "But understanding it does not make the structure seem any more *right*."

Ernest nodded. "But it does make me believe that maybe these artificial black holes of yours do exist," he said, looking at Jack. "A structure like this makes artificial black holes almost seem plausible."

"It looks alive," said Anthony.

"The pillar?" said Jack. Never in his life had he seen a structure that looked less alive, more artificial and obviously constructed.

"No," said Anthony. He pointed down at the open expanse between them and the base of the pillar. "Them."

From the moment they'd entered this portion of Alpha's

picoverse, they'd seen them, both back in North America, and now at the Equator. From a distance they looked human, but when you got up close they were obviously not. Part machine, part biological, their faces smooth and featureless, they moved through a dead world, up and down the streets, silently shuffling, not interacting with one another, human-like mannequins going through a pathetic imitation of life.

"They're just machines," said Ernest. "And not even very good machines," he added. The things were falling apart, many of them with missing limbs, plastic skin worn away in spots, most of them no longer walking on anything resembling feet, but on ankle stumps, some so damaged that they no longer even walked, but dragged themselves along, using their hands and what few fingers may have remained.

Anthony shook his head. "They're not alive as individual entities, but they are as a *whole*. There is a pattern to their movement, a structure, and even what appears to be a purpose, the whole thing shifting and transforming. That motion is reflective of an intelligence."

Jack squinted. He saw none of that, just the huge expanse before them and what he estimated had to be tens of millions of the humanoid machines randomly marching about. But he knew better than to dismiss what Anthony was saying. "So what do you suggest?" he asked.

Anthony gave a quick scan across the plaza then at the pillar. "That we get across the plaza as quickly as possible and into the pillar."

The pile of bones was nearly up to their knees, almost all of them broken, just remnants of bones. Jack kneeled down and picked up a handful of the bits. He could tell that most of them were the bones of small creatures, probably birds, but there was one larger shard, something that looked like a piece of jawbone. He turned it over in his hand and saw a molar still imbedded in it. "Human!" he shouted, holding it up for the others to see, the sound of his voice barely carrying over the roar of the moving machines.

He stood, looked out into the plaza, and tossed out the jawbone. It was only a matter of seconds before it was splintered, and the shards pulverized. Jack knew that was exactly what would happen to them if they fell, if one of the machines knocked them down.

"No other way across," said Anthony, who had been staring out at the plaza. "Look," he said, pointing not at the machines, but at the floor of the plaza. "See the regions that are not as worn down as the others?"

Jack bent down to get a closer look and could see that the stone floor of the plaza, made out of what looked like massive slabs of granite, was in fact worn in places, the pattern resembling a highly convoluted floodplain—shallow trenches bordered by slightly raised regions. Some trenches were deeper than others, intersecting in spots, as if the pathway had changed over time, new paths cutting into the old. But he knew that water had not worn down the massive slabs of granite. It was *them*, wandering about.

Looking down at his feet and kicking away at the mound of bones, Anthony exposed the ledge that they stood on. It was built of the same granite as the plaza—seamless, flowing down into the plaza, nearly a foot lower than the ledge.

"Worn away!" shouted Ernest, who had also cleared a region of the ledge and, kneeling down, was feeling the smooth stone with the palm of his right hand.

Jack understood. The entire floor of the plaza was nearly a foot lower than the bone-strewn ledge they were standing on—worn down by the machines. He knew a process like that would take thousands of years—tens of thousands of years. The bones and the worn granite told Jack that probably nothing had successfully negotiated the plaza for millennia.

"Follow me," shouted Anthony, who suddenly stepped out into the plaza, closely followed by Katie.

"No!" shouted Jack. Reaching for her, he missed, instead running his outstretched fingers into the metal-hard shoulder of a machine. First one machine and then a second stepped between him and Katie as she continued to follow

Anthony. He had no time to think, could only react. He stepped into the plaza, was shoved by a machine, lost his footing, hit the granite pavement, and screamed as a machine stepped onto his right hand, its foot gone, a worn nub of ankle momentarily pinning him to the ground. And then the machine moved on and Jack felt himself pulled up by the hair.

"Follow them!" said Ernest. He let go of Jack's hair and pointed at Katie.

Jack stumbled forward, right hand cradled against his chest, only partially aware of the fact that Ernest had probably just saved his life, as he darted around a headless machine and closed in on Katie, who herself was pushed up against Anthony.

Ernest then shoved him from behind. "We won't last long out here!" he shouted, punctuating the shout with a painful sounding *ooof*, as a passing machine hit him in the side. "Anthony, how long to get to the pillar?"

"The time is not fixed, the pathways for a given individual not totally predictable!" Anthony shouted without looking back, concentrating on the machines moving all around him, veering left and right, turning and twisting, at times even stopping, sidestepping and moving backward before moving forward again. "As far as I can tell, it takes one of these machines on average about twenty years to cycle between the edge of the plaza and the center!"

"Twenty years!" shouted Ernest.

Jack was certain that at best they had only a few minutes before they were trampled.

Anthony moved hard toward the right and stepped over a crawling machine. Just as he stepped over, he paused and, reaching out to his left, grabbed onto a passing machine and tugged it toward himself, turned it nearly ninety degrees and then pushed it on its way in a new direction.

"We don't have twenty years!" yelled Jack, wincing, his vision momentarily tunneling as something struck him in the side of the head.

"We won't need it," answered Anthony as he began to

run forward, sidestepping machines, pushing one to the right, another to the left, and then stopping altogether and holding on to one. "Help me, Jack!" he shouted. "We've got to keep *this* one here."

"What's going on, Anthony?" shouted Jack, as he grabbed on to the machine, which was now frantically scraping at the granite ground with the remnants of a left foot and a right ankle stump.

Both Katie and Ernest came up behind them, and also seized onto the struggling machine. Anthony didn't look at them, but looked beyond them, at the machines spread out all around them, at the sea of metal and plastic. Still holding on to the thrashing machine, but jumping up and down, Anthony detected a far-off motion, like a wave in an ocean, only this wave was produced by the bunching and parting of the machines.

"Let him go!" said Anthony, who released the machine that quickly hobbled off. "We've finally been detected!"

From their left, a solid wall of machines sidestepped all at once, moving toward them. "Help!" shrieked Katie as the wall of metal and plastic first crashed into her.

No one could help her. There was no time. As the wall hit them, they were picked up, a nearly infinite number of hands grabbing them, passing them over the heads of the machines, moving them in the direction of the center of the plaza.

"Don't fight them!" screamed Anthony.

Jack rolled face forward, flipped over, hands grabbing his wrists and ankles, tossing him forward, new hands grabbing and pulling, throwing him across the heads of the machines.

"Supplies are to remain in the staging area."

Jack rolled over onto his back, not yet able to stand. He was bruised from head to toe. His right shoulder felt nearly dislocated, and blood ran into his right eye.

"You will be returned to the staging area."

Jack reached up and wiped the blood out of his eye,

certain that must be the reason for the obvious distortion of the creature standing before him.

"Supplies do not cause deviations," it said as it bent down toward him. It was translucent, made from what looked like slabs of stained glass, with trapezoidal eyes made of prisms, from which streamed rainbow light. "Supplies?" it asked, reaching down and trying to grab Jack.

Despite the pounding ache in his shoulder, Jack rolled to his right, slamming into Katie, and half standing, pulled her up along with him. They stood at the base of the pillar, the structure rising up forever before them. The machines had passed them from hand to hand, head over head, finally dumping them at the pillar, in front of this machine.

"What happened?" asked Ernest, pushing himself up, angling his head back, and seeing the stained-glass creature for the first time. He scuttled back on all fours, pushing himself up into a crouch only when he was certain he was far enough away so that the thing couldn't make a grab for him.

"Supplies are to remain in the staging area," it said to Anthony, pointing out across the plaza and at the ever-moving machines.

Anthony stepped between the creature and the others. "We are not supplies."

The ground beneath them suddenly rumbled, and Jack felt himself pressed down, his stomach dropping, his knees almost buckling. Katie almost fell and grabbed his right shoulder, the one that already felt as if it had been torn from its socket.

"I am Artist," said the creature. "I require supplies."

It waved a translucent glass arm in the direction of the plaza. Jack turned and almost fell, stumbling backward. They were now several hundred feet above the plaza floor, an entire ring of granite around the pillar having risen up, taking them with it.

"Supplies are to remain in the staging area until called for," said Artist. "I was informed that four supplies would arrive."

Below and to the east echoed a low rumbling, and then the roaring clash of metal against metal rolled over them. Jack turned. At the edge of the plaza he could see an open patch of ground, a region totally devoid of the machines. The opening was at first circular, then transformed into a square, followed by a pentagon, and then flowed back again into a circle. With each change in geometry came the crashing sounds of metal as the machines collided into each other, making room for the open plot of plaza.

"Who informed you?" asked Anthony.

"Alpha," said Artist.

"What?" said Katie, letting go of Jack for the first time since they'd been lifted into the sky. "Alpha is dead," she said.

"Alpha provided the codes," said Artist. "Identification was made. Alpha informed me that supplies would be arriving and then departed for transportation."

Anthony continued to move, keeping himself directly between Artist and the others. He looked over his shoulder. "Artist is not fully aware," he said. "It must be referring to Alexandra. She was probably able to use Alpha's identification codes to make this thing believe that she was Alpha."

"Supplies must remain in the staging area," said Artist and started to move toward them, but then stopped, looking into the plaza. "The pattern has deviated. It is unstable."

Jack looked down, and realized that unstable was a totally inadequate way of describing what was taking place. The region of open space continued to transform into various geometrical shapes, but with each cycle the size of the open space grew. The machines were getting pressed more and more tightly together, the ones in the very middle getting crushed, metal and plastic being torn apart, a line of broken machinery piling up.

Anthony smiled, hoping that the gamble was about to pay off.

"Supplies cannot alter the nature of the art," said Artist. Its head began to turn back and forth, first looking over the plaza and then back at Anthony. It did this several times, finally stopping to look at Anthony. "It is the nature of Artist to create the pattern, to generate an aesthetically pleasing mix of function and form."

It turned and looked once more out across the plaza and then back at Anthony. "You have altered the pattern."

"I am the *new* Artist," said Anthony. "Those supplies are no longer required. They are damaged and need to be replaced. I will create the new pattern."

Artist took a step back, angling its face, catching the sun, and sending shafts of green and blue light toward Anthony. "I am Artist. I am responsible for the staging and preparation of the supplies. It has *always* been my designation."

"Are you controlling the *new* pattern?" asked Anthony.

"No," said Artist.

"Who instigated the new pattern?" asked Anthony.

"*You* instigated the new pattern," it said. It stepped to its left, moving toward the edge of the platform. "The supplies are being damaged. More supplies are required," it said and turned back toward Anthony. "*New* supplies are required."

"I will acquire the new supplies," he said. "I will establish the new pattern. I am now the Artist."

To the west, a building nearly thirty stories high suddenly leaned, and sounds of explosions filled the plaza. A wall of scrap metal and plastic almost as high as the building had washed up against it, imploding it, pushing the debris along with the collapsing building back into the city.

Artist looked at the collapsing building, at the billowing cloud of dust and then out across the plaza where most of the machines now lay motionless, shattered, bits and pieces gathered up like snowdrifts. Only a few hundred thousand machines still moved about, climbing across the mounds of debris.

"*You* are Artist," it said to Anthony, and then turning, took the several steps it needed to get to the edge of the platform and then stopped, the tips of its stained glass feet hanging over the edge. "You have systems access," it said, and then stepped forward, falling, turning, rolling, sunlight glistening, reflecting from its colored surface.

"Destination?"

The four turned, the voice having come from behind them. In the seamless exterior of the pillar there was now an opening. They could see nothing within, just a diffuse white light spilling out. A line of green pulsing arrows appeared beneath the surface of the granite, heading into the pillar.

"Please follow the arrows," said the voice. "A short wait will be required before the elevator returns from Geo level."

They walked forward, following the arrows. Jack craned his head back, looking up at the vertical pillar that vanished in clouds far above. The elevator was returning from Geo level. He knew exactly who had taken the previous elevator ride. Alexandra was still well ahead of them.

SECTION III
CHAPTER 4

The height made Katie dizzy. She kept her hands wrapped tightly around the chair's handholds and tried not to look down, but it was *impossible not to look*, she realized, in the same way that it was impossible not to look at a car accident.

She estimated that they were at least ten thousand kilometers up, the Earth curving away from them, the Rocky Mountains visible on the northern horizon, cutting a jagged line from south to north. None of it looked real. It looked like an Earth fabricated out of papier-mâché that had then been struck by a hammer, shattered, and cracked. The point of impact was right where the Sonomak lay buried on the eastern slope of the Rockies.

The shattered region was expanding, pushing west to the Pacific and east to the Mississippi. Terrified, she was certain that at any moment those cracks would spread south to the Equator and that the four of them would cease to exist, or a chunk of the pillar beneath them would vanish, replaced by a chunk of upper atmosphere or vacuum from another picoverse, and they would go rebounding away in space.

"Can you see the pattern, Mother?" asked Anthony. He was seated next to her, perched on the edge of his chair, leaning against the transparent view port ringing this entire section of the elevator.

Katie gulped, reached toward him, while still holding on tight to her chair with her other hand and grabbed his shoulder, pulling him back into his chair. "Please, Anthony," she said, momentarily closing her eyes, forcing back a wave of nausea. "Please sit back."

Anthony grinned at her and pushed a thick swatch of his slightly too long blond hair out of his eyes. "I didn't know you were afraid of heights," he said. His expression suddenly turned thoughtful. "I suppose that there is a lot that I don't know about you."

Katie winced, the comment physically hurting her. "And so many things that I don't know about you." She took a quick glance back out the window, and could see that the horizon was slightly more curved than it had been only a minute or two before. The elevator was quickly moving them up the pillar. The spiderweb-like cracks running across North America continued to grow. Most of the island of Cuba was simply missing. "What pattern do you see?" she asked.

Anthony pointed to the north, to where Katie thought the Mexican–U.S. border would lie, if there were such a thing as Mexico or the United States in that portion of the continent now. "Do you see that burned orange region, shaped like a triangle but with the top lopped off?"

Katie looked, searching for the piece of geography he described, in the same way that she might have looked for a piece of jigsaw puzzle. Finally she saw it and nodded.

"Watch carefully," he said. "It is just about to fragmen into four nearly identically sized pieces. Draw an imaginary line between each of the opposing vertices."

Katie imagined the lines, and as she did, it was as if the planet read her thoughts, the lines appearing just where she had imagined them, the burned orange trapezoid trans

formed into four smaller regions, one colored a deep green
and the other three, distinctly different shades of blue.

"And what about the base of the Pillar, can you tell how
stable it is?

Anthony smiled. "No problem," he said. "This far south,
it should actually be good for several more days."

"How do you know?" she asked.

"Think of the picoverses as soap bubbles, all coalescing,
coming together, and this Earth, what we see beneath us,
is a flat plane slicing through all those bubbles. As the
bubbles break, shift, and coalesce, the geometry of the
changing bubble structure is projected on that plane."

Katie nodded, understanding the words, but still not seeing how he could know *how* the bubble universes would
coalesce. How could he look down at the Earth and trans-
pose the physics that described each collapsing universe
and simply know the resulting geometrical structure?

How could he calculate such a thing? she wondered for
just a moment, but quickly suspected what the answer must
be. "You don't actually solve the equations that express
what is going on down there," she said as she pointed down
toward Earth.

Anthony shook his head. "No," he said. "I know how
the equations behave, understand their temperaments, their
likes and dislikes, know how they react to different circumstances. But most importantly, I know how they interact
with each other. The equations defining each picoverse
have a unique personality, and when multiple personalities
interact, it is fairly easy to predict the outcome."

Katie didn't understand. By nature she was a number
cruncher, lived and died by the least significant bit. The
transformation that Nadia had brought about in her skull
had made her even more of a cruncher. She could no more
understand the *personality* of an equation than she could
turn herself inside out.

But Anthony could.

"And back in the plaza, you understood the underlying

equations, the *personality* of the math which was moving those robots about?"

"Exactly," said Anthony. "I saw Artist through its art, through the movements of those machines. And when I saw it, I knew how to change it, where the critical path existed, where an almost insignificant deviation in the pattern would cause a total collapse of the entire structure."

Katie smiled and let go of her chair, reaching out for Anthony, holding on to both of his hands. "I don't understand it, Anthony," she said, and then let go of one of his hands and reached up to his forehead, pushing back his hair. "Are you wired so differently from the rest of us?" she asked. "Gris told me that you were transhuman," she whispered, as if to say it aloud might make it true.

Anthony smiled. "All too human, I'm afraid." He looked out into space, past the Earth, into the darkness. "I don't know how to stop her, don't know what it is that we'll find at Jupiter, and certainly don't know if it is at all possible to use what we find there to repair the damage that's been done."

"The damage that *I've* done," said Katie. She let go of his hand and sat back in her chair.

Anthony turned to her. "No," he said, shaking his head. "Jack was right. The collapse *needed* to happen," he said, listening carefully to the words he spoke, having not consciously even thought of them before he spoke. He didn't understand why he said it, but it felt right. "There are reasons for all this."

"I pray that you're right," said Katie.

"Excuse me."

Anthony opened his eyes. For just an instant he did not know where he was. A face filled his field of view.

"You need to wake."

"I don't sleep," said Anthony. He pushed himself back in his chair, knowing that despite what he had just said, he *had* been asleep. For a moment he could touch the dream he'd been having—an alpine meadow circled by snowy peaks, the air crisp, cold, but the sun striking his back, warm and comforting, the scent of animals thick in the air, adrenaline suddenly pumping, the hunt about to begin. And then it was gone, as if it had never been there at all.

"I know you don't sleep," *she* said.

He looked past her, down at an Earth that was now a sphere, so small that it appeared as if he could reach out and take it in his hand.

"Take it if you wish," she said.

Anthony leaned forward, pushing out his right arm, knowing that his hand was about to be stopped by the pillar's viewing window. He pushed his hand farther out, not able to find the window, his arm stretching, lengthening, his hand impossibly distant. And then he felt his fingers wrap around the Earth, could feel the warm waters of the tropics in the palm of his hand, the frigid ice from the North Pole stinging his fingers, and the gritty roughness inside his index finger that was the Himalayas. He pulled the Earth toward him, sitting back in his chair as he did so. He examined the Earth, slowly turning it, and stopping when he came to the angry-looking wound that spread out across North America.

"It's begun," she said.

Anthony nodded, agreeing with her, knowing that something had begun, something that could not be stopped, but perhaps something that could be *guided*. He looked up at her. "Is this a dream?" he asked, holding the Earth up toward her.

She smiled and sat down in a large, red velvet chair that had not been there a moment ago. "Perhaps an altered state would be a better way to describe it," she said.

"Who are you?" he asked.

"No one of importance," she said. "Just a device to explain to you the trivial little facts that seem to comfort those who travel between the planets." She smiled.

At that instant Anthony saw the transport system connecting all points within Alpha's solar system. He saw the pillars rising up, not only from Earth, but on all the terrestrial planets and the moon. And at each pillar hub, at that halfway point up the shaft, he saw the large spinning ring, adorned with the little light sail craft, powered by lasers, those used for the short-range transport between the pillars and the interplanetary transports.

Worlds.

The transports, the size of small moons, were actually hollowed-out asteroids, whose orbits moved between the inner and outer solar system, the little worlds designed to carry goods, cargo, and passengers between the planets.

"You are the first passengers in nearly fifty thousand years," she said.

Anthony remembered the plaza around the pillar, the bones and the decaying, age-worn machines, waiting to be taken up the pillar and then transported across the solar system.

"No need for them any longer," she said. "Everything was built, the Sonomak completed, nothing left to do until the operator arrived."

"And am I the operator?" he asked.

"You might be," she answered. "Or it might be any of the others."

"Where is Alexandra?" he asked, frightened at the prospect of her being the operator.

"Far away," she said. "She is already in transit."

"She wants us dead," said Anthony, "She wants everything dead, to have never existed. She must be stopped."

"None of that matters to me. My job is transportation. I am to see that the operator is delivered to the Sonomak. If you are *all* delivered, then I will be assured of having completed my function."

Anthony stood and looked out the window—nothing but darkness. No stars in this world. Even the Earth itself was gone, transformed into a shattered sphere that he clutched in his right hand. He turned it slowly, imagining all the other earths, the other picoverses Alpha had created, all the earths that were now crashing down upon each other. "The Pacific is so large," he said. Placing the tip of his index finger on Japan, he put his outstretched thumb on the thin bridge of land connecting North and South America. Anthony held up the Earth, placing it between him and the woman, holding it out at just the right distance so that it seemed to cover her head, making it appear as if the Earth rested on her shoulders. "Who gave you your instructions?" asked Anthony. "Who told you to transport the operator to the Sonomak?"

She stood from her chair and walked off the edge of the elevator platform, passing through the viewing window that no longer seemed to exist, and floated out into the blackness of space, quickly receding, growing ever smaller, until nothing remained but a shimmer of reflected sunlight. Then she was gone. "It was the operator who instructed me, who told me fifty thousand years ago that all of you would be coming and be in need of transport."

Anthony laughed. "You are damaged—we've been in the picoverse for only a matter of hours," he said, not quite sure why he found this funny. "And if one of us is the operator, then how could one of us have given you instructions fifty thousand years ago?" He stepped forward and ran into the window that was back in place. The Earth he held in his hand crashed against the window, the sphere shattering, transformed into a cloud of sparkling dust that hung in midair.

"The operator was present then," echoed her distant voice. "The operator has returned. You must remember."

"Wake up, Anthony."

Anthony opened his eyes, sat up, stood, pushed at the hands trying to hold him, then spun around and pressed himself up against something hard and unyielding. He blinked, focused, and looking down toward his feet for the shattered, dusty remnants of the Earth, saw nothing, and then turned to look outside the viewing window. The Earth hung below him. "I was dreaming," he said.

"It must have been some dream."

Anthony turned. Katie and Jack stood in front of him,

Katie looking concerned, reaching out, hesitating, and lowering her hand. Beyond her, Anthony could see Ernest. There was something wrong with Ernest. Something had changed.

"Ernest?" he asked.

Ernest shook his head and moved away, turning, stopping only when he came to the viewing window, leaning against it, pressing his forehead to the glass.

"What's wrong with Ernest?" asked Anthony.

"He won't say," said Jack, quickly looking over his shoulder toward Ernest and then back at Anthony. "We all had some sort of dream, met some virtual character that is part of the transportation system, but seemed to be much *more* than part of the transportation system."

Anthony nodded.

"Attention!"

Anthony jumped, nearly knocking Katie to the floor in the process.

"Please follow the green lines to departure bay 18."

"I guess that would be us," said Ernest, the expression on his face a dark one. He did not look at the others, but began to march off toward the elevator exit, following the green pulsing arrows that had materialized in the floor. "Wouldn't want to keep our lord and master waiting," he said.

Katie, Jack, and Anthony all exchanged glances, but said nothing as they fell in behind Ernest. Anthony watched Ernest move, suddenly not recognizing him at all. Something in his gait, in the way his arms moved, in the way his single boot and mechanical foot hit the floor seemed so totally wrong. He was suddenly certain that the man he had known for almost his entire life, the closest friend he had ever had, the person who had been more of a father to him than anyone else, was gone.

Anthony did not know who they were following.

He only knew that it was *not* Ernest Lawrence.

•   •   •

They stood in the docking bay overlooking the spacecraft, a thing that was all sail, literally square miles of what looked like gossamer aluminum held together by spiderweb-like wires. There were no engines; none would be required. At the hub of the pillar lay a powerful laser, a device capable of punching holes in small asteroids. But rather than being used to shatter asteroids, the laser light would play out across the sail, the light pressure accelerating the craft, hurling it away from Earth and to the distant orbiting transport that would then take them outward to the Sonomak. In the center of the solar sail was a pod, an elongated sphere of aluminum that looked barely big enough to hold the four of them.

Swish.

Doors parted, and the interior of the pod was exposed. Anthony walked in first, lowering his head to enter, taking the seat nearest the front, the one before what he assumed was a control panel. He squirmed into the seat and felt it conform to his body, actually pulling him down and back, positioning him in a reclining position. His hands sank into the fabric of the chair, disappearing. He lay back in his seat and became enveloped, the warm fabric wrapping him in a snug cocoon. For just a moment he felt claustrophobic, tried to lift his hands, to pull the material away from his face.

But he didn't.

He was already asleep and dreaming.

Jack and Katie quickly succumbed, swallowed into their own cocoons.

Only Ernest remained awake. His fingers played across the console in front of him. Alexandra *had* set a trap for them. The craft's navigational system had been tampered with. Ernest quickly reprogrammed, running through the system's database, searching for the location of the *correct* transport.

The *Hirku-Ashi* had long ago left the inner system and was nearly out as far as the orbit of Mars. There were easily a dozen other transports that were closer, which the sail craft *should* have targeted for. But Ernest knew none of those would do. He checked the light craft's consumables; the retinal display played across his eyes.

Close.

But they could make it. The *Hirku-Ashi* was just within the limit of their range. He set the coordinates and then relinquished control of the ship to its automatic systems. His seat engulfed him, pulling him under. He dreamed. *Nightmares of lives best forgotten.*

SECTION III
CHAPTER 5

*The hatch of the sail's pod opened slowly—far too slowly for Al-*exandra. She kicked at it several times and then rammed her shoulder against it. The hatch continued to slowly open, the mechanism totally oblivious to her attempts to hurry it. Before it fully opened, she dropped down on all fours and scrambled out beneath the rising hatch. She stood, and rose up off the floor to a height of nearly a meter before floating back down. She was inside the transport, a hollowed-out asteroid, very near the axis of the slowly rotating rock, where gravity was at a minimum. She took several running jumps down the hallway to what appeared to be a large window, which she hit hard. Even though she was nearly weightless, she still had mass; her momentum was unchanged. "Damn," she said as she pushed herself back.

A world spread out before her. She guessed that the asteroid was shaped something like a potato and was rotating around its long axis. The docking port, where the sail had landed, was at one end of the axis. She had an unbroken view of what appeared to her to be a hollowed-out space that ran at least fifty kilometers to the far end and had a diameter of at least ten kilometers. The inside walls of the world glistened, alive with motion, reminiscent of the machines that had marched around the pillar. Huge swatches of window were opened to space, bringing in reflected sunlight that was focused to a point at the center of the trans-port, creating the appearance of a burning sun. She looked away from the artificial sun, instantly putting it and every-thing else about the transport out of her mind. "I require assistance!" she said, as she turned her back on the pano-ramic view.

To her left, a portion of the wall recessed and then slipped out of sight. A human-like figure stepped out, one that she recognized as being like the ones wandering around the pillar's plaza, but this one looked new. It wore a bright orange jumpsuit and pale blue slippers.

"Welcome to transport *Eden*," it said, sounding cheerful. "Your personal quarters have been prepared. You may wish to have a meal before you are put in stasis for the journey."

Alexandra stepped toward the machine, bobbing up and down a bit as she did so, not yet comfortable in the low gravity. "No stasis," she said, not knowing exactly what that meant, but knowing that she had a great deal of work to do and that there would be no time for rest.

"But the trip to Europa station is nearly a year in length," the machine said. "You are the only human on board, and as such the psychological isolation may be damaging. It is recommended that you submit yourself to stasis."

Alexandra was in no mood to argue with a machine, especially one that was so stupid as to believe that she was a mere human. "I need access to this transport's computer systems," she said. "I need to be put in communication with the facility at Europa," she added, wanting to find out as soon as possible just how this new Sonomak operated, and what she would have to do to fire it and control it.

The machine stood, facing her, motionless, as if waiting for further requests.

"Now!"

The machine turned. "Please follow me," it said.

"This isn't a transport, just a hollowed-out asteroid," said Katie. She waved her hands first at the stars above and then at the woods all around. *"This is a world."*

"I'm *way* too old for this," Ernest said, almost laughing at just how ironic that statement really was. He looked away from the campfire and into the dark woods. He still hadn't told the others what he'd dreamed, of what he'd *learned*. He hadn't yet been able to roll it around enough times in his own mind. Telling the others made no sense to him until he could understand it himself.

Jack tossed a branch into the fire, sending up a twisting column of twinkling cinders into the nighttime sky. Anthony leaned back and, picking up a handful of what he thought to be some sort of blueberries from the wooden bowl that he'd fashioned earlier in the day, he began to pop them into his mouth one by one. "You're not getting too old, Ernest," he said. "You're getting too soft."

The old Ernest would have laughed at this.

Ernest stared at him, looking through the fire, staring so hard that Anthony thought he might be able to look right through him.

What has happened to Ernest? Anthony asked himself once more.

Jack and Katie laughed and snuggled closer together. The night air was cold, despite the roaring fire.

"We've been through this before," said Ernest. He pointed a stick across the fire at Anthony, deliberately changing the subject. "Give the predators a few more days to pick up on our scent, to realize that there is a new type of food wandering the woods, and we'll soon find ourselves beating off very nasty carnivores with wooden clubs and homemade bows and arrows. The last such adventure cost me a hand and a foot."

In response, Anthony picked up several arrows he'd already fashioned, flint tips tied into place with rabbit gut and adorned with feathers provided by something that had looked like an undernourished chicken. Whoever or whatever this Ernest was, he seemed to have the full memories of the Ernest he had known. "This is paradise compared to the last world we found ourselves so abruptly thrown into," he said.

Jack leaned back, letting his head drop into Katie's lap. She rubbed his forehead and ran her fingers through his hair. Above him, stars burned bright and steady. He knew it was an illusion, probably nothing more than some sort of high-powered lightbulbs hanging in the null-gee center of the asteroid—the *Hirku-Ashi*. Beyond them, far above them, lay the other side of this inside-out world.

"That fire has gotten a bit larger," said Jack. He pointed past the stars.

"It must be a wildfire," said Katie, angling her head back, looking directly above. "It's so much bigger than all the other fires."

"No," said Anthony. "The strength of the big fire has been varying all night. There's a pattern to it, a cycle." Anthony tossed another small piece of wood into the fire, causing the campfire to flare briefly, as it shot out a plume of sparks. "That's what's happening on the other side."

"But that's no small campfire," said Katie. "It's at least one hundred kilometers away."

Anthony nodded. "You're right," he said. "I'm sure that what *they're* tossing in that fire are more like entire trees rather than these little broken branches."

"Exactly," said Ernest. *"They."*

"Any idea who *they* might be?" asked Anthony, turning toward Ernest.

Ernest shook his head.

Anthony was certain that he was lying, that he knew exactly what lay on the far side of the horizon—on the other side of this inverted world. And Anthony himself felt that he could almost see what waited for them. He'd known this place from the moment they'd awakened, from the moment he'd looked out into this mountainous world of snow-covered peaks, alpine valleys, and thick pine forests. This had been the world in his dream. There was a reason for their being here. He knew that they were not supposed to spend the year it would take to travel to the Sonomak hiding in a metal cubbyhole.

There are no random acts.

Anthony tossed another log onto the fire and then lay back, resting his head on a pillow of pine needles. "And to be ready for what waits for us, I suggest that we all get some sleep."

"Ready for what?" asked Ernest.

Anthony looked up into the sky and at the fires burning on the other side of the world. "Ready to learn what this world has to teach us."

"Keep low," said Anthony to Katie, who crouched next to him, both of them pressed up against the fallen trunk of a massive sequoia. He motioned with a quick nod, letting her know that she could take a quick peak around the edge of the tree.

"A deer," she said.

"And enough meat to keep us in supplies for several days," he said, his stomach growling as he said it. He estimated that they'd moved better than one-third the distance around the circumference of the world and were less than a couple of days away from where they saw the nightly fire. But as they'd moved nearer, the game they'd been hunting had become more skittish, more frightened, much better equipped to elude them.

They hadn't seen anything much bigger than high-flying birds in the last two days. There were plenty of signs of game, droppings and tracks, even trails worn through the underbrush. But the animals had stayed far away.

This deer stood in a clearing, visible from mid-chest to head, contentedly munching on a nearby bush. Anthony looked to his left and held up a shard of flint he had carefully polished and chipped nearly a week ago. He caught the sunlight from above and signaled to Jack, three quick flashes telling him to start flanking the deer, to move around and behind it and start flushing it in his direction.

He then turned and gave Ernest the same signal.

"Get ready," he whispered to his mother, making sure that his arrow was secure in his bow and looking over, visually checking hers. "If we miss this one, we might be eating twigs and grass for dinner tonight."

"I'm sure you already know just where the deer will move, and have us positioned so the poor stupid thing will practically run over us," she said.

Anthony smiled. She was starting to understand him.

"Ahhhhhh!"

Anthony whipped his head around to the left, knowing that it was Ernest who had screamed, and knowing that had not been the scream of someone who was trying to spook a deer. He quickly looked back at the deer. It was staring directly at him. And then it lowered its head and went back to pulling leaves off the bush it had been working on for the last fifteen minutes.

At that moment, Anthony understood what was happening, knew why that deer had been so still. It was no *wild* deer. He stood and lowered his bow, letting the arrow fall to the ground. He raised both his hands high above his head. "Get up, Mother," he said. "Drop your bow and move slowly. Don't make any threatening motions."

Katie stood. "What is it?" she asked. Looking all around, tripping through spectrums, searching far beyond the capabilities of human eyes, she saw nothing but thick woods.

"We weren't the hunters, here," he said. "We were being hunted."

"By what?" she said, her voice full of alarm.

"By them," said Anthony, motioning to his left with a nod of his head.

Katie turned, still seeing nothing.

A man stepped out from behind a tree that was less than ten feet away from them. He wore a swatch of animal fur wrapped around his crotch, a necklace of sharp teeth around his throat, and held a large, tree-limb club in his right hand.

"It's a caveman," said Katie, not quite believing what she was seeing.

"A Neanderthal," said Anthony. The sloping forehead, the heavy brow, and the receding jaw left no doubt. He was about to elaborate, when from behind, something struck him in the head. He was unconscious before he hit the ground.

"Not very industrious," said Ernest. Leaning against the thick branches that made up the cage, he peered out at the nearly fifty Neanderthals that slept pressed up against each other. To Ernest they resembled little more than a pile of skin and fur, out of which deep rumbling snoring sounds emerged, and the occasional flailing hand. "No wonder they went extinct."

"Except for this little tribe that finds itself shuttling between the inner and outer solar system," said Jack. Also pressed up against the branches of the cage, he worked with a piece of splintered wood on a strap of leather that held the branches in place. "I don't know what they cured this leather with," he said, tossing the stick across the floor of the cage, "but it's tougher than nylon rope. We aren't going to cut our way out of here."

"And tunneling doesn't look like much of an option," said Ernest. He stomped on the rock on which the cage was placed. But it wasn't even a cage, just an upside down box in which they'd awakened after being ambushed in the woods. He imagined that it would take nearly a dozen Neanderthals to actually lift the thing. But he also knew that even if they could escape the cage, there was no escaping the reason they'd come to this asteroid.

Ernest had programmed the lightsail himself.

He had been unable to do anything else; it had been a command he found himself unable to refuse.

"The only way out is if Anthony and Katie can figure something out," said Jack. Looking to the far side of the clearing, past the sleeping Neanderthals and at the massive pile of lumber dumped into the huge fire pit, he then peered into the woods. "Anthony should be able to come up with a plan."

Ernest sighed, and he wondered if Jack really knew so little, of what both of them were. Why hadn't he told Jack what he'd been shown in the dream? He didn't know, but felt that this still was not the right time. In whatever game they were playing, being *forced* to play, he was not about to give up an advantage without getting something back in return. For the time being he decided to continue playing along, *masquerading* as Ernest Lawrence. "If they're out there," he said. "If they weren't already captured and eaten by these creatures."

"We don't know that they're going to try to eat us," said Jack.

Ernest pushed himself back from the wooden bars in order to see Jack, to make sure that he got his point across. "They're cannibals, Jack. You can see the pile of bones as easily as I can. These *animals* eat each other." He pointed through the limbs of the cage at the mound of bones piled at the edge of the clearing, a mound so large that it was nearly a small hill. "Those aren't the revered bones of the dearly departed," he added. "Those are half-eaten carcasses."

There was no arguing with that. The pile was made up mostly of Neanderthal bones, some so old and weathered they were little more than fragments, but a few were quite fresh, tendons and gristle still holding them together. "But they might not eat us," said Jack, not so much trying to give Ernest some hope to cling to, as to give himself hope. "We're not Neanderthal."

"They hardly look like discriminating eaters." He pointed again toward the sleeping pile of Neanderthals.

One was no longer asleep. A male child, no older than two or three, crawled from out of the pile, stood, and then ran over to the mound of bones. Reaching in, tugging at the bones, taking a few licks and nips at what he could find, he soon gave up, and moved toward the cage. In his left hand he carried what looked to be an upper arm bone.

"Don't spook him," said Jack. "If we can get hold of that bone we might be able to use it to get out of this cage."

Ernest gave a little laugh. "Of course," he said. "Perhaps we can fashion a weapon out of it and make our escape by beating all those Neanderthals to death before they skewer us on a spit."

Jack gave him a look, telling him to be quiet. The child approached slowly, stopped about five meters from them, and then crouched down. "Arrrrk," he said, sounding to Jack like a dog clearing its throat. He then laid the bone down in the dirt in front of him, and began gently to rock back and forth on his feet.

Jack poked his hand out between the timbers of the cage, pointed at the bone, and then motioned with his fingers, trying to get across to the child that he wanted it.

The child glanced down at the bone and then back at Jack. The little Neanderthal reached down and, poking at the bone, pushed it a few inches toward Jack.

"See," said Jack, "he understands."

The child then reached back down and pulled the bone back toward himself.

"Oh, he understands," said Ernest. "The little monkey is playing with you."

The child cocked his head to the left. "Hoot," he said, and then looked at the bone and back at Jack again.

Jack fluttered his fingers. "Bring it to me," he said.

The child stood, pointed at Jack and fluttered his own fingers, perfectly mimicking Jack.

"Monkey see, monkey do," said Ernest.

Jack was about to tell him to shut up, was tempted even to give him a hard kick, when a stiff breeze suddenly hit him in the face, carrying with it the heavy scent of sweat and salt that seemed to permeate the Neanderthals. Dirt and pebbles blew up before the child, thick dust suddenly coalescing into a little dirt devil, spinning fast and furiously.

"What?" said Ernest.

The bone was picked up in the miniature tornado, suddenly spinning itself, blurring, rolling end over end so quickly that it could barely be seen. And then the dust devil vanished, just as the child turned and ran.

The bone flew through the suddenly still air, hitting the side of the cage, only inches from Jack's hand. Jack reached out, grabbed the bone, and pulled it into the cage. He sat back, cradling it, running his fingers over it.

"What just happened?" asked Ernest.

Jack looked up at him. "You know exactly what just happened," he said. "That *monkey* of yours generated that wind and used it to pick up the bone and throw it at us. He did what none of us could possibly do, did what I've seen only one other person ever do."

"Anthony," said Ernest.

SECTION III

CHAPTER 6

"Wake up, Ernest."

Ernest opened his eyes, felt his shoulder being shaken, and rolled over, knowing that something was wrong. A thick cloud of dust hung in the air, and the camp echoed with shrieks and hoots. "What's happening?" he asked. Pushing himself halfway up and crawling over to the side of the cage, he looked out into the camp's central clearing.

"Visitors," said Jack. "And Half-Lip looks mighty upset about it."

"Good," said Ernest, certain that anything that Half-Lip didn't like would be good for them. Ernest peered out of the cage. The entire tribe was there, all on their feet, hopping up and down, creating the billowing dust that had floated toward the cage. Hooting and screaming, hitting the ground with branches and shaking fists, they were all focused on the far end of the clearing, where five Neanderthals stood.

"The visitors?" Ernest asked, pointing at them, unable to tell if they were the new arrivals—the Neanderthals all looked alike to him. One of the few exceptions was the one they had started calling Half-Lip, who was missing most of his lower lip and a large swatch of skin down to the tip of his chin. Half-Lip appeared to be the leader, seemed to have access to all the females of the tribe, and was continually barking at and cuffing the other males.

"Yes," said Jack. "Everyone woke early this morning, in an agitated state. There was a lot of random motion and snapping and quarreling with each other. Then about five minutes ago, the first of these new guys appeared at the edge of the clearing. A new one has been coming in about every minute, and Half-Lip's tribe has been getting more and more wound up with each arrival.

Half-Lip stood directly between his tribe and the five newcomers.

"Shreeeet!" he howled, made a run toward them, got within about ten feet and then stopped in a cloud of dust, and shook both his fists at them. He then turned around and walked back to the rest of his tribe, moving slowly, confidently, as if in no hurry to get back to them, or concerned that he had his back to the five.

"Confident monkey," said Ernest.

Jack was just about to agree, but didn't have the chance. He saw something happen to Half-Lip, saw him momentarily tense, the muscles standing out through the thin layer of hair that covered his back. His head cocked first to the left and then to the right, and then he angled his head back, sniffing at the air.

"Hooooot!" he shouted, and jumping up, came down hard on the heels of his feet and began to paw at the dirt.

A sixth Neanderthal stepped into the clearing.

"That *runt* has him all upset?" asked Ernest. He pointed at the newest arrival.

Jack was also confused. He was much taller than the rest of the Neanderthals, by nearly a foot, but *runt* was still an apt description. This male looked nearly fifty kilograms lighter than the rest of the adult males, not sharing the gorilla-like physique of the other Neanderthals, actually looking rather slender. But he was still very much a Neanderthal, the sloping forehead, bony brow, and receding jaw leaving no doubt. And unlike the other males, all of whom wore some form of adornment, bones and necklaces, feathers and glistening bands of flint, this one wore nothing.

"Skinny has Half-Lip worried," said Ernest.

Jack nodded. Half-Lip kept taking several small steps toward Skinny, and then retreating, back stepped, not showing his back to *this* Neanderthal.

Skinny held up his right hand, waved it in the air several times, and then lowered it, pointed a finger first at Half-Lip and then at the cage holding Jack and Ernest.

"Oh, oh," said Ernest. They'd spent four days in the cage. They'd been fed, given water, but otherwise totally ignored except for the few children who would occasionally wander by and stare at them for a few seconds. "Skinny's got plans for us." Ernest suddenly shivered, remembering something, a phantom memory resurfacing.

Skinny had given him the destination codes for the light-sail.

Skinny had forced him into coming to the Hirku-Ashi.

Half-Lip looked over at the cage, then back at Skinny. He gave a little, flat-sounding hoot, and then stepped back toward his tribe, moving through the crowd, and coming to a stop once having passed through them. He sat down in the dirt.

Skinny and his group also sat.

Some of the tribe had dispersed and trotted over to the massive fire pit. As Jack and Ernest watched, the females of the tribe got down on all fours in the center of the pit and began to push and shove at the dirt and ashes, revealing what looked like flagstones, each nearly a meter across and roughly circular in shape. Not satisfied to just unearth them, children brought over gourds filled with water and various animal skins. Small amounts of water were poured onto the stones, and the skins used to wipe them clean.

"A twelve-by-twelve grid," said Jack, seeing the perfectly square pattern that the stones made. From beyond the fire pit, Neanderthal males came up the hill carrying logs. But these were not just any logs. These logs were obviously specially prepared, all bark removed, the wood gleaming, looking polished, the ends of each log flattened.

"What game are they playing?" asked Ernest.

Jack wasn't certain yet. The logs were all about the same diameter, perhaps one foot, but their length varied from two feet, up to nearly ten feet. The log-carrying Neanderthals hauled the logs up to the flagstone grid and carefully balanced them on the stones, and then ran back toward the pit to get other logs. In just a matter of minutes, 144 logs sat erect on the stones. Jack could sense no pattern as to how they had been laid out, the height of each log different, no apparent relationships between them, other than the obvious periodic spacing between the stones they rested upon.

Half-Lip and Skinny stood and started to walk through the standing logs, at times stopping to rest a hand on one, or to bend down and inspect how it rested on the stone beneath it. Skinny was the first to step out of the array of logs, exiting on the side nearest where he and his five companions had entered the clearing.

Members of the tribe screamed and hooted, waving fists in his direction.

Skinny didn't seem to notice, but instead looked over at the cage, nodded at Jack and Ernest, and then angling his head back, looked up into the sky and at the other side of the world.

Ernest looked away, not wanting to make eye contact— actually too frightened to make eye contact.

Half-Lip slowly walked out of the maze of logs, touching each one he passed by, and finally stood outside the checkerboard grid. His muscles tensed, and at that moment all of the Neanderthals became silent, all of them simultaneously sitting down.

"Shreeeeek!" screamed Half-Lip as he suddenly ran forward and hit a tall log with his shoulder.

The log began to tip, to fall forward and to the left, missing all the logs in the next row in, but just clipping the side of a log in the adjacent row, starting it careening to the left, while the log that it had just hit rebounding to the right.

It was at that moment that Skinny made his move. Half a dozen logs were in motion, falling, although none of them had actually hit the ground yet. Skinny ran into the collapsing array, three rows in, and with his right foot, gave a log of about his own height a firm kick.

Jack watched the log jerk forward about six inches, sliding on the polished stone beneath it, but not falling, not so much as wobbling. Then he couldn't see it as all the logs began to topple, the falling ones striking others, those that hit the ground rolling, colliding with others. Some logs were flipped high into the air, turning end over end, and then came crashing back down, some of them hitting so perfectly that they stood again, balanced, only to once again be hit by another falling log.

"It's like a game of dominoes," said Jack, not referring to the real game of dominoes, but to the game which kids would play, stacking them up in intricate patterns and with the push of a single domino, start them all falling—but this was much more. It was hard to see because of the rising dust and the still moving, tumbling logs, but he could start to see a pattern emerge, small regions of the artificial forest once again standing.

One last log fell, one of the largest, nearly ten feet in length, and as it hit the ground it just nicked the tip of a short log already lying there, kicking it into the air, flipping it end over end, and then planting itself firmly on a vacant stone, the sound of wood smacking against rock making a loud, hollow banging sound that echoed through the otherwise silent Neanderthal camp.

"My God," said Ernest.

Half of the logs had been knocked down, lying between the other half that were standing upright. But it was not just any *half*. Every *other* flagstone had a standing log on it. And along each row, logs descended in height, the tallest on the end of the array nearest Skinny, and the smallest on the side where Half-Lip stood.

"He did that," said Ernest. "He *made* the logs fall that way."

Skinny slowly walked around the logs, looking at them, as if admiring what he'd created, the pattern that he had generated, nodding his head. As he walked, Half-Lip turned and ran, disappearing into the forest.

"That's it?" asked Ernest. "Did Skinny just take the tribe away from Half-Lip by controlling what those logs did, by forcing them into that pattern."

"I think so," said Jack.

But then Half-Lip came running back into the clearing, holding in his hands a large chunk of obsidian, its black surface sparkling. Half-Lip hoisted it up, holding it high above his head.

"Uh-oh," said Jack, suddenly certain that the bloodless coup, which they'd just witnessed, was about to turn very bloody.

Skinny turned to face Half-Lip and folded his arms across his chest, not showing the slightest care or concern that two hundred kilograms of berserk Neanderthal was running at him with a massive chunk of glass-faceted rock. Half-Lip hurled the obsidian at Skinny, and it fell short, partially imbedding itself in the ground just in front of Skinny.

Then Half-Lip hurled himself into the air.

And he too fell short, his head cracking against a razor sharp edge of the obsidian sticking out of the ground. It cut through his skull, cleaving it from just above the brow to the back of his head, almost down at his neck. Half-Lip's brain spilled from his open head, landing directly between Skinny's feet. Skinny reached down, and pushing fingers into the pink mass, pulled up a handful of Half-Lip's brain and stuffed it into his mouth. He did not even chew, but wolfed it down, like a ravenous dog.

"Hoooooot!" roared the Neanderthals.

Skinny stepped back, and the other Neanderthals descended onto Half-Lip's corpse, pulling it apart, tearing and ripping, eating it raw in a feeding frenzy.

"Did Half-Lip do that on purpose?" asked Ernest. "Did

he throw himself on that rock and split his own head open?"

Jack nodded, knowing that was exactly what he had done. But as bizarre as that display had just been, he'd already put it out of his mind and instead stood up, pushing his face up against the bars of the cage. Skinny stood before them. Gray and red remnants of Half-Lip's brain dripped from the Neanderthal's thick chin whiskers.

Quicker than Jack would have thought possible, the Neanderthal's right arm moved, his fist slamming into Ernest's face, knocking him off his feet and into the back of the cage. Jack was about to go to Ernest, who lay sprawled and unmoving in the back of the cage.

"It's been a long time."

Jack turned back toward the Neanderthal. "I'm taking you out of here," said the Neanderthal, his voice deep and gravelly, the words sounding misshapen and alien coming out of his too large mouth. "I've already collected Anthony and Katie and have them safely back at my camp."

"Who are you?" Jack managed to ask.

The Neanderthal stepped nearer, pulled himself right up to the bars, only inches away from Jack's face. "Don't recognize me?" he asked. "I'm disappointed. I would have expected more from my *Creator*."

They'd walked all afternoon and far into the evening, led by Skinny, who called himself *Tek*. They eventually stopped at a small clearing with a stream running next to it. The Neanderthals provided a meal, mostly dried fruits that one had been carrying in a large skin pouch, along with fatty dried chunks of some sort of meat.

The moment the meal was done, the Neanderthals toppled over into a pile, snorting and snoring before they even hit the ground. Ernest too was soon asleep, but kept his distance, curled up at the base of a tree far away from the Neanderthals.

Jack and Skinny had not spoken since Ernest had regained consciousness. Jack sat down next to Tek, who was picking at a scab on his right shin. "Explain it to me," said Jack.

Tek looked up from his leg. "Some things I know, some things I don't. Believe me, *I've* forgotten far more than is even imaginable—both deliberately, and just as a consequence of the finite capacity of what I've got up here," he said, as he thumped on his sloping forehead. "You should certainly understand about choosing not to remember," he said, sounding cryptic.

"Forget about what I've forgotten and tell me what *you* know," said Jack.

"So impatient," he said. "One of the many annoying personality traits of humans. A day doesn't pass that I don't offer up a small prayer of gratitude for having merged that inferior form with the unique, but somewhat undeveloped abilities of the Neanderthal. Truly a case of the sum being much greater than the parts."

Jack *was* losing his patience and felt tempted to jump on the Neanderthal and pound *his* head against the ground until he explained what he knew. But Jack held himself back, knowing that if it ever came down to a fight between him and a Neanderthal, even this hybrid one, that it would be *his* head getting beaten to a bloody pulp.

"Am I correct in assuming that you now realize just a bit of what you are, that you came from the Makers' universe?"

There it was, thought Jack. First Alexandra, and now this Neanderthal. Jack nodded. "That's what I've been told."

"Think about what that means, Jack. You've been here since the *Big Bang*." The Neanderthal barked and hooted several times. "In actuality, I suspect that you've been somewhere well *before* the Big Bang." Again he barked and hooted. "But all this depends on how you look at it. I choose to view it from the perspective that *you've* always been somewhere."

"Explain it so I can understand it," said Jack, again feeling compelled to jump on the Neanderthal and beat the truth out of him.

"You are an *immortal* being, Jack. There are certain important consequences of that fact, such as when the Sonomak was fired and Alpha's picoverse generated, a version of you was also born into that world that *should* still be alive today."

That's right, thought Jack.

He had believed what Alexandra had told him—it felt right, knowing deep down that he had in fact been in the universe since its birth. But he had thought no more of it than that. It was as if he was not letting himself think about it. He had chosen to believe that the version of himself in Alpha's picoverse had died all those thousands of years ago, along with everyone else from the twenty-first century. Alpha had insisted that the *incarnation* of himself had died at the hands of Alexandra. But could Alexandra really kill him? Could anyone really kill him? If he had survived throughout the thirty-billion-year history of the universe, it seemed awfully unlikely that something would have been able to kill that duplicated version of him in the last hundred thousand years spent in Alpha's universe.

"Yes," said Tek, nodding his head, sensing that Jack was beginning to understand. "This leaves you with a bit of a paradox. Exactly *where* is that version of you that should live in this universe?"

Jack slowly shook his head as he looked into the Neanderthal's pale blue eyes, suddenly realizing just where this other self might be, suddenly *knowing* who that other self must be.

"Wrong," said Tek. "My lineage, though quite bizarre, does not include you."

"Then who and where?" asked Jack.

"Well, for an immortal being you pulled off an amazing trick. You died, long ago. In fact, it was within a year of the time this picoverse was born."

"What?" asked Jack, now totally bewildered.

"I was there, about seven years old at the time. You along with my mother, my father, Beong, and Tanaka were put in front of a wall and shot. You'd shown Alexandra how to shut down the wormhole from this side, and she was done with you. They made me watch. You took a single shot in the head and that was that."

Jack blinked—several times. "Then you are . . . ?"

Tek nodded. "That's right. Although one hundred thousand years separate me from what I once was, at the moment of your death, I *was* Anthony Wittkowski."

Jack shook his head. "No, that is impossible. Anthony *evolved* into Alpha, not into you."

Tek reached over and thumped Jack on the forehead. "I *was* Anthony, who after ten thousand years became Alpha, and who then became something *else*. That part of Anthony, that frightened, ego-driven, hurt, and damaged part of myself, the part that could no longer stand up to the loneliness, withstand the solitude, put himself to sleep, waiting for you to *return* and rescue him."

"And you are?"

"I'm what remained, the portion of consciousness that ran the machines, governed the solar system, put out the trash, and generally did the trillions and trillions of things needed to keep a little empire going. And then I moved beyond those mundane housekeeping duties and looked for my *own* path of escape, moved far past my original, inferior packaging." He smiled, exposing large, yellowed Neanderthal teeth.

Jack pointed upward, not actually pointing at the far internal horizon of the *Hirku-Ashi*, but actually pointing out toward space. "You built the Sonomak? You collapsed both Jupiter and Saturn?"

Tek grinned. "The one and only."

"And you saw that other version of me die, saw that bullet go through his head and kill him?"

"As dead as dead could possibly be."

"But if I am who and what you say I am, then how could a bullet have killed him?"

Tek barked out a gentle laugh. "I said that a bullet went through his head, and then he was as dead as dead could be. I never said that the bullet actually resulted in his death.

I suspect that he simply passed through to some other universe, leaving that chunk of meat behind. Mere mortals such as myself require immense machines to move between worlds. For you, I'm certain that with the touch of a finger, you could simply walk through the most impenetrable barrier, into whatever universe you choose."

Jack looked down at his hand, at the fingers that *had* touched the void between what he had thought was his universe, and Alpha's universe. His touch *had* opened the wormhole.

"What am I?" asked Jack.

"I have no idea," said Tek. Standing up, he beat some dust out of the scraggly fur of his pelt. "All that I do know is that you started the ball rolling, and that it is up to the rest of us to figure out how to stop that ball before it rolls over us, destroying everything in its path."

"And why would I do that?"

Tek barked out another laugh. "Only a fool would attempt to understand the mind of the Creator." Turning, Tek walked away from the fire and into the night.

SECTION III
CHAPTER 7

"There is no exact solution!" screamed Alexandra.

Io twisted, distorted, seas of molten sulfur exploding upward, spewing from the moon, being pulled down into the twin vortices in front of it. Cracking from crust to core, the moon spit out mountain-sized shards of ice and iron, its surface rippling, layer after layer ejecting into space, being swallowed by the twin black holes.

Alexandra attempted to control the destruction.

The start of the process had been easy enough. She'd begun with one of Jupiter's outermost moons, Ananke, giving it a gentle nudge, thrust generated by a few precisely placed matter-antimatter explosions, pulling it from its orbit, sending it down the gravitational well of the two black holes. But Ananke was not intended to be a meal for the holes. Instead, it collided with another moon, Leda, much smaller than Ananke, transferring momentum, sending that little moon hurtling into Io, blasting it out of its orbit and sending it toward the holes. That she could control, could use the living computer that filled the seas of Europa to show her how to manipulate the trajectories of the colliding moons.

That had been easy.

Io passed between the black holes and ruptured, spewing out crust, mantel, and core, the bulk of it vanishing over event horizons. But a small fraction, several trillion tons of high-density rock, slipped between the gravitational maelstrom generated by the holes and launched at an appreciable fraction of the speed of light.

Tens of thousands of pieces, all with different trajectories, and all with a near-infinite number of potential impacts, which in turn would cause further impacts. *All* of which had to be controlled.

"No!"

The number of calculations became *boundless*; not even a moonful of machinery would be able to track and predict the trajectories. And they *all* had to be controlled—those hyper-speed shards of Io needed for the next phase to blow Ganymede and Callisto from their orbits, their trajectories continually altered and guided by impacts, as they in turn accelerated toward the black holes. Just missing the black holes on their first pass, the gravitational tug of the moons would pull the holes apart, starting them on their own oscillating pathway, triggering them to begin their dance, the gap between them first widening and then narrowing. And with each pass, the region between the holes would be gravitationally stressed to the point of rupturing space-time—different trajectories, different ruptures in space-time.

"Null set," a voice whispered in Alexandra's head as she watched Io's ricocheting fragments spinning before her out of control. "No distortion achieved for these inputs."

"I know," she snapped at the voice. "Always a null set," she said. She'd run the simulation hundreds of times. Not only was she incapable of controlling the trajectories of the black holes in order to rip apart the fabric of the universe in a controlled manner, she was not able to do *anything*. No picoverses, no wormholes, not the slightest distortion in space-time. She could not control the black hole's trajectories.

Too many variables.

Alexandra pulled back, her face coming out of the flesh-like interface, making smacking sounds. She blinked, focusing on the control panel and then lowered her head against the console.

"Would you care to try again, Operator?" asked the computer.

"I would *not* care to try again," said Alexandra, finally having to admit to herself that she could not control the computer, that something was *missing*. "Why can't I control the damn thing!"

"Instructions, Operator?"

Alexandra slammed her fist against the console once more. It was always the same response. *Instructions, Operator?* She'd tried to hide from this for nearly ten days now, desperately wanted to believe that she could be the operator, that she could control the Sonomak. But she could not. At that moment, she knew that she had no choice. What the machine needed, was *the* Operator. And she was certain who that had to be.

Jack.

She sighed. "Can you locate the present position of the lightsail that departed after mine?" she asked the computer, knowing that it and the oxygen-starved corpses within it now floated somewhere well beyond the orbit of Mars.

"Presently located in docking bay 37, Sunside axis of the *Hirku-Ashi* transport."

Alexandra sneered and raised up her right fist, prepared to bring it down against the console, but instead, slowly lowered it. "Manifest?" she asked, certain that the craft must be some sort of cargo drone, a piece of hardware making the journey between the pillar and the transport.

"Four passengers," said the computer. "Jack Preston, Katie McGuire, Ernest Lawrence, and Anthony Wittkowski."

"Son of a bitch," said Alexandra. "He reprogrammed the sail, discovered my tinkering." She stood, feeling for the first time in days that she would be able to complete her mission, that she could see a solution through the tangled web of possibilities. It would be so much easier to pull the needed information out of Jack's brain if it were still alive, rather than having to reconstruct it from his dead carcass.

"I require transport to the *Hirku-Ashi*," she said.

"When do you wish to depart?" asked the computer.

"Now!" She was about to turn, when she stopped and slowly sat down. "No," she said, and rested her hands against the console. "I require *assistance* in my trip to the *Hirku-Ashi*," realizing it was her underestimation of Jack's abilities that had put her in this current situation. She would not make that mistake again.

"Nature of assistance?" asked the computer.

"Firepower," she said without hesitation. "Massive firepower."

"Organic or inorganic?" asked the computer.

Alexandra smiled. "Show me what you've got."

Ernest leaned back, feeling almost good for the first time since arriving in the asteroid. According to Tek, Anthony and Katie would soon return to the camp, and they would all be reunited. He bit into a piece of fruit, a cross between an apple and a pear, and watched Jack examining the array of flagstones with the central clearing.

This was the first time that he'd been alone with Tek. His jaw still hurt where the Neanderthal had hit him, and under normal circumstances, dealing with that smack in the face would have been the first order of business.

But these were not normal circumstances. "You see the world differently," he said to Tek.

Tek was crouched in front of him, eating his own fruit.

He did not bother looking at Ernest, did not need to examine facial expressions and other subtle nonverbal hints.
"We are not human," he said.

"You are *Neanderthal*, real Neanderthal?"

"What the Neanderthal might have been had they been
left alone by you *Homo sapiens*," he said. Reaching down
to his right thigh, he pulled off a tick, an annoying little
bloodsucker. He smashed it between thumb and forefinger
and then popped the remnants into his mouth. "Natural talents and genetic potentials brought to the fore with a bit of
manipulation, and then just a dash of Homo sapiens added
to smooth out the Neanderthal rough spots. The result is a
race much more evolved than you humans."

"More evolved?" asked Ernest. "Who built this ship?"

"It was *monkeys* just like yourself," said Tek, using the
same insult that Ernest directed against the Neanderthals.
"So irrational, so chaotic, so boundless, that you require all
these devices to inflict boundary conditions on your behav-
iors. There is a core of randomness in you that can only be
described as *psychotic*. Your thought patterns and responses
to situations sometimes show absolutely no correlation to
the reality you are confronted with. And at some level you
recognize this defect, so you build these devices to bring a
degree of predictability and order into your lives. It is this
defect that dooms you and has brought you to this point of
total destruction."

"It is that *defect* that allowed humans to build this
world," said Ernest.

"Exactly," said Tek. "And we are a part of this machine
that the human species built—one more machine in an endless sequence of machines, all of them built with the intent
of giving you the illusion of control."

"And the purpose of this grand machine?" asked Ernest.

"A device," said Tek. "A device built to help aid you in
your quest of repairing the damage you have so thought-
lessly unleashed on the universe."

"That doesn't answer my question," said Ernest.

Tek shook his head. "You and Jack, alike in so many

ways. Is the weight of all those memories simply too great, or is it some core of laziness or indifference that lets you blissfully drift through eon after eon. You don't even seem to remember the dream we shared."

Ernest said nothing.

A part of him had continued to hope that the dream he'd had while rising up the pillar had been just that, a dream. He really wanted to be Ernest Lawrence, really wanted to be a human, really wanted to be just a man. He sighed, knowing that he could no longer escape the truth. There had been so much more to what Tek had shown him in the dream other than Alexandra's sabotage and the correct co-ordinates to reach the *Hirku-Ashi*. So much more.

"The memories are more like dreams," whispered Ernest, as if he didn't want to be able to hear himself speak.

"And what are those dreams?"

Ernest closed his eyes and leaned back. "It was only two days after the stars had vanished back in May of 1925, and it seemed as if half the Bay Area was on fire—the panic, the riots, the fear and hysteria overwhelming everyone. I had been trapped in downtown San Francisco the night the stars vanished and had spent the next two days walking, working my way down the west side of the Bay, hoping to make San Jose by nightfall, so that the next day I could start back up the east side of the Bay and toward Berkeley." He stopped talking.

"And what happened?" asked Tek. "Were you somehow killed?"

Ernest nodded and reached up and rubbed the right side of his head, just above the ear. "I didn't see the person who shot me, don't even know if the bullet was intended for me. But the effect was the same. It wasn't really painful, but I was down on the pavement, dying, my entire body numb, my vision blurring, when suddenly a man stood above me, reaching down, cupping his hands around my face."

"Who was it?" asked Tek.

"I guess it was Jack," he said. "It didn't look like Jack,

but I know it was Jack." He stopped talking and looked over at Jack, who was still examining the flagstones.

"And you know it was Jack, *because* . . ."

Ernest turned his head and focused on Tek. "Because those hands cupped around my face reached into me, reached deep, and Jack passed *into* me, almost behind me. What had been Ernest Lawrence was still there, but was of total insignificance compared to the entity that now occupied this body," he said, reaching up with his right hand and pounding his chest.

"And until I reminded you, you believed that you were simply Ernest Lawrence and that the bullet had not in fact cut right through your head, killing you, but had merely grazed your skull."

Ernest nodded.

"I can now see bits and pieces of the places Jack has been, where *I* have been," he said. "But at the time I couldn't see any of that. Jack was there, but deep in the background, pushing me, prodding me. He was the one responsible for my working with Heisenberg on the Sonomak. He was the one who made me go out and find Anthony."

Tek nodded. "Now I want you to answer as truthfully as possible, with the memories you now have. Did that part of you that is Jack help in the building, in the *understanding* of the Sonomak?"

Ernest closed his eyes, drifted through the dim memories, and slowly began to shake his head. "No," he said at last. "That was just me and Werner, and the hints we received from Anthony. Jack didn't help."

Tek nodded. "I didn't think so. He won't help us. He might nudge a bit, and bring some critical ingredients together, but he will not open any doors for us."

"What are you talking about?" asked Ernest.

"We're on our own here," answered Tek. "If the pico-verse collapse is to be stopped, if Alexandra is to be stopped, if the universe itself is to be saved, it will have to be done by us. Jack will not help." Tek paused and then pointed at

Ernest. "The part of you that is Jack will not help."

"Why?" asked Ernest.

Tek shrugged his shoulders. "I suspect it is because that is the way Jack wants it. And what Jack wants, Jack *will* get."

"I still don't understand," said Ernest.

The Neanderthal leaned back, closed his eyes, and began to squirm in the dirt, trying to get comfortable, as if preparing for a nap. "I think you will soon enough," he said. "Your friends are back."

Ernest stood up, looked around, turning, seeing only Neanderthals in the compound. Two skinny ones were walking toward him. "Where?" he asked.

"Right in front of you."

Ernest blinked, stepped back, tripped and fell, hitting the ground hard.

"Don't you recognize us?" asked the closest of the newly arrived Neanderthals, pointing first at himself and then at the female standing next to him. "After all these years, Ernest, is a bit of fur and a restructured skull enough to fool you."

"Anthony?" he asked, looking up at the Neanderthal. Then, turning, he looked at the little female next to him, more child-sized than adult, with glistening crystal eyes. "Katie?" he said.

They nodded.

"How?" he asked in a stammer.

"The how is simple biomechanics, a bit of DNA manipulation," said Anthony, bending down toward Ernest. "What matters is the *why*."

Ernest didn't have time to ask why. As Anthony reached down, he revealed in the palm of his hand a small piece of metal, liquid looking, glistening and almost alive. He pressed it against the side of Ernest's head.

Ernest collapsed.

Drip.

Ernest opened his eyes. Thunder rolled and echoed inside

his head. He squinted and rubbed his eyes. Above him, the branches of a tree flowed outward, spreading, multiplying, each break point leading to others, diameters narrowing, twigs flourishing, myriad leaves dancing in the breeze.

Drip.

The droplet fell from the tip of a leaf, landing beyond his gaze, but the sound echoed as it splashed in a pool. He had been listening to that drip for a long time, from long before he regained consciousness. It was not a steady drip, or even a melodic, rhythmic drip. The time interval between the *drip-drip-drip* was chaotic, random, each drip uniquely influenced by the ever-changing breeze, altered by the way the previous droplet wetted the leaf, forever changed by fluctuations in humidity and the slow dimming of the afternoon sun. But Ernest didn't need to understand the why, didn't give a second thought to the how. All that mattered was seeing the pattern where none was apparent, integrating all the effects without considering any of the causes.

Now, thought Ernest.

The droplet hit.

Again, thought Ernest after an unspecified time passed.

The droplet hit.

Once more, whispered the voice inside of Ernest.

The droplet hit.

"You need to be careful, Ernest. Your brain is no longer wired the same."

Ernest blinked and rolled his head to the right. Two Neanderthals sat next to him. He had a great deal of trouble focusing on their faces. What he saw, somehow sensed, were the spatial, temporal, and even chemical relationships that existed between them, distance, scents, twitch of muscles, center of mass, hair pushed by the breeze, all of it integrating, those relationships defining the two Neanderthals.

"It's Anthony," said the larger of the two Neanderthals. "You need to rest. The Neanderthal DNA template has not quite completed the integration of your Homo sapiens DNA, and your mechanical parts make the whole mix even more complicated. You should try to get more sleep."

Ernest raised his right hand, holding it in front of his face. He slowly closed his eyes, the image of the thickened, dark fingers, and the tufts of fur-like hair quickly giving way to thoughts of the location of the hand, of *his* hand, with respect to the two Neanderthals. He slipped into a multidimensional landscape, a savannah moving toward the outer solar system, the grasslands colored in hues beyond the visible spectrum.

"It's too damn slow," complained Alexandra as she peered into the monitor showing the array of glass-coffins, all of them draped in a thick latticework of tubing and electrical connections.

"The rate of growth is limited by fundamental biochemical realities," said the computer. "There are thermodynamic limitations which dictate the maximum rate of tissue growth, and chemical uptake at synaptic junctions cannot be pushed beyond the current rate without damaging the neural networks."

Alexandra slumped back in her chair, and the pain in her stomach suddenly worsened, forcing her to wince. For a moment, she mistook the hunger pangs for something infinitely worse, for some sort of gut-level clairvoyance that space itself was about to dissolve around her in another collapsing picoverse. But nothing happened, and the gnawing in her stomach continued. She looked at the upper right quadrant of the monitor, the one that received its feed from a Lunar Nearside base, its sensors focused on the earth.

What she saw had little resemblance to the earth she had known, where she had been trapped for nearly four million years. A massive continent-spanning piece of the planet was missing, the void going down nearly to the planet's core, exposing a white-red boiling froth of liquid metal that spewed out into space, as if the planet was vomiting up the contents of its stomach.

She could not imagine what was holding the planet together, wondered why it hadn't already shattered and spewed itself out across the solar system. But she knew that she was seeing only a single aspect of Earth; that in reality there were probably dozens of them intersecting, merging, and flowing across each other, as the picoverse collapse continued, the planet probably achieving added stability, anchored by so many other picoverses. But she knew it could not last forever. The collapse would eventually consume the earth she saw, along with all the earths being sucked down into the vortex, and then the tear would continue to move outward, devouring the entire solar system.

And from there it would move into the universe beyond.

"How long until they're ready?" she asked.

"Forty-three days," replied the computer.

"Damn it," she whispered as she rubbed her stomach, knowing there was nothing she could do to speed up the process, knowing that she could not take the risk of going after Jack without the help of what was growing in those quartz coffins. She'd downloaded all files of the *Hirku-Ashi*, and knew that nearly twenty thousand genetically enhanced Neanderthals filled that rock, twenty thousand evolved brutes that she was certain Jack would now control. They would do everything within their power to stop her from getting him. That was exactly what *she'd* attempt to do. She expected nothing less of Jack.

She slowed herself down, practically stopping all metabolic reactions. Each external hour passed in what seemed like seconds.

SECTION III
CHAPTER 8

Tek finished his slow climb up the hill and dumped himself in the short grass, rolling over onto his back, closing his eyes, and letting the warm sunlight soak into his dark hide. "Do I sense jealousy?"

Jack shrugged his shoulders and dropped himself into the

grass next to Tek. On the plain below, he watched Anthony, Katie, and Ernest play. Tek's morning lessons were over, and the three were now left to themselves. As Jack watched, Anthony rose up into the air, holding onto a canopy of palm fronds sewn together, a blast of wind catching the Neanderthal-parasail and pushing him into the sky.

Katie and Ernest danced below him, their motions setting forth an avalanche of air molecules, building pressure waves, guiding wave fronts, funneling the resultant vortex beneath Anthony's sail.

"Perhaps just a bit," said Jack. He watched Anthony hover nearly fifty feet above the ground, slowly rotating, his hairy legs beating at the air as if he were riding an invisible bicycle. Jack held up his right hand, examining it, looking at the pale, hairless skin.

Tek rolled onto his side, facing Jack. "It was your own doing, Jack. I know you have no conscious understanding of it, but at some level you did not want to make the transformation, so you were able to block the Neanderthal template from taking hold."

Jack shook his head. "But Ernest changed," said Jack. *"And he is me."* It had been a week since Ernest had made the transformation, and since Tek had told him of Ernest's true history. Jack had been able to accept the situation rationally, but not emotionally. Ernest was simply Ernest.

"It's true that he is another version of you, the one that woke in the Soviet-dominated picoverse," said Tek, "but he's an extremely pale image, just enough Jack left within him to move things along, to intervene when something needs to be done. He is basically still Ernest Lawrence. I suspect that the only *true* Jack is you, the original who did not wake in a picoverse. And you did not want to be transformed, to become an active player in this little game."

"Why?" asked Jack.

"You manipulate, guide, give a nudge here and there, but you do not really intervene to force us into any *particular* action."

Jack was not so sure of that. "What about Alexandra?"

he asked, searching distant memories, shadow lands so
murky and faded that he could not be certain that they had
ever been real. "At some point in the past I altered her,
changed the core reason for her being. She was a device
placed on Earth to make certain that humans never develop
the ability to manipulate space-time." He paused, letting the
words seep deeply into his head.

Images flashed, as if momentarily illuminated by lightning bolts.

A café in Paris.

A less than three-decades-old Eiffel Tower threw its afternoon shadow down the Avenue de Suffren, and a light
scent of rotting fish and mildewed wood drifted in on the
breeze that rolled off the Seine.

Humans were nearing the transition point—that break
where the old reality, discovered by Galileo, Newton, Faraday, and Maxwell, was about to give way to a deeper
understanding—*the understanding that not all things could
be understood.*

Henri Becquerel had discovered natural radioactivity, understanding for the first time that not even the fundamental
elements themselves were permanent, but could decay into
other elements. The mystery hiding within the atom was
being solved: Thomson had discovered the electron, Ruth-
erford the proton, and now Bohr had synthesized these discoveries into the first primitive model of the atom. Humans
were entering into that regime where dimensions were
small enough and energies great enough that the *absolute*
no longer existed and that ultimate reality was defined by
probabilities. And then there was Einstein—special relativity, the basic relationships between mass and energy, and
the mechanics of objects moving at appreciable fractions of
the speed of light were already in hand. Jack had been
watching Einstein carefully, accessing his notes through
spies. The man would be a pivotal player in what was about
to transpire. He was less than a year away from synthesiz-
ing a general theory of relativity, showing that the gravity

associated with a mass was an artifact of the mass's ability to distort the fabric of space-time.

Only a century lay between the invention of the steam engine and the first glimpse of distorted space-time.

They were advancing so quickly. Combining their understanding of the atom with a mass's ability to distort space-time would start them down *the* pathway. In fact they were already on the pathway. Only active intervention would stop them now.

Jack could see something of the future, peer beyond the horizon and see where these new discoveries would take the humans. But he did not want to look too closely, because the future that was unfolding was not his. He could see just enough to know that if the humans were left to follow their ferocious curiosity, they would in all likelihood destroy themselves before they mastered the mechanics of space-time manipulation. But he could not be completely sure.

He sighed.

Usually it was so simple, the future so obvious. Intelligence was typically an evolutionary dead end. Like a spark fanned to a roaring fire, unless controlled and tempered, the outcome was almost always total conflagration. Such intelligence needed active intervention to save them from themselves, either allowing time for the species to evolve to the point of some degree of self-control, or allowing the world to spawn another race, giving another species a chance to make the *leap*.

But occasionally a species showed the potential for survival without intervention, and he always felt compelled to give them the chance to define their own future. Only one thing stood in the humans' way—the *Controller* that the Makers had placed on this world, to keep its dominant species from developing the ability to manipulate space-time. But these humans might just survive without the manipulation of the Controller. So he had to act, to intervene in the Makers' experiment.

He looked across the table. A beautiful woman, dark

skinned, with almost black eyes, the only color, her bright red lipstick. He could not remember her name, but that was not important. What was important was that this woman would no longer stand in the way of the humans, but would actually help them create their future.

"I want to thank you," said Jack, "for the insightful reports you have been relaying to the Makers," not bothering to explain how he had intercepted them, or even why he would want to intercept them. "I believe you are correct in your assessment of this species, that there is something unique about them, something *special*." Until called to this world, Jack had been far away in both time and space, those memories so distant, so buried, so alien, that they could not actively interface with that aspect of his consciousness when in human guise. He reached across the table toward the woman. No one else in the café saw him reach forward, this motion not quite taking place in the physical reality where humans currently dwelled. Jack touched her forehead.

His fingers passed through shimmering panes of rainbow-colored glass.

"I'm sorry," he said in a whisper, knowing that no one could hear it.

"And why are you sorry?"

Jack blinked, and Paris had vanished. Tek squatted before him.

"Why are you sorry?" asked Tek again.

Jack peered into the future, saw the infinite possibilities unfold before him. An infinite number of paths. And yet they all seemed to lead to the same place. The physics would allow nothing else. The humans had started something that could only be stopped in one way. This Earth, and all the earths created by the Sonomak, would not survive.

They *could* not survive.

The humans had pushed too hard, too fast—far exceeding the potential he had seen in them only a century earlier. And he had let them, had encouraged them, had hoped that the dim possibility of success would become the final future reality.

But now it was too late.

He now understood why Alexandra's old programming had been rebooted and his tampering removed. This too was his doing, a fail-safe device placed inside her back at the meeting in the Paris café. If the humans were allowed to continue, the fabric of the greater universe would be at risk, and all the countless worlds with their own species would be devoured. That couldn't be allowed.

He had given the humans their chance.

And they'd failed.

"I'm sorry," he said again and then reopened his eyes. "But you're right. I will not interfere. Humans will determine their own future." Jack forced a smile. A plan, an inevitable sequence of events that would bring this experiment and this species to an end began to unfold before him. He would miss them. He had come to like them.

Some he had even come to love.

But that meant absolutely nothing.

"You've remembered?" asked Tek. "You *know* who and what you are?"

"Enough," said Jack. "More than enough."

"Then time is very short," said Tek.

Jack nodded.

"A log is just a log," said Tek.

Anthony, Katie, and Ernest sat in front of him, students before the teacher.

"A log possesses minimal personality, has no free will. There is mass, density, dimension, and texture. Combine those meager aspects with the tug of gravity, and the direction and force of the breeze, and you can control the outcome, touch a single log and make the others do your bidding." Tek pointed behind him, at the 144 stones.

But there were no logs on the stones today.

Instead there were thirty-six Neanderthals, each occupying a single stone in the central six-by-six region of the array. Some sat, some stood, some crouched. A few were even curled up, asleep, snoring loudly.

"But these have free will, a desire to be."

Resting on his haunches, Ernest squirmed.

"Bored?" asked Tek, focusing on Ernest.

"Yes," he said, and then pointed at the thirty-six Neanderthals. "Time is limited, and you are wasting what little of it we have on this."

"And you would suggest?"

"We need access to the Sonomak simulator." The three had been given a brief overview of the Sonomak that was composed of the twin black holes and the remnants of Jupiter's and Saturn's moons. They knew what had to be done, that the trajectories of the black holes had to be controlled in order to gain access to the fabric of space-time, to mend the rip that was chewing its way out from the dozens of collapsing earths. "Moons, rocks, trajectories, and gravitational gradients are what we need to be thinking about—objects with no free will, objects that simply obey the rules of physics."

Tek's lower lip pulled up above his upper lip, the Neanderthal equivalent of a human smile. "Ninety-two naturally occurring elements," said Tek. "That's all there are. Those elements are used in the fabrication of logs, moons, and *Neanderthals*. The only thing that differentiates these objects is the way in which those elements are put together, in the complexity of the construction."

"We've heard this before," said Ernest.

"And I guess you will hear it again," said Tek. "There comes a point in all systems when the complexity becomes sufficient to allow the system to cross the boundary between simply being an object, and becoming an object with free will."

"The Sonomak does not have free will!" shouted Ernest, standing up.

Tek shook his head and said nothing. He always said nothing when the argument reached this point. "The exercise is quite simple," he said. "You will be allowed a single action in order to remove all thirty-six Neanderthals from their stones."

Ernest shook his head, refusing. At his core he believed in particles, in fields, in the hard-and-fast rules of physics. He'd come to accept, and even appreciate, the new realms he had entered, places where patterns were revealed beneath layers of chaos, but this exercise was meaningless. "It cannot be done," he said, as he pointed at the Neanderthals, "and even if it could, that would not bring us one step closer to successfully operating the Sonomak."

Katie looked up at Ernest and then over at Anthony. She felt herself in the middle, both literally and figuratively. "He built the machine, Ernest," she said. "He understands it better than any of us and should know what it will take to operate it."

"Then let him knock those thirty-six monkeys off their perches!" shouted Ernest.

"Ernest," said Anthony softly. "The Sonomak will have free will."

"It is a machine!"

The answer came to Anthony so clearly, with such certainty, that he couldn't believe that he hadn't seen it a week earlier, when Tek had first presented them with the concept of a machine with free will. "But *we* will be operating it," he said. "We will be a *part* of it. It will be *our* free will which will allow the Sonomak to work."

"What?" said Ernest.

"Watch," said Anthony. "With a single action I can remove all thirty-six of those Neanderthals from their stones."

"Impossible," said Ernest as he looked over at them and examined just a few of the infinite number of permutations of colliding Neanderthals, all of them acting and reacting in ways that could simply not be predicted.

Anthony shook his head. "Creeeech!" he shouted. "Kat-at-ak!" The thirty-six Neanderthals focused their attention on him, those that had been asleep, waking, and standing. A Neanderthal near Anthony stepped off his stone. Others quickly followed.

Katie smiled, exposing her big block teeth.

"What are you doing?" asked Ernest.

"Just what Tek asked us to do," he said. "I took a single action, and as a result the Neanderthals are no longer on their stones."

Ernest squinted, his eyes nearly vanishing beneath a thick bony brow.

"I asked them to step off of the stones," said Anthony.

Ernest shook his head. "That's cheating," he said. "You know what Tek wanted us to do." Ernest paused, scratching at his pelt, suddenly not so sure of himself. "And how is this suppose to help us with the Sonomak?"

Tek nodded to the Neanderthals, who quickly returned to their stones. "Keep yourselves focused on your objectives, on your *true* objectives," he said. "If you don't know precisely what it is that you want, you'll have no hope of finding it."

Ernest rolled his eyes. "More psychobabble," he said.

"Perhaps," said Tek. He spun on the ball of his left foot, while pulling his right leg up, his right foot suddenly waist high. The foot caught Ernest square in the gut, throwing him off his feet, hurling him backward.

"Umph!" was all that Ernest could manage as he crashed into what felt like a fur-covered rock that he knew must have been one of the thirty-six Neanderthals. As he hit the ground, face first, he could hear the sounds of a riot, screams and hoots, grunts and squeals, and the heavy thuds of Neanderthals hitting dirt.

"No," Ernest said in a whisper, pushing himself up, shaking his head back and forth, and sucking down a deep breath. A few of the Neanderthals were standing; the rest still sprawled on the ground. Not a single one remained on the stones. All had been knocked off; the chain reaction had begun when he collided with the first Neanderthal.

"Class dismissed!" said Tek, not turning to look back.

"What are you?"

Jack didn't turn, didn't appear to respond in any visible

fashion, but his guts knotted and his breathing quickened. He had been waiting for this conversation. He was actually surprised that Katie had held herself back for so long. But he could no longer read Katie as he had once been able to. The combination of the Neanderthal genetic template and the mental alterations that had taken place when she had linked with Nadia had turned her into something he couldn't quite fathom.

He no longer knew her, but he still loved her.

He sat atop a bluff, looking down at a sloping plain speckled with Zebra-like creatures. He had been watching a small group of Neanderthals play with them, herding them into a circle, chasing each other, full of fury and motion, but getting absolutely nowhere.

Katie sat down next to him, pulled up a large clump of grass and, stuffing it into her mouth, along with the clod of dirt still attached to the roots, pushed it between her left cheek and teeth. The grass produced a mild narcotic effect on the Neanderthal physiology. Katie sucked hard on the grass.

Fright.

She was certain that what she felt, what she *had* felt toward Jack, was now meaningless. She knew that there was no *him*. And yet, she still loved him.

Jack still did not turn, did not want to look at her. "You didn't ask *who* I am, but *what* I am." Then he turned and looked into her crystal eyes. "Is the gulf between us already that large?"

Katie nodded. "What do you see when you look at me Jack? Am I a bacteria, a virus, just snippets of mobile DNA? What am I, compared to you?"

"I'm a man," said Jack.

Katie shook her head and sucked hard on the wad of grass in her cheek. "That's your current guise, the skin you're wearing at the moment. But that skin isn't *you*."

"But it is," said Jack. "There are some dim memories, but most of it is beyond my understanding. I experience the world through this skin, think about the world with the brain in my skull."

"And I do the same," said Katie in a sad voice, tapping the side of her head with a fur-covered hand. "And what is inside me tells me that what you really are is something beyond my comprehension."

Jack shook his head again. "I'm not. I've chosen not to be something beyond you. I am human."

She stood. "That's exactly it, Jack. You have *chosen* to be human. You have *chosen* to operate at our primitive level. But that was and *is* a choice under your control. Tomorrow you may choose to be something else, may choose to be what you really are."

Jack nodded, not knowing what to say. He could never find the words, never knew what to do when relationships started to crumble.

"Are you one of the Makers? Is the entire universe a little experiment of yours?"

Jack shook his head. "I don't *believe* I'm a Maker."

Katie put her hands to her hips and squinted at Jack, quickly tripping through a wide range of spectral inputs. "Well, don't strain yourself trying to remember, Jack," she said, her anger flaring. "You wouldn't want to do us any favors by figuring out just who you are, how you're involved in the destruction of billions of lives and entire worlds. I wouldn't want you to actually do something about it."

"It is not up to me to do something about this," said Jack. He knew just how feeble that sounded. "This is an opportunity for *you* to do something, to create your own future." He did not, could not tell her that he was now certain that humans had no future.

"Thank you!" she screamed, the shrill shriek in her voice lifting up into a range that only a Neanderthal could possibly produce. Turning, she stomped down the grassy hillside.

Jack lowered his head to his knees. "This is how I've always done it," he whispered. He wondered if it was always this hard, this painful. He suspected it was. And he suspected that this is why he did not let himself remember his own past.

"It's about time," was the last thing Ernest said before the interface wrapped around his face, pulling at his fur, sucking him down, flowing across his open eyes, its millions of atomic-width tendrils worming around cell walls, crawling down the optic nerve and then erupting into his brain.

Ernest hung in free space—*totally free space*.

The sun burned to his left, a yellow electric arc of negligible size. Io hung below and to the right, an angry-looking ball of yellow-red sulfurs, volcanoes spewing out a noxious mixture of toxic metals. Far away, the feeble sunlight caught several small moons, the rocks reflecting in dull yellows. He flipped. Bottom became top, up became down. The twin holes hung in front of him. He could of course not see them, those eaters of everything sucking down all matter and energy, the ultimate vacuum cleaners. But their throats glowed, that region where the infilling matter was torn apart, blasted, the bits and pieces accelerated, spewing out their own light before being swallowed.

"L-holes," he said, not wondering how he was able to talk in the vacuum of space, but simply marveling at the reality he had theoretically predicted.

"Enough sight-seeing."

Ernest turned. Three Neanderthals hung some five meters in front of him—Katie, Anthony, and Tek.

"For this training session," said Tek, "you will not rely on the primitive optics in your skulls. The Sonomak will see for you."

Ernest winced, lurched back, the onslaught of visual information slamming him in the head. The spectrum ran from the X-ray hornet's howl enveloping the holes, to the dull monotone groan of long wavelength radio waves oscillating throughout the picoverse, like ripples in a fishbowl.

"Track initial conditions," instructed Tek.

Ernest managed a groan as he drowned in the data—more than twenty thousand discrete objects, all moving, all emitting radiation, all *potentially* interacting with each other.

"The system you are observing is unstable. Use the initial conditions you find to instigate a process to set up a runaway oscillation in the twin black holes, which in turn will rupture space-time and open a wormhole to Alpha's picoverse."

"Impossible," Ernest barely managed to say, as he drowned in the data.

Movement.

Ernest felt it, detected it in the subtle blue and red shifts of bodies accelerating, trajectories being *manipulated.*

Carme, Sinope, and Lysithea—three rocky moonlets suddenly on the move, being guided, trajectories all closing on the big moon of Callisto.

Ernest turned, physically pushing against the onslaught of data, swimming upstream in the white-noise torrent. Through the haze and static, he saw Anthony spin about, arms stretching, hands vanishing in the distance. He gave Sinope a corrective shove.

"I can do it!" shouted Anthony.

Ernest hoped he could, because he suddenly knew that he himself never could. The possibilities were infinite, the potential trajectories greater than infinite. He knew with full certainty that even if all the computers in this universe were tied directly into his brain, that he could not control the chaos engulfing him.

Carme and Lysithea collided—two moon-sized eggs rolling into each other, the impact shattering both, the shards recoiling in all directions. Ernest wailed, feeling his head rupture as the trajectories of the *millions* of rocks recoiling from the impact were driven down his optic nerve. His skull shattered.

"No!" shrieked Anthony.

For the briefest of moments, Ernest wondered how he could hear Anthony, how a brain without benefit of its skull, exposed to the hard vacuum and the searing radiation ambient of the twin black holes, could keep processing data, how it could remain *conscious*.

That was the last thought he had.

SECTION III
CHAPTER 9

"The Earth now has four moons," said Anthony. He stared into the image hanging in front of him. "Four, that is, if you include that partial chunk of moon over there," he added, as he reached out and cupped a sliver of moon in an orbit far above the others.

Jack nodded.

"The process is accelerating," he said. He blinked his eyes several times and fluttered his fingers, those commands allowing him to peer into the heart of the simulation, the one that deconvolved the image being received from the big optical array mounted on the *Hirku-Ashi*'s sunward side.

The image before him exploded, the shattered and bloated Earth being peeled back layer by layer, those portions of earths from the different picoverses being mathematically sliced away and made to hover by themselves. Crust, core, oceans, vast deserts, spewing magma—snippets and slices from the different universes that were collapsing in on themselves to form a composite earth pulling apart.

"Parts from at least twenty-six different picoverses," he said. Turning his head to the left, he drank in a red torrent of data. "Distortions extend outward to the orbit of Mars." He turned to look at Jack. *"Venus is gone."*

Again Jack nodded.

Anthony stared at him, tried to stare right through him, wishing for a moment that he had his mother's eyes and the ability to see across a nearly infinite spectrum. But he knew that ability would not let him see what he needed to really see, would not let him see *inside* of Jack.

"I said that Venus is gone, Jack."

"Time is getting short," Jack answered.

Anthony turned in his seat, putting his back to the shattered images of Earth. "I don't think we can do it, Jack," he said in a whisper. "It's been nearly two weeks in the simulator. We've been able to generate a few low-level distortions and ripple space-time in the vicinity of the holes, but we have not come even remotely close to generating the sort of stresses needed to form a wormhole capable of breeching the universe."

"Too much data?" asked Jack.

Anthony shook his head. "If that were only it. More data could be handled by more machines."

"Then what is the problem?" asked Jack.

Anthony pushed himself back. "It's not our ability to crunch the data," he said. "It is in the *way* that we crunch the data, in knowing which piece of data is the critical piece, which grain of sand when moved in just the right way will unleash a chain of events capable of rupturing space-time. We can't do that."

Jack nodded. If Anthony could not do this, then he doubted that anyone could. The humans were not yet capable of this, not even after their minds had been transferred into the physical structure of the enhanced Neanderthal brain.

"When we entered into that sea of machines surrounding the pillar, I could see the overall system constructed by the collective movement of all those machines. Understanding how the system functioned allowed me to find the most vulnerable element within the system in order to bring the whole thing crashing down," said Anthony.

"*The* grain of sand," said Jack.

"Yes," said Anthony. "Given enough time, we might be able to do it. But even assuming that, all we would have actually done is to escape this picoverse. We still need to repair the damage that's been done, to seal this imploding region of space-time, to stop it from devouring the universe."

Jack nodded.

"Tek has not been able to run the simulation successfully, though he's been trying for the last fifty thousand years," said Anthony.

Jack didn't answer, knowing there really was nothing else that could be said. If Tek could not operate the Sonomak after fifty thousand years of trying, then it would be simply impossible for the others to master it in only a few weeks. Jack knew that he had no choice, but he would not act until the last possible moment.

He owed them that much.

He would allow them to be masters of their own fate until he had absolutely no choice but to step in and fix the damage, by making certain that the damage never took place.

"Even if we don't suddenly wink out of existence, replaced by another chunk of space-time as the picoverses continue the collapse, and if we do reach the Europa station in time, we won't be able to operate the Sonomak. We'll just have to wait there until this picoverse is devoured."

"A solution may still exist," said Jack.

"Is there something that *you* can do?" asked Anthony.

Jack shook his head. He had suspected that this was why Anthony had asked to meet him in the viewing room. He had hoped that Anthony had called him here to tell him of some breakthrough, of some unseen turn of events that would save the humans.

But there was one thing that Jack would have to do. Moving between this picoverse and the universe was a trivial matter for him. He was built to move between universes; it was as natural to him as opening a door and walking outside. Much more difficult would be the actual sealing of the space-time breach that was currently devouring the picoverses and would eventually unleash itself on the greater universe.

Very difficult.

But he knew what had to be done. He had studied the Sonomak and knew that it would be quite capable of generating an extratemporal wormhole within the universe itself, one whose throat opened into the universe at a point in time well before protohumans ever dropped down from the trees.

So easy. *Done so many times before*, he realized.

A small piece of solar debris, something with a diameter on the order of ten kilometers could be easily nudged from its orbit and sent earthward. The strike would be sufficient to reset evolution's clock, to wipe the planet clean of higher life-forms, but let those hiding in the dark come out and have their chance.

He remembered now.

Earth was so fertile, the potential so vast. How many times in the past had he been forced into this exact situation, into stepping back, wiping the slate clean and starting over? At least a dozen, probably more. The last had been nearly sixty-five million years ago, the impacting rock removing all possibility of those brainless, violent behemoths ever evolving into the graceful, beautiful creatures who would eventually tamper with the fabric of space-time.

And then there was no turning back.

Entire worlds were created, each a work of art, a dream turned to reality.

An unstable reality that they could not control.

He'd been forced to reset the Earth's clock, to step ten million years into their past and obliterate their future with a single falling rock. Then the chaos of evolution took over, eventually bringing humans to the threshold.

Now he would have to do it again.

"I don't think I will ever be able to operate the Sonomak," said Anthony. "But I can see enough of the pieces of the puzzle to know that *you* can operate the Sonomak, that you can open the tunnel back into the universe. You can do that, Jack."

"Not *for* you," answered Jack, standing, turning his back on Anthony and walking out of the viewing room.

"You started all this, Jack!" yelled Anthony. "And now you won't help us stop it!"

Tek sat back in the leather couch, sinking in deeply. He put his furry Neanderthal feet up on the coffee table, and took a deep pull on his bottle of beer. Ancient memories, those stored away well before he accepted the Neanderthal template, tried to tell him that the beer was crisp, and a bit dry. But the Neanderthal taste buds insisted that the beer was too sweet and flat. He took another long drink, reminding himself that there was much more to beer than the taste—alcohol had the same effect on the Neanderthal brain as it did on the human brain. Tek needed to relax, and at the same time to focus.

Focus very hard.

He was only moments away from learning if a plan begun nearly one hundred thousand years ago was going to have even a *chance* of working. He took one more long drink. "I thought this place might afford us a degree of privacy," he said as he swept the beer in front of himself, indicating the apartment. "It is also a place where I've learned to feel comfortable, having spent a great deal of the past one hundred thousand years here."

Anthony stood at the window, looking out into the night. In the distance, between two redbrick apartment buildings, he could see the United States Capitol Dome bathed in bright light. He turned around to face Tek. Behind the beer-drinking Neanderthal was a roomful of bookcases, choked to overflowing with books, and beyond it a kitchen, complete with dirty dishes stacked on the counter and a refrigerator that occasionally emitted a high-pitched squeal. "Jack's Washington apartment?" he asked.

Tek nodded. "At least as close as I can come to it."

Anthony nodded, not really caring about Jack's apartment. He kept himself in the here and now, knowing full well that his face and hands were enmeshed in the Sonomak Simulator Interface and this place had no more reality than did the Sonomak *control* zone—that simulated chunk of space where they hung free in vacuum, *attempting* to control the Sonomak.

"So, what did you want to talk to me about?" asked Tek, just barely managing to keep control of himself.

Anthony walked away from the window and sat down in a floral-fabric-bound monstrosity, sinking in until he could feel springs poking at his back. "I cannot operate the Sonomak," he said, and then paused, choosing his next words very carefully. "*We* cannot operate the Sonomak."

"Oh," said Tek as if this was of no consequence.

Anthony nodded. "I can sense you in the Sonomak simulation—a phantom imprint of every attempt you made to generate a wormhole."

"And?" prompted Tek.

"You couldn't generate a wormhole."

"Quite true," said Tek. "And that is why I brought all of you here, so that you could operate it."

Anthony leaned forward. "That's obvious," he said. "It's just as obvious that none of us can operate the Sonomak." He pointed at Tek. "I am what you once were, nearly 100 thousand years ago. Do you really expect me to be able to do something that you can't do? If you can't operate the Sonomak, then there is no way that I can."

Tek leaned forward and put his near-empty beer bottle on the coffee table, deliberately missing the coaster. Sitting back, he gently clapped his hands. "Congratulations," he said. "I could of course have told you this the moment we met, but you wouldn't have believed it then. I could already sense the growing arrogance in you, that self-assuredness that would eventually lead to total megalomania." He paused and looked past Anthony into the Washington night. "I was eventually able to remove those negative characteristics from myself," he said. "I let them stay in Alpha's carcass, while I took the best that remained and transitioned into this wonderful form." He waved a hand over his hairy hide. "But of course I did not completely sever the connection with Alpha. The disgusting creature proved so useful, not only for luring Jack back into the picoverse, thereby releasing Alpha back into the greater universe, but following the directions I'd buried deep within him so well. He created just the right world to banish all of you into, and then went on to create all those other lovely picoverses, enough to guarantee that once the inevitable collapse began, there would be sufficient threat to the greater universe that Jack would be *forced* to act."

Anthony opened his mouth to speak, but said nothing.

"I cannot operate the Sonomak, and you cannot operate the Sonomak. In fact, there is nothing born on Earth that can operate the Sonomak."

Anthony nodded. "Obviously so, or else you would have found that individual and had him operate the machine long ago. It is just as obvious that you believe that the only one who can operate the Sonomak is Jack."

"Naturally," said Tek. "But certainly you must realize that Jack doesn't need something as trivial as those spinning black holes to escape this picoverse."

Anthony sat back.

"Jack can move between universes as easily as we breathe. It was that ability that allowed him to enter into Alpha's picoverse after it had been sealed from within."

Anthony walked across the apartment, clearing his mind.

Pieces came together.

"Jack is *your* tool," he said.

Tek grinned, exposing his big yellow block teeth. "None of us can escape the picoverse. There was only one entity that could, the entity that is responsible for placing us in this predicament in the first place, the very same entity that will not willingly help us."

"But why have Alpha fabricate all the picoverses? Why didn't you just make your escape when Jack first reopened the wormhole back to the universe, when Alpha did?"

"Escaping the picoverse is not really escaping anything, since it doesn't take us away from the Makers, or from Jack."

Anthony nodded. "You never constructed the Sonomak intending to use it to escape the picoverse."

Tek nodded. "Jack will do that. And then he will use the Sonomak to generate an extratemporal wormhole into our past, to destroy us while we still swing through the trees, allowing the universe to go on without benefit of us."

"How can you know that will be his plan?" asked Anthony.

"I've had one hundred thousand years in real time. I have *thought* this through. The Sonomak is uniquely configured to generate an extratemporal wormhole once relocated back in the greater universe. Jack will be aware of this."

Anthony considered that for a moment. "So you have provided him with an easy means to erase us, before we even drop down from the trees?"

"Exactly," said Tek. "Jack will take the Sonomak back to the universe and use it to destroy the *human* race."

A pattern emerged, a nearly infinite number of puzzle pieces suddenly snapping into place. Anthony slowly smiled. "What you're planning won't be easy," he said.

Tek nodded. "Few things worth doing are."

SECTION III
CHAPTER 10

"Katie?"

Katie rolled over, untangling herself from the pile of Neanderthals she had been snuggled up against, and walked toward the center of camp and the twelve-by-twelve obsidian flagstone grid. The night was bright, a full moon hanging along the central axis of the *Hirku-Ashi*, casting hard shadows, the landscape textured in infinite shades of gray.

"I'm leaving, Katie." Jack floated in midair, about one meter above the center of the flagstone grid, legs folded and hands placed in his lap. "I've done all that I can, all that I will allow myself to do. The future rests in your hands."

Jack's lips had not moved, yet the words echoed in her head.

She realized she was asleep and this was a dream.

"You didn't have the guts to tell me this when I was awake!" she shouted, standing on tiptoe so she could look into Jack's eyes. "You caused all this, opened the way for us, and now you won't help us."

Jack shook his head. "You and Horst are the ones responsible. You were the ones who entered into energy domains that stressed the fabric of space-time."

"*Stressed the fabric of space-time—we ripped* it clean through, you son of a bitch! And unless you help us stitch it back together, entire worlds will vanish!"

"I can't do that."

"You can do anything you damn well please. Go back and fix it, don't let us run the experiment in the first place. Smash the first damn Sonomak into a billion little pieces."

Jack shook his head. "If it hadn't been you and Horst, then it would have soon been another group. It was inevitable. Regardless of the starting conditions, given your curiosity, your drive, and your innate intelligence, *if left to yourself*, you will always reach a point at which some member of your race will begin to manipulate space-time."

"Then don't leave it up to us. Unleash an army of Alexandras to keep us in line, to prevent those experiments."

Again Jack shook his head. "The function of the Controllers is to make certain that a species does not destroy itself as it evolves, as it moves toward its potential pinnacle. You reached the point where you showed yourselves capable of manipulating space-time, of transcending to something incredible, something so rare and precious. To make that transition you needed to master the power you had unleashed."

"We obviously *can't* control it."

"That appears to be true, but has not yet been conclusively demonstrated."

"Conclusively demonstrated!" she shouted. "Right now

there are worlds devouring themselves, billions being simply erased. I'd say that pretty conclusively demonstrates our inability to control this power."

"I will not step in and take away your chance to create your own destiny. You did not stumble upon this. You have propelled yourselves toward it, sought it out, done everything imaginable, sometimes even unimaginable, to peel back layer after layer of the unknown to understand all that can be understood. I will not stand in the way of what your species so obviously needs. To stop you now, to save you from yourselves, would eventually destroy you, breaking you as a species."

"And if we can't fix this mess ourselves?"

"Then your species will cease to exist."

"And that will be our destiny—total oblivion!"

Jack floated upward, rising into the moonlit sky. "Yes."

"I hate you!" she screamed, as she dropped to her knees and pounded her fists against an obsidian flagstone. "You are a compassionless, arrogant, wanna-be god, and I pray to whatever power that *really* runs all of creation that someday you will come face-to-face with it and be kicked right on your ass!"

Katie opened her eyes, wide awake. Anthony's face was only inches from hers, his own eyes open. "Jack's gone," she said.

"I know," he said, nodding his head. "I shared the dream."

Katie sat up. "We will beat that son of a bitch!"

Anthony looked up at her. "Maybe," he said. "But it will require you to do the one thing that you fear the most."

SECTION III
CHAPTER 11

Katie still found it uncomfortable wearing clothes. After so many months as a Neanderthal, with nothing but a wispy layer of fur separating her from the rest of the world, the thick orange jumpsuit she now wore felt like a suit of concrete. Had there been a choice, she thought that she would have preferred to keep at least some of the Neanderthal DNA, but the plan called for her to return to a pure Homo sapiens form, although the modifications made by Nadia still remained.

She sat back in the gel-supported seat, barely sinking in, the location of the *Hirku-Ashi*'s docking port so close to the asteroid's central axis of rotation that the spin-generated gravity barely produced a tenth of a gee.

"It's begun."

Katie turned her head. She had been the first into the transfer craft, while Anthony and Ernest still stood on the loading bay dock. Just past them stood Tek, the left side of his face enmeshed in the thick interface goo that neurally connected him into the *Hirku-Ashi*'s systems.

Holographic images flashed before them.

In the distance, thunder roared, and Katie could feel her gel-filled seat quiver.

"Alexandra and her associates vaporized a nearly one-hundred-meter-diameter section of the *Hirku*'s forward bulkhead and are closing in quickly on our central encampment. If the hole is not closed, the pressure will drop below breathable levels in less than eight hours."

Katie leaned her head forward, resting her chin on her chest.

Grabbing on to the door lip of the transfer craft, Anthony hoisted his furry right leg into the craft. Katie was not sure if Anthony would be able to take the three-gee acceleration they would be traveling at. His rib cage stood out clearly beneath his hairy chest, and hip bones protruded from dark skin that looked as if it had been heat shrunk over his backside. She did not understand the exact nature of the endless simulations that Anthony, Ernest, and Tek had been running in the Sonomak simulator for the last month. She was not part of that program, had given up the Neanderthal template that would have allowed her to interface with both the simulation and the Sonomak.

She had another task to perform.

Anthony dropped into his seat, and Ernest followed.

They were still nearly one hundred million kilometers away from Europa and the Sonomak, and the *Hirku-Ashi* would take nearly another three months to get there. They didn't have three months. Alexandra's attack had forced them to act. But they had planned for this, the transfer craft ready and waiting, the vehicle little more than three seats strapped to a high-efficiency fusion reactor. Flip the switch, the reactor powered, and the energy liberated from the fusing of hydrogen atoms was transferred to heavy mass xenon atoms that were blown out its backside.

So simple, thought Katie, preferring to dwell on the craft's fusion engine, rather than on what would happen when they reached Europa. Accelerating at three gees, the craft would take them fifty million kilometers in fifteen hours, then flip on its axis and decelerate at three gees for another fifteen hours, slowing them down over a distance of another fifty million kilometers in fifteen hours.

Using such a craft could have taken them from Earth to Europa in a matter of days, and when Tek had first shown them the craft, she had wondered why they simply hadn't taken it from Earth to Europa in the first place.

One look at Anthony and Ernest told her why. Tek knew that they had needed these past months to learn and grow, to transform themselves both inside and out into something that *might* be able to operate the Sonomak.

Tek walked up to the open hatch of the craft and peered in. "You know what you have to do," he said.

The three nodded and the hatch closed.

No good-byes were said.

Katie listened to the hiss of hydraulics, a sharp push to the right of the craft as it was ejected from the *Hirku-Ashi*, and then she was slammed in the chest, air exploding up her throat and erupting from her mouth and nose. She sank deeply into the seat. She turned her head and looked at Anthony. Eyes shut, jaw clenched, his chest slowly rose, and then quickly fell. She watched long enough for the slow, apparently painful process to repeat itself several times. "Thirty hours," she said in a hiss, forcing the air up her throat.

Anthony said nothing. Breathing was difficult enough; talking was beyond the realm of the possible.

*Tek walked quickly along the corridor, the holographic image keep*ing pace with him, hovering several meters before him, showing scene after scene of Alexandra and her advancing forces moving up the axis through the *Hirku-Ashi*, vaporizing everything in their path.

And then there were the Neanderthals.

They sat, quietly, peacefully, gathered in tribes and smaller family groups, seated in clearings, and beside streams. They had lost the conflict the moment Alexandra and her forces had entered the asteroid.

The Neanderthals knew this. There was no point in fighting.

Tek sighed. The very ability that let them gaze into the tangled web of the future, to generate a desired outcome from a nearly infinite number of starting conditions, was their greatest strength—and also their greatest weakness.

Humans would fight even after the fight had been lost.

Neanderthals stopped fighting the moment they believed the fight had been lost.

Both characteristics were fundamental to each species, wired directly into them at the most basic level. He could not be certain, but he believed that this was the fundamental reason why the advancing Homo sapiens that had poured out of Africa had been able to so quickly eradicate the Neanderthals.

Tek hoped that the combination of the two, the blending of both characteristics would be enough to see Anthony, Ernest, and Katie through, to give them the ability to stand up to Jack.

Turning the corner of the corridor, he dropped down to the floor, and crawled into an open tube protruding through the wall of the corridor, the opening barely large enough for his wide shoulders. The transport system buried within the *Hirku-Ashi* had been designed for use by its smaller human builders.

He gave the commands.

The walls of the tube closed in around him, wrapping him in a tight-fitting cocoon. Acceleration slammed at him, driving the blood out of his head, and then just as quickly he felt himself falling free, almost floating as he was hurled through the thick skin of the *Hirku-Ashi*.

He knew where Jack would be waiting.

Jack blinked and returned. He did not know where he had been. He sensed the world about him, breathed deeply, and accessed the Hirku-Ashi's onboard systems.

It had started.

He corrected himself. *It was about to end.*

"You did not go with them," said Jack.

Tek stepped into the clearing, panting. The air pressure was dropping quickly, a hard wind now tugged him in the direction of the *Hirku-Ashi*'s forward section, where Alxandra had breeched the hull.

"Their chances of succeeding were slim enough when you were with them, showing them how to work the Sonmak. Without you, even those slim chances are greatly reduced."

Tek nodded. "They will not be able to operate the Sonmak."

"Are you certain?" asked Jack.

Tek attempted to catch his breath, but now found it impossible. "I could not operate the Sonomak to escape the picoverse." He paused and shivered. The *Hirku-Ashi* was losing not only air but also the heat held in the air. "It was never my intent to use the Sonomak to escape the picoverse."

This did not really surprise Jack; he had suspected as much for at least several days before he had left the others, before he had retreated *elsewhere*. "And your intent was?"

"Twofold," said Tek. "First it was a lure to bring you here, to the *Hirku-Ashi*, and to let you see the Neanderthal. I wanted to give you an understanding of their potential, of what they might have become if they had not been eradicated by the humans, and allow you the opportunity to consider what they might become if you would let them live."

"You expect me to save them now?" asked Jack, sweeping his right hand out before him.

"No," said Tek. "I expect you to save them at the *beginning*." Tek sensed where Jack had interfaced with the *Hirku-Ashi*'s systems and uploaded information to him, information that had taken him nearly one hundred thousand years to construct. Part of that data contained his own personal logs, the details of his journey, and his personal evolution, merging the best of what it was to be human with the best of what it was to be Neanderthal.

"Impressive," said Jack. "You have it pinpointed to an exact time and spatial coordinate. I don't think I could have done it much better myself."

Tek eagerly nodded, and started to wheeze. "It's the perfect near-Earth asteroid. The barest nudge will send it on its new course, sending the six-kilometer-long chunk of iron and nickel right into the heart of central Africa, 12 thousand years before the *humans* fired *their* Sonomak," he said, the tone of his voice full of contempt.

"And Homo sapiens will be destroyed before they ever leave Africa, before they spread throughout the rest of the world eradicating the Neanderthal," said Jack.

"Exactly," said Tek. "I have it all set up, all the parameters in place. I've spent fifty thousand years specifying every variable. All you need to do is transport the Sonomak back into the universe and activate the system. Homo sapiens will never exist, and the collapse that is currently devouring the picoverses and will soon erupt into the universe beyond, will never have been generated in the first place. It will solve all the problems that the humans have generated. And it will give the Neanderthals their opportunity, *our* opportunity, to show you what we are truly capable of. It is the Neanderthal branch of humanity that will take the Earth to the next evolutionary level, and not those visionless Homo sapiens."

"An interesting proposal," said Jack. "But we still have the matter of Anthony, Ernest, and Katie. I must give them their chance, let them attempt to operate the Sonomak, to attempt to solve this problem."

"I understand," said Tek. "But they will not even attempt to operate the Sonomak. Anthony and Ernest now have the ability to see the possibilities, to truly understand their limitations. There is enough Neanderthal in them to force them into accepting the inevitable when faced with it. When attempting to fire the Sonomak, they will see that they can never successfully operate it, and they will give up. They will surrender to you."

"Are you so sure?" asked Jack.

Tek nodded. "They will not fire the Sonomak." Of that Tek had absolutely no doubt.

"Agreed then," said Jack. "If they don't use the Sonomak, then I will use it as you suggested and give the Neanderthals their chance."

Tek sagged and fought to get his breath.

"You of course realize what your own fate is, what inevitable pathway you put yourself on when you stayed behind to plead the Neanderthals' case to me."

Tek nodded and turned. Ice now hung on the pine trees. The sky was incredibly clear, not a cloud remaining, nothing to blur the horizon or to obscure his vision of the fluttering *creatures* dropping down out of the sky.

"I . . ."

Jack lurched back, hit by a wall of steaming air and finely shredded Neanderthal debris. He jumped up, wiped the gooey mush off his face, and waited for a moment. The creatures landed around him, a dozen, human-avian-machine hybrids, all with weapons trained on him—ugly stubby guns whose tips sputtered and spit small balls of lightning that quickly evaporated in the thin air.

"It's over!"

Alexandra dismounted from the back of one of the creatures, pulling off a helmet, dropping it to the ground, and striding forward.

"And how is that?" asked Jack.

"I am about to intercept the craft in which your friends attempted to make their escape. They will be killed unless you help me repair the damage they've done. And once they're dead, I'll eviscerate you and drain you right down to the last neuron."

Jack smiled. "I have other plans."

He snapped his fingers and rainbow light flashed throughout the *Hirku-Ashi*. The creatures vanished, shunted away to an alternate region of space-time. Alexandra stood in the clearing, facing Jack alone.

"You can't do that!" she yelled, stepping forward and firing several glassy tendrils from her forehead, all of which struck Jack in the right eye. "You will help me shut down the universe. The Makers demand it!"

Jack smiled.

Alexandra collapsed into a heap of fine glass crystals which the thin breeze swept away into the forest, and would soon carry into the vacuum of space.

Jack vanished in a maelstrom of rainbow light.

SECTION III
CHAPTER 12

Three days.

Anthony and Ernest had not moved, at least not the parts of them that Katie could see. Seated before the Sonomak console they were encased in heavy gray goo, their heads totally enveloped, arms sunk elbow deep, and everything below the waist wrapped in a thick, bloodred fabric that sprouted from the floor.

Their exposed chests quickly rose and fell.

Rivulets of sweat ran through the matted fur on their backs.

Katie paced, making yet one more transit of the control room and the banks of equipment that could only be described as being alive. It moved, actually seemed to breathe. If she leaned up against what looked like a floor-to-ceiling covering of thickly corded pink muscle-like fiber, she could feel it twitch, spasm, occasionally detect waves rolling along its surface. Embedded in the living wall were body-shaped receptacles, suggesting where hands, feet, and heads should be inserted.

She again had to remind herself that this was not the equipment, but merely the interface that connected the Sonomak operators to the hardware that would initiate the firing sequence of the Sonomak, starting the initial trajectories of rocky fragments along the paths that would eventually set the twin black holes on their mission to rupture space-time.

Katie continued walking, moving to the back of the interface room and to the viewing window. Despite what Anthony and Ernest had told her, she was still having trouble accepting what she was seeing.

The object luminesced in hues of blues and greens.

There was no sense of distance, no reference structures, nothing recognizable to be used to judge the size of the thing. It looked solid, and by any normal standards it was. But down at the atomic scale it was a tenuous honeycomb, a latticework of cadmium, tellurium, and sulfur, through which the salty seas of Europa percolated.

They were thirty kilometers beneath Europa's permanent ice cap, at the interface between the ice and the sea that flowed around the entire moon, a mineral-laden ocean nearly two hundred kilometers deep. And throughout that massive sea, one with far greater volume than had ever existed on Earth, ran the honeycomb latticework, spanning the entire girth of the moon.

Like the interface that filled the far wall of the room, the honeycomb latticework was alive, powered by the heat rising up from Europa's core. The energy that had once been generated by the tidal forces exerted by Jupiter, now came from the twin black holes. Bathed in the warm glow from beneath, and nourished by the salt-heavy water flowing through it, the latticework lived, electrons flowing from node to node of each atomic intersection of the sulfur, cadmium, and tellurium interfaces.

The latticework was a mind, fabricated over millennia under Tek's direction, designed to observe, suck down data, and interpret the trajectories and potential collisions of a nearly infinite number of objects. It was the hardware to which Anthony and Ernest had been interfaced for three days, attempting to set up the initial conditions that would start the black holes on their space-rupturing trajectories.

For three days Katie had walked, sat, slept, eaten the tasteless bricks of food they had brought and drunk from a small pool of water that would appear at the rear of the interface room.

She waited, not knowing if her time for action would come within the next few minutes, or the next few days. Katie lowered herself to the floor and, in an action that had become pure reflex, reached up to the top pocket of her orange overalls and checked to make sure that the Virtuals were still there.

She would be needing them, she hoped.

"They've reached their limit."

Katie spun around on the smooth floor. Jack stood less than five meters in front her, dressed in an orange jumpsuit indistinguishable from hers.

Here we go, she thought.

"They've been in the interface far longer than the system was ever designed for," said Jack. "It is supplying them with nutrients and water, and carrying away wastes as designed, and could continue doing so for millennia, repairing their bodies at the cellular level and even at the genetic level if necessary."

Katie nodded nervously. *Come on Jack, let's go*, she thought.

Jack tapped the side of his head. "But they won't be able to withstand it mentally, their cognitive states getting lost in all that," he said, as he half-turned and swept his hand toward the viewing window, at the latticework that ran so much farther than the eye could possibly see. "They are dying. They passed their maximum mental capabilities almost two days ago. They could not operate the Sonomak then, could not determine the correct initial conditions, so they certainly cannot do so now."

Katie stood. "That's it then?"

"I'm afraid it is," said Jack, sounding incredibly sad. "You are not able to escape the picoverse on your own and have absolutely no chance at stopping the collapse and correcting the damage."

"And now you will *correct* our mistakes?" asked Katie.

"I'm afraid I have no choice," he answered.

A shudder ran through the interface room, one so slight that Katie thought she might have only imagined it. Jack took half a step toward her, then stopped, quickly looked around the room and angling his head back, looked up at the featureless ceiling. "You're home," he said.

Anthony and Ernest dropped to the floor, kicked back, forcibly ejected from the interface. They slid half a dozen meters across the floor, their unmoving bodies slowly coming to a halt.

• • •

"I felt it," said Ernest, only partially conscious, his eyes not yet open.

Katie had dragged both Ernest and Anthony back to the corner of the interface room, at first certain that both of them were dead. But they were still alive, their breathing ragged and shallow, their bodies hot and sweating. For nearly the last three hours she'd been wiping their foreheads with a moistened sleeve of her jumpsuit, and dripping water into their mouths from her cupped hands.

"Ernest?" she said, shaking him gently. "Wake up," she whispered, and then looked down to the far end of the interface room. Jack stood before the interface wall, a thin tendril of goo running from it to the back of his head. He did not look in their direction, appeared totally oblivious to anything that was taking place in the room.

Between them hung a holographic image of the black hole system, all of it in motion, Io shattered nearly two hours ago, and large fragments of Callisto already sucked down into one of the holes.

"He's started it," said Katie.

Ernest attempted to push himself up, his arms shaking, then giving way, dropping him back to the floor. He slowly opened his eyes. "We sensed it," he said, and then half closed his eyes, as if the act of remembering was simply too exhausting. "He pulled us and the entire Sonomak out of the picoverse." His eyes opened wide. "We saw it, our globular galaxy hanging above us, filling the sky, running to Europa's far western horizon."

Katie simply nodded. "Good," she said. *They had escaped.*

Again Ernest tried to push himself up, and this time managed to sit. "What's he doing?" he asked quietly, looking across the interface room and not at Jack, but at the holographic display. Small flares of light sparked as minuscule shards of moons slipped toward one of the hole's event horizons.

"I think he's doing *it*," she said.

"Help me up," said Ernest, trying to stand.

For a moment Katie hesitated, not wanting to leave Anthony's side.

"We've got to know," said Ernest.

Katie took a deep breath, turned and tugged Ernest to his feet. He draped his right arm over her shoulders, and she half guided, half dragged him to the display.

Ernest knew that at the display's resolution, only ten to twenty thousand of the largest objects would be visible, the billions of smaller fragments too small to be seen here. Ernest stared, searching for the pattern.

The scene was quickly changing.

Most of Io was now gone.

Several shards, probably several hundred kilometers in length, streaked across the width of the display, moving at a significant fraction of the speed of light, shimmering in azure light, suddenly winking out of existence as they were sucked down the throats of the holes. Ganymede, still nearly whole, wobbled, tugged out of its orbit, its crust peeling off, and began swirling down the impossibly steep gravitational gradient generated by the holes.

Ernest slowly turned toward Katie. "He's running Tek's program,"

"You know?"

Katie and Ernest turned.

Jack stared at them. "What did Tek tell you?" A half-dozen pink tendrils erupted from the interface wall and slammed into the back of his head, staggering him for a moment, pushing him forward, almost pushing him off his feet. "Why would he tell you?"

Ernest looked down at the holographic display.

Ganymede was being sheared in half, swallowed, its metallic core shattering, needle-like fragments of quickly solidifying iron spewing out.

Jack's body shuddered, a head-to-foot twitch that almost dropped him to the floor.

"Move," said Ernest as forcefully as he could, pushing at Katie.

She looked across the room at Anthony, who still lay on the floor. She shook her head, her body language pleading, begging with Ernest not to force her to do what she knew had to be done.

"It's the only way," said Ernest.

She backed up, moving away from Ernest and Anthony and toward the viewing window, as she reached into her top pocket, pulled out the Virtuals, and slipped them on.

"Tek could not possibly tell his *real* plan to you," said Jack. "The Sonomak was not designed to escape the pico-verse, but to be used to fabricate an extratemporal worm-hole to Earth's past."

Ernest nodded, smiling.

"Used to go back in time, to the point at which Homo sapiens were just leaving Africa," said Jack. "That event will be stopped. This world, this time, will belong to the Neanderthals."

Katie looked over at Ernest. "What?" she said. "Neanderthals!"

"No!" shouted Ernest, suddenly moving, passing through the holographic display, the remnants of the black hole system swirling all around him, knowing at that moment that Tek had lied to them, had used them. "Back to *our* time!" he screamed.

Jack shook his head.

For just an instant, Katie thought she saw a smile start to form on Jack's face; the ends of his mouth just began to curl up. But then his eyes grew large.

"Go to him!"

Katie managed to turn her head. Anthony was half sitting, propped up on one elbow, his eyes open to slits. "Go to him!" he screamed again.

Then Katie saw nothing. *The interface room vanished.*

IV. HOME

Half to forget the wandering and the pain,
Half to remember days that have gone by,
And dream the dream that I am home again!
—JAMES ELROY FLECKER (1884–1915)

CHAPTER 1

Go to him.

Anthony's last words were all that existed. There was nothing else. No light, no dark, no weight, no sense of touch, not even thoughts.

Go to him.

Falling.

Static flowed over her, through her, tearing at her with jagged, razored talons. Shredded, inverted, and finally reassembled, gravity tugged at her, dropping her down a shaft of swirling salt and pepper.

"Uhhhh!"

She hit hard, landing flat on her back, her head cracking against something that gave just a bit, the sounds of splintering echoing in her ears. Still surrounded by a storm of salt and pepper interference, she blinked.

The Virtuals locked.

Salt and pepper gave way to a rolling rainbow, and then to four fixed quadrants. Through the upper right quadrant a few white clouds hung in a yellow-tinted blue sky. She blinked again, and the clouds were inspected through myriad spectrums, the yellow-tinted air scanned for particulate and emissions.

"Pollen," she said.

She pushed herself up, sitting. A skyline swung into view. The light from the overhead sun threw rainbow hues from the pillar-like building that dominated the skyline.

Bank of America tower.

"Back in Atlanta." She stared at the tower, not quite able to accept what she was seeing. Just before the wormhole had grabbed her, she'd been certain that Tek had double-crossed them, that he had engineered the entire effort to

destroy mankind, to make a new world for the Neanderthals.

The Bank of America tower loomed large.

Tek had not lied to them, but to Jack.

Looking around, she found herself sitting on a partially
shattered slab of rain-rotted plywood, a few streaks of the
original black paint still visible, but now mostly colored in
hues of gray and mildew-green. To her left was a massive
segment of galvanized ducting, and to her right, a half-
dozen large liquid nitrogen tanks, stripped of their pressure
gauges and relief valves.

She'd been returned to her roost, to the top of the Nunn
physics building. *How had Anthony managed it, how had
he been able to thread the extratemporal wormhole through
all time and space to deposit her in just this place?*

It was incomprehensible.

Anthony had claimed that he could do it, that he could
see the pathway, manipulate the nearly infinite number of
tumbling rocks and moon fragments to guide the wormhole
to just this place, but a part of her had never really believed
it. A part of her had expected to be swallowed by the wormhole and erupt from the other end somewhere in the vacuum of space.

But he'd done it. And now she had to do her part.

"Clock?" she said.

The Virtual clock materialized in front of her.

12:37 p.m.

Beneath the clock hovered the date—*June 23, 2007.*

She nodded her head, her body understanding a few seconds before her mind could integrate all the facts. She *had*
been returned to the beginning, just as they'd planned, to
the start, to the point in time in which all the damage, all
the planetary-spanning destruction, could be stopped.

The first firing of the Sonomak that had transformed the
machine into a carrick knot was only a half an hour away.
If that firing could be stopped, then all subsequent events
would be altered.

At least that was the theory that Anthony believed.

The paradox was the grandfather of all paradoxes—literally. Step back in time and kill your own grandfather. His death would mean that you had never been born and would not have existed in the first place to travel back in time to kill him. Therefore you could *never* kill your own grandfather.

Cause and effect would not allow it.

At least *within* a given universe. But the math and physics were not clear when one passed from universe to universe. Anthony was convinced that under these circumstances causality could be violated, that she could rewrite the past.

12:39.

She jumped off the wooden platform and bounded for the roof exit, hitting the door with all her weight, running down more than a half-dozen steps before the door was fully open. And then she slowed herself down, knew that there was time. They'd gone over the steps she would take what seemed like hundreds of times, worked it out to the last detail. She just had to follow the plan. There would be no explosives hurled into the Sonomak lab, or bashing in of Horst's skull moments before the Sonomak was fired.

Subtlety.

She could not risk revealing herself to anyone here. Her very existence was a concrete demonstration that alternate universes existed. She polarized the lenses of her Virtuals, transforming them into highly reflective mirrors, and then took them off and looked into the reflecting surface.

Crystal eyes.

Hair at least six inches longer than it had been back in June.

The bright orange jumpsuit she had never worn in this world.

She could not be discovered and had to disguise herself to appear as she had been back in June 2007. She started down the stairs again, heading for her office. That would be a safe place for the moment. She knew that her other self was already down in the Sonomak lab, preparing for the test firing.

12:40.

She took the stairs one at a time.

Katie reached up, snugged the Virtuals against her face, checked the lower right quadrant to make certain one more time that they were set to maximum polarization, so that it would be impossible for anyone to actually see her eyes, and then she stepped around the corner.

Horst.

She stopped and stared. He walked slowly toward her, head down, arms behind his back. Katie could not believe how plump he looked, so snug in his black suit, his black hair was so thick, his face unlined, each step he took so steady and forceful.

So alive.

So unlike the embittered, broken man that he had become before his death. Katie smiled. *Before his death.* Not now. She could stop that, stop it all. She ran a hand through her hair, hoping that Horst would not notice the misshapen haircut she had just given herself, and pulled the lab coat tightly around herself, not wanting any of the orange jumpsuit to show through around the collar.

She walked quickly toward him, her shoes slapping against the floor, certain the noise would snap him out of his deep concentration, out of his prepresentation ritual. It didn't. She walked right into him, the two colliding.

"Umph!" Horst back stepped, stumbled, and almost fell.

Katie reached out for him, wrapped her arms around his more than ample waist, and kept him from toppling over backward.

"What's wrong with you, Katie?"

He pushed her back, and Katie could see confusion in his face.

"Nothing," she answered.

She knew that she was taking a risk on multiple levels, knew that he had seen the *other* Katie only moments before at the other end of the Van Leer building, and might wonder how she had gotten ahead of him so quickly and without having passed him.

He studied her for a moment. "What's so important that you chased me all around the building, that you couldn't wait a few minutes for me to get back to the lab?" he asked, sounding annoyed.

Your death and the destruction of this Earth along with so many others.

She was tempted to blurt it out, but resisted, knowing that approach would only lead to confusion, and confrontation. If Horst found out who she really was, what had happened, he would never be able to resist firing the Sonomak. She had to be more subtle, play for time, making certain that the Sonomak was not fired today, and then work out a plan to sabotage the Sonomak, to keep it off-line until the funding ran out and the program was killed.

Horst stared at her, a puzzled look on his face. "Is there something different—"

"I know what you plan to do," said Katie, cutting him off, attempting to distract him from whatever differences he had noticed between her and the other Katie.

"Oh," he said. He raised his right eyebrow. "And why should this concern me?"

"Because if you run all forty-eight accelerators you will in all likelihood not get an incomplete burn—the alignments have not been sufficiently checked, and the software isn't going to be able to compensate the beam steering quickly enough."

"And just how do you know this?" he asked.

She thought quickly, not wanting to make this story too complicated, to get trapped in some inaccuracy or lie. But she had to be convincing enough to make sure that they did not power up the Sonomak for the demonstration. "I've run the simulations, checked the tolerances. Unless all beams hit dead on you'll fall far short of the twenty million degrees."

Horst stared at her, and then stared through her.

At that moment Katie was certain that she had gotten through to him. "You can't run all forty-eight accelerators," she said, hammering home what she hoped would be the critical point.

Horst reached up with his right hand and pulled at his chin and slowly paced back and forth. "How long do you think it would take to check out beam alignments, to run a few low-level tests with all forty-eight accelerators to check out the system?"

Katie's shoulders sagged as relief flowed over her.

"I think we can do it in a week," she said.

Horst stopped pacing, nodded, and reached into his pocket, pulling out a DVD wallet. Unsnapping the wallet and thumbing through it, he pulled out a DVD and held it up to her.

"Power surge—forty-eight accelerators," said Katie as she read the disc's label.

"It will make it look as if we attempted to run all forty-eight accelerators," said Horst, "but just as we start, the system will abort, claiming that there was an input power surge. The Sonomak will shut down, I'll give a little song and dance about Tech's power grid problems, and then beg for a week's extension for the demonstration." He smiled.

"Good," said Katie, knowing how totally inadequate that word was to describe the ultimate disaster that had just been avoided. For just a moment, she expected to feel herself wink out of existence, having just created a future in which she would not exist.

But that did not happen.

Causality can be violated.

That is what Anthony had told her, and he appeared to be right. The math was beyond her, the physics and insights something that only Anthony seemed capable of understanding.

"Now get back to the control room," said Horst. "Don't let on to the others what we are going to try to do. I need their reactions to be genuine in response to our little power surge."

Katie nodded, turned, and trotted down the hallway. She felt so buoyant, so relieved, to know that worlds had been saved, that her family had been saved, that Anthony would not have to experience twenty years of pain and torture. Just before she got to the end of the hallway, she turned, and smiled at Horst, even waved to him.

She then cut around the corner.

Now things would really start to get complicated.

She had not thought this part all through yet—she had not really believed that she would get this far. She knew that within a matter of hours Horst would confront the Katie of this world about their conversation on why the Sonomak could not be fired. And she would of course deny remembering anything about it. Things would quickly start to unravel.

And she would have to intervene again, possibly kidnapping Katie and taking her place, to ensure that the Sonomak was never fired. A part of her mind, at a level just below consciousness, began to assemble the plan.

But she reserved the conscious part of her mind for something far more important. Anthony, *her* Anthony, the six-year-old she had lost, was somewhere on campus at this very moment, brought here by Miss Alice.

Jack disengaged himself from the interface wall, the pink bundles dropping from the back of his head, hitting the floor to the accompaniment of a wet smacking noise. He stared at the two Neanderthals for just a moment, and then looked *far* past them. He smiled. And then he laughed, a deep, rumbling, belly laugh, one that doubled him over.

"You used me," he said. Straightening back up he walked toward them. "You couldn't do it yourself, couldn't control the Sonomak to escape the picoverse, so you *used* me."

Anthony pushed himself up, just barely managing to sit. He feebly waved his furry right hand at Jack, motioning with it, as if he held a screwdriver in it. "We could not build the actual tool, so we built the circumstances that would bring the tool to us."

Jack nodded. "Very good. You escaped the picoverse and *redirected* the extratemporal wormhole. I didn't see the subtle divergence in Tek's program, never suspected that he would intend the wormhole's throat to intersect at a time other than the one most critical for the destruction of *Homo sapiens*." He angled his head back and sniffed at the air, ignoring the stink of fear and sweat and the rubbery tang of the interface wall. He smelled the currents of space-time, the ebb and flow of the collapsing extratemporal wormhole, and the gentle, quickly damping echoes that drifted through the fabric of the universe.

"You sent her back to the beginning?" he asked, looking confused. "Why?"

"Take another sniff," said Anthony. "The wormhole has collapsed, but space and time are still weakened, not totally recovered from the breech of the wormhole. A weak connection still exists between where she went and where we intend her to be going."

Jack smiled. "Very good," he said. "Very, very good. This is so much more than I ever expected, so much more than I ever thought you capable of."

"Underestimated your playthings?" asked Anthony.

"Never my playthings," answered Jack.

"*Pets* then," said Anthony, suddenly sounding bitter.

"Perhaps children might be the more apt description," said Jack. "*Arrogant* children," he added, the expression on his face darkening. "I can quite easily bring a stop to all of this, redirect another extratemporal wormhole, and reset evolution's clock, sweeping you away as I have so many others who have failed."

"You could, but you won't," said Anthony. Slowly standing, and then hobbling over toward the interface, he stopped only when he came directly in front of Jack. "Have we not proved ourselves, have we not earned the right to be left alone, to become what we wish to become?"

Jack smiled, stepped aside, and let Anthony pass.

Anthony pushed his hands into the interface wall, felt the warm pink bundles wrap around his head, and was once again floating in the void. The holes danced, swinging around each other, spiraling ever closer, the in-fall of shattered moons feeding them energy, the space between them tearing apart with each pass, spitting out snippets of alternate reality that quickly collapsed and spewed back a steady stream of matter and radiation, the twin relativistic jets exploding outward from the central core of the spiraling black holes.

Anthony slipped deeper, let the movement, the relationships, the flow of both matter and energy sweep over him, tasting and sampling each of the billions of shards of shattered moons that spun around the holes.

One large fragment remained, a sizeable chunk of Callisto, its core spewing out molten metal from its far side, while the near side glistened, a several-kilometer-thick layer of just-exposed ocean already freezing in the cold vacuum, ice geysers exploding as the freezing surface expanded, the strain buckling the ice fields, hurling shards back into space.

Fragments were redirected, the twin jets exploding from the dancing holes used to redirect rocks and moonlets. The chunk of Callisto was swept into the maelstrom, torn apart, the region nearest the holes sheared apart, torn right down to the atomic level, while the trailing edge was tugged along, oblivious to the fate that awaited it in only a handful of seconds.

The nearest hole swallowed the Callisto shard. The momentum transfer nudged the hole ever so slightly closer to its twin just at the exact moment when the two reached the nearest approach.

Event horizons merged.

For just an instant, a single, distorted, dumbbell-shaped hole hung among the destruction. And then momentum tore them apart once again, and the space between them ruptured, the energy gradient between them greater than anything the universe had experienced since its own birth.

A new universe erupted, one laced with a tangled,

spatial-temporal network that touched the universe at myriad points in both space and time.

And dragged into this new universe, reeled in along the weakened corridor of the extratemporal wormhole that had taken Alexandra back to the original Earth, were all the picoverses that Alpha had created. But space was not sufficiently weakened for the worlds to thread the already narrowing umbilical that connected the two universes.

Something more was needed, a surge from the Earth itself, a re-rupturing of the extratemporal wormhole that had carried Katie back to Earth. Anthony suddenly felt it, the throat widening, the worlds passing through. "Thank you, Father," he said.

Then the connection closed, pinched off, forever separating the two universes.

And in the process, the fissure in space-time that the collapsing picoverses had instigated winked out of existence, like a snake swallowing its own tail, until nothing remained.

"Couldn't have done it better myself," said Jack, the sounds of his voice drifting away into the void.

Anthony hung in the vastness of space, the holes gone, consumed in the formation of the new universe. Nothing remaining except for the weak sunlight that reflected from the few remaining icy shards of moonlets that the holes had not swallowed.

"Good-bye, Mother," he said in a whisper. "Don't *lose* him this time."

Beautiful day.

Katie sat on the upper outside balcony of the Student Union, overlooking Tech's Central Quad. Just a bit past 1:00 and the lunchtime crowds were starting to thin, a few students running, late for the start of class, but most still milling about, talking, sitting, throwing Frisbees, still eating, or lying in the grass and soaking up the early summer sun.

Katie saw all that, but did not pay attention to it.

She watched Anthony.

The lenses within the optical column of her crystal eyes distorted, pulled apart, and the scene before her narrowed as it magnified, Anthony fixed at the center of her vision. Seated in the grass next to Miss Alice, he had a large coloring pad in his lap that he diligently scribbled across with a red crayon.

So alive.

So real.

Katie nulled out all noise, stepped down the receptors in her peripheral vision, and focused all her attention on Anthony. Blond hair tossed about in the warm breeze. Scab on his left cheek, the wound healing from *last week's* encounter with a wayward high-speed paperclip expelled from his recently constructed paper clip dispenser. A smudge of dark jelly in the left corner of his mouth, the telltale sign of Anthony's favorite lunch—what he insisted on calling a peanut butter and jelly sandwich, despite the fact that he despised peanut butter and would not allow any actual peanut butter in his *peanut butter* and jelly sandwich.

Blue eyes, so focused, so intense, so full of life.

Katie felt tears roll down her cheeks, thankful that even though her new eyes did not require the moisture that tear ducts provided, the modifications forced upon her had not eliminated them. She stood, only marginally aware of the other students around her, and pushed her way to the guardrail that surrounded the cafeteria's upper deck, trying to move just a bit closer to Anthony.

He looked up, directly at Katie.

Her head snapped back; she automatically decreased visual magnification, and ducked down, attempting to hide behind a chair. Anthony continued to look up at her.

No, *past* her.

Katie turned, reestablished auditory inputs, reaccessed her peripheral vision, and searched for whatever had caught Anthony's attention, suddenly afraid that it was someone that they both knew, perhaps Horst, or even the *other* Katie.

She saw nothing, just a flock of starlings rising above Van Leer Engineering.

Suddenly the chair she was clutching rattled, and she picked up a high-frequency whine, something that would have been inaudible to her old brain. She started to stand, started to turn. Her vision momentarily blurred, distorted as if she was seeing everything through superheated air. A coed standing directly in front of her, an acne-faced undergrad who barely looked sixteen, shimmered.

And then vanished.

Wumph!

The air was pulled out of Katie's lungs as she was dragged toward an adjacent table, the rapid change in air pressure pulling her across the tabletop, dumping her to the ground, and still carrying her along, entangling her in a mass of hysterical, screaming students and upended tables and chairs.

Crack!

White light momentarily saturated her Virtuals, but by the time she stood, having pulled herself up and out of the pile of students and furniture, her vision had cleared enough to see the dark, oily looking cloud rise up over the Van Leer Building.

"Oh my God," she said in a whisper. "What did you do, Horst?"

Van Leer was gone. The entire building, all five floors, was reduced to a pile of smoking rubble and a few protruding, twisted, and, in places, even *melted* steel girders.

"Horst!" she screamed. "You fired the damn Sonomak!"

For a moment everything froze in place as Katie's panic drove her to clock at her highest possible speed. Horst *had* fired the Sonomak. She'd not stopped him, had *not* been able to change the past. Had Anthony been wrong?

She paused.

Had Anthony lied to her?

Had there really been no way to stop the firing of the Sonomak, of altering the past? But that made no sense. What was happening now, the destruction of Van Leer was not something that *had* happened. Things had changed, and in some horrible, unexpected way. She knew that she would have to figure this out later. Now there was something far more critical.

She slowed her internal clock again and let herself catch up with the world.

Turning back toward the Quad, she watched a steady downpour of concrete dust and particulate rain down in a thick fog. Straining to see through the settling debris, she rastered her vision from the far infrared to the ultraviolet.

"Anthony!"

She couldn't see him, could barely image any of what she knew had to be hundreds of people running across the Quad.

Movement. Shimmer of rainbow-tinted oil flowing across water.

Despite the summer afternoon heat, she shivered. She stepped her spectral response far up the spectrum, until the entire Quad was enveloped in near-darkness, nothing visible except the high energy X-rays that her eyes were tuned to.

A wormhole, its throat sputtering X-rays, materialized some ten feet above the entrance of the Boucher Material Science Building.

Crack!

An arc of lightning lanced across the Quad, spitting and flaring a shower of X-rays as a second wormhole emerged, this one biting into the corporate Coca Cola fountain that dominated the central Quad. Water hissed, vaporizing, more screams rising up as the scalding water spewed over the crowds.

Katie turned and ran back into the darkened cafeteria, quickly shifting her vision into the infrared, able to easily see in the dark, jumping over tables, bodies, and mounds of spilled food, over the entrance turnstile, down the stairs, and out the front of the Student Union.

"Anthony!" she shouted into the dusty twilight.

Crack!

A wall of blast furnace heat hit her on the left, picked her up and slammed her into several running bodies, all of them then crashing into a row of trash cans. To her left, no more than twenty feet away, a new wormhole had gouged a deep trench in the concrete stairs leading down to the Quad, spitting out a torrent of steam and heat-distorted air.

She blinked, attempting to focus.

A figure emerged from the wormhole. At first she thought it was some sort of muscle-bound monster, pointing a weapon. But as the figure moved forward, she could tell it was a human, wearing some sort of large bulky suit, like a spacesuit, and the weapon was obviously some sort of sensor device.

She stood and ran. "Anthony!" she shouted, running down the stairs, tripping on the last step and sprawling across the lawn. The smoke and concrete dust were beginning to dissipate, and she stood, getting her bearings, moving toward the left and the middle of the Quad where she had last seen Anthony.

"Anthony!"

In front of her, a large oak, one of the many that dotted the Quad, was uprooted, the trunk shattered. She could see several students pinned beneath the limbs, some still moving, some obviously dead.

"Anthony!"

She turned, heard something above the screams and sirens, the hiss of superheated water, and the continual crack of thunder. She ran around the tree, tripping over limbs, over students, a shattered bench, and the twisted remains of a bicycle.

"Anthony!"

"Mama!"

She dropped to all fours, crawling into the debris of the fallen tree.

"Where are you, Anthony?"

"Mama!"

To her left and much louder. She tore away at branches, pushed herself through the tangle, and a splintered limb seemed to reach out, grab her right cheek and cut a deep gash. She pushed on, and then saw a sneaker protruding out of a thick wad of twisted wood.

A sketch pad.

"Anthony!"

The sneaker moved, and Katie tore at the branches, ripping away leaves, tossing the debris over her head, behind her and to the side.

"Mama!"

And suddenly Anthony was in her arms, snuggled against her chest, trying to bury himself within the torn remnants of her lab coat. "Miss Alice is hurt," he said. "Hurt *bad*."

Holding on to Anthony, she pushed herself forward. Miss Alice lay motionless, face down, covered mostly by branches. A splinter of wood, nearly two inches thick protruded from the back of her skull. Reaching forward, Katie pulled at her shoulder, trying to turn her over. But she would not budge, pinned to the ground by the wooden shard driven through her head. Grabbing her by the neck, Katie felt for a pulse, knowing that she would not find one.

She did not.

Katie crawled backward several feet, sat, and looked into Anthony's tear-streaked face. "Did Miss Alice park in the usual spot, did she park in my spot?"

Anthony nodded, and Katie, still holding on to Anthony, began to crawl out from under the shattered oak tree. Her assigned parking spot was back by the Tech Tower, the administration building, far away from the remnants of the Van Leer Building. Each morning as she had made the long trek from her car to her office and labs, lugging books, portable computers, purses, notebooks, and the myriad academic debris required in her day, she used to curse the parking officials and their utter stupidity at assigning her a spot so far away from Van Leer.

At that moment she thanked them, and whatever gods had been responsible for the computer blunder that no one had been able to correct. That far away from the rubble that was now Van Leer, the jeep should be safe, and the extra set of keys in place, hidden safely in the cubbyhole beneath the front right fender.

"We're going, baby," she said. "Far away from here."

SECTION IV
CHAPTER 2

Katie smeared the dark gel into her red hair, and then began to pull a comb through it, working the dye in. She looked up in the rearview mirror. For the moment there was nothing she could do about her crystal eyes, but the jet-black hair, and the tanning cream that transformed her normally paste-white, freckled skin into a color that resembled light milk chocolate would have to do.

She believed that they weren't looking for her *yet*.

But that would quickly change. At best she had a day of anonymity remaining. It was less than three hours after the *Event*, as the media had already labeled it, and not only had all of their pictures been blasted across the networks, but an actual Vid recording of the final minutes before the lab had been vaporized had been leaked from the DOE TP storage facility and was being played over and over again.

The world knew that the firing of the Sonomak had triggered the Event. The world also knew that those responsible for the Event—Katie, Horst, Beong, and Aaron had been vaporized in the process.

But Katie had also been at the Student Union at that time. How long would it take someone to remember having seen her in the cafeteria when she was also being recorded in the lab? It would not take long for the authorities to note the discrepancy. There were enough Vid recorders mounted throughout Tech as surveillance devices to keep students secure, as well as enough personal Vid recorders to have picked her up dozens of times at places where she couldn't possibly have been.

They would find out.

They would come looking for her, wanting to know how she could be in two places at once. And she knew that the moment they saw her eyes she'd be whisked away to some deep and secret debriefing center from which she'd probably never emerge.

And then Anthony would be alone again.

She would not let that happen. *Never again.*

"How's that burger?" she asked, leaning around, looking into the backseat.

Anthony sat buckled into his seat, the partially eaten remains of a Kiddee Meal strewn about him, as he played with the cardboard container it had come in, transforming it into some sort of origami creature. "Good," he said. Not looking up, but wiping at his mouth with the back of his right hand, the wiping doing little except to further spread around the ketchup that already covered his chin.

Katie smiled and leaned back in her seat. The jeep was parked in the lot of a CVS pharmacy, located in what a shotgun-peppered sign had told her as she exited Interstate 75 was Beautiful Rocky Face, Georgia. They were about twenty miles south of the Tennessee border and 150 miles north of Atlanta.

The drive to get this far had been a slow one, the interstate traffic heavy, people already starting to flood out of Atlanta. They were not certain what had happened at the Georgia Tech Campus, but the initial reports prompted many to hop into their cars and head north, south, east, and west, anywhere that took them away from Tech.

Katie lowered her Virtuals back over her eyes, chopped the display to feed sixteen simultaneous channels and watched them all, downloading the photons that struck her retinas, letting her rewired brain shift through the torrent of information and pull out what was important, what had the potential for directly affecting her and Anthony.

More than 150 Portals had been detected. Portals were what they were being called, but Katie recognized them as wormholes. At first the news media had crowded right up to them, a few eager reporters pushing cameras right into the throats.

But that quickly stopped.

A few reporters crossed the threshold and simply vanished, their Vids and various equipment, those hardwired back to the world, recording what took place on the other side. In one, a woman reporter suddenly found herself in what looked like a stainless steel bubble, and as the Vid kept recording, she was disintegrated by a purple mist that rained down on her. In another, a little fat reporter with a toupee flopped over his face found himself in a dense, thick pine forest, where something mechanical, spiderlike, and nearly ten feet tall erupted from out of the thick woods, and seized him.

Once those Vids hit the nets, reporters backed away. Then the police and military cordoned off the entire campus, but not before things had started coming *out* of the portals.

Machines.

People.

Things that almost looked like people.

Katie did not know *how* this had happened, but she knew *what* had happened. The wormholes connected this earth to the *other* earths, to the ones that Alpha had created.

But there was so much more to it than that.

Katie had seen the girl disappear at the moment of the explosion. That gave her a hint of what else had happened. Driving up the interstate, she used a part of her mind to focus on the traffic, on the mechanics of moving the car as quickly away from Atlanta as possible, while she used another part of her brain to search for *anomalies*.

Within a matter of minutes, it was obvious to her that this was not her earth, not even her universe. This world had a population of only seven billion people, not the nine billion that had populated her earth. On this earth, not a single extraterrestrial signal had ever been detected, despite the fact that an active search program had been ongoing for nearly fifty years. President Clinton had actually completed *two* terms. The very universe itself had changed. This one was only about thirteen billion years old, and smaller than hers by better than a factor of two.

And then there was the matter of the Planck constant.

Of all the anomalies she'd encountered, this one was the most unbelievable. The Planck constant was different, more than one billion times *smaller* than what it *should* have been.

The firing of the Sonomak had somehow pulled this earth and those other picoverses into an entirely new universe. This was a new universe, one that she was certain Anthony and Ernest had created from the Sonomak. All of the earths had been placed in it, some thirteen billion years after its actual birth, connected to each other through a network of wormholes. The fabric of space itself had been altered, the Planck constant shifted to an incredibly smaller dimension.

Katie knew that had been deliberate.

In such a universe, the negative energy densities needed to spawn a new universe, to make a bridge between this universe and another would be at least a billion times greater, a density that she believed would be physically impossible to achieve, even if using the black hole technology that Tek had built, assuming someone could operate it. This universe was theirs, and she suspected theirs alone, built for them, and designed so that not only could they never escape, but nothing could burrow in from the outside. Not the Makers, and maybe not even Jack.

Katie sighed and slipped the jeep into drive.

She did not understand it all yet, but knew where to look to find the rest of the answers she needed. "Still buckled in?" she asked, looking over into the backseat.

Anthony looked up at her, dropping the convoluted chunk of cardboard into his lap. "Where have you been, Mama?" he asked.

"Far, far away," she said, "But now I'm back and will never leave you again."

Anthony nodded, satisfied.

•   •   •

Jack pulled a quarter out of Anthony's left ear.

"How'd you do that?" asked Anthony.

Jack looked at him, his face filled with a deadly serious expression. "Simply magic, taught to me by Eastern Mystics I encountered during my trek to the hidden Valleys of the Himalayas."

"Really?" asked Anthony, sitting back. "Magic?"

"Oh yes," said Jack, just managing to hide a smile. "That was quite a few years ago when I made my trek, and I'm quite rusty. Levitation, mind reading, and bending spoons by sheer mental concentration are things that I'm sure I could do if I started practicing again, but I've been so busy these past few years, and had so little need for those skills that I just can't do them anymore. But pulling money out of thin air is an essential skill in my line of work, one that I practice every day."

Anthony nodded solemnly.

Jack handed him the Vid remote. "Excellent cartoons on channel 128," he said and then paused. "But they might not be on. They've preempted just about every other channel with what's happening back in your old neighborhood of Atlanta, and I suspect that maybe even the cartoons might be cancelled."

Anthony flicked on the screen, paying only partial attention to it, as he looked at the quarter Jack had just given him, and, reaching up, he pulled at his right ear, checking for whatever other coins might be lurking there.

"You're good with children," said Katie as Jack walked toward her.

"It helps to think like one," he said, sounding cheerful, as he sat down on the couch next to Katie. Then he looked at her seriously. "I'm not *your* Jack."

Katie nodded.

She'd known that from the moment she had located Jack, well before she had even been able to meet him this night. There was no Jack Preston at the DOE. Jack Preston of this world was a second-term U.S. senator from California She'd uncovered that after just having passed through

Knoxville as she continued her drive north. She'd almost lost control of the jeep, just barely missing the rear bumper of an eighteen wheeler hauling onions.

This was not her earth, not her universe. She did not understand the mechanics of the transformation that this earth had experienced. But the results were obvious. Her earth, from her universe, when forced into this new universe, was slightly altered to fit into this new reality. No ET signals had ever been detected. This universe was much smaller and younger. And it had *always* been this way on this earth. The realities of the two universes had melded, creating this new earth, a new reality. But the process had not been a perfect one.

Two billion people no longer seemed to exist on this earth. Where they had gone, if they had ever really existed, except in her mind, she did not know. And of those who did remain, many had different personal histories.

Jack Preston was not a DOE contract monitor, but a senator. It had taken her nearly two days to make contact, but once she'd gotten through to him, he had met her within the hour. The government was looking for her. Jack knew she was of critical importance in understanding what was taking place in Georgia.

What she'd told him in the last four hours had at times been unbelievable, but each time he thought he had reached the point of simply not being able to take in any more of her fantastic story, he looked into her eyes, something obviously from another world, and was able to continue listening.

He needed to hear more.

"I do not believe that there is any part of me that originates from *elsewhere*," he said. He looked over his shoulder at Anthony and the Vid. There were no cartoons, just some military types pointing at charts and satellite shots of the Tech Campus. "But I do believe your story." He looked back at her.

Katie nodded, certain that the person seated next to her was Jack Preston, *the* Jack that *her* Jack would have been had he not been *infused* with whatever otherworldly entity had taken him over, eventually swallowing the Jack she had known, that she had *loved*.

"And I will help you and Anthony."

Katie sagged and slid back into the couch. This Jack had the power and the visibility to make sure that she didn't simply disappear, that she didn't lose Anthony once again.

"But before I go public, and even before I reveal to the government who and what you are, I need as much information as you can offer." He reached forward and almost touched her, but then pulled his hand back. "The more I know, the better I can help. The two of you should stay here for the next few days, and I want you to write down everything you can recall, every detail, every thought, every feeling you experienced."

"Do you want to know it *all*, really feel it *all?*" she asked.

Jack slowly nodded, surprised at his own reaction, the feelings of familiarity, even attraction he was feeling toward Dr. Katie McGuire. He'd known her now for only a few hours, but somehow it felt like so much longer, as if they had met before.

And in a way, in a bizarre and otherworldly way, he realized they had met before. But he had to keep reminding himself that he was not her Jack, was not the Jack who had the power to move between universes, who was ultimately responsible for the *fabrication* of this universe.

"See it from the inside?" She reached up and tapped her right eyeball. "I can show you *everything*."

Jack sat back, certain of what she meant, knowing that he couldn't refuse, couldn't let the opportunity pass to experience something of this other version of himself, of this godlike Jack Preston.

"You will feel what I felt," said Katie, pausing, looking away from Jack. "How I felt about *you*." Again she paused. "Such an experience may change you, may alter the way that you feel about yourself." She said nothing more.

But Jack knew that there was something more, something

left unsaid. "It might change the way that I think about you, how I *feel* toward you."

Katie nodded.

Jack was not impulsive by nature; he was a planner and a plotter, considered every step very carefully before he actually took it. But suddenly a desire to take a risk filled him. The feeling was almost alien, and for a moment he wondered if he was in complete control of himself, if someone or something else was forcing him to act recklessly, impulsively.

He didn't care. That too was a very non-Jack-Preston-like response.

"How long will the procedure take?" he asked.

"Perhaps a minute, but you will be somewhat disoriented for an hour or two after as the information integrates with the rest of your mind."

Jack smiled nervously. "What would *your* Jack have done?"

Katie smiled back. "It doesn't really matter," she said. "What does matter is what you want to do."

Jack nodded. "Do it."

"When?" Katie asked.

Jack took a deep breath. "Now," he said. He didn't have time to take a breath, and just barely saw the thin glass tendril erupt from Katie's forehead. He didn't feel himself fall back into the couch.

She showed Jack *everything*.

And Jack *remembered*. Thoughts, images, feelings, filling him not only through the link connecting him directly with Katie, but through another link that had suddenly materialized, one so much more tenuous, but infinitely more powerful, one that reached right through the fabric of the universe and touched a place infinitely far away.

"Katie?" he whispered.